The
Devil's Ribbon

Also by D. E. Meredith

Devoured

The
Devil's Ribbon

D. E. Meredith

MINOTAUR BOOKS
A THOMAS DUNNE BOOK ✎ NEW YORK

This is a work of fiction. All of the characters, organizations, and
events portrayed in this novel are either products of the author's
imagination or are used fictitiously.

A THOMAS DUNNE BOOK FOR MINOTAUR BOOKS.
An imprint of St. Martin's Publishing Group.

www.thomasdunnebooks.com
www.stmartins.com

ISBN 978-0-312-55769-0

First Edition: November 2011

10 9 8 7 6 5 4 3 2 1

For Mum and Dad—with love, always
le grá go deo

Acknowledgments

As ever, Charlie Meredith for everything; my two fantastic boys, Joseph and Rory; wise owl and friend, Natasha Fairweather. Plus: Anne Wilk, Mary Meredith, Kathleen and Alec Laver, Helen Calcraft, Freya Newbery, Gaby Chiappe, Julie Major and the Bike Club, Tim Sibley, Amy Fletcher, Caroline "Is your Mum working? Don't disturb her . . ." Stack, Jennifer Joyce, Sarah Ross (and all those suppers). A huge "Grazie" to Francesca Polini, "Go raibh maith agat" to Eoin O'Neill and my cousin, Lorna McPhearson, and "Merci beaucoup" to Melanie Lanoe; thank you also to Elizabeth Piedot, Naomi Klein, and Phil Michel. A special mention to Marika Lysandrou and her timely input. Big thanks also to my agent, Kevin Conroy Scott, for your insight and advice; Sophie Lambert, and everyone else at Tibor Jones.

Most important of all, a huge debt of gratitude to my brilliant editor, Peter Wolverton, and especially, Assistant Editor Anne Bensson—for your crystal-clear direction, support, encouragement, smart suggestions, and endless advice, but most of all, for writing "ha, ha, ha . . ." on the notes when it was supposed to be funny.

I am also very grateful for the meticulous work done on the final draft by Jane Herman and Kevin Sweeney. For their wonderfully evocative designs, a thank you to David Baldeosingh Rotstein and Rich Arnold. Also, Bridget Hartzler for her work behind the scenes, and everyone else involved in *"Hatton and Roumande"* at Thomas Dunne and St. Martin's.

An extra-special mention to Claire Wilson, and her lovely ladies at the St. Margaret's Book Club.

They are going, going, going from the valleys and the hills,
They are leaving far behind them the heathery moor and mountain
    rills,
All the wealth of hawthorn hedges where the brown thrush
    sways and thrills.

They are going, shy-eyed cailins, and lads so straight and tall,
From the purple peaks of Kerry, from the crags of wild Imaal,
From the greening plains of Mayo, and the glens of Donegal.

They are going, going, going, and we cannot bid them stay,
Their fields are now the strangers, where the strangers' cattle
    stray,
Oh! Kathaleen Ni Houlihan, your way's a thorny way.

—*Ethna Carbery, "The Passing of the Gael"*

The
Devil's Ribbon

Prologue

Nothing but shadows and an eerie stillness in the heat of a simmering night as a figure stoops under a lintel and makes his way
quickly, through a labyrinth of alleys, before finding Berry Street
and heading north along the Farringdon Road. For a fleeting
moment he pauses and looks over his shoulder, to be seen briefly
against the backdrop of a Smithfield's butcher's shop. His face
mottled like the pox in the dark of its window. A sharp jaw, full
lips, skin drawn tight over jutting cheekbones, and grasped
tightly in his hands, a book. Musty pages from another lifetime,
another world away and on its broken board, just one word—
Liberty.

Four hundred and twenty prayers are inside. Cries in the
dark, ghosts from his past, but tonight some of those prayers are
about to be answered, as he heads out of the city, past Finchley
Fields, walking at a terrifying pace, his head down, continuing
faster, faster. He isn't wearing any boots as he sweeps past the
numerous slop houses, slums, and taverns of the Holloway
Road, where it grieves him to say that according to the newspapers, and that wonderful British institution, *Punch*, the Irish

smell of piss, live eighty to a room and keep pigs in the privy. *Well, that's the Irish for yer, yer honor. Savages, the lot of 'em.*

But this man is heading to where the rich folk live. Up Highgate Hill, still hogging the shadows, he smoothes on gloves so when he leaps over a wall, he bounds up from his haunches like a cat, not making a sound, not leaving a mark, as he pushes on through the meadows which are humming with night insects, moving at a swift pace past the spiked gates of The Necropolis.

Pitch black, the stars overhead like needles, lucent and shimmering. White Lodge. At the back of the house, he loiters, looking through a window at an older man who's slumped over what looks like a mound of parliamentary papers, Points of Notice, bills from the estate, an essay by Carlyle, *In Memoriam,* and other testaments to a dire lack of faith.

Is the man sleeping? Or is it simply a love of laudanum?

The killer double checks the poison which he keeps in a vial, knowing this death to be inelegant, mockingly cruel but, more important—fast.

He gives the door a sharp kick and it swings open with ease. The older man doesn't move a muscle, but remains asleep, blissfully asleep—as the killer looks around the study to see back copies of *The Nation,* others of *An Glor.* Up above him, a map of Ireland, and on a little table, buttermilk, a plate of soda bread, and two sherry glasses, left untouched .

The killer lays a hand on the sleeping man's shoulder and whispers his name, but nothing comes back. *Gently does it,* he thinks, filling up the needle and giving it a tap. Down the hallway, silence. The floor above him, silence. Not even a mantel clock.

He leans in closer, *"Gabriel?"* He's so close, he can smell a spicy pomade, the toilette of a gentleman, but this gentleman man will never be clean until . . .

"I'm here, Gabriel. Wake up."

A drowsy look of surprise.

"*You* . . ." say laudanum eyes.

"*Save your prayers for the devil,*" the killer says, as he plunges the poison inside.

1

"The skin is <u>cold</u> and often damp, the tongue flabby and chilled like a piece of <u>dead meat</u>. The patient speaks in a plaintive <u>whisper</u>, tosses incessantly from side to side and complains of intolerable weight or <u>anguish</u>. He <u>struggles for breath</u>, points out the seat of his <u>agony</u>. If blood is obtained at this point, it is black, oozes like jelly, drop by drop. Toward the close, the patient becomes insensible and with a rattle in the throat, <u>dies quietly</u> after a long <u>convulsive sob</u>."

All was silent in the morgue, save the scratch of a nib, as Professor Hatton copied out a passage from one of his well-thumbed medical journals, underlying words which reminded him not of the symptoms of cholera, but of his father who'd died on a suffocating night, reminiscent of this one.

He was pale, when his sister Lucy had taken his hand. "You did everything you could, Adolphus."

"Yes, but it wasn't enough," he'd replied bitterly, as they'd stood among the handful of people who'd gathered by the newly dug graveside, watching as the coffin was lowered, knowing prayers were a comfort to some. He'd stared at the Hampshire earth and the worms made violet by the spades, thinking if there was a God, then how could this happen . . . . again?

Bone-tired, Hatton shook away the bad memory and forced his wandering mind back to his work, which was money well earned but giving him the damnedest headache, as he wrote on a neat, square of paper, "Note to self—alimentary canal, entry point? Sphincter muscle? Exit? See Mr. Farr's work, *London Medical Gazette*, page 12—Broad Street Pump—*how does cholera travel?*"

Outside, there was a sudden sound of wheels on cobbles, the creak of a chain and a harsh voice crying in the dark, "Bring 'em over 'ere. For pity's sake . . .'ere, I say . . ."

Not more bodies, he thought. It was midnight and he'd only just finished cutting the last lot, making the cholera count what— twenty? He checked his notes—yes, twenty—which wasn't enough to call it an epidemic yet, which was good news for Infectious Diseases, but for him? Well, thought Hatton, that was a moot point.

The harsh voice came again—

"Don't lift the cover. Wheel it over there. There, I say. Leave the bodies by the water pump. Fussy devil? You ain't heard the like. He'll 'ave your guts for garters, if anyone touches that padlock."

Hatton's chief diener, Albert Roumande was on the far side of the mortuary, a question in his eye to which Hatton said, "I know, I know, Albert. I'm going." Outside, in the moonlit yard, an arc of stars framed a paltry gang of body collectors who were gathered in a round with torches in their hands. Hatton snatched one of the torches. "For pity's sake, put the damn flames out. Then for heaven's sake clean yourselves up a bit. There's a real risk of infection, here. Especially you! Have you learned nothing from us, lad?" The young man in question stood to attention, removing his cap in a quick show of deference, as Hatton shook his head at the youth's disheveled appearance. "Monsieur Roumande has a mountain of work for you, so hurry yourself. Where have you been anyway? You've been gone hours already."

"*Excusez-moi,* but Monsieur Roumande said he needed me to visit Newgate, sir, and then go on to the Irish nests in the slums, where I heard the fever bell ringing. Shall I help shift the bodies, Professor?"

"Well, that's *your job,* isn't it?" said Hatton, cross, because he'd done a fifteen-hour stretch already. "Get the corpses into the mortuary, quickly, then it's hot water and carbolic for the lot of you. No hands anywhere near the mouth, until you're done with the cadavers and washed. Do you understand me, Patrice?"

The boy nodded, contritely.

"Very well, get on with it," said Hatton, wiping a swathe of sweat from his neck, because the air in the morgue was uncomfortable and fetid, but it wasn't much better out here, he thought. St. Bart's Hospital had been built as a sanctuary for the sick on the ancient meadows of Smithfield, a holy place of medieval monks and healers, but the "smooth" fields had long become a market, and the market had long become a herding place for animals and a slaughterhouse for a thousand dead sheep, a million disemboweled pigs, the split carcasses of cattle. But it was a different sort of death tonight that demanded Professor Hatton's attention.

Back in the cutting room, Albert Roumande wobbled precariously on a rickety chair, risking life and limb, but determined to hang up another posy of dried herbs to drive the scent of death away, because as chief diener—a word meaning only "servant of the morgue"—his work covered all matters of sanitation, odor control, preserving and pickling, the procurement of newfangled instruments, knife sharpening and bookkeeping. Added to which, being a man of rare intellect and an avid reader of everything from *The Lancet* to *The London Medical Gazette,* when it came to understanding the nuances of anatomy, in truth, he was barely a whisper away from Professor Hatton himself.

Roumande jumped down from the chair with remarkable dexterity as he announced, "If the summer keeps up at this temperature, we'll soon be awash with corpses. But where and how to store them without buckets of ice?" He scratched his head. "That'll be the next problem. The heat is choking the city, but at least we've someone committed to help us, at last." He turned to their apprentice, Patrice. "But no peace for the wicked, eh? Go and get those cadavers onto the dissection slab, lad, and then I've got a treat for you."

The boy wiped his hands on his apron and beamed, "A treat? For me, monsieur?"

"Learning and erudition, Patrice. You've been with us for almost a fortnight now and you can't always be scrubbing and mopping. Put on some gloves, don a mask, and you can observe your first cholera cutting. Is that permissible, Professor?"

Hatton nodded, happy to leave such matters to Albert Roumande. A man who excelled not only in all things to do with the running of the morgue, but whose sage advice was something Professor Hatton—the younger man, at thirty-five—had come to rely on. For example, on how to raise children—"*With love, Adolphus, nothing but love.*" On how to sharpen a knife, "*Always, Professor. Against the blade.*" On matters of dissection, "*I think you've missed a bit, Professor.*" And matters of the heart, "*Like birds needs the sky, and stars need the moon, a man needs a wife, Adolphus . . .*"

But tonight was not a night to contemplate matters of the heart. There was work to do. Standing under a sign which said *Perfect Specimens for an Exacting Science*—cherry red on Prussian blue—Hatton carefully inspected an array of surgical instruments, embossed with the doctor's initials—*ARH esq.*

"The smallest, I think, for the child's gut," Hatton said to the sliver of silver in his hand.

"I agree with you, Professor," said Roumande, rolling back his sleeves. "Here, Patrice, step up to the cadaver. See these scissors? They are typically used to separate the membranes out from the muscle. Each fold, each cavity may unlock a secret. Step forward, but touch nothing. Observe the organs carefully because later we shall expect you to draw them."

Hatton prepared to delve in, to feel the flesh rip against the blade, and the muscle melt against metal. Muffled behind his calico mask, he said, "See here, as I draw the blade," Hatton sliced the torso of a young Irish girl, creating a purple slit, a seeping Y, running through the skin down to the pelvis and then back again to her right breastbone. Roumande stood ready with a large pair of coal tongs, peering over the corpse and adding, "A perfect skin flap, and the infection is clearly denoted by the telltale blood. It resembles crème de cassis, *n'est ce pas?*"

The youth spluttered, "*Excusez-moi,* monsieur. *S'il vous plait.* Please, wait . . . wait a moment, monsieur."

"I have him," Roumande crooked his arm around their apprentice. "Here, steady now. Sit down for a moment, but what on earth's the matter? You've seen umpteen dissections before."

Patrice put his head between his legs and retched into a nearby bucket, wiping his mouth, "*Excusez-moi, excusez-moi . . .*"

"Is it the girl that upsets you? Or the fear of these infected bodies?"

"It's the black blood, like a witch or the devil's . . ."

"Cholera isn't the prettiest." Roumande patted Patrice on the back, and then turning to Hatton, said, "The smalls will be more interesting for Mr. Farr, don't you think? And we're in luck tonight for we've a couple of babes, here."

Hatton didn't reply, his eyes still intent on the girl.

"Lost in thought, Adolphus?" asked Roumande.

Hatton shrugged, "You're right, Albert. We should concentrate on the smalls." He pointed his scalpel at the micelike shrouds. "And I'd wager those babies are twins."

"My thoughts exactly, Professor. To compare the onset of fever on cadavers of the same nature will perhaps be worth a few extra guineas for Mr. Farr? And I couldn't sleep tonight if we dissected the girl. She must have been a sight for sore eyes, before the cholera took her."

She was maybe fourteen, girlish yet womanly, on the cusp of life before she died, thought Hatton, as Roumande bent down to study the girl a little closer, saying, "There's a priest in Soho might be willing to bury her. Though where he puts them is a mystery, for they can't be buried in the confines of the city." Roumande turned to their apprentice. "All cholera corpses by rights should be incinerated. The Board of Health insists upon it. And yet here lies the prettiest of creatures, an innocent and a Catholic, as well. Well, what do you think, Patrice? Do we burn her like meat?"

The morgue wasn't a democracy, thought Hatton to himself, and not all opinions mattered. Hatton was all for self-improvement, being of humble origins himself, but there were limits. And more to the point, was this dead child really worth the trouble? But before Hatton could say any of this, the lad spoke up, "I know the priest. It's Father O'Brian at the Sacred Heart in Soho who buries them. Special dispensation for Catholics, Professor, because in death we don't like to be burned, monsieur."

Professor Hatton lifted a handful of the dead girl's red gold hair. Auburns curls, pallid lips, and lids of ash. "Very well, take her to the priest, for she's at peace now. But mind yourself, Patrice. We've strict rules for cholera cadavers. There's still the curse of disease upon her, so tell no one what you have on the cart. Only the priest, Father O'Brian, do you hear? If we can give one of these poor children some dignity, so be it."

An hour passed, as Hatton sat quietly, not fighting the sense of loss which always overcame him after so many gone forever. In the winter, he would pull up his chair close to the huge stone grate.

A roaring fire would warm his body, if not his soul. But this was summer. No fire was lit. The cholera girl had been delivered to the priest and the lad was back at his station again, as Hatton shut his eyes, listening to Roumande, slipping in and out of French, with his "*Oui!* Attention! Do it like this" and "*Mais, non! Non, non, non. Ecoute.* Do it like that."

They had worked together long enough for Roumande to know that the professor needed a pause for contemplation on life, and what it really meant when it ended.

The filigree watch in Hatton's fob pocket ticked.

Perhaps twenty minutes passed before the professor found the wherewithal to stand up, brush himself down, move over to the chipped enamel sink, and peer at himself, noting the worn-out face of a solitary man.

"It irks me," said Hatton, still looking in the mirror.

"What's that, Professor?" asked Roumande.

"Mr. Farr specifically asked me to do the cholera work, and yet all my findings must be checked by Dr. Buchanan, our hospital director, but he's a physician and knows nothing of pathology. He simply wants to ingratiate himself with Mr. Farr and all those eminent gentlemen at the Board of Health."

Roumande shook his head, "It's been a long night. You're tired, Adolphus, and still upset about the girl."

"No, Albert. It's not just the girl. Our budget review is tomorrow at nine, *remember?*"

Roumande gave a shrug, *but of course.*

Moving over to his desk, and opening a drawer, Hatton found his favored chisel blade. "The usual squabbling at the trough, Albert. You should see the other doctors and their sycophantic ways. It's a disgrace." He nicked the wood; little shards were flying up. "They come to the meeting laden down with chocolates, bottles of Cognac, cigars for Dr. Buchanan, but I shan't do it. There's no dignity in it, and anyway"—he stabbed the desk, hard—"forensics isn't a priority at this hospital. Never shall be, never will be."

Roumande didn't answer, because Professor Hatton had been this way for a while now—that is to say, peevish and irritable. Ever since their last proper case, which hadn't gone well. Roumande cursed the day that dandified policeman, Inspector Jeremiah Grey, had arrived at The Yard. And if Roumande closed his eyes, he could still hear the inspector's Welsh squeal ricocheting off the paneled walls of the Old Bailey and see his friend, Professor Hatton, head bowed in the witness stand, as the judge shouted, "Order in Court! Order in Court! I will have order in Court . . ." While Inspector Grey was a spit away, screaming like a girl, "But you're our expert witness. So say it, damn you! Say it! Say they are indeed the victim's digits in the biscuit tin, or step down, Professor Hatton."

But Hatton was a man who understood Truth and could never testify to evidence he suspected had been planted, even if that meant a murderer walked free. After the case was dismissed and the accused found "not guilty," Grey had waited for them, just outside the Court and seethed, "That's right, Hatton. Walk away, just as that murderer's done. You should have spoken up, you should have been definitive, you should have said something, *anything*—not stood there like a lemon. And tell me, Professor, what is all this forensics *for* if not to help me?"

Hatton had turned to face him, trying to remain calm, "That was the first time I'd seen those fingers, and it appears your evidence came out of nowhere. Mr. Tescalini *found them*? Simply stumbled upon them? I really don't think so, and please, Inspector, don't ever put me on the spot again like that. It's extremely unprofessional."

Grey was wrestling with a sweet wrapper, shoving a bonbon into his mouth, as if his life depended on it, as he said, "Cast dispersions on our methods if you like, but we found the tin, hidden in a bedpan and . . ."

Hatton shook his head, "Inspector with respect, I checked that room . . ."

"I'm a policeman and my job is a simple one—to send the

guilty down and get results for my superiors, anyway I can. Not be left with egg on my face by a supercilious prig like you."

Hatton had shaken his head with disgust and then whistled down a carriage, ignoring the inspector's last remarks, who, in turn, had ignored Professor Hatton for these last six months.

It had been a bad day; a long, bad day for St. Bart's.

But work must carry on and so Roumande sighed and, turning back to Patrice, said, "My fingers grow thicker with each year and the professor has no time for sketching anymore. When it comes to the most important of our tasks, we need young blood. So come."

Albert Roumande led the boy down a short passageway, to a room no bigger than a cell, whose walls were papered with a variety of anatomical sketches, and on a wooden table, a collection of pencils, quills, inks, and other sketching material plus a number of organs, displayed provocatively on white china plates. The "gallery," as Roumande liked to call it, was lit by a single oil lamp. There was a scent of mold and old blood, masked by the sharper cut of turpentine.

Roumande pointed to a freshly cut lump; claret jelly in the morgue half-light. "The professor is keen to capture any unusual aspects to the alimentary canal and the sphincter muscle. You've heard of the theory of miasma, of course?"

The apprentice nodded, because frankly, who hadn't? That diseases like cholera were caused by the foul air of London and the great stink rising off the river.

"Well, that's one line of thought, but it's our belief that cholera is, in fact, waterborne. The body count this summer is no epidemic, but it could easily become so. The professor's work is to gather statistical data in relation to how cholera travels, anatomically speaking. But tell me, because I'm curious. Before you came here, what did you know of the human body? You seem to have a certain talent."

The youth smiled, "Thank you, monsieur. Coming from you, that's high praise indeed. Your reputation on the Continent is second to none, which is partly why I came here. To learn from you, monsieur."

Roumande was not without a modicum of vanity. Despite himself, he puffed his chest out a little as he said, "I strive to be the best, of course," then quickly added, "but only for the sake of the cadavers. One must always remember, these corpses were once somebody's child. Never forget that."

"I won't, monsieur."

"I've lived in Spitalfields for over twenty years and there was revolution in the air when I left in '32, as you well know. But I've honed my skills here, in London, because the Metropolis is a sick city, Patrice, the sickest city on earth. And a violent one, too."

The apprentice nodded, "I knew only a little of the dead, before I came here, monsieur. In Paris, I worked as a body collector, and before that, when I lived in Marseille, I had a job in the Jesuit hospital of St. Jean's, where I became accustomed to cadavers, but I was nothing as grand as a diener."

"So you're from the South, then? I thought as much," said Roumande, enjoying the opportunity for a lighthearted chat for once, and reminiscing about the old country. "My great, great-grandfather was the first diener in Paris, who learned his trade at the steps of the guillotine. We've had assistants in the past, but they've been butchers. A few Irish, a couple of English, even the odd Negro, but none has had the artistry which we require. The apprenticeship is ten long years for a reason. The skill of a diener must be learned, honed, perfected. And you are how old, did you say?"

Patrice pulled his shoulders back, "I am almost eighteen," he said proudly.

"Eighteen, eh?" Roumande looked at Patrice as if he was surveying a horse at a country fair, weighing up the value of him. His dark curls and good looks were what Roumande's wife might call Byronic. A certain kind of male beauty, which at eighteen was fetching enough, but by forty or so would be long gone, turned to swarthy as Roumande had become.

"You'll be nearly thirty by the time you qualify. But you're still quite happy to wait?"

"I believe patience is a virtue, monsieur."

"It is," Roumande put his arm around the lad and drew him closer. "But in this trade, so is passion, dedication, and a flexibility of mind, which doesn't care what polite Society thinks. If you stay with us, you'll need to grow accustomed to taunts, because they call us scoundrels, body snatchers, the devil's magicians. And when they're not insulting us, the living would rather ignore us, as if we didn't exist at all."

He paused, as the murky chasm of the morgue closed in on them. "But beneath the cobbled streets, down each bend and turn of an alley, from unmarked graves come ghostly whispers from the dead. Close your eyes and listen. Well? Can you hear them whispering your name? Can you hear them calling you?"

The apprentice, his eyes closed, answered,

"Yes, monsieur. *Je peux les entendre.*"

Roumande, satisfied, said, "As I can. And it's our work, and the work of Professor Hatton with his new science of forensics, to give the dead a voice that all the world can hear, by seeing everything, by missing nothing. So, open your eyes, Patrice, and draw."

2

ST. GILES

One hour till dawn and the lamps in The Flask were dimmed, the tallow candles burned to nothing. Two men and a boy, sat in a huddle in a corner, hunched over dirty pints of what looked like porter but could have been gin; it was too dark to make out the difference. John O'Rourke, an Irish hack, looked at his watch then growled like a bad-tempered dog, "Where the devil is O'Brian? We take huge risks showing our faces, even here. That priest treats us all as if we are nothing."

Jasper Tooley, a cripple child, slugged back a gulp of his drink, saying that he needed to be off soon, or his pa would surely miss him and then there'd be hell to pay. Meanwhile, the third in the group—a young man, smartly dressed, with a tumble of red curls and a freckled complexion, said, "Calm yourself, for we know where he is. Father O'Brian is tending to the sick in the rookeries. Cholera grips our people. Five more dead were found tonight and word is the bodies were treated like animals. Snatched, they said, and taken to St. Bart's to be hacked to pieces, all in the name of science."

"Jesus, Mary, and Joseph."

"Yes, but we're fighting back this time." Damien McCarthy had a quill and a map spread out in front of him, and had circled an area in green ink which said "Piccadilly." "It'll be the English cut to ribbons when the time comes, John, and it's fast approaching."

"The sooner the better," said O'Rourke. "Our people are starving again in the home country. We should strike now. Parliament's in recess and the Lords are off in the country to fuck dogs and sodomize their women. And they call *us* savages."

At the mention of the word *sodomize*, the boy blessed himself and looked to Heaven, which was a moldy spot on the ceiling.

"You think I'm joking?" John O'Rourke eyeballed the lad. "They're a filthy nation of perverts and liars. Sure, doesn't your father like to call himself British when it suits him, though? When he has a contract to win, am I right?" The boy was ashamed of his pa but said nothing, only looked into the dregs of his drink, as O'Rourke continued, "Still, you might yet redeem your family's name and die an Irish martyr, eh?"

The poor boy's eyes grew wide with terror, but Damien added in a gentler voice, "Take no notice of Mr. O'Rourke. None of us are going to die and he's a foul-speaking gentleman at the best of times. Isn't it the nature of these pen pushers? Am I right, John? Isn't it in the heart of you to be rather too free with your powers of description?"

O'Rourke sucked on a small clay pipe. "But I wrote a fine piece yesterday. Did you read it, Damien? It was on the latest developments in Westminster, and as usual I mentioned your wonderful brother."

"Ah, yes. The Appeaser of Highgate? But you've no need to worry about Gabriel. There's no love of Union politics anymore. I was in Ireland only a month ago and the tide's moving toward our way of thinking. Toward a single, free, and liberated Ireland. The time is coming, John. I know it."

And the time was coming. There was revolution in the air. Irish prisoners transported to Australia were rising up in the goldfields of Ballarat, and in America, roaming in gangs, arming themselves, and here in the slums of London, discontent was simmering and John O'Rourke could feel the lust for change, he could cut it with a knife. Irish liberty would rise out of the ashes of the famine and their draconian masters, the British, would pay for what they'd done. A thousand years of oppression—The Tara Hill rebellion, the Battle of the Boyne, the Three Rocks, Ovidstown, and the bloodletting of Ballinamuck.

As God was his witness, O'Rourke knew the facts, all right. He wrote about them every day of his life. The words rattled around in his brain, grew in his heart like a malodorous cancer—by the end of 1848, after the deadly spores of the potato blight, one million lay dead, another million banished to the far corners of the earth, to live in squalor, to languish under the heat of a foreign sun, to be exiled from their own land, to be laughed at, spat at, mocked.

O'Rourke narrowed his eyes. "A guinea says Gabriel McCarthy MP will get his comeuppance for his liberal sensibilities. His speeches about perseverance and waiting for liberty make me retch. Waiting for what? Waiting till the English wipe us out completely? It's hard to believe sometimes that you're brothers. He sits in The Commons, like his father before him, preaching to our people about achieving repeal, not through the blood of martyrs but," he cleared his throat and did his best Donegal accent, "*tru legil and constitutional means and lickin the hairy Inglish arse, yer honor . . .*"

"To my eternal shame, my brother is his father's son," replied Damien with a smile. "Whereas, I . . ."

"Jesus, Damien I've heard it all before. *The little babby of the McCarthy clan, livin' in the corner of yer brother's house but free to have opinions of yer own?* Well, aren't you the lucky one?"

"Some say it might be the making of me, John. That I'm a free spirit."

O'Rourke laughed and sat back in his chair, "Oh, and let me guess who's been putting those romantic notions in your head.

She's married to him, you know. He'd cut your throat if he knew your thoughts, brother or no brother. You know the rules. Till death do they part."

Damien dipped his quill in the ink, "I'll not discuss Mrs. Mc-Carthy in this low company. Times were such, she had no choice but to marry my brother. Anyway, pay attention. We'll need the device placed round about here"—he stabbed the map with his quill and smiled.

The crooked boy blessed himself again, and John O'Rourke went to clip his ears, but the boy looked back with such contempt that the sometime editor of *An Glor* and regular contributor to the marginally more respectable *The Nation* decided not to antagonize this puppy any further. The Flask had long since been a place for secret meetings of the Irish political variety, but they needed to be mindful. Spies were everywhere. Even here in St. Giles, which was an underworld, a law unto itself. Thousands of Irish lived here, the poorest of the poor, in what was termed the rookeries. A labyrinth of squalid boardinghouses, a little north of Soho, its pavers heaving with rubbish, screaming children, half-dressed costermongers, and prostitutes, but all proud to be speaking their own language, following their own religion.

But being poor meant two things in John O'Rourke's book—easily radicalized but also easily bought. And, thought O'Rourke, there was something about this boy which wasn't quite there. There was definitely something missing. He wasn't entirely *reliable*. These were dangerous times to put your trust in a twelve-year-old bookbinder's son. Still, if the boy turned out to be as useful as Father O'Brian promised he'd be, then O'Rourke was willing to take the risk, for the time being at least.

The journalist pointed at the map, "And this jeweler's shop? How well do you know it?"

"Well enough," answered Damien. "Why only last week I accompanied Mrs. McCarthy there. Gabriel, as ever, was far too busy for her, but we walked arm in arm quite nicely, and I helped her pick a diamond brooch. Very becoming, it looked, too."

O'Rourke laughed, a scoffing sort of laugh, as Damien wrote "Burlington Arcade" on a separate piece of paper and drew an impression of arches.

O'Rourke lit his pipe, "Did O'Brian say when the device might be ready?"

"There are still one or two mechanisms which needed adjusting, and I left him to it. He only went off with it in his pocket after this mass this morning!"

O'Rourke could feel his sense of humor slipping. "Well, he needs to hurry himself. The anniversary of Drogheda is July 12, which is just three days from now. Anniversaries work best. Sends the message home where it hurts. Just get the package back from his saintly hands, and I'll deliver it myself. It's time."

"Amen to that, Mr. O'Rourke. But I'd love to see how far you'd get without me."

The men swung around to a low voice that rolled across the darkened tavern like thunder. The priest was standing by the door, his hands covered in dirt.

"Jesus, Father, don't go sneaking up on us like that," said O'Rourke. "Why didn't you announce yourself?"

The priest threw his head back and laughed, "Sure, I only wanted to listen to the washerwomen, for that's what you sounded like. You need to mind yourselves. As far as I remember, the punishment for sedition in this godless country is death by hanging."

The priest pulled up a chair. He was a tall man and found it difficult to get comfortable. He stuck his legs out, making the others pull back, putting a black leather pouch gently on the table, and John O'Rourke instinctively reached out, but the priest was quicker. "Jesus. I wouldn't go touching that, John, unless you want to blow your own head off. It's a finely tuned device. And I for one think the anniversary of Drogheda is a grand idea." His voice grew louder and he seemed afraid of no one, as he stood up in the middle of the tavern and seemed to fill the very air, the very space around him. He'd been a soldier once with his ramrod back, his massive chest, his hands the size of shovels and feet the size of boats. "I'll not stand dissention in the ranks, do you understand me? Does anyone have issues with that?" He looked directly at the journalist. "Well, John?"

John O'Rourke cast his eyes to the ground, "Whatever you say, Father."

"And what about you, Damien?"

"You know I'll follow you to the ends of the earth, if it wins our people liberty."

"And you, lad, what do you say?"

But the cripple boy's attention had been taken by a moth that had settled on the table ledge. The moth was perfect, fresh burst from its chrysalis, its armored body like a wasp. A luminous wasp.

"It's a death's head moth, Father," said the boy, looking up from the fluttering creature, slightly lost to the world. "It makes its home in the rotting trees up in Finchley Fields. It's a rare beauty to find in the middle of the city, Father."

As quick as flash, the priest grabbed a glass and with a sharp twist, severed the moth's head from its body. He smashed it underfoot, saying, "Forget about the moth and repeat after me—*Clan shan van vocht* . . . if you are in favor, say aye."

The men stood up to join their chief, but the boy stayed sitting on his chair, bereft, till he was grabbed by the collar by the priest who glowered, "Pay attention, child. I'm in no mood for any more nonsense. Sure, just look at my hands . . ." His palms were thick with dirt. "I've just been burying a pauper girl who died of the cholera. She was left outside the Sacred Heart, with a note addressed to me, begging for God's Mercy. Too late for that, I'd say, but I buried her anyway. It's not mercy she needs now, but sweet fucking vengeance. So, repeat after me, if you are in favor . . ."

"Aye!" The men thumped the table, fist on fist.

"The twelfth of July, then," said the priest. "Motion carried."

3

Just as he closed his eyes and fell deeply into a moonlit dream, Mrs. Gallant, Hatton's landlady, was rapping sharply at his door with that irritating little tap of hers.

"It's almost nine o'clock, Professor."

Damnation, Hatton thought as he leapt out of bed, galvanized by fear of Dr. Buchanan's barking voice, sure to greet him as he entered the hospital director's dominion, the last and the least.

"No breakfast, Mrs. Gallant. Not today," Hatton yelled as he heard a clattering of dishes from behind him and momentarily caught the sweet scent of bacon in the air, knowing he would have to make do with a bitter coffee from the grinder's stall by the hospital gates.

The professor headed down Holborn, not waiting for the omnibus, rushing along Charterhouse Street, on and on, till at last he caught a glimpse of St. Paul's golden dome in the distant haze. Sweating buckets, he could hear in his head his feeble excuses for arriving at the budget meeting . . . he pulled out his pocket watch . . . half an hour late.

At the sight of the hospital gates ahead of him, Hatton broke into a run and thought he heard a Special blow a whistle in his direction, but darted into the safety of the vast building, where the entrance hall's sparkling mirrors showed fleetingly his shirt stuck to his skin, his tie unloosened, his hair all over his face, and as for his hat? His new brown derby? Missing. In short, Professor Hatton was a mess and hardly worthy of a pay rise, if the cut of his trousers was to be judged.

"Enter," said the gruff voice of Dr. Buchanan. Hatton stepped into the director's room in the newly painted South Wing, which was full to bursting with physicians and their unspeakable smugness.

"Aaah . . . Professor Hatton. How good of you to join us, at last. But alas, we've finished already. In fact, we didn't have time to discuss *your* particular requirements." Hatton's heart sank because he knew what that meant—budget cuts at the morgue. "And anyway you're wanted elsewhere. Inspector Grey arrived a full fifteen minutes ago and he didn't come alone. So, off you go, and get freshened up at once. You're a monster mess, sir. It doesn't do for St. Bart's professors to present themselves in such a shambles to The Yard. This is the most eminent hospital in London and we have a reputation to uphold. Really, Professor . . . it doesn't do at all . . ."

"Professor Hatton. What a pleasure, sir. What a pleasure indeed. It's been far too long. And despite some professional disagreements in the past, dare I say that I have missed you so? And I'm here because I urgently need your counsel. It's a very intriguing case . . ."

The man decked out in a blue waistcoat, tangerine breeches, and a sumptuous tartan coat was clearly no stranger to the morgue. Despite an absence of more than six months, Inspector Jeremiah Grey had positioned himself to make his little speech of "rapprochement" not on Hatton's chair—which would have been bad enough—but on the professor's desk, his legs crossed, just so.

It was true, thought Hatton, that Grey's predecessor, the late

Inspector Adams, and he had never been friends. Indeed, far from it. So, when word came that Adams's replacement would be a religious man, coming from Cardiff of all places—a city of Methodists, God-fearing, hardworking, straitlaced people—Hatton had heaved a huge sigh of relief. At last, a senior policeman in London they could rely on. But Jeremiah Grey soon proved to be a law unto himself.

The inspector had been at The Yard less than a week when the rumor mill started. First, that this new detective was strongly suspected of planting evidence, and second, that he hadn't come to London alone.

Hatton had been busy at the slab when he confessed, "No, Albert, I haven't met him officially yet, but it appears he has an assistant with him. An Italian, of all people. A Mr. Tescalini, who isn't on the pay roll of The Yard but is some kind of valet to the inspector."

Roumande had been eating a jambon sandwich at the time, but stopped mid-bite, "A valet, Professor?" he'd swallowed, mustard smarting his eyes. "Isn't that a little unusual?"

Hatton wiped his hands on a cloth as he answered, "It most certainly is. A policeman's salary is paltry. Even a senior detective like Grey will earn, what? Three hundred pounds a year at the most, which isn't enough to keep a personal manservant. And if the stories are true, I've heard this Italian carries a gun. Odd for a valet, don't you think? A valet normally carries a clothes brush, some shaving cream, a diary for keeping appointments, a little money, perhaps."

"A gun, you say?" Roumande was rightly perturbed.

Hatton moved over to the sink to wash himself down, "I've also heard that the inspector, far from being the epitome of Christian piety, is rather something else." But then Hatton swiftly added, not wanting to jump the gun, "But I don't want to prejudge him based on the usual Smithfield gossip. We must give this Welshman the benefit of the doubt until we make up our own minds, based on the evidence of actually working with him."

But the "evidence" turned out to be indisputable. As the months wore on—and they had worked together on and off for almost two years now—the inspector revealed himself to be a man who skated on thin ice, relished it even. Grey was as slippery as an eel and seemed to have his own incomprehensible modus operandi, which involved disappearing witnesses, testimonies lost or slightly tampered with, evidence vanishing before miraculously appearing again with "Just in the nick of time, Professor . . ." or "Like a rabbit from a hat, this one . . ." or something along the lines of, "Well, you could knock me down with a feather, but when Mr Tescalini went back to the lady's drawing room, there was this letter knife simply dripping in her husband's blood. Test it, would you, Hatton?"

The blood, almost certainly a rabbit's. But as far as Grey's superiors were concerned—various politicians, the Yard commissioner, Lord this, and Lord that—this new inspector got results and sent umpteen to the gallows. Crime rates came crashing down, arrests went soaring up whether it was felons, rapists, armed robbers, fraudsters, garrotters—and who could argue with that? Hatton had tried and duly paid for it. But perhaps it was time, thought Hatton, to let bygones be bygones and start again with a clean slate, if not for his sake then for his department's.

But it wasn't really any of this history or, indeed, the ornamental draping of a Welsh detective on polished walnut which demanded the professor's attention. Hatton had to look twice, but no, he knew he wasn't mistaken. It was the inspector's tie which caught his eye, the pattern, even by the inspector's standards, being somewhat unusual.

"Yes, my dear Professor. You are not mistaken." The inspector, leaned forward "They're dancing girls and they are definitely cancanning. Mr. Tescalini and I recently experienced the delights at a private party in Paris. A case took me there, as a case has brought me here. Monsieur Roumande, be a good fellow and fetch the professor a chair."

Hatton didn't need a chair, waving the offer away; but for politeness sake, he ventured, "So how is Mr. Tescalini? Still working for you, then?" Hatton couldn't hide the sarcasm in his voice, for he loathed the man. Hatton was a scientist, not a phrenologist, and tried not to judge a book by its cover, but Mr. Tescalini was no ordinary cover. For a start, the Italian's countenance was unnaturally pale and his eyes, which were very close together, were always shifting, never resting, never still, as if he was watching out for someone—or something. His form was squat and solid, but not in a reassuring way. More like a primed musket ball, ready to blow.

Grey, ignoring Hatton's tone, peeled off a lavender kid glove and answered with a wry smile, "Thank you for asking, Hatton. Mr. Tescalini is *splendido, belisimo, magnifico, stupendisimo.*"

"I see," said Hatton, adding, "Glad to hear it," not really caring either way and quickly turning his attention to a male form laid out on the slab to see at once the feet were slate colored, as were the hands.

"Cholera?" Hatton asked, as it was an obvious question.

"He was admitted as such, Professor," said Roumande.

Hatton turned to Inspector Grey, "And this a *police matter,* Inspector?"

The detective's face was blank. "Please, Professor, just take a look at him. There's a five-guinea wager at stake here."

Hatton detected a faint smile under the policeman's well-brushed mustache, clipped privet-neat against a thin upper lip. Inspector Grey had clearly decided that this body was not so infectious, for his face and mouth were bare to the room. Nevertheless, Hatton rolled back his sleeves, washed his hands, and put on a clean apron, one of many which hung from a set of meat hooks behind the entrance door, and according to hospital procedure, a protective calico mask. Albert Roumande looked at his friend, his eyes peering over his own mask, a scrunch of intelligent lines around them, questioning.

Hatton looked at the corpse, which was in a state of extreme rigor mortis, and recognized him at once, because his face had been on the front cover of *The Times* only days ago. Underneath a film of gray, there was a distinctive, bluish tint to Gabriel McCarthy's face.

Hatton made a small initial incision to see the blood run freely, and immediately removed his mask. Roumande quickly followed suit, saying in an exasperated tone, "The Yard wouldn't let me take off my mask until you concurred, Professor, but it's clearly not cholera. So you see I was right, Inspector," Roumande swung around to face the detective, "Five guineas, monsieur, and it's your round."

Grey's high-pitched laugh spliced the room, "Your diener is quite the betting man, and put a guinea on arsenic, but I upped the stakes a little. As we know, arsenic is a slow poison, administered little by little and manifests itself with cramps, cold sweats, bellyache, and so on. But according to the wife, her husband had shown no signs of being ill. That his death was sudden. But I'll let you play detective, because I need to be crystal clear on this, from the very beginning. You see the man before you? You take my point, Professor?"

Yes, he took the point, because Hatton knew this man. Gabriel McCarthy MP was an Irish Unionist and so considered a friend of the British. The two countries had been forged into one, the Act of Union, described in *The Times* as a "delightful marriage" but viewed by many as nothing less than a rape. Emancipation for Catholics was promised but not given, rebellions were quelled with the gun. The Unionists vaguely talked of Repeal but only by legitimate means. But these moderates were the Old Men of Ireland with their aristocratic manners and respect for the Queen. Secret societies with names like The Oak Boys, The White Boys, and Ribbonmen had long since gathered in the bogs and glens of Ireland plotting revenge, but now they had morphed into a hiss on the streets of St. Giles, Whitechapel, Soho, Southwark, Saffron Hill—a hiss of Gaelic—*Fenians*.

There was a definite tint to the MP's face, but it wasn't the

Blue Death. Hatton bent down and smelled the dead man's mouth. There was no mistaking the sourness, as he announced, "It's strychnine, gentlemen. *Strychnos nux-vomica,* in its purest form. Vile and bitter to the taste, even in minute proportions. Muscular convulsions tighten the neck muscles here"—Hatton pointed to the area of the throat—"leaving this terrible look upon his face as if he has seen something too awful to imagine."

"Like he's seen a ghost?" asked Inspector Grey.

"Exactly, Inspector. Death in less than ten minutes. He would have been unable to shout for help almost as soon as he imbibed it. He'd have staggered about the place, crashing into furniture, his back arching into the agony of opisthotonos before he hit the ground, which explains these minor lacerations and bruises to his arms and legs. This bluish tint to the face is not fever of any description. It was his last fight for breath."

Hatton asked Roumande to turn the gas lamps up and position them directly over the body. The Y cut was quickly made and Hatton was about to wrench back the rib cage when, instead, he slowly lowered his knife and hesitated, feeling the tension, knowing that the rookeries in London were already simmering with Irish unrest, and what he was about to find might tip London into open warfare. A whisper in the confessional, a whistle in the street, or a poster of Gaelic scrawls across the window of a tavern in the Seven Dials. And what would start as a rumor—*murder*—would surely end in more violence still. The murder of a Unionist could act as a trigger for open rebellion. If McCarthy could be so easily killed, why not the others who stood in the way of a liberated Ireland?

"Get on with it," said Grey, impatiently. "What are you waiting for?"

"Just thinking, nothing more," said Hatton.

"Your lead, Professor," said Roumande, peering at the corpse. "Although if I may suggest, some intestinal mucosa would tell us for sure. Patrice, leave the blood bucket for now and fetch the Eaton and Spencer."

How Roumande had secured this magnificent microscope, Hatton didn't know and he didn't care to know, as it cost more than half their yearly income. Nut brown and polished to a shine, the instrument was left standing on its own special table, to be used only in matters of forensics.

Hatton peered down the lens of the Spencer, his fingers curling around the viewing rods, the instrument astounding him with its precise and extraordinary clarity, leaving little room for doubt. The mucosa was clear of any fever, but the gut samples would take a little more scrutiny.

"The Marsh Test, Professor?"

"Yes, Albert. Bring me the Bunsen burner."

Grey was intrigued, for it was well known that this method was reserved for detecting traces of arsenic only. He watched mesmerized, as Hatton selected a glass test tube in the shape of a capital U and, using a dropper, added a little sulphuric acid and a gram of zinc and, with steady hands, took a tad of the gut muscle and dropped it into the tube. Roumande lit the Bunsen, the blue flame illuminating a small plate, which the chief diener held up as if it was a mirror. Grey hovered, Patrice not far behind, as Hatton held the tube as close as he could to the plate, and then after a count of, "Are you ready, Professor? *Un . . . deux . . . trois . . .*" Hatton pulled the stopper out, like a champagne bottle. Instantly, the gas revealed itself against the gleaming white, like a miniature storm cloud, which was not the shiny black of arsenic, but sepia.

Hatton allowed himself a triumphant smile. "The amber stain of strychnine, Inspector. I'm yet to write up a definitive paper for *The Lancet*, but several experiments here at St. Bart's have now demonstrated that this test is not only accurate, but it's flexible as well. I've used it now, successfully, for a number of different poisons."

"What about his hands?" Inspector Grey asked, moving closer to the slab, his cologne so strong it made Hatton double take. It was a distinctive perfume and held memories of a bordello in

Pall Mall, a place where, two years ago, the professor had finally been summoned to meet this new member of The Yard, and from the start things hadn't gone well.

Despite his reputation, as reported in *The Metropolitan Police Gazette* and *The Daily Telegraph*, as an indisputable "Giant of the Law," at first sight, Inspector Grey had been somewhat of a disappointment. Standing on the steps of the blood-drenched bordello, Hatton had thought him diminutive, unmanly, a natty dresser but not in an agreeable way. A blue silk suit clashing with a primrose waistcoat, Grey had picked his way around the decapitated corpse of the prostitute as if he was a ballet dancer, barking orders to his servant—Mr. Tescalini—a bullish-looking man with meat cleaver hands.

Hatton had tipped his hat at the Italian, who'd tipped his own battered derby back with a curt, "*Buongiorno, professore. Mi fa molto piacere conoscerla.*" Before marching up the steps and grabbing the owner—an unfortunate, highly rouged madam—into a corner where squeals and shrieks were emitted along with the dulcet tones of, "I'm not giving you's a penny, not a damn penny, you's rascalian, Italian, dough-faced, fat arsed . . ." Another shriek, followed quickly by, "Iris was like a daughter to me . . . how dare you's insinuate that I would touch a hair on her head . . ." The sound of a furious thump had followed, and the well-bosomed lady seemed to be all of a swoon and displaying a great deal of purple petticoat. Out of good manners, Hatton quickly averted his eyes, but not before seeing the Italian doff his hat again, but this time toward the inspector, which appeared to be some sort of signal known only to each other. Hatton, being new to this pair, was at a loss what to do next and simply watched, dumbfounded, as the inspector appeared to wink and then run his index finger across his own lily-white throat like a . . . well, in retrospect, like a surgical knife.

Grey had steered Hatton away from the fracas with, "I brought him with me from Cardiff. Rarely go anywhere without him, you understand, because Mr. Tescalini's a marvel, Professor, a marvel but he speaks very little English. He can understand us perfectly well though, can't you?" Grey had looked over his shoulder, raising his voice as if he was talking to a child, "Can't you, Mr. Tescalini? He listens. Others speak, which can be useful, but *ma il suo inglese e' terribile, signore. Dobbiamo assolutamente ripassare il passato remoto.* And yes, thank you, Mr. T, but that's enough now. That's quite enough now, so pleeeessse . . . put the lady down." The inspector had turned duly back to Hatton with, "Anyway, I've called you here because such is the nature of this prostitute's many influential customers, an arrest must be made quickly and to help me . . ." Another wink followed, this time for Hatton. "I shall require a forensic sweep, Professor. Leave no stone unturned." Famous last words, because many stones were left unturned on that particular case. But that was a different story.

Grey's voice echoed around the morgue and brought Hatton back to the present, who answered, "The hands, did you say, Inspector? Well, they certainly look as if fever's upon him, but I think you will find that the distinctive coloring is caused by something else."

"Is it dust of some description, Professor? That's what your French fellow here suggested. His hands and feet seem to be covered in the stuff."

Roumande was quickly at the end of the body with a small nailbrush and a thin sheet of paper, as Hatton continued, "Roumande's right. It's from a grate. Quite clearly ashes, though we'll need to run some tests to be sure. We're able to break down the molecular structure to some extent, although our methods are new."

Hatton asked Roumande if he would be so kind as to get the sample bottles, and quickly turned back to the detective, knowing on the next point he could be decisive.

"You have a murder victim, Inspector. It's been made to look like cholera but it's penny gaff stuff. Perhaps whoever did this thought the body would be burned in a fit of panic. It's quite a reasonable assumption, given the way people are behaving in the city in this infernal weather. Reason and logic have left the city. I hear daily reports of Londoners refusing to cross the river by bridge or use the paddle steamers. But where was he found, Inspector? You never said."

"In his study, Professor," answered Grey, impressed by the theatrics of it all and moving with a lingering smile out of the way of Patrice, who was busy slopping out the blood bucket, before moving on to his next job, a pencil behind his ear.

Grey stroked his mustache. "Well, whoever did this didn't count on the nature of the wife. It was she who calmly organized for the body to be brought here, for a doubt clouded her mind as well. It seems she's heard of your new science, Professor, and insisted that we bring the body here to be properly examined. I told her I wasn't entirely convinced. Yours remains a voodoo science but, well, at this stage, I have little else to go on. I'm prepared to give you another chance, bury the hatchet, all forgiven and forgotten, eh?"

Hatton didn't reply but only swallowed these snide remarks, because money was short and opportunities like this one thin on the ground, as the inspector continued, "So, are we finished here? I'm sure poor Mrs. McCarthy will want the body back, and as there's no fever here, things can proceed quickly once we've signed the necessary paperwork. You'll get back to me on any more samples, Professor, and I assume I can call upon your services as I investigate this case? On the usual terms, of course. I presume fifty guineas will suffice?"

Hatton bowed at such a generous offer.

"Well, let us hope," continued the inspector, "for all our sakes, there's a simple explanation here, and this gentleman's demise is nothing to do with politics."

Hatton laughed, not able to help himself, "Nothing to do with politics, Inspector? Surely it would be everything to do with politics? The 'Appeaser of Highgate'? Isn't that what they called Gabriel McCarthy?"

The inspector shrugged, "He was useful to the British government, but no man is indispensable. Gabriel McCarthy was a man of compromise, a Unionist, and so not wedded to repeal like these so-called Irish Nationalists. In my opinion, they should hang the lot of them. Are you a political man, Professor?"

Hatton shrugged. He occasionally wrote to *The Times*, read essays by Carlyle, knew the works of Bentham, and got into the odd contretemps in a Smithfield tavern if the subject mattered. He'd signed petitions when they came his way—the banning of public hangings, the abolition of slavery, better education for girls, vaccination programs for the scourges of diphtheria, smallpox, and so on. But on the whole, science was his concern, not politics.

The inspector continued, "I'll tell you what I think, then, shall I? That Britain is a mighty nation, chosen by God and Providence to lead the world, but as to the Irish? In my opinion, they're worse than the Negroes. Have you seen the way the Irish live? Like pigs, Professor. They're a nation that cannot even feed themselves."

Hatton looked at the scalpel in his hand, "We rule them by martial law, Inspector. Anglo-Irish politics has become a poison in our midst. I cannot even walk through St. Giles these days without fear of having my throat slit, just for being an Englishman. Men of compromise are badly needed. Gabriel McCarthy is a terrible loss."

Grey adjusted a solid gold cuff link, "Hmmmm. Well, the volatile nature of Anglo-Irish politics was ever thus. But you're right. These are dangerous times, so for the time being at least, the less said outside these four walls, the better. So, is that all, Professor?"

But Hatton wasn't finished with the body. "If this is a murder case, and I'm to be called upon, Inspector, then I'm sure you understand it's not simply a matter of money."

Hatton looked at Roumande for support, who took the cue, and stepped forward to flank him, "As you know, despite the recent upset with those digits in the biscuit tin . . ."

"The victim's you mean . . ."

Hatton tried to bite his tongue, but this time he simply couldn't, as he said, "In my opinion, Inspector, as the expert witness on that case, those digits you found so miraculously, halfway through the trial, could have been just about anyone's. They weren't necessarily the victim's, and you damn well know it, Grey. They were so badly severed, so decomposed, so knocked about among the biscuit crumbs, as to render them useless, and whatever you might think of me . . ."

Grey sighed and adjusted the fit of his waistcoat fussily.

Flustered, nevertheless Hatton pressed on, "Yes, whatever you might think of me, whatever you say behind my back among your colleagues at The Yard, we still retain a reputation for excellence at St. Bart's, and I must ask, or I should say insist, that I go to the crime scene, as soon as possible. I'll also need to do a complete and total autopsy. There can be no funeral until Wednesday, at the very earliest."

The policeman pulled a face, but he was not one to throw away the opportunity of help so lightly. The performance of the plate and Bunsen burner might do very nicely, should such evidence be required in court.

"Very well," agreed Grey. "Go ahead, Hatton. I've a busy day ahead, so do what you must. I'll send a carriage to St. Bart's to fetch you once I have spoken to the widow. Rest assured, the crime scene will remain unmolested. I shall see to it myself. But time is pressing, and I must attend to another case." He turned to Roumande as if to seek his opinion. "A missing chef? He, too, is a Frenchman from Spitalfields and famous for his gateaux. His name is Gustave Pomeroy. Perhaps you've heard of him, monsieur?"

"Pomeroy? No, Inspector, but then I rarely go to restaurants and I don't like cake," replied Roumande. "Except for my wife's, of course."

"Well, you are missing out, sir," insisted the inspector. "For this skilled gentleman is highly sought after by the ladies of this town. He was due to deliver a private dinner of grand proportions for

Mrs. Holford and the philanthropist Tobias Hecker. In aid of work-house children, and rumor had it that Her Majesty might attend. Well, the cooking maestro never arrived, and neither did our Queen, so the ladies were doubly disappointed. And it seems this Pomeroy chap has disappeared into thin air. No sign of the chef at his lodging house in Spitalfields, or at his restaurant in Piccadilly, and the ladies, Hatton, the ladies . . . they are verging on hysteria. As if I haven't got better things to do, but you see, gentlemen, there's no wriggling out of it. And Mr. Tescalini is very fond of madeleines, which is an incentive of sorts, I suppose. So, yes, I must be off."

And with that, the inspector threaded around Patrice, who was standing in the way, head down, busy with a mop and bucket, his sinewy arms glistening from splashes of water as he whistled to himself. The inspector gazed for a second too long, then made a sound like "Grrrr," before whirling his pocket watch, lasso like, into his top pocket and hurrying out of the morgue.

It was noon.

"Sorry, Professor. I wasn't listening," Roumande was standing by the corpse, scratching the top of his head.

Hatton answered him, not getting up from his desk. His belly was rumbling and his patience thinning. "I said we're done here this morning, Albert. Quite done. We'll continue after lunch."

"Done, Professor? But there's something here that intrigues me. What say you to his mouth? It's not quite right, Professor."

Hatton tried to mask his lack of patience. "His mouth is a grimace, which is quite normal for a person who has swallowed a large quantity of poison. Perhaps you could show Patrice how to fix it before delivery to the widow?"

Patrice put his mop down and hurried over to help.

"You seem a little tense, Adolphus. Is there something wrong?"

"No, friend," Hatton already regretted his shortness with Roumande, especially in front of their apprentice. "A little tired perhaps, and this morning I had some bad news. Dr. Buchanan has decided to postpone our budget announcement until the autumn, although the scarlatina experts are sitting pretty, of course. I know I sound cross, but really, I spent forever on the figures, by which I mean of course that *we* spent forever on the figures."

Roumande raised a bushy eyebrow. "And he hasn't even looked at them, Professor? Not even noted the rising cost of embalming? Or our suggestions for introducing this new method of fingerprinting?"

"I couldn't even see them presented on the table, such was the scattering of crumbs and coffee cups. But there you have it. Why expect more from that oaf? As a physician, he's only interested in infectious diseases."

"Indeed. Well, that's most disappointing, for it throws all our plans for forensics to the wall, unless I can think of some other way to raise money. At least we're back in favor with The Yard. But, Adolphus, I must press you on Mr. McCarthy. Is there not something strange about his face? Aside, that is, from the grimace of poison?"

Hatton looked at the face with more attention. "It does look unusually swollen, but we've already established, quite precisely, the cause of death from the gut samples. The hairline is never quite the same once the face is taken off."

"I think we only need to open his mouth, Professor."

Hatton looked at McCarthy again. Was Roumande right? It was normal for the visage to be puffy, but perhaps around the mouth there was something else? There was only one way to find out and he secretly chided himself for not noticing, unprompted, as this was his normal exacting approach. He hated to make excuses but he'd slept little and was still out of sorts.

"The rigor is advanced because of the poison, and the jaw will be clamped like a vice . . ."

Roumande already had the pliers ready. Hatton took them and pushed the tip through first, between the dead man's lips, until he heard the click of metal on enamel. "Pass me the thinnest blade we have, Albert. Let me just see if I can push it through here." He leaned under the chin and twisted the knife. The jaw snapped open, crocodile fashion.

"You're right, my friend. McCarthy's had more than his breakfast it seems . . ."

"What is it, Professor?"

"It's what I feared," Hatton said, pulling a long line of silk from the dead man's mouth. "You know what this means, don't you, Albert?"

"That we must see it properly, Professor," said Roumande, telling Patrice to open the morgue door, quickly, so they could dry the ribbon in the sun. It was wet with mucus and old blood, disguising its true color.

"*Mon dieu,*" Roumande gasped. It was boiling outside, the hottest part of the day. Hatton joined his friend to examine the silk, which began to dry instantly and morph from black into a vibrant green, which was a calling card Hatton had seen before. Three years ago, when an off-duty English soldier had sauntered into a tavern, saying it was easy to get a fuck in Kerry, for a slice of toke, and my oh my, weren't those colleens as beautiful as they were willing? Any orifice you damn well liked. Whatever was your pleasure, and they called themselves devout Christians. The soldier arrived on the slab an hour later, scalped, his ribs crushed, his heart cut out, and an emerald green ribbon in his mouth.

Ribbonmen, thought Hatton. *Fenians.* And he remembered, the ribbons which he'd first seen in Edinburgh, ten years ago. Worn in the hats of the gangs of so-called Ribbonmen, who claimed to be political activists, but they were nothing more than a band of felons, outlaws who ran things as they wanted in the Irish quarters of any city they came upon. The emerald ribbons, worn as a measure of solidarity with other groups of peasants across the sea, who ran roughshod the length and breadth of

Ireland, attacking English troops with anything to hand—pickaxes, shovels, even boughs of hawthorn. Was it all now returning to the very heart of London? Were they here to break the Union, as they once threatened they would be?

4

LIMEHOUSE DOCKS

Just past midday, and the sun shimmered on shards of steel. At this point, the river was a mercurial sea, choppy and brackish. At low tide, mudflats would stretch for miles toward the marshes of Essex, a squelching melee of whelks, fish heads, bits of old china, Venetian glass, Roman pennies, and, occasionally, bodies. Emerging from the wash, blackened tree stumps was all that was left of primordial swamp—now drained, pummeled, and transformed into the docks of the greatest city on earth. London.

Oyster catchers skirled and seagulls screamed, as barges lolled past, sails unfurled, sculls sliced through the water like swords and Russian ships from Memel and St. Petersberg lugged their way to the artificial lakes, filled with wine, barrels of porter, brandy. Meanwhile, leaning against a wall, John O'Rourke was dressed in a shabby velvet jacket, sucking on his pipe, oblivious to the clatter of carts around him, the roar of a train overhead, the stevedores and dockworkers hollering, as crates crashed to ground, ropes snapped. He was concentrating hard as he unraveled a scroll of paper, ignoring a boy who was begging at his heels and an old sailor, who had a bright red parrot on his shoulder and was doing the damnedest jig. A little along the way, foremen were shouting from a roster and those who couldn't hear their names were clambering on each other, waving their hands, desperate for any kind of work.

O'Rourke glanced briefly in their direction, knowing that when it came to politics, men who were starving, with nothing to lose, were ripe for the picking. He checked his own worn pockets for a few florins to give to the shop steward, who he'd quote in an article soon to be penned. O'Rourke wrote like a scholar, and his lip curled at Mr. Hecker's, the mill owner, dreadful use of grammar, but that was the English for you. *Philistines, the lot of 'em, yer honor*. But the rehash, by the time he'd embellished it for the second edition of *An Glor*, would set these slums alight. This foreign land of belching smoke would bend to Irish will, sooner than it thought, if things went according to plan.

A tap on his shoulder and O'Rourke swung around to find Damien McCarthy, not his usual fresh-faced self but bug-eyed and haggard.

"Jesus, Damien. You look terrible and you don't smell too good, either."

"I'm done in. I've not been home since our meeting at The Flask. I've been walking the streets for hours, thinking about what's going to happen. We're really going to do it this time, aren't we, John?"

O'Rourke nodded curtly, shoving the scroll at his friend. "Read it, Damien. If you should have any doubts . . ."

"I don't have any doubts, John. Sure, it was just of matter of when. So," said Damien, "what's all this about?"

"You'd hardly call the man a poet," sneered O'Rourke, "But he makes his point all right."

Damien flattened the paper with his hand and read—

From the Office of: Mr. Tobias Hecker, Esquire
Salmon Lane
Limehouse.

To Whomever It May Concern:

Irish workers have recently requested the following—arm guards, a penny rise in wages, compensation for machine injuries incurred whilst on the properties what belongs to Mr. Hecker and . . . here's the nub of it . . . one Sunday off a month.

Mr. Tobias Hecker—Philanthropist, Most Charitable at Heart—says there will be no time off. Not now, not never and more's to the point that a NAIL this VERY MORNING was found in one of his Custard Creams and forthwith, the mill gates will be locked.

Signed, Your Most Eminent etc. etc.

O'Rourke snatched the leaflet back. "Mr. Hecker has already advertised the jobs to Poles, Italians, even the Chinks and Negroes. Most of the Irish will be gathered at the usual tavern by now."

"I know the one. The Salty Dog?"

"Where our boys will be supping their pints but with a bit of organizing, God Knows, they'll be willing to fight. I'll get the shop steward, O'Reilly, to get the men working on banners. O'Brian has blunderbussers, a couple of rifles, gun powder. He keeps it all in the sacristy at the Sacred Heart, would you believe? So, are you with me?"

"I'm with you, John, but what about O'Brian?"

"It was his idea in the first place. O'Reilly, the shop steward, is one of his flock. The chief wants a piece in *The Nation* by tomorrow. Says it'll be vital to garner some sympathy here among the Quakers and anyone else who'll listen to us."

"Carrot and stick, so to speak?"

"Always. So, are you ready, Damien?"

"Lead the way."

They quickly found the tavern, where the two men pushed their way through the grumbling crowd, a heaving morass of hate, as Damien McCarthy told them to be quiet and leapt onto a nearby table. And was it any wonder that these men were willing to listen? McCarthy with his Dublin education reminded the men gathered of another, Daniel O'Connell, who'd led the monster marches back in '47, only this aristo boy was younger and far better-looking.

"Men of Ireland. Listen to me. I'm here on behalf of the Irish National Brotherhood. The chief's heard of your plight and is begging you'll not be taking this lying down this time . . ."

"We don't want any trouble," said a voice in the crowd. "We just want work and to feed our families."

"We can't survive without the mill," said another.

"Our children will starve," said a third, desperation in his voice.

"But not if you take the revolution to them," cried Damien. "This could be the beginning, lads. Just think on it. A free and liberated Ireland? Can you imagine such a thing? We'll burst the factory gates wide open and take the jobs anyway. Hecker owes you that. Men have died on the mill working for what? Pennies? We need to quell men like Hecker and hit them where it hurts, on their own turf. So are you willing?"

The men started to argue among themselves, but some of them were nodding, others cursing the hated mill owner, who'd boasted that he helped the Irish back in '48. Claimed he'd given them free corn and sat on a charitable works' committee. "What of it?" said the younger men who had been babes at the time and could remember nothing akin to any kindness.

Damien reached out to the men and reminded them of all they'd suffered at the hands of their English landowners. The bloody flux, swollen bellies, the stench of famine, fever, living on nothing but grass and berries for year on year, dead babies left to be nibbled by rats and mothers torn apart by dogs. *An Gorta Mor*—the time of famine.

"Go home and talk to your womenfolk, but tomorrow, myself and Mr. O'Rourke—that's the gentleman scribbling at the table over there—will be back again first thing and we'll bring guns, explosives, axes, cudgels. Clan Shan Van Vocht. If you are with us . . ."

The room exploded, hands slammed on the tables, men thumped the walls with their fists, and only a few slipped out with their heads down, shuddering to the resounding cry of "Aye."

5

HIGHGATE VILLAGE

It was two o'clock in the afternoon when Hatton opened the door to a Scotland Yard hansom, expecting to see the diminutive Welshman, hopefully dressed in something more appropriate. It wasn't unusual for Inspector Grey to do at least one costume change during the day. It was well known that Grey kept a rack of Savile Row suits and Jermyn Street shirts hung up in a store cupboard somewhere at Number 4 Whitehall, Scotland Yard.

"I can express myself, or blend in as required," Grey once told Hatton. "One must be ready for anything and Mr. Tescalini keeps my clothes just so. He's a marvel, Professor. Every policeman should have one."

And Hatton was sure, after this morning's eye-aching display of gregarious tartan, he would find Inspector Grey out of his tangerine breeches and head to foot in woven sobriety. But to his surprise there was no Inspector Grey at all within the carriage, sartorially elegant or otherwise.

"*Buongiorno,* Signor Hatton. *Andiamo!*"

It had been six months since the professor last laid eyes on

Mr. Tescalini. Had he got fatter since the performance at the Old Bailey? Hatton wasn't sure, but Tescalini's bulbous head—partly bald, partly badger bristle—and tombstone face still looked the same. Did the man not sleep, he wondered? Hatton had never seen such darkened circles under the eyes, not even in the mirror when he'd been up for two nights on the trot, which was normal at the morgue.

Mr. Tescalini pulled the tatty tails of his ancient frockcoat about his rump. He made a hasty apology in Italian mixed with faint mutterings of English to say that Inspector Grey had gone ahead to Highgate several hours ago, as he was so concerned about "*la bella*"—Hatton presumed the widow.

Hatton shrank into the far side of the coach, uncomfortable at being so close to a man who had once been a suspect in a particularly brutal murder case, even though the Italian had been declared entirely innocent of all charges. This accusation being a particular cause for concern, during a meeting in Inspector Grey's office Hatton had brought the matter up.

They'd been alone in the Criminal Investigation Department sipping coffee at the time, as Hatton had ventured, "Not many policemen have their own servant, Inspector."

"Hmm . . . what did you say?"

"I said, not many . . ."

"Yes, yes," the inspector answered, turning away and looking out of a nearby window. "I'm very lucky, I suppose. Mr. Tescalini has been my assistant for quite a while now. Five years or so. There are a great many Italians in Wales, did you know that?"

"No, Inspector, I didn't know that. So, may I ask, how did you come to hire him?"

The inspector smiled, clearly reminiscing as he said, "I met him down at the docks in Cardiff. It was a beautiful day, July 24, 1853. Off a boat, he'd come, from a far-flung island called Sicily, where families have strong ties. Blood ties, Professor. But blood ties can go array and he'd faced a terrible danger there, which we can never speak of. He'd stowed away on a brig and found himself stranded in Wales of all places, working as a stevedore. He has strong arms, big muscles, have you noticed?"

Hatton shrugged, *Not so you'd know so.*

"Well, Professor, he does. And he has a nose for fashion and the cut of my jib, which is so often the way with these Latin's, which is why he does the valeting. I had a very difficult case on when I met him, involving a number of nasty individuals and a gang of thugs who were on my tail, threatening my very life, and I was in need of some protection, and my errr . . . Auntie Sally . . ."

Hatton leaned forward, "Your Auntie Sally? Where does she come in?"

Grey twisted a gold cuff link. "Nice lady. Presbyterian. Well, she left me a little rhino and as a detective, I have needs, Professor, which The Yard doesn't cater for. This job comes with certain dangers, I make enemies, and as a bachelor I have little time to take care of my toilette, which is something I take considerable pride in. In short, I needed an assistant who could look after me, in more ways than one."

"I see," said Hatton.

Grey leaned across the table. "Of course, he's not officially part of The Yard, but as the years have gone on, Mr. Tescalini has made himself indispensable and I've grown rather attached to him, despite these scurrilous rumors about him being a killer, which is pure rubbish! He's an excellent fellow, which is why I brought him to London, because Mr. Tescalini is a truncheon, Adolphus. A human whistle. If there's danger about, Tescalini will protect me, for he has eyes in the back of his head and he's as loyal as a dog."

In the past, Hatton had often wished that Mr. Tescalini was at least versed in more than just a smattering of the mother tongue, but as he looked at him now—ashen, sweating, and prodding his gums with a toothpick—it occurred to the professor that this lack of English was, in fact, a blessing.

They sat in stony silence all the way to Highgate Hill, until the Italian shifted on his seat and pointed, "Aaah! *Bellissimo cimitero. Ammirevole*, no, Professor Hatton?"

"The Garden of the Dead, Mr. Tescalini. Is that what you are pointing at? Yes, it is very delightful, but I have never visited it myself."

Mr. Tescalini seemed to understand and nodded in sympathy, but the conversation was abruptly called to a halt as the carriage came to a stop and the driver cried out, "Whoa there, my beauties."

"Quanto costa, signor?" Mr Tescalini asked politely to the driver, doffing his battered derby.

"A shilling to you, Mr. Italiano," responded the driver. "And we'll call it no more. A very good day to you, sir."

Hatton was always surprised how very politely everyone spoke to the detective's assistant, because his presentation to the world certainly didn't invite such manners.

The gate to the house was already open, a hand-painted sign decorated with a twist of tenacious buttercups announcing very prettily, *White Lodge*. There was a long gravel pathway winding to the house, past poppies, daylilies, delphinium, and a flush of hollyhocks and scrambling over an ornate wheelbarrow, terra-cotta pots, little topiary hedges, a spread of jasmine and honeysuckle. Hatton took a deep breath and filled his lungs with the perfumed air, and for just a second listened to the delightful drone of honeybees.

But there was no time to spare. Mr. Tescalini rapped on the door, his ham fists pounding, and it was instantly opened by a Special in a blue uniform with gilt buttons, who ushered them into what Hatton thought must be the study. But the curtains were shut, as was tradition with death, and the rheumy light offered him nothing.

"Please see to the drapes, Mr. Tescalini, for I cannot work in the dark."

A rush of light, and Hatton almost jumped out of his skin to see Inspector Grey sitting on a red leather and mahogany chair.

"How very like you to draw the curtains, Hatton. But you're quite right to illuminate the matter, and you're exactly on time."

Hatton looked askance at him. "On time, Inspector?"

"For a communion, Hatton."

The inspector spun the chair and faced him. "There is a mood of unease here, and I'm a great believer in the telling nature of sensation, when an unexpected death occurs. I know you are of a more scientific inclination, Professor, but as I sat here in the dark, on the dead man's chair, certain feelings began to form. They are not clear yet, but my initial hunches are rarely wrong."

Mr. Tescalini stared at Hatton, his bloodshot eyes challenging the professor to nay say these spiritualist connections, but Hatton simply let the mesmerism nonsense float, saying, "So you have a sensation, Inspector Grey? And yes, houses often do convey feelings. But what did the widow tell you? Anything of note?"

Inspector Grey smiled, and lit a wafer-thin cigarillo.

"That Gabriel McCarthy was a man under strain, Professor. It seems there were financial issues, which out of kindness I did not let her dwell on. But the widow is already fretting about the cost of shipping the body to the family estate in Donegal."

"I see," said Hatton, wishing the inspector would stub his cigarillo out. This was a crime scene, and any trace of a vital odor that might linger in the air and lead them to a killer would be destroyed, masked at the very least.

"There's also a brother," Grey continued. "He has apparently lived with the couple since they married, having no place of his own. The widow says she hasn't seen him since yesterday evening, and on that point, I must confess that I pushed a little and she became most distressed. Most agitated. She wrung her delicate hands, tears flowed, and she told me that the brothers were at loggerheads—over money, over politics, over being here in England, and other things besides which I can only guess at. All this"—he looked at his pocket watch—"in under an hour. She was a tap, Hatton. After I adjusted the valve of her emotions, a veritable tap. And such an outpouring that I felt the poor Mrs. McCarthy should rest a while before we cursed her with any more questions. But back to forensics, Professor. Unfortunately, it appears that the room has been tidied."

The inspector was right. There were no upturned chairs and no sign of struggle. The fireplace had been swept, the carpets brushed, the whole place smelling, he now noticed, not of the inspector's cigarillo but of household disinfectant. Damn, thought Hatton as he sighed, taking his notebook out. "It's a shame the maid got in before us, but forensically speaking, poison is a quiet death. It leaves no bloody footsteps for us to follow. We may have to make do with your sensations, Inspector."

Hatton shook his head at the devastation of the crime scene, a room cleared of all possible clues, and put his notebook away. He turned to the desk where the inspector was still sitting, rifling through official-looking papers.

"Have you looked at all his correspondence?" the professor asked, hoping for something.

"There is little here to interest me," said Grey. "A copy of that despicable newspaper, *An Glor*, with bits of blarney torn out and a pile of parliamentary papers. A scattering of newspaper clippings, not entirely cleared from the grate. But there are no immediate state secrets. Nothing to pinpoint a political motivation, but I'm quite sure Gabriel McCarthy had his enemies. Appeasement rarely wins friends, and in that regard, I shall be most interested in talking to the brother."

"Who I assume will inherit everything?"

The detective sat back in the chair. "Yes, Hatton, everything. But it's a mixed blessing, as far as he's concerned. A struggling estate in Donegal, mountains of debts, and an unwanted seat in the House, should he decide to take it. Although it's well known that Damien McCarthy's views are not his brother's, so that isn't likely. He's a thorn in the Union's side, and a very vocal Repealer. But there is another prize, which I believe is a tradition among the Irish gentry."

"A prize, Inspector? What sort of prize?"

"It appears that he might also inherit the widow. You know what a village is like for tittle-tattle. But at this stage, it's nothing more than a rumor. "

The detective paused, looking out toward the verdant garden, and spoke as if to himself. "She is a dark and most enticing flower. And as such, provides the younger brother with a clear motive and my favorite sort of murder—*La crime passionnel*." The inspector carried on looking out of the window for a moment before turning back to Hatton. "So yes, the brother must be treated as a prime suspect, unless your gatherings of evidence, such as you can still do, suggest otherwise."

Hatton looked briefly over his shoulder and checked that the door was shut before he ventured, "I'm not sure this is a crime of passion. Monsieur Roumande and I finished the final autopsy only an hour ago. This death has a signature. A very clear one. May I speak freely, Inspector?"

"Well, there's no one to hear us."

In the corner of the room, Mr. Tescalini was stuffing a small iced cake into his mouth. There was a china cup balanced on his knee. On the table next to him was a Bible and a little stack of books—essays by Carlyle, Mr. Tennyson's *In Memorium*. Hatton realized there was no easy way to put it.

"There was a ribbon in Gabriel McCarthy's mouth, Inspector, and the ribbon was green. Surely this means only one thing?"

"A ribbon, you say?"

The inspector visibly shuddered, his face twisting like a gargoyle, as he jumped up and spat, literally spat, saying, "Then damn those fucking Irish scum to the bottom of the sea, but I thought we'd seen the last of them. The Irish Republican Brotherhood? Isn't that what they call themselves now, and there's another word, isn't there . . . and the word is—"

There was a knock and in the doorway stood a fresh-faced maid laden down with a tray.

Grey was transformed—as if he hadn't been speaking at all.

"Ah, excellent. French Fancies. My absolute favorite. It's the combination of sugar and violets I find so irresistible."

The maid set the rattling tray down, and began to pour the tea, saying, "Mrs. McCarthy cannot sleep, sir, as you suggested. She heard the gentlemen's voices and wanted to meet them."

A young woman came into the room behind the maid, her voice steady. "I am here already. Thank you, Florrie. You may leave the tea. "

The woman was dressed in black, with skin the color of milk and lips damson red, as if she'd been chewing them. Her eyes were swollen from crying and she begged, "Please, do not stand for me, gentlemen, but sit. As I shall," she said as she fanned herself. "Forgive me, I needed to speak to you but I am not so well today."

She found an easy chair, helped by Inspector Grey. "I'm not usually lost for words." She fanned herself a little more, as she turned to Hatton. "You must be the doctor from St. Bart's? My husband, sir, when will you return him to me?"

Was it so obvious that he was the guardian of the dead? Hatton supposed it must be, as he said, "The body of your husband will be with you soon, Mrs. McCarthy. I will deliver him myself."

She was twisting her fingers in agitation, shaking her head, which was a tumble of black locks, a little unkempt, as she said, "I haven't yet spoken to Gabriel's brother about the funeral and there's no instruction in the will, but England was not his home . . ." Her voice trailed off. "I cannot yet accept that Gabriel is dead." Her body suddenly folded, as she let out a muted groan. Rather than having left the room as she'd been bid, the maid immediately sprang to her mistress's aid. "You need some more tonic, madam, or some salts . . ." The maid looked at the men with accusation in her face, but the widow pushed her away. "Don't smother me. I will speak to these men. Now please, Florrie, leave me." Mrs. McCarthy pulled herself up again, brushing down the black gown, which had ridden up a little, hinting at the slimmest of ankles, a petticoat, pushing the fallen locks away from her face.

"I am calm," she said. "Perfectly." She looked directly at Hatton, who felt uneasy under those dark and questioning eyes. Was it her eyes? Or a particular look? What was it? Under the intensity of her gaze, he looked away, but having already stolen a glance at her face, which had made Hatton silently gasp, felt sick to his stomach.

It wasn't that she was exquisite. Her skin was dewy in the heat, wet with perspiration, wan with emotion—but that wasn't it. Nor was it the groove of an elegant clavicle or the fine line of her throat. It was something else. He looked again, to see a face he was sure he knew. The cheekbones were sharper, higher. This jaw was more defiant, the lips darker, fuller. She must have seen him or felt the gaze, because instantly, her fingers fluttered across her collarbone. Hatton noted a wedding ring and looked away.

"Are you quite all right, Hatton?" It was Grey. "Open a window, Mr. Tescalini. Our professor has also gone quite pale, but a gasp of Highgate air should cure him."

Hatton felt foolish. Had he been staring? He deliberately moved a little away from her, but still caught a hint of something in the air? *My God,* he thought, it was the very same. What was it? He tried to grasp it. Nutmeg. The scent she brought into the room was sweet like nutmeg.

But still holding him with determined black eyes, she continued, "Tell me the truth because I'm not a child. It wasn't cholera, was it, Professor? Do you know what killed Gabriel?" she hesitated. "Do you know what caused that look of terror on his face?" and with a slight choking sound, she buried her own.

Trying to concentrate on the scientific findings and not on the beauty of the widow, Hatton answered as straight as he could, blinking back a vision of his father's farm, a dusty ditch, and up ahead an oak tree carved with initials and a heart. "The grimace on his face, I will explain in a moment, madam, but the blackening of his skin was ash from a grate."

"Ashes from a grate? What a strange thing, but why on earth would anyone do that?"

Concentrate, thought Hatton. *Just answer her. She is not the same. She is different. Quite different.*

"To panic those that found him, and you see," he said, surveying the room, "your maid has scrubbed this room for fear of cholera, I presume. But if I may, I would still like to take samples from the fireplace. The ash is likely to match, I think."

She leaned forward a little, her pert figure poised at the end of the easy chair. "You can do that? You have the expertise?"

Hatton replied, as the memory of another time and place morphed into the present. He said emphatically, "We are making great strides in that direction. There are a number of tests I can do when I get to back to St. Bart's, but only with your permission?" She nodded, of course. "Was the room like this when you found your husband?"

"He was lying on the floor, Professor, already cold. I've told Inspector Grey all that I know." She hesitated and seemed to be thinking, and then continued, "Yes, a chair had been knocked over, that was all. Florrie must have tidied things up and shut the window, after I sent a message to Scotland Yard and they arranged to take my husband to St. Bart's."

"Did you hear nothing last night? We estimate his time of death was around midnight."

"No, Professor. I heard nothing. I brought him his supper, I bid him good night. I always wear this," she pulled up a watch on a golden chain, as if to prove herself. "The last time I saw my husband alive it was just gone eight o'clock. Gabriel often worked late, but he never disturbed me. This is a large house, and I must confess I took a little something last night and I'm a heavy sleeper, anyway. Gabriel begged me to get a dog, in case something like this happened. We are a well-known family, unpopular because of the Union, and he said an intruder might—" She started to cry, dabbing her swollen eyes with a handkerchief. "My husband is . . . he was . . . a very thoughtful man. Inspector Grey has told me, Professor, that you think he was murdered."

Her voice had flattened out into an odd monotone, which Hatton now recognized. Somebody must have given her opium to calm the nerves. Or that dreadful quackery they called Parker's Tonic, which he recalled from his training days was a potentially lethal combination of thirty grams of opium, a dash of ether, Ipecacuanha wine, a splash of chloroform, and six fluid ounces of rose hip syrup.

"Yes, madam, I'm afraid it was almost certainly strychnine. Is there any in the house? Perhaps the maid would know? It is commonly used as rat poison, or in gardens to kill the weeds, and accidents occasionally happen."

She turned her eyes toward the window, but didn't answer, the merest impression of a frown.

"Take your time, Mrs. McCarthy. Don't vex yourself."

It was Inspector Grey, his tone soft and soothing.

"The mind plays tricks but I think you know a little of my husband's life, Inspector. You must know what I am thinking?" Her voice grew more resolute. "That this was an act of punishment."

Hatton watched the inspector crouch down at her side, strangely intimate, and as she tilted her face toward him, there was passion in her eyes. "You knew his politics, Inspector. It was no secret that he was committed to his fellow countrymen, but Gabriel was a Unionist, and this won him many enemies. He was prepared to wait for freedom. In Ireland we say *Fan tamall,* and how rare is that among the young?"

She spoke as if she wasn't young herself, although Hatton guessed she was little more than twenty. Twenty? How old must Mary have been when he last set eyes on her?

Mary, thought Hatton.

A name and a girl he hadn't dared think of for so many years, but he thought of her now.

In the blink of an eye, he could see her clearly, skipping along by the hedgerows near his father's farm, calling him to join her. She was fifteen, the beginnings of a woman, and he must have been, what? More or less, the same. *Mary, Mary, Quite Contrary. How does your garden grow? With silver bells, and cockle shells, and pretty maids all in a row.* Pretty maids? Whose mind was playing the trickery now?

"Passion can be a hard thing to bear," said the widow. "It can be a burden. But Gabriel was prepared to work with the British, and keep the Union strong. He had worries, he was often tired, and he had a workload which took its toll, but he had everything to live for . . ."

Yes, thought Hatton, he could see that, and at that he wanted to reach out to comfort her, to take her hand as he had taken Mary's, but he kept to his designated place and only asked, "So, there's no strychnine in the house, Mrs. McCarthy?"

"You're right to keep me to the point," she answered. "I run the house, but I don't keep a tally of every item. I leave that to Florrie. We have traps for vermin, I think. Yes, I'm sure Florrie always uses traps. But perhaps . . ."

"What, madam?" said the inspector.

"I think we might use poison on the lawn." She stood up and moved to the window. Hatton's eyes followed her, thinking she wasn't exactly the same, she had nuances which were different, quite different. There was an inner strength in Mrs. McCarthy, despite her grief, determined as she said, "My brother-in-law likes the feel of the soil on his hand. We are Irish and to my people, land is everything. He prunes the roses, cuts the grass, and does the work himself, and he does it with a good heart. A gift to me, he says. Gabriel wished he wouldn't, but there were so many daisies on the lawn that, yes I'm sure, that he may have used something to keep them down."

The inspector, not taking his eyes off the widow, "Daisies, you say? Well, when your bother-in-law finally returns, I need to speak to him. He's been out all night? Bit odd, isn't it?"

She looked suddenly terrified. "My God, Inspector, he's not a suspect, is he? They're brothers and Damien's a committed Christian, Inspector. I can't entertain the thought that . . ."

Inspector Grey was studying the garden.

"Did you choose those particular roses, my dear?"

She looked confused but answered, "Damien planted them, Inspector. They're a French rose."

Grey smiled. "Ah, yes, Félicité et Perpétue. A wonderful rose for the position. A rambler longs to be warm. It needs to be south-facing. May I compliment you, just a little?"

And Hatton watched as the widow opened her mouth to speak but instead changed her mind and remained silent. The inspector took a step toward her, and for a moment Hatton thought the detective might kiss her hand, but he did nothing of the sort. He only offered his deepest condolences as he opened the door and guided Mrs. McCarthy out, returning one minute later, sticking his head back around the door saying, "Gather any evidence you can, Professor. Do a sweep of the kitchen, any store cupboards, the cellar, those potting sheds beyond the lawn, and it goes without saying, the garden. Another hour alone with me and she will be a tap, a veritable tap . . ."

Hatton was left in the room alone and sat on the edge of the easy chair as the widow had done. The room was overbearingly warm as he briefly shut his eyes, to hear his father's voice, echoing through his mind—

"Stay away from those children, Lucy. I've told you before."

His sister Lucy was indignant. She'd been darning stockings at the time, in the farmhouse kitchen. "It's not I that plays with the tinkers, Pa. It's Addy. I'm forever warning him not to."

"Well, Adolphus?"

"They're only here for the summer, Pa, and will soon return to Ireland. They're only here for the hop picking."

His father shook his head, "That's not what the neighbors say. They say the tinkers are stealing."

"*With respect, Pa . . .*"

"*What's that? Who've you been listening to? A tinker's word, against our neighbors? Just remember that it's our neighbors that lend a hand with the hay, that bring us eggs when our hens don't lay. It's our neighbors that we rely on, that have stood with our family through thick and thin, when your poor, dear mother . . .*"

Adolphus hung his head and muttered, "*Mother always said it was wrong to look down on traveling people. That tinkers brought good luck, a bit of color and spirit to the Shires.*"

"*Don't talk to me of your mother. Do you understand me? Your mother has gone. Forever and I won't—*" His father raised his trembling hand, as Adolphus lowered his eyes to the ground. "*Stay away from the tinkers, do you hear me?*"

Lucy piped up, mischief in her eye. "*It's only one he talks to, Pa, and she's as pretty as can be. The blackest hair you've ever seen, like a raven, and the whitest skin, but as for that accent, 'Would yer be sparing me a jug of wartair, for I'm terrible parched, beggin' yer pardin, Missy . . .*" Her voice was taunting, an older sister's revelry, and at this moment, Adolphus hated Lucy with all his heart as she sang, "*Mary, Mary quite contrary . . . Addy is in luu . . . huvvvvv . . .*"

Quick as a rat, Adolphus turned on Lucy, grabbing a thick blond plait.

"*Pa! Pa! Hellllpppp . . . Get off me, Addy, or I swear . . .*"

A sharp bite to his arm finished the matter.

"*You're not too old to go to your rooms, both of you. And Adolphus, I'll belt you into a month of Sundays if you ever go near that tinker girl . . . it'll bring nothing but trouble . . . stay away from her . . .*"

Hatton sighed and opened his eyes, knowing as he looked through the window at the glorious garden, that Mrs. McCarthy wasn't the same. Similarities, yes, but she was no double, no doppelganger. Mary hadn't come back from the grave. The black hair, the white skin, those dark, questioning eyes—were just an echo.

Hatton stood up and got on with his work. His work of death. His work of observation, brushing, measuring, and collecting, of noting and deciphering. He did his best, scrutinizing every corner of the room and, as he went about his work, breathing in the fresh air from the opened window and the scent the widow had worn, heady in the summer air. And almost despite himself, he ran his hands over the back of the easy chair where Mrs. McCarthy's head had rested, and gently using tiny silver tweezers, retrieved a long strand of iridescent hair. Hatton put it in a bag and labeled it *Item 1*, knowing he would keep it, perhaps look at it again when he got back to the morgue. Might it be useful? Might it tell him something? Might he put it with another he had kept? But that would be odd, he thought. Yes, in this heat, the mind played tricks on one.

6

SOHO

The floor Jasper Tooley knelt on was hard. There was no cushion upon it, but he guessed on the other side of the grill there was a crimson one for the priest. The priest, thought Jasper, deserved cosseted knees, for he was the *Representative of God on Earth.* Head down and hands clasped in the presence of such an earthly deity, the boy whispered, "Bless me, Father, for I have sinned."

In the other chamber, a small tallow candle threw a lick of dirty light up behind a mouthing silhouette. A gloomy face, an outline of lips and lashes. The gruff voice which came back cut him off with, "Well, whatever you've done, I absolve you from your sins, in the name of the Father, the Son, and the Holy Spirit, *Gloria Patri, et Filio, et Spiritui Sancto.* Amen."

"Amen."

"What time is it?"

"It's four o'clock now, Father."

Despite the heat outside on the streets of London, the Church of the Sacred Heart was cold. Jasper did what he was told, which was three Hail Marys and five Our Fathers, but before he managed to finish his prayers, he was hauled up by the scruff of his neck and pulled roughly into a dark corner under one of the vaulting aisles, as the priest hissed, "Where have you been, anyway? We've work to do and you smell rank, you smell of dead men."

"It's glue from the bindings, Father. It's made from animal bone and smells like the devil. I only came here to tell you that I went for a quick drink in the rookeries, and there's rumors flying around like mad. They're saying Gabriel McCarthy's dead and also that there's trouble at the docks. That Mr. O'Rourke is on his way there now."

There was a slight pause, an intake of breath, but when the priest spoke, he was matter-of-fact. "Sure, I knew it already about Gabriel, and if you ask me, it's been a long time coming, and I gave the order to O'Rourke to pay a visit to Limehouse. Nothing happens without my knowledge. See here"—the priest pointed to his skull—"all seein' and all knowin'. I sent O'Rourke to the docks a couple of hours ago. But speaking of the devil, have you seen Damien? I haven't laid eyes on him since last night."

The boy stuffed his hands in his pockets, looking at the floor, saying nothing.

The priest tucked an oily black strand behind his ear. "Well, it doesn't look good, one brother dead and the other not seen for dust. The police will be sniffing about, though those cowards don't dare come into St. Giles. We'd fucking kill them if they did. This is our turf now."

The pair of them—odd shadows on the walls of a very tall priest and a very crooked boy—made their way past the Stations of the Cross, stopping to genuflect before they crossed the nave of the church and disappeared into the sacristy, where the priest de-robed, then said "This way" as he opened an arched door at the very back of the room.

Outside the church it was still a drowsy summer afternoon.

The other boys waiting for the catechism were sitting in the church garden, shaded by apple trees, and beyond the trees an unruly bed of snapdragons, poppies, and other jeweled petals—which the priest didn't heed at all because he was far too busy counting heads, like an expectant schoolmaster.

"So who's got what, then? Come on lads, cough it up. I can't run this place on air. I've told your mammies, before. I need money."

A cap was passed around, with the usual paltry offerings dropped in of farthings, bits of old stale toke, and excuses made as to why one or two of the lads had nothing to give, their families having been cleared out already by the gombeen man.

The priest spat, "Of course, it's fucking Monday, isn't it? What did he take, this time? Steal the roof over your head? Well, he would if he could. Gregory Mahoney still comes here to church, the sniveling wretch, begging me for forgiveness. Well, shall I give it to him, boys? In spades? Shall I pay him a little visit he'll never forget? I've a mind to, because God knows he's deserving enough."

Father O'Brian knew everyone in the Seven Dials and what they owed this world and the next. He made a point of it, and as if Nature reflected his thoughts, a cloud must have passed briefly over the sun, because the air felt suddenly cold. One of the boys shivered, another giggled, as the priest's wiry shape cast a threatening shadow across the lawn.

If the boys were pale, they grew paler. If they were quiet, they grew quieter. "Stay away from that devil, boys. He's no better than a Jew, a Jesus murderer. Understand me? And if you see him coming, run and hide, scatter like the wind, get to the hay barn and lay down real quiet. Keep the babe from crying, because ssshhhh, he's coming . . ." One of the boys said, "I need to go the privy, Father." But the priest, ignoring him, whispered, "He's coming. Gregory Mahoney's coming over the brow of the hill, do you see him, boys? Oh yes, he's coming with that miserable cur, but have you seen him kick that cur? It's a wonder the creature's still alive . . ."

One of the boys began to wail as the priest jumped up, threw his head back, laughed and said, "Why only last week that bloodsucker came into mass, sniveling and saying, 'It wasn't me that hurt the colleens down on the beaches, Father.' And do you know what I did to him? I hauled him up, like the traitor he is, and told him that he was going to hell."

The boys were blessing themselves, their eyes out on stalks.

"That traitor not only raped, he killed his own people with promises he made about a New World which were lies, all lies. Anyways, enough of that. Let's think about the future." Holding up three fingers, Father O'Brian continued with his class, "So, off the top, what are the three R's toward Irish liberty?"

"Ribbons," shouted one of the boys. "Green ribbons!"

"Revenge!" shouted another.

"Revolution!" said a third.

"Exactly," said the priest. "You've been listening well. So, can anyone add to this?"

Jasper put up a faltering hand.

"Yes, you—Jasper Tooley, from our little cell of one in Clapham."

"Errr . . . readies, rhino, and religion, Father."

"Hmm, not bad, but there's another thing. Very important this, and I need a word in your shell like—alone."

The other boys at the catechism instantly scattered, the crippled child left skulking under the shade of an apple tree, and for a moment the priest looked at this child with his rickety spine, who briefly reminded him of so many others who were long dead, burned in a pyre or buried in quicklime. He pushed his sorrow down and said, "Word is your family's now binding books for the British government?"

Under the glare of the priest, the boy almost physically shrunk.

"You don't need to answer because I already know," the priest winked, knowingly. "Did you and your pa have a nice cup of tea with the chief clerk of Her Majesty's Home Office, Mr. Amersham, then?"

The boy stuttered, "But I swore, Father. I swore on pain of death. Mr. Amersham made Pa sign The Limitation of Speech

Act. He was very particular and asked all sorts of questions before giving out the contract, which is worth *five hundred guineas.* You're not Catholics are you, he said? My pa said emphatically no, sir. That we are, God forgive me, Father"—he hung his head and whispered—"*Church of Ireland.*"

The priest's face was stone. "How dare you utter those sacrilegious words in this holy place? Don't you understand that Church of Ireland doesn't exist? It's a British invention, a colonial invention, and that's why your mammy sends you *here* for catechism, to be a proper Catholic. Is your brain crippled as well? I thought you artisans were educated. Jesus, Mary, and Joseph."

Suddenly gripping the boy in his vicelike hands, Father O'Brian raised his eyes skyward, "Am I right or am I wrong? Did you, or did you not, sign a contract with the Home Office this morning at precisely ten o'clock?"

The boy was amazed, thinking this man was like a God who could see every move he made, every place he went, every thought in his head. The Home Office contract was a secret. It was confidential work and worth a fortune to his pa. But Jasper knew he'd no choice but to confess, so lowering his head as if in prayer, he said, "You're right, Father. My family took a large order of bookbinding from the Home Office today, including files going back ten years to the times of famine. *An gorta mor,* Father."

"So, the rumors are true. How many files, would you say?"

"A veritable cartload, Father."

The priest leaned in a little nearer. "Anything pertaining to something called the *Gregory Clause?*"

"The Gregory Clause? I don't know about that. The files are all piled up in the bindery in Clapham. There are heaps and heaps of them and their guts are hanging out. Gregory Clause? Now you come to mention it . . ."

"What?" O'Brian rasped, practically salivating.

The boy, having recovered a little, was not without insolence. He eyeballed the priest, "First I need to know, will you be taking me to Lourdes? Will I get to meet the little Bernadette girl, who cures the sick? *Like you promised me, Father.*"

The priest went to pull the boy's ear, but then thought better of it, saying, "Don't push it, Tooley. Gregory Clause. Yes or no?"

"Yes, Father."

The priest patted the crippled boy on the head. "You'll make us a fine little foot soldier one day. The Home Office, eh? So, Senior Intelligence Officer Jasper Tooley, take a pen and write this down." He cleared his throat and repeated. "'The Gregory Clause 1847.' Got that, lad? The exact detail of this clause has been denied on a number of occasions, but Mr. O'Rourke and I are sure it exists. But we need to see it. We need to see how they did it. We need to see who sanctioned the tumbling."

7

HIGHGATE

The day had been a long one. The house in Highgate offering very little in terms of forensic evidence, but nevertheless Hatton had taken three samples of household ash, a variety of bottles from the cleaning cupboard, and what Mrs. McCarthy claimed was her husband's draught—a small, blue bottle containing laudanum. The sun was just beginning to dip as Hatton wandered into the meadows of White Lodge, which were ablaze with poppies, iridescent dragonflies, beewhals, and butterflies. Getting his notebook out from his medicine bag, he added "antimony" to the lists of common poisons he'd already found, or knew he would find with a bit more quizzing of the maid. Mercury and arsenic in the household paint, hydrochloric acid, morphine for bouts of indigestion, tincture of Belladonna for ladies' complaints. All highly toxic, yes, but not enough to kill a man, and no sign of that deadliest of all—crushed from the seeds of an Indian deciduous tree—*nux-vomica.*

But knowing all the time that murder left an imprint and that to doubt, to look again, to ask questions, always questions, and to look beyond the obvious was all that mattered. Death would speak to him, he just had to listen. But right now, all Hatton could hear was the burring of chickens as he bent his head under a lintel, stepping into the cooling shade of one of the outhouses, an ancient half-forgotten place which smelled of dry hay, rushes, and something he knew at once–the cut of turpentine.

Leaning up against a wall was an easel, a few pots of paint, some brushes, and a number of half-finished paintings. Brightly colored oils of romanticized places and one in particular which caught his eye, having the air of a Constable about it—a river-scape, a muddy beach, a dear little skiff named *Liberty* nestling under a weeping willow, and in the distance, what he knew to be an ait—a river island.

Her voice made him jump when it came.

"Are you admiring my paintings, Professor?"

She was wearing a linen smock with a thick, brown leather belt around her waist. Her hair hung loose in a most becoming way, and her feet, he noticed, were bare. "My poor, dear husband wasn't one to stand on ceremony, Professor, and I could no longer wear those heavy mourning silks. The heat is making me ill."

Hatton was embarrassed. "It's not for me to judge, madam . . ." clearly averting his eyes. There was a strong, bright light behind her which melded the dove gray dress into practically nothing, a diaphanous shift.

"No, it's not for you to judge, though I find the English often do," she said, stepping out of the light, her dress becoming thick again, in the shadows of the outhouse—the long line of her thighs, the curve of her hips, the nip of the waist, other things, secret things, disappearing again.

He hung his head with shame at his lascivious thoughts, and at the same time was cross that the young woman would appear like this, unannounced, to creep up on him like that. For heaven's sake, couldn't she see he was working? That he was a busy man and she was interrupting.

"I am interrupting you," she said. "But your inspector is talking to Florrie for so long, and I came out here to think. My mind is tormented with questions, Professor, so many questions. Was there something I didn't do, something I didn't say, something I should have heard but didn't? That in some way, Gabriel's death is my fault. Please, Professor . . . do whatever you must . . ."

She leaned against the wall, as if she might faint.

Hatton was aghast at himself. This was a young woman in obvious distress, and he was a doctor and should behave like one. She needed to sit, to have something for the shock, but not those damn quackery tonics used for feminine hysteria. A glass of brandy would be better. He would see to that in just a second, but before heading to find the maid, he took her arm and steered her to a milking stool, saying, "Please, Mrs. McCarthy, rest awhile."

She looked up him. "Florrie gave me a draft and I'm not used to such things. I feel a little dizzy." He took her wrist to feel the pulse. "Don't take any more of that tonic, Mrs. McCarthy. It's full of morphine and Indian hemp. Overdoses are not uncommon, so I strongly suggest, steer clear of it."

"I will, Professor," she said, as he held her wrist and looked into her eyes for a second too long.

"Ah there you are, Hatton . . ." Inspector Grey was suddenly under the lintel. "I thought I might find you out here. We shall be off now, Mrs. McCarthy, but I'll be back the minute your brother returns, so as soon as he shows himself send a message to The Yard, clearly marked for my attention, Room Three, Second Floor, Criminal Investigation Department."

As they got into the waiting carriage, Grey was initially effusive, grabbing Hatton's arm with, "The widow was a tap, a veritable tap. Far be it for me to say, but as a confirmed bachelor, I seem to have a way with women, a natural affinity with the fairer sex. Couldn't stop the little woman talking . . . on and on she went."

Oh, do be quiet for once, thought Hatton as Grey complied and lapsed into silence for most of the journey back to the city, only every now and then letting a self-satisfied smirk break over pencil-thin lips, as he remembered something Mrs. McCarthy had done, or something she'd said.

Hatton had to steel himself. It was a lonely fact that, apart from brushing past nurses on his way to the morgue, the demands of his work ensured he had little opportunity to enjoy the company of women. Until now, he'd rarely let this thought bother him, so intent was he on work, but as he looked out of the window, at the flat line of the sky and the density of buildings, he remembered:

He'd been fishing in the brook for hours when he heard a long, low whistle, thinking it was the village dolt, Eddy Stoates, come to scare the fish away. But then a peep, peep, peep like a bird and the snap of a branch. He thought no more of it but cast his rod again, intent on landing a trout, but then another flitter and a shower of tiny pebbles, breaking the surface of the water.

That does it, he thought.

It was time he taught that dolt a lesson. He loathed the village boys at the best of times. Their heads were full of nothing, and it was sheep that moved in a herd, not men. Addy dreamt of escape, a different kind of life, and this shady brook was his secret place, a place to be quiet and think about his future. He didn't want to be a farmer, a life driven by the elements and seasons, the lay of the land, the bland demands of soil prices, hungry pigs to feed. He dreamt of higher things, but this thought was broken by another shower of pebbles and a girlish laugh.

"Hey you?" he cried, but she was gone in an instant. Addy threw his rod down and went after her. A flash of black hair, she ran like the wind up the grassy bank, but he was a damn good hunter when he put his mind to it. "Got you!" he said, as the girl—and she was a girl despite her strange appearance—fell to her knees then turned around to face him, saying, "Saoirse . . ." Her breathing came in sharp little rasps as he held her to the ground. "You scared the fish away . . ." He grabbed her wrists

*tighter. "Who are you? What do you want?" "Saoirse . . ." "I
don't understand you? Speak English." He held her there for a
few more seconds, pinned beneath him, his legs straddling a thin
body in rags. There was a storm coming, electric in the air, a crack
of thunder, clouds rolling in. His breath running faster than hers.*

*"I speak the Queen's own English," she said, wriggling free of
him. "I speak Latin, as well. All Irish do, maaaster." The "maaaster" said with a sly smile. The girl brushed her ragged dress down
as if it was the best Indian silk. She had flowers in her hair—
speedwell and purple mallow. Ophelia, he thought, laughing to
himself. "Sure, the fish could see you coming for a mile. I was
standing on the bank watching you. I could teach you how to
tickle them straight out of the water, if you want me to."*

*Hatton laughed out loud. "I'd like to see you try. A girl who
can fish? Now I've heard everything. You're Irish aren't you?"
She curtsied, lower than she should have done. "My people are
here for the seasonal work, yer honor. There's nothing at home."
She twisted her foot in the ground and sighed. "We're here for
the hops but I slipped off half an hour ago." She looked at him,
with defiance in her eyes. He walked off, thinking girls are stupid and a waste of good fishing time, but she followed him and
continued to seek him out and follow him for that long hot
summer, and when summer was out, he was of a different mind
altogether.*

*She drew him into her world. Each night he'd leave the house,
while the others were asleep, to visit the camp on the edge of hop
fields; flames of fire under a dark luminous sky, the sound of
rapacious fiddling, and, in the middle, a people gone mad, wild
with drink and dancing, Mary festooned with ribbons, golden
bells around her heels.*

*She was always questioning why the moon controlled the
waves, why the sun rose, was it true what people said about the
layering of the earth? She told him stories, but said they weren't
stories, but legends—ancient legends of a noble people, with their
own language and their own ways, downtrodden by his. He'd be*

angry with her and she'd only kiss him and tell him, "It's of no matter, Addy. A hundred years ago. All forgiven and forgotten."

He should have heeded his father's warning.

The accusation came on the brow of a hill. Eddy Stoates had come out of nowhere, red-faced, spitting, "That Irish bitch of yours is stealing. Her whole family is. Our milk's gone sour, the hens ain't laying, my ma's silver brush has been taken from the dresser."

Eddy Stoates was leering at her. "So, what have you got to say for yourself? But I'll let you off a thrashing if you give me whatever you're givin' Addy Hatton, here . . ."

Hatton rounded on him, saying he would give him a pummeling if he didn't take every word back and, for good measure, Mary said, "He'll not be bothering me, Addy. Pogue mahone, Stoat face . . ."

"Irish bitch."

Addy was quick, running at Eddy Stoates, leveling him, his fists raised for more. "Apologize, right now——"

Mary was quicker, laughing her head off and grabbing some itchy hay, sticking it down the boy's shirt and calling him a scarecrow. "That'll teach you a lesson." The boy kicked her and wrestled himself free and slunk off. "You'll pay for this . . ."

Addy brushed himself down. "Are you all right, Mary? He didn't hurt you, did he?"

She smiled. "Is Troid e an Saol! Life's a fight, Addy. We saw him off though, didn't we?"

If only he had seen her home, back to the bosom of her family, but after talking for a while, he gave Mary a farewell kiss and left her on the path. He had studying to do, he said. September loomed and his pa had finally raised the capital for boarding school. "Of course you must go." She squeezed his hand. "Grab this opportunity with both hands, Addy. You can be whatever you want."

"I want to be a doctor. To study science, chemistry, anatomy and go to Edinburgh, where the best work is done."

"And you shall," she said, skipping off, her figure getting smaller and smaller, merging into the hedgerows.

Not enough evidence they said, as a cold-blooded murderer walked away from the magistrate's court. Eddy Stoates had always been violent, a real temper on him, a dog teaser, a kitten drowner.

When they found her, she was hanging from a Hawthorne tree, the speedwell in her hair, spoiled with blood. The coroner said she'd been raped before she was hung. There was a bloody footprint in the ground, marks around her neck, a crushed larynx but still not enough evidence they said to hang a seventeen-year-old English lad. Hatton's pa had shaken his head in disgust as he left the gallery, and swore there was no justice in the world—"A peasant," he said. "That's what our so-called neighbors called her. I'd like to string them up myself." And Lucy sobbed and sobbed and said, "My poor, poor Addy . . ."

Not poor Addy, Hatton thought. And whenever he a saw a fish jump, starlight break the density of trees, summer shadows skip before him, campfires, a country fiddle—he thought of Mary, and of what could never be.

"Have you ever eaten at Verrey's, Professor?" There was a long pause before the detective repeated, "Professor, you're away with the fairies. I just asked you a question. Would you be so polite as to answer me?"

Hatton murmured he had little time for such things, nor, sadly, the money.

"Well, we shall dine there tonight," announced Grey. "I have to interview Monsieur Pomeroy's sous chef."

Hatton didn't reply, his mind flitting again to a long, hot summer, twenty years ago.

"Professor, please! Pay attention. Our missing chef? The Pomeroy fellow hasn't shown his face for over a week and I'm getting quite a lot of nudging by the ladies of this town and sharp prods from Mr. Hecker."

Hatton rubbed his eyes and tried to concentrate. "Mr. Hecker? Remind me, Inspector?"

"The mill owner and flour magnate, up in Limehouse. Mr. Hecker and Gustave Pomeroy were well-acquainted, it seems. Hecker is an influential man and has a number of important friends at The Yard, including the commissioner."

Hatton wished the inspector would cease with this nonsense, but the policeman didn't, he barely took a breath. "And I am sure you know, Professor, Verrey's is the very best French restaurant in town."

From the depths of the carriage came an enthusiastic "*Si! Magnifico!*" from Mr. Tescalini, who leaned forward, his moon face suddenly very close to Hatton's.

"Everything's on the house tonight," said Grey, as the carriage slowed to a sweltering stop. "So, Hatton? Can I count on your company?"

Hatton felt flushed from the insufferable heat of the carriage as he said, "If you must have me there, although I can't see what St. Bart's has to offer to the Mysterious Case of the Missing Pastry Chef."

The inspector smiled. "Either way, it will be good for us to talk about the wider implications of your work. Where all this *forensics* is going? Some of my superiors think your science to be nothing more than wizardry. That I must keep an open mind and look at other things. The competition?"

"Competition?" Hatton was aghast, for he had none in London. The only other forensic experts were in Berlin, Amsterdam, and Paris.

"Spiritualists and table tapping, phrenology and the alienists," Grey paused. "All of these new disciplines offer insight into crime, and so you see, this McCarthy thing is rather a test for you and your unusual methods. You've let me down before, Hatton."

Hatton's face burned at the words, but the inspector continued, "But don't fret, because if you perform as required and forensics proves itself, I may even consider reinstating your retainer. It makes planning so much easier, and I've heard you've been looking at this novel idea of fingerprinting?"

Hatton was reluctant to proffer an opinion on something not yet empirically tested. "It has potential, I suppose."

"Well, what about White Lodge? Any fingerprints there? Have you got something in that bag of tricks of yours which allows you to measure such things? Don't shy away from the new, Hatton. If you get stuck, don't hesitate to ask. Get your clever fellow, Roumande, to help, because rumor has it he's almost as good you, anyway. I'm teasing you, of course!"

Hatton's knuckles gripped white. "As you well know, the crime scene was completely devastated. The study polished within an inch of its life. Roumande is the most excellent of dieners, but his presence today wouldn't have made any difference. People don't understand the first thing about forensics, Inspector. But," added Hatton, "the maid did mention that two crystal glasses and a decanter filled with sherry were out on the desk, as if the victim was expecting someone. Of course, she'd cleared them away by the time we arrived."

"Well, the wife made no mention of any visitors," said the inspector. "Only that the brothers argued yesterday, over money and politics. Perhaps the older brother wanted to clear the air before they retired for the night and was waiting up for the other. Did you look at the content of the glasses, Professor? Have you tested them for smears?"

This smacked of Grandma sucking eggs, thought Hatton, telling him things he knew to do already. "The taste of strychnine is bitter, and it can't be disguised, even in sherry. I checked the glasses, of course, but they hadn't been used at all; still, just to be sure, I'll look again at the morgue."

"So, anything else or are we clutching at straws here?"

Hatton looked at the large evidence bag he'd placed at his feet. "There's the ash, of course, and a number of books found in the study that might be of interest." Hatton took out an essay by Carlyle, a novel by Mrs. Gaskell—*North and South*—and a leather-bound copy of *In Memoriam*. "From the theme of the subject matter, it would appear our MP had lost his faith in God. The essays and poetry relate to Christian doubt, Inspector, which is hardly surprising after Mr. Darwin's shocking revelations this month. Westminster talks of nothing else and Mrs. Gaskell is very vocal on the problem of urban unrest."

"But Mrs. Gaskell's concern is with Manchester and The North, not London."

"Yes, Inspector, but there's plenty of unrest in the rookeries. Perhaps the MP thought by reading this work, he could learn something."

"Indeed."

"But this is all conjecture. All I really have to go on, forensically speaking, is the cadaver. But," said Hatton flicking through one of the books, "if we could lift the smudge of a fingerprint off one of these pages, then who knows what story these books might *really* tell. Sadly we are a long way off that, Inspector, but if you are happy for me to experiment? Push the boundaries a bit?"

The inspector gave a curt nod.

"Roumande has recently returned from a lecture at the University in Lyon, where . . ."

And for a minute, all other thoughts were forgotten, as Hatton basked in a brighter, braver future where his new science was in the ascendance. Where justice would be done.

"Excellent, excellent. These flights of fancy might help inform how best we should present the death of Gabriel McCarthy. For *present* it we must, and with the least hyperbole possible."

"Present, Inspector? I'm not sure I follow you."

"Come, come, Hatton. I think you do. I've already discussed this with Sorcha. That's her name, by the way. Sorcha, meaning radiance, and she is, don't you think? I've never seen a widow who was more becoming in the face of death. Is that a sin, do you think, to think such a thing? Well, religious quandaries aside, the radiant Mrs. McCarthy is in complete agreement that the death of her husband should be presented initially as 'natural causes.' Thus allowing us to do our work, free from the whirligig of politics."

Hatton was astounded. "But he was murdered, Inspector. To present his death as anything less would be a lie."

Inspector Grey sat back firmly in the carriage, and momentarily caught the eye of Mr. Tescalini, on whose enigmatic features hovered the very faintest trace of a smile.

"It isn't exactly a lie, Professor." Inspector Grey leaned forward, placing his hand firmly upon Hatton's thigh. "The strategy is expedient and will purchase time. Time to identify all possible suspects, all possible leads, all possible possibilities. And when the right moment is upon us, and the opportunity for political exploitation passed, we can correct our initial conclusions, announce the guilty, and close the case. In the blink of an eye, for both of us, a stupendous success."

"Retainer or not, I cannot sanction this." Hatton forced himself free of the thigh embrace and went to open the carriage door, rattling the handle this way and that.

Oblivious to the professor's distress, Inspector Grey continued, "Tell me Adolphus, are you aware of what the date is?"

"For heaven's sake, Inspector. It's July 10, and I wish to leave the carriage," Hatton said, still wrestling with the lock.

"And so July 12 is just two days from now. I see that date means nothing to you, does it? Please, leave the door. I need your attention for just a little longer."

Damn this man, thought Hatton, but he sat back, crossed his arms, and said more emphatically, "Very well. Let's hear it, then. What of the date?"

The inspector said, "It's an anniversary of the bloodiest kind. Drogheda? The battle of the Boyne? Cromwell versus the Irish? Does that ring any bells or are you such a committed Englishman that you do not let such historical trifles invade your consciousness?"

"I understand you perfectly well, Inspector, but to lie . . ."

"Make no mistake, just as I am a servant of the Law, you, sir, are a servant of The Yard. You found the ribbon and understand its meaning. In two days' time, as is tradition, Protestants will be dressed in orange, marching in Liverpool, London, and Manchester and thinking if a Unionist MP can be so easily killed by Fenians, then who next? And it will be the Battle of the Boyne for sure, or that is what the Ribbonmen would like, but not on my watch, Professor."

Hatton shrunk back in the carriage and looked grimly out of the window.

"So, I think we have an understanding," said Grey, "And I assume dinner is still agreeable? Excellent. Nine o'clock sharp and don't be late."

"So there you have it, Albert. The death is to be presented as 'natural causes,' in exchange for money." The two men were in the "gallery," at the far end of the mortuary, to the side of them, a number of rudimentary sketches of organs in different states of decay were pegged on string, draped as if washing on a line. Roumande peered closely at a cross-section of a dissected heart which clearly depicted—in intricate detail—Tardieu spots, indicating asphyxiation of some kind. Hatton peered at the image as well, taking in the smattering of carmine pinpricks.

"But from what you say, to fund forensics we can't rely on The Yard, but I'm quite convinced we have other skills to sell, some of which could demand a high price. For example . . ."

And from a small side table, Roumande picked up a detailed black-and-white portrait of a flayed male cadaver—a gaping torso, head thrown back, mouth slightly open (as if in postmortem ecstasy), its entire chest fully exposed.

"This is astonishing, Albert." Hatton took it, held the sketch up to the light. "This is from *Gray's Anatomy*, surely? But I don't recall this plate. Where did you get such a thing?"

"He's done an excellent job, don't you think?"

"This work's been done by Patrice? Already? Can it be possible?"

Roumande took a quill and tapped at the bottom of the page, where the assistant's name was clearly signed in a tidy hand.

"I asked him to do the entire cadaver, last night, and he's been drawing all day at incredible speed, for there are more here. The infant's alimentary canal we asked for, a bloater's eyes, the unborn fetus of a dogfish. Look around you, Professor. He's done nearly everything on our shelves. All of our treasured specimens in a matter of hours, snatching the time to draw when he's not busy with other, more pedestrian things."

Hatton looked at his pocket watch and repeated, "Incredible . . ."

Over the years, Hatton and Roumande had put together an impressive collection of organs pickled in laboratory glass, some of them displayed, others hidden from view, kept bolted down in the basement. The dissected brains of criminals, the lungs of a two-headed dog, the genitals of rapists, fish gills, frog spawn, lizards the color of milk.

"He's a rare talent. And he has already caught the attention of Dr. Buchanan. You may recall our director has a governor's meeting coming up? A fund-raiser for the hospital? With a number of Americans coming?"

Hatton nodded.

"Well, Dr. Buchanan is preparing a leaflet to give them on the history of St. Bart's, and I have suggested a flat fee of ten guineas for illustrations by Patrice. And you know how very vain Buchanan is, so I suggested a portrait of our hospital director for the front cover. Dr. Buchanan is beside himself in anticipation of a masterpiece. With your agreement, of course."

Roumande looked rather pleased with himself.

"And you would like a slap on the back, my friend? A round of applause from our cadavers? Well, you shall have it. As long as Patrice doesn't get ideas above his station—his work at the morgue comes first."

"My thoughts exactly. The young lad, by the way, is turning out to be the most excellent student. He's done a range of errands for me, with speed and accuracy. He is very self-reliant and has a great enthusiasm for pathology. We must hold on to him, and this extra work will be a way of showing him we value his talent."

"And it's ten guineas a throw, you say?"

"Ten guineas, yes, but a retainer would offer us more. Times are hard, Professor, and I can understand Grey's reasoning for wanting to keep McCarthy's murder quiet for as long as possible. It's a tinderbox in the slums."

At that moment, a large horsefly settled on Roumande's bare arm; he slapped it hard. "Damned flies!"

"Are you sure you won't come with me to Verrey's?" asked Hatton, a little more gently. "It might do you good to get out of the morgue."

"Sadly, it's out of the question," said Roumande. "McCarthy will need embalming tonight before we deliver him tomorrow. and I've got some new methods to try. It's quite the fashion in Vienna to mix a little morphine with the other preservatives. It makes the waxy pallor creamier, and from what you've said, we should do our best for the widow."

"Point taken, but what we really need to crack is the ribbon, Albert. Is there anything distinctive in the weave? What dye was used to get such a vibrant green? Where was it bought? Questions, Albert, always questions."

Roumande followed Hatton back through to the mortuary where the ribbon was pinned on laboratory glass, ready for viewing under the microscope. Hatton peered again, twisting the viewing columns. "I drew a blank at White Lodge. There was no trace of strychnine anywhere, but I'm sure the ash was taken from the grate, then smeared on McCarthy's body at the crime scene, *postmortem*. The killer, or killers, hoped that when the body was found, it would be burned. So why bother with the ribbon at all? Why increase the risk of being caught? Why leave a sign?"

"As he collapsed from the poison, monsieur, he'd be sure to see it coming."

Hatton turned around to see that their apprentice was back, mop in his hand. Hatton was impressed. "Exactly, Patrice. The poison is intense; the MP would be in agony, lying on his back, but for ten minutes, his eyes would be open. The very last thing he'd see would be the silk, the very last thought in his head would be some sort of a message from the Fenians—if it was the Fenians. But not all ribbons are the same. You live in Spitalfields, Albert, which is full of weavers, correct?"

"They're on their last legs, Adolphus. Most of them retired or gone to the wall. The weaving industry is practically dead among the Huguenots. Madame Roumande buys her haberdashery at the docks these days, straight off the boats, from Chinese traders. It's a damn sight cheaper than Spitalfields, or if it's just ribbons for the girls, we go to Petticoat Lane. I'll ask Sylvie what she thinks of all of this, when I get home tonight."

"They sell the finer ones in Piccadilly, monsieur. The shops there are like Aladdin's Cave, it's a wonder to see, it's . . ."

"Yes, yes," said Hatton, sure that he was on to something. "You're right, but the shops in Piccadilly will be shut by now, so let's start on this particular line of thought tomorrow. I want the ribbon measured, width ways and length ways. First thing in the morning, I'll analyze the molecular structure as best I can. What chemicals have been used to get this vibrant green? Where this particular silk hails from? Handwoven or factory made? Anything we can find out about the silk might just help lead us to the killer . . ."

8

ST. GILES

Father O'Brian was chanting the evening mass in Latin to a packed church when the rock was hurled through the window, gashing the skull of an old woman, who fell to her knees with a scream. Across the black-and-white floor of the nave, shards of indigo glass mixed with splashes of red wine and communion wafers as O'Brian raced down the aisle to see the hastily scribbled messages, already stuck on the door of his church—*No Popery. Death to All Catholics.* But the culprits must have been younger and quicker than he. He tore down the notices, but not before seeing the steaming dog turd left on the steps of the porch. He grabbed a parishioner and told them to do the usual—"Clean it up, fast. This is the fifth time this month." He grabbed another, "Take whatever money's in the sacristy and get Mrs. Murphy to Dr. Gilbert on Neal Street, quickly."

The furor was over in an instant, the blood and glass swept from the nave. The parishioners dispersed as O'Brian went back into his church, bolting the door behind him. There were prayer books scattered about, the stink of incense in the air as the priest made his way slowly, but with intent, toward the sacristy, where the black pouch was just where he'd left it.

He waited for a second, to hear outside—a horse whinny, the sound of shouting—but he was sure the church was empty, pin-drop silent, as he eased the device out from its resting place, with the delicacy of touch he used to save for women, before he became a religious man.

A raw recruit at seventeen, he'd been drummed into the army by the British to fight their enemies in Europe, for a few shillings a week. A stroke of luck in retrospect, because he'd learnt a thing or two on the battlefields, before he took to the cloth. Like how to swim in a bloodbath, fire a bullet from a musket, and win the loyalty of men, but more important, to understand chemistry, which was something of a hobby. O'Brian knew nitroglycerine was unreliable at the best of times, guncotton no better. One accidental bump, one unfortunate shake and . . .

"That's not what we want now, is it?" he said to himself, tick-tock, ticktock in the one hand, and in the other, well, it didn't take a genius to work out the flowing—

$$3HNO + CHO + O + 6H (NO) + 3H10$$

Did it?

9

PICCADILLY

Hatton stood on the steps of Verrey's, looking down at his best boots, which Mrs. Gallant had polished to a shine. He'd walked from Bloomsbury to Piccadilly, the boots pinching a little, and along the way couldn't help but notice several chaperoned ladies lift their eyes fleetingly to his, reassuring Hatton that his evening dress was, thank goodness, flattering attire.

But there would be no couture competition with The Yard, because here was Inspector Grey delivered to the steps of Verrey's by a gilded barouche. Operatic might describe tonight's garb, with his muffler, his silk white tie, and the fashionable cut of his suit, all elegant lines. He was smoking a cigar. He was swinging a cane. The inspector looked dashing. "Yes," muttered Hatton to himself with envy, dashing was the word.

"Here we all are then, Professor," said Grey, Mr. Tescalini by his side. "Nine o'clock, precisely. So, shall we dine?"

They stepped inside Verrey's, where peacock dresses shimmered, fans fluttered, and ringlets curled and kicked. And it took a second for Hatton to adjust himself to the gay laughter, the clinking of glasses, and the *hurrahs*, as dish after dish was paraded through the gilt and crystal restaurant. As the little party made their way to the table, it was all that Hatton could do, as a gentleman, to avert his eyes from a sea of alabaster clavicles and diamond-strewn décolletage.

Inspector Grey, however, did nothing of the kind.

"How delightful you look tonight," he said, as his puckering lips brushed eager hands. From a less silver-tongued man it might have seemed rehearsed, but from Grey's mouth, the ladies took it as the most delicious compliment and held their palms to their hearts in reply, or pretended to hide behind featherings of ostrich.

"So," said Grey, waving away his adoring fans. "Have you decided yet, Adolphus?"

"I'll have whatever you're having," said the professor, glaring at the menu with its *au this* and *à la that,* thinking *helllllpppp* because he was from Hampshire, dammit.

Meanwhile, Grey talked ten to the dozen, only forking in the odd mouthful as he discussed, at huge length, the missing pastry chef. "The most celebrated chef in London and lost, disappeared, gone, vanished into thin air. Are you sure your diener hasn't heard of him? By all accounts his disappearance is completely out of character. Monsieur Pomeroy was a master of his art. No money worries, no creditors, no skeletons in the cupboard, but hardworking, disciplined, and highly religious."

But Hatton wasn't interested in chefs, celebrated or otherwise. It was another case he wished to talk of.

"So as I was saying, Inspector, the silk could be the key. A number of murders have recently been solved on the Continent, where an item of clothing found at the scene has led directly to the killer. There's the fingerprinting we can try, of course, and there's another test, a new test involving nitrate acid which—"

The inspector interrupted him, "Very innovative, I'm sure, Professor, and when the fingerprinting's ready, I'd like to go and do a proper forensic sweep of Gustave Pomeroy's home in Fournier Street."

Hatton sighed. He wasn't getting anywhere, so he gave up for the time being and allowed himself to relax a little and enjoy *Timbales d'Asperges*, whipped into the palest green imaginable. Even Inspector Grey paused, eating a mere teaspoon, to exclaim, "Now this, my friends, should be illegal."

Next up *Sole à la Dieppoise* (buttery and ghost white), then a positively melting *Escalopes De Veau à la Crème* accompanied by scatterings of braised chicory, followed by a variety of other delights concluding with two desserts. At which point, the sous chef arrived.

Grey stood up. "Ah, Monsieur le Chef! May I say that this evening, your food has surpassed all our expectations. Isn't that so, Professor?"

Inspector Grey beamed at Hatton and toasted the table with an effervescent, "Good health, gentlemen! Please, please, Monsieur le Chef, sit down and join us."

"I mustn't stop, Inspector. I only came out to apologize in advance for our paltry desserts, because without Monsieur Pomeroy at my side, I've only been able to produce two tonight. *Salade de Fruits*, which as you can see is predominantly *Tropiques,* and our usual chocolate offering of *La Gloire de Verreys*."

Inspector Grey jumped up, grabbing the sous chef's arm. "I'm not a lover of *Les Desserts*, I shall leave that indulgence to my colleagues. A quiet word with you is all I require, sir."

The sous chef nodded. "Anything, Inspector. Gustave is the best of men. We can't imagine what's become of him. His reputation's never been better. Although his wife had recently died, he was deeply religious and that, perhaps, helped him recover from his grief, especially these last few months, where he seemed to be almost happy. Why, he was even whistling at work. His disappearance makes no sense at all. I fear something terrible might have happened. Perhaps he's been hurt and is lying somewhere injured, completely helpless, right now—"

"Well, that's why we're here, monsieur. To find him," said the inspector, steering the sous chef back toward the kitchen, and leaving Hatton with a slice of cake and some slithery-looking melon. And like the melon, the room began to swirl. *Such delightful ladies, such exquisite tables, such opulence. Now this,* thought Hatton looking around him, *is Society,* as he slugged down another drink and imagined how his life might be with professional success, perhaps even a wife by his side. Why the devil not? He, too, could be in demand, not simply by the dead but by the living. And it occurred to Hatton that he'd been too long in the mortuary, too long in the morgue.

But these wine-soaked thoughts were suddenly interrupted by a man of the most inappropriate kind, who lumbered over to Hatton's table, dressed in a squashed Tom Bowler and wearing the expression of a madman. Sending cutlery flying and without an introduction, the John Bull figure sat down and blurted, "Damn that Inspector Grey. No, sir, as one Englishman to another, I'll not be quiet for that Methodist taffy. I shall sit here until I've got what I came for. Scotland Yard is supposed to help people like me and protect *my* interests." He banged the table. "I pay my bleedin' taxes!"

"My dear fellow, calm yourself," said Inspector Grey, who came charging up behind him. John Bull turned around and spluttered, "Now listen to me, Grey. I shall not be quiet. As you know, I am a plain man, very plain, and it's taken me several hours to find you. I want my money and I'll give you the usual ten percent, of course, if you secure it for me without any fuss. He may be drunk, he may be dead, he may be in cahoots with other rookery thugs. They may have split the lot and gone back to Ireland, but a deal is a deal, come on now, shake on it and say you'll help me, Grey . . ."

Grey stroked his waxed mustache, "Thirty percent, Mr. Brown. Deal or no deal?"

"Damn you, Grey, you drive a hard bargain. Very well, deal, but we must go to the rookeries right now and not after . . . what is this? Pudding, is it?"

Tescalini nodded, shoveling in the gateaux.

The inspector smiled, "Let me introduce you to my friend here, Professor Adolphus Hatton. If this rent collector's being difficult, there are three of us tonight. Who knows how drunk he'll be, or how rough? But this man is a doctor, young, and full of vim, which might prove useful when we get to the slums."

It was at that moment that Hatton realized how profoundly drunk he'd become—not only had he cleared all seven plates, but he'd also finished every glass and failed to notice that at Verrey's once the last sip is taken, another glass is poured. And so Hatton, when asked if he was happy to go with them to the Seven Dials, simply nodded, followed by a slurred, "No bother at all . . ." and turning to Mr. Tescalini promised the Italian that they were brothers in arms and that if there was trouble, he would, "Fight to the end, Mr. Tescalini! *E Viva Italia!*"

Grabbing his cane, Hatton stumbled to the door and tumbled out of the restaurant, to be hit in the face with a night-air thump. He hovered on the edge of the pavement for less than a second and then led the way for them, in a slightly swaying gait, along Regent Street, turning east toward Soho.

But as the walk progressed, Hatton returned to his senses, because it occurred to him, hadn't he just chopped through six victims of cholera, from this very spot? The Seven Dials was a den of thieves, felons, and garrotters and the prime location for his body collectors to find corpses. Piled high, Patrice had told him. Piled high and slumped up against doorways and bundled into corners. And wasn't it here, only two years ago, where they had found a man so sliced about that when they removed him they needed a trowel?

"So this is the place then, Mr. Brown?" asked Inspector Grey, his voice a whisper.

"The rent collector's place is just along this alleyway a bit," replied Mr. Brown, who owned a few doss-houses here but rarely came to visit, and certainly never alone. "Locals call him the gombeen man, and he collects money for all the landlords around these parts. Mr. Hecker, the mill owner, owns everything to the North of the Charing Cross Road. I've just a few tenement blocks here in the Seven Dials. Mahoney was supposed to deliver my money hours ago, but he didn't show up. I presume, Inspector, you're suitably armed?"

Inspector Grey patted his dinner jacket. "You know that I wouldn't have offered my assistance in the rookeries without a loaded pistol, Mr. Brown. But I'm not at liberty to swing it about. It's standard issue, of course, but The Yard doesn't want to get itself a reputation for the reckless use of firearms. Mr. Tescalini and our dear doctor are here. No firearm will be necessary."

The men hovered on the corner of a street, actually little more than a passage, leading off into a darkened alley. To the other side, a huddle of jutting-out buildings, half-timbered, battered brick, and shattered windows.

"Steady now, Professor," said Grey. "By God, this stench is unspeakable. Mr. Tescalini, do you have a kerchief? I presume, Mr. Brown, the rising vapors from your picturesque tenements do not offend you? No, friend," said the inspector "do not answer that."

Inspector Grey pressed a hand-stitched, linen handkerchief to his mouth, and after breathing deeply, handed the lemony cloth to Hatton. Cadavers arrived at St. Bart's in hideous form, encrusted with feces and other reeking fluids, but this was the rot and decay of sewer creatures. One privy to thirty families and a year of slops, which had seeped through the cracked and uneven pavers; a ripe mixture of dead dogs, vermin, and a fug of infectious diseases.

"Come now, Inspector," said Mr. Brown. "It isn't so bad. And there's no one about. They're drunk, or suppurating quietly in their own filth, for it's nearly all Irish in this quarter."

The inspector asked curtly, "Have you a light or a candle perhaps, for there seems to be a shortage of gas lamps?"

The landlord shook his head. Mr. Tescalini disappeared for a moment, returning promptly illuminated by a swinging lantern.

"Ever inventive, Mr. Tescalini. So, gentlemen," continued the inspector, "are we finally ready?"

Tescalini gave Mr. Brown a quick shove toward the lodging house, making the landlord totter forward. They followed him as he mounted rickety wooden stairs to a door patched up with planks of wood and rusty nails. "Mind your step here," said Mr. Brown. "I haven't quite got round to sorting out the floorboards. Mr. Mahoney's just two doors along."

There was a faint coughing coming from somewhere, but in the gloom it was difficult to tell exactly where it was. "There's no fever here, is there?" the inspector's terse whisper filled an echoing void.

"No, Inspector. Some of my tenants are laborers at the tannery, while others just cough and splutter for the sake of it. You have my word, Inspector. The Board of Health's been here. There's no more cholera. It's burned itself out."

Tescalini held the lamp up a little higher, illuminating a door which bore no name—just yellowing paint and splintered planks, hinges which were green with algae and a cobweb of dirt.

Tescalini knocked. No answer, but from above their heads more coughing, louder now, and then a thwack followed by a howl, and a shout of something in a tongue Hatton thought he recognized. He shuddered. *Mary, again.* Was she following him? Because the words she had first spoken to him were so similar. He tried to recall it. *Saoirse,* he thought. Yes, that was the word.

"Try again, Mr. Tescalini." Inspector Grey's voice was monotone.

Another bang, still nothing.

"Stand back," Grey commanded.

Instantly a lightning sideways leg kick, so acrobatic and powerful that it seemed to come not so much from Mr. Tescalini as from some other, much younger, perhaps oriental man. And with a "*Prego,* senore!"—the door came crashing down.

"No need for a pocket pistol," said Grey. "Someone's been here before us."

There was an odd calmness to Grey's voice, and a thick, pungent aroma in the air, which Hatton knew well, along with the sound of buzzing.

The blowflies and bluebottles hovered over a body cleaved through the middle by a spade, veins and intestines spilling like worms from the yellowing flesh. The spade glittered silver and shiny in the throw of the lamp and all about the corpse was scattered money.

"He's sliced in two, Professor." The inspector was leaning over the body, his kerchief pressed close to his mouth. "And the punishment's been delivered on collection day, so we have a building full of suspects. This is the umpteenth butchering in these quarters, although none done, I think, with such ferocity."

Behind the professor, a laugh from the Italian and the sound of guts coming up, which Hatton presumed to be the landlord, Mr. Brown, delivering the contents of his stomach to the floor.

Hatton caught site of the dead man's supper. A chipped plate of bread and a morsel of cheese, two tin mugs and a roach which had been flattened to the plate, its wings broken off. *Disgusting creatures,* thought Hatton to himself, smelling the mugs to detect that it was definitely pocheen. Hatton didn't know which he cared for least—the roaches or that devil of a home-brewed drink. One of the mugs had been drained to the dregs, the other, untouched. The man's skin was dung-colored, thin as parchment, the torso severed by the spade. Hatton looked at the dead man's hair, threads of tawny brown.

"His hair is dyed," said Hatton.

The inspector nodded. "Indeed, and alopecia, too, which is not a pretty sight. His face . . . what do you make of it? It has terror upon it, but there's also something else . . . like he's seen a ghost . . ."

Hatton didn't reply, but instead set to work as best he could. The body hadn't just been hacked in half—around the crotch, there was too much blood. Swallowing a slight gob of nausea caused by the wine, he used the tips of his fingers to tug at the sodden rags of the man's breeches and saw that the man has been mutilated. "They've cut off his testicles, Inspector. Someone has neutered him."

"Neutered?"

"Yes, neutered like a dog, with scissors or maybe a surgical knife."

Hatton started on the basics, measuring the length of the body, but stopped in his tracks when he came to the dead man's hands. He examined them more closely, in particular the nails, thinking to himself, *Veal, this corpse is veal,* a term he'd coined for labeling abnormalities. The hands were deformed in a way Hatton had never seen before. Under his breath, he muttered, "Gold dust . . ."

"I beg your pardon, Hatton?"

"Nothing, Inspector. Only that the violence of this crime surpasses anything I've seen before. I need the body back at the morgue, but first of all I need Roumande."

"Monsieur Roumande, at this hour? For a rent collector? My dear Professor, you are over egging the pudding . . ."

"This is not just any kind of killing. Look."

Hatton crouched down among florins, pennies, and glints of silver. "I make this thirty pieces. Thirty pieces of silver, Inspector. Count them yourself, but please, whatever you do, don't touch them."

The inspector crouched down as well, "So, a little touch of religious mockery, here?"

"Judas Iscariot, Inspector. A traitor to his own kind, and I wonder what else we'll find?" Never without his medical bag, Hatton bent down and undid its little padlock, smoothing on a pair of well-worn gloves, and began to look under the tables, the edges of the bed, opening cupboards and draws to see crumbs, rat droppings, rusty cutlery, and . . . "A prayer book"; he blew off the dust. "Hasn't been used for a while but there's an inscription in here. *On Receiving His First Holy Communion, Gregory Michael Mahoney, 1792. Our Lady of Sorrows, Ardara, Donegal.*"

"Ardara, Donegal, you say? Isn't that the very place where Mr. McCarthy's from?" The inspector turned around to look at Mr. Brown, as Hatton's eyes followed him. "What do you know of this man, Mr. Brown? He was a rent collector, a usurer, a gombeen man. Anything else we should know? Who else did he work for, apart from you, I mean?"

"Mr. Hecker, the mill owner. I've already told you so. He has a number of ventures along the river in Limehouse—a biscuit factory, a flour mill, shipping interests and land abroad, as well, I think."

Grey got his notebook out and, with a tongue as pink as a cat's, licked the end of his pencil. "I know him, of course. In fact, I'm doing a little job for him because a friend of his is missing. Monsieur Gustave Pomeroy?"

The John Bull man shrugged.

"Do you happen to know if Mr. Hecker has any connection to Donegal?"

Was the inspector on to something? Hatton's eyes narrowed, as he watched a little closer.

"If you know him, why don't you ask him?" said Mr. Brown. "He's always at the mill, rarely leaves his office. Busy is as busy does, Inspector. You don't get rich but digging potatoes, do you, Grey? That's what we English understand, but these Irish are lazy good for nothings. I heard Hecker laid off his whole workforce yesterday. About time. Maybe he'll give the jobs to some desperate English boys and show a bit of patriotism."

"I couldn't agree with you more, Mr. Brown." Another lick and then the inspector said, "Do you know if the gombeen man brought his family to London? Or were they left behind in Donegal?"

The landowner wiped his puke-smeared mouth, his voice thick with spittle. "There's no one. No family at all. He was universally loathed. Why, even his own church rejected him. The local priest had ex-communicated him years ago. Mahoney was sobbing like a big, blabby baby when it happened. Said the local priest had written to the Vatican . . ." Mr. Brown hoiked up a great gob, spat, and wiped his mouth again. "Thirty pieces of silver, eh? Sounds fair enough for a wretch like him, but I still want my money."

"Not so hasty, Mr. Brown." The inspector blocked the way. "Perhaps you've heard the term *forensics*?"

"Can't say that I have . . ."

"Well, we've an expert in our midst and police work takes precedence over greed. All that money is evidence."

"The devil it is. You'll answer for this, Grey, sure is eggs is . . . urggghh . . . get him off me, you great Italian lump . . ."

Mr. Brown promptly dispatched, Hatton sent a message to Spitalfields and waited for Roumande, who burst in half an hour later with, "I came as quick as I could, Adolphus," before looking at the body and giving a long, low whistle.

"That's exactly what I thought, Albert. I wanted you to see him fresh. He's been sliced in half, like a knife through butter, and there's exactly thirty pieces of silver here. And there's more still. Grab a lantern, Albert, and then pay attention to the money . . ."

Roumande held the lantern aloft. The room was a dark cavern, a void of low-flickering candles, dark shadows on the wall, but as the light grew stronger, he saw pools of silver, lucent and shimmering.

Roumande rubbed the stubble on his chin. "Is it glitter?"

"I'm not sure, but keep the flame well away from the spangles, Albert. I think it might be some sort of chemical. I'll check when we get back to the morgue. Look about you . . ."

Roumande spun on his heels, holding the lantern higher. "It's everywhere . . ."

Hatton nodded, "We need to seal the place off till we know exactly what it is. It's on his prayer book, in the drawers, on the bed, the table, all over the corpse. I didn't notice it at first, being too busy looking at specifics, but when I stood back a little and *really* looked . . ."

"It's almost beautiful . . ."

"It is, Albert. Like a kind of fairy dust, and look, there's more here . . ."

Hatton handed him the prayer book. "A definite link, I'd say. Grey thinks so as well. The inspector plays his cards close to his chest, but I could see it in his eyes. Both victims are from the same place in Donegal."

"So Grey should ask the wife. Did this moneylender work for the McCarthys? Did the victims know each other? Did they help each other? We know already that the MP had debts. Maybe this gombeen man loaned McCarthy money, dirty money, and this is some kind of gang thing . . ."

Hatton shrugged. "That's a line of inquiry for The Yard to follow, but I'll give Grey a prompt when I get him alone. He's upstairs talking to the tenants, but our priority is Mr. Mahoney here. He needs shifting."

Roumande was by now bending under the table to double-check the blood splatters, "Impossible, Adolphus. It's the first Monday of the month. Payday, so there's no collectors anywhere. Not even the grubbers tonight. They'll all be dead drunk by now, in a flash house, the lot of them."

"First light, then. What do you think? Pretty clear I'd say."

Roumande emerged from underneath the table. "A whack with considerable force, for the blood to travel that far, Professor. These splatters are dense and show quite clearly the murderer hit the victim from the left, and as there are no splatters directly behind you, so he must have stood exactly where you stand now, his body acting as a shield."

"Exactly. He stood directly by this wall and raised the spade thus, and he must have been right-handed, wouldn't you say?"

"The tilt of the spade and the splatters would suggest so, Adolphus. And what about hair, footprints, tufts of fabric?"

"Nothing. I've drawn a blank, which in itself is odd, don't you think? This glitter is everywhere and yet not an alien mark, not a whisper of anyone here at all."

"But this place is drenched in blood, Adolphus, so you'd think there'd be a print somewhere. Outside, perhaps along the corridor?"

Hatton shook his head, "There are no smears leading away from the body, so we know the killer's taken his time after the butchering and cleaned it up. Cleaned himself up, too, most likely. I've already been down the corridor with a lantern and out into the yard. Of course, we'll need to double-check when it's light, but I can find no handprints, footprints, or drenched clothes anywhere. The killer must have stripped, washed, and then disposed of his clothes. You'd think the other tenants would have heard the screaming. Or seen something."

Roumande gestured toward the tin mugs. "Maybe they don't care who did it, or are not inclined to say? And he wouldn't have howled after drinking a mug of that stuff. A quart of pocheen, a shove, and an old man like, who weighs what? Less than a feather? He would have gone down like a ninepin. But as unpopular as he was, he's definitely had a visitor. Two mugs, Professor."

"Well-spotted, Roumande." It was Grey, back again. "A man with no friends, no priest, no wife, no children, no styling advice, and yet . . . like our Unionist MP, a visitor and both from a place called Ardara. All grist to the mill. And speaking of mills, seems Mr. Mahoney here worked for Mr. Hecker up in Limehouse. I'll pop up there tomorrow. I need to talk to him about the lack of progress I'm making on this damn Pomeroy case. Good job, it's not payment by results, eh? Anyway. God . . ." The inspector stifled a yawn. "What a night. Are we done here? Had a good poke around, have we?"

"As much as we can for now, Inspector. But I'll require the body first thing tomorrow. There's a clear link, don't you think?"

"Donegal, you mean? Possibly. I'll ask the wife, but," the inspector stifled another yawn, "we all need some shut-eye. Monsieur, have you done the fingerprinting thing?"

Roumande shook his head, "Alas, no. I cannot just 'do it,'

Inspector. There are a number of tools involved. Charcoal, a fine brush, sticky paper. I came straight from Fleur de Lys in Spitalfields . . ."

"Tomorrow is another day. There're a couple of cabs outside." Grey ushered the men away from the room. "Mr. Tescalini will board the place up. Call it a policeman's hunch, but if these murders are connected, the timing's worrying. This could be related to the anniversary of Drogheda, which means the killer or killers aren't finished yet. If it's a crescendo they're after, we have twenty-four hours until . . ."

Hatton didn't like the look on Grey's face. "Twenty-four hours, Inspector? Twenty-four hours, till what?"

The inspector didn't answer, only turned to his assistant with a glib smile. "Signore, take heed of our professor here, which means no burning of candles, no flames, matches, or lanterns anywhere near that glitter stuff. Bolt down the door and seal it. Good night, gentlemen." The inspector raised his hat, shutting the door firmly behind him, but didn't move from his spot, only stood firm, his back pressed flat against the door, waving them off. "*Buona sera,* the lot of you. Until tomorrow."

10

Hatton had a fitful night of dreaming, a terrible thirst, and a digestive problem so acute he had to reach for his chamber pot, so when his bedside clock said five o'clock, he decided to rouse himself and head for the morgue. The dawn was painted with a crisscross of coral-tinted cirrus. A sharp chorus of gregarious sparrows made Hatton's head pound, but he managed to stumble along and, arriving at the mortuary room, found the door to be ajar.

"Good God. You almost gave me a heart attack. What on earth are you doing here?"

"*Excusez-moi . . .*" Patrice muttered, springing up from the bed he'd made on one of the dissection slabs. Had Hatton not been so weary, he would have rounded on their apprentice, but he only said, "Tell me, Patrice, that you've not been here all night?"

"*Non, non,* monsieur . . ."

Hatton embarked on a lecture about hospital standards, but the angst-driven sentences only made his head pound and the boy was clearly not following, so he simply said, "Oh for heaven's sake, go and find a coffin for Mr. McCarthy. There's an ebony one right at the back of the store cupboard. The best one, do you hear me?"

Hatton walked over to the main dissection slab and pulled back the shroud. Gone was that look of terror, and instead the MP seemed at peace, and on his face, a kind of sereneness. Hatton leaned a little forward, thinking to himself, what was this look? A dead man's blessing? Hatton pushed the image of Sorcha McCarthy away as unpalatable, but there she was, the image of her back again. And he remembered what Roumande had said to him a while ago, hunched over late-night drinks in a nearby tavern.

"You say you are made of stone, but no man is made of stone, Adolphus. So, you can honestly say, no woman has ever stolen your heart?"

Hatton's defenses, so carefully constructed over the years, had started to fracture a little. His father had recently died. He'd felt stripped bare to the world as he said, rather bitterly, "I have little time for such trifles. I cannot talk of frivolous things."

Roumande swirled his double brandy, looking into its amber glint, as if the secrets of the world might be contained within. "Love is far from frivolous," he said.

Hatton had moved uneasily on his chair, as he'd answered, "Work takes precedence. I had a sweetheart once, but it was long ago."

Roumande smiled, leaned forward. "You never told me you had a sweetheart. I'm all ears, Adolphus."

Hatton had had more than a couple of drinks that night and was on the verge of confessing but what was the point? It wouldn't bring her back. Instead, he felt his eyes prick but swallowed hard and only said, "I'd rather not talk of it if you don't mind, Albert."

Looking at Hatton's face, all twisted up, Roumande had known better than to ask any more but simply said, "It's etched on your face, Adolphus, whatever you say. Mark my words, friend. If you can love that hard, it will happen again."

Was it a warning?

Or a tempting of fate?

"Monsieur? Are you sure you quite are well? You seem a little pale, as if you have a malaise, Professor?"

Patrice's words jolted him back to the present.

"Get on with your chores, Patrice. The walls need washing, the floor needs scrubbing. Then go to Smithfield and buy two new blood buckets. These others are cracked and we've another body on its way, so be quick, and before you go, put some more of that flypaper up." The boy grabbed a flyswatter and wacked three fat bluebottles, and then with a leap in the air, smashed a flurry of mosquitoes. "Good work," said Hatton, impressed.

"They're coming off the river, Professor, and the rotting meat of Smithfield. The Board of Work should do something. I cannot keep the numbers down and we're infested with body mites."

"A good lashing of chloride of lime will work. Make sure you do all the corners, around the windowsills, and seek out any eggs under the tables, behind the specimen jars. Be vigilant, Patrice. We need to keep on top of it."

"But surely, monsieur, it's also the responsibility of the state and the work committees, but they do nothing to help us. The stall traders and costermongers talk of nothing else. The boards are overpaid bureaucrats, do-gooders but do-nothings, lining their own pockets and it's we, the people, who are suffering in this terrible stink . . ."

Hatton laughed to himself. This lad was spending too much time with Roumande. Hatton was a dissenter when it came to science, religion, and politics, but in his humble opinion, all the great thinkers were forced to stand alone—Thomas Beddoes, Galileo, John Hunter, Edward Jenner, but as to Roumande?

Roumande was a different fellow altogether.

A Frenchman for a start, Catholic by birth, a Huguenot by nature, a revolutionary sympathizer, a self-improver, a believer in The State. But this was England not France. Boards of this and boards of that were all very well, if they got the work done quicker, but it was the power of free speech and free will that made the greatest advances for society. The rest was just . . . piffle. On that thought, Hatton picked up his pen, dipped it in his trademark indigo ink, and was just beginning to write up his notes, such as they could be after a night fueled by too much rich food, champagne, and—

"The air is cooling a little. Clouds are rolling in. Jean-Paul— you will remember, he's my eldest, Patrice—has constructed the most wonderful barometer made with a jam jar and a slosh of red wine. The wine rises, as the air density increases, thus telling us there's a storm brewing. He's a clever boy. Takes after his father, I'm told!"

Roumande had burst through the door, slightly bedraggled and unshaven, but with the huge tidal of energy, which was his particular trademark.

"So what are we doing here? The ribbon from yesterday, Professor? Or shall I go straightaway and get the gombeen man?"

"How are you feeling, Albert? After last night, I mean?"

"Full of vim, Professor. Whereas you, Adolphus? You don't look too well."

Hatton struggled up from his desk. "Nothing another shot of powders can't sort, but enough of me. Did Madame Roumande have an opinion?"

"Factory made, she said. The weave is even, the length and breadth completely uniform. Indian silk, she says, and as to its green? I checked last night before I left the morgue."

"You move way ahead of me, Albert. That was my job," Hatton said, a little testily.

"Verrey's called you, Adolphus, and the Zeiss called me. It's high levels of arsenic, as you would expect, that lends the silk such vibrancy. A very nice color, Sylvie says, but nothing special. You can pick up it anywhere, apparently."

"Hmph," said Hatton, and then added, "Very well. But I want to do the coins before you go, Albert. Patrice, what are you doing standing here like a dolt? Go and get the buckets like I asked you to."

"*Oui,* monsieur."

Roumande cleared his throat.

Hatton sighed, "Yes, Albert?"

"Learning and erudition, Professor?"

"Oh, very well, he can watch, only for a bit, mind. So . . ."

The coins were florins, crowns, and guineas—thirty in all. Hatton turned the viewing columns, increasing the aperture so the glitter burst into a universe of stars. "It's a dusting of silver firmament, like a meteor shower scattered across these larger molecules, which are some sort of acid, I think. I studied chemistry, of course. But this combination is odd . . . and I'm not sure where it could have come from. Was it scattered for some reason? Was it dropped? Silver nitrate is normally used by artisans, mirror makers, druggists, and the like."

Roumande spoke, "Maybe the killer brought the traces in with him on his shoes or on his coat? But if the killer is Irish, they tend to be costermongers, not artisans."

Hatton bit the top of his thumb. "Quite possibly, but there are a number of Irish bookbinders, aren't there? And I know for a fact that there's a pharmacopoeia off Soho Square which is called O'Reilly's, in great big lettering, so I presume they're Irish, too. We must keep an open mind as to the nature of the killer. But this combination of acid and firmament . . . I've never seen it before. However, I know just who to ask. There's a brilliant chemist name of Meadows who I studied with at Edinburgh.

He's in London, now. Where are the back issues of . . . ah, yes . . .
I remember . . ." Hatton rushed over to one of his shelves,
jumped on a stool, and grabbed a huge pile of scientific periodi-
cals. Flicking through a tatty copy of *The London Chemical
Gazette,* he smacked a page with the flat of his hand. "I have it!
Professor Andrew Meadows, recently made a research fellow at
University College. An excellent chemist but a notorious drunk,
and word is he experiments on himself, like many of his ilk."
Hatton pulled out his filigree pocket watch. "He shan't be up at
this hour though, and it's been a while since I visited him. The
poor man has been treated shoddily over the years, moved from
pillar to post, city to city, basement to basement. He explodes
things and experiments on puppies, upsetting everyone. But science is science. Truth is what we seek, not approval."

Silver nitrate, he thought. Some sort of acid? But what's this
got to do with a gombeen man? And an MP? There seemed to
be a link, but what was it? Perhaps another dead man from Donegal was just coincidence, after all? There were thousands of
Irish in London making a sheer fluke entirely possible. He
wracked his brain. Silver nitrate was used for cauterizing bullet
wounds . . . eye drops for blindness . . . making mirrors . . . pho-
tographic images . . . silver ornament and artistry . . .

Outside the morgue, somewhere down a hallway, a clock
struck nine.

Patrice, who had been watching all the time, stepped back from
the Zeiss and muttered, "Mr. McCarthy's coffin needs to be put
upon a wagon, monsieur. We need to make haste to Highgate . . ."

Roumande turned to the boy. "Go to the market, get the buck-
ets and return quickly, then. Make haste. I'm going to the slums."
He caught Hatton's eye. "The gombeen man is *veal,* Professor.
Did you spot it?"

Hatton allowed himself a smile. "I most certainly did."

"Then I'll be off. Oh, and Adolphus, if I may be so bold, it's
a lady you're visiting, remember? A very pretty one, I've heard
and—" Roumande pointed hastily at Hatton's tie.

"Thank you, Albert," Hatton answered, rushing to their only mirror, pasting down his hair and hastily reknotting the tie and quickly adding, "You're a true friend. By the way, Albert, a quick word please, now the boy has gone."

Roumande put up his hands, "Before you say anything, I gave permission for the lad to stay. Not my best decision, I admit, but the lad had nowhere to go last night. He's hardworking, well-mannered, and intelligent. We're damn lucky to have him. One night only, I said. But he'll stay at Fleur de Lys tonight and the next, till he finds a suitable lodging house. Sylvie likes him and my girls, when I introduced them to him, dear oh dear." He shook his head in a fatherly but disapproving way. "It's true to say, they were all over Patrice like flies on . . . hmphf . . ."

"You took him to your house?"

"For cherry cake and coffee, a few days ago. I felt he needed a little French hospitality, being so far away from home. Of course, I shouldn't say such things about my own darling daughters, but the fussing and the giggling at everything he said verged on hysteria. I can see he's a handsome lad, but I've told them, a couple of nights at Fleur de Lys and then, as charming as he is, he has to go."

"And stay well away from your daughters?" Hatton smiled.

Roumande opened the door of the morgue. A crack of lightning burst across the sky. The diener pushed his derby down. "My dear Adolphus, you can read my mind."

11

LIMEHOUSE

The cab with the greased-out windows was heading east, over the ruts and cobblestones of dockside. Bits of old turnip and cabbage leaves clogged the road, a church spire slanted gray in the distance, as a hushed conversation continued. The priest's voice was low but thick with anger. "We need to turn the screws, mount the pressure. The Tooley boy did well to get the file. It was there in his father's bindery filed under *I* for Ireland, but it should have been under *M* for murdering bastards. So, what did I tell you? I was right about the British, wasn't I?"

O'Rourke had a pipe in his mouth, and felt a little queasy as he read *Her Majesty's Government: Highly Confidential*. He took the pipe out, spat a tad of baccy across the floor of the cab, and hesitated, as a dark world unfolded. He shut his eyes for a brief second, breathed surely, steadily—voices in his head, echoes of the dead—but carried on reading anyway, "*A New Plantation in Ireland—The Gregory Clause 1847.*"

But the priest was impatient, his voice now quaking, "Let me summarize it for you, John, because though it's hard to believe, it shows quite clearly that the British deliberately chose to pro-

long the famine in order to annihilate a race. Rid a land of popery. To, and I quote, 'use the famine as a mechanism for reducing
surplus population.' That is, to destroy an entire people by evict-
ing unwanted tenants from the land, when we were weak, when
we could barely stand . . ."

O'Rourke ran his fingers along the lines of the *Gregory Clause.*
"They really did mean to kill us, didn't they?"

The priest nodded. Said "They did," and then used the cuff
of his frock coat to rub the window clean. "Jesus, it makes me
sick to think of it. But look at them now. Our people are out in
droves; we might be poor, but we're a very literate race, and if
the English wanted to wipe us out, they didn't achieve it. And
at the right time, in the right place, the details of this file will
be a propaganda victory written up in one of those papers of
yours." There was a huge crowd of men milling around by the
dockside, the beginnings of a battlefield. "Did you circulate the
handbills, by the way?"

O'Rourke pulled a handbill from his pocket. "Damien
printed three hundred copies. Usual things—*Down with the
British, Death to all Millers, Tiocfaidh ár lá!*"

"And it shall, John. The day is fast approaching because tomorrow is the anniversary of Drogheda. Cromwell slaughtered
our people like dogs two hundred years ago, but the tide is
turning . . ."

"I'm counting the hours and can see the headline now."
O'Rourke shut the file and patted it, knowing that with a stroke
of his pen, this story might easily be summarized as, "It's a fucking coup d'état, O'Brian." To which the journalist quickly added,
"Begging your pardon, Father." The priest opened the door of
the cab, jumped out. "Couldn't be better, could it? Come on
now. I've a speech to make and a riot to start."

O'Rourke watched the priest leap up onto the makeshift po-
dium. He certainly looked the part in his flowing black robes
with his Danton passion and a voice that was louder and more
commanding than the gathering rain clouds. *Tiocfaidh ár lá!*

was the rallying cry. *Ten years, I've been waiting for this*, thought the journalist, and despite the heat rising off the pavers, O'Rourke was in a different world, as he blinked into the angry mob to see not the gray and brown of factory workers, but veils of snow.

The harsh winter of '47. A frozen, merciless world where crows squabbled over ripe pickings, bones moaned in a blurring wind and a robin flitted between the trees, among the bright red berries, as snow feathered John's lashes. He was freezing to death out here, barely able to stand after the soldiers dragged his family from their cottage. "Tumbling," they called it, like a game you might play with your sweetheart in the hay barn. From where he lay, John could smell smoke and feel walls battered in by crowbars, hear screaming and see in the distance half-naked women running for their lives. Is that my mammy? Tell me that's not my mammy, he cried. He was sixteen at the time and John knew if he'd a loaded gun, he'd have shot the lot of them. A bullet through the head and he would have jumped up and down on their English corpses and spat on their graves. Instead, he lay helpless, famished as he was, and did nothing.

But not today. Today was a day for action.

A roar went up. *"Tiocfaidh ár lá!"* And the priest was back at the journalist's side with, "Hail another carriage, John. We need to get out of here, quick before the cavalry arrive. We're heading west this time, to Piccadilly." The priest patted his pocket. "Fucking terrifying to think what's in here. One false move and . . ."

"Jesus, O'Brian. *Is ag magadh fum ata tu?*"

The priest smiled, sticking his great legs out, clapped his hands in slow motion and mouthed, "No, son. I'm not kidding you, because one false move and . . . boom!"

12

HIGHGATE

Hatton got out of the carriage in Highgate. The body wagon was directly behind him, Patrice at the reins and the inspector up ahead, who greeted the professor with "And how do you fare this morning, Adolphus? After last night, I mean? You look a little tired. You were on the ran tan, sir. Completely drunk before we found that body. Blood sobered you up a bit though, didn't it? When we left you with Mrs. Gallant I thought you were in the safest of hands . . ."

"Mrs. Gallant? I don't remember seeing her . . . the last thing I remember was the gombeen man, Mr. Tescalini nailing down the door, the waiting carriage . . ."

"I fear you were slumped against the window all the way to Gower Street, dribbling a little and talking to yourself about some girl called Mary, and we had to stop from time to time but Mr. Tescalini helped. He's not here this morning, for the poor man needed a little respite after such a night. To cut a man in half? It would take a regular pair of hands for that kind of shoveling, a pair of Paddy hands, no doubt, for have you seen the size of some of those fellows?"

Hatton didn't reply, still struggling to remember how he'd got home last night. All he could remember, to be honest, was the forensic highlights.

"It's the combination of potato with buttermilk that makes them that way," continued the detective. "It's all they eat. And that's the reason they only have themselves to blame. We did what we could during those terrible times. Gave them free corn, set up work committees, relief programs, soup kitchens, and we even had the foresight to distribute recipes for cooking the corn. And they still insist that we did nothing."

"Recipe cards? Well, they couldn't eat those, now could they, Inspector?" Hatton said sniffily, his headache worse than ever. Thinking, recipe cards for the starving? He'd never heard of anything more ridiculous.

But Grey was of a different mind, "No, Hatton, they couldn't eat them, but they might have used them. The fussy devils claimed they found the corn we sent unpalatable. That the corn, badly cooked, not properly milled, killed the babies. But it is *mettle*, in times of crisis, that keeps a nation great. They should have stopped with their moaning and taken a note out of our book. By rejecting what we offered, the Irish only had themselves to blame." Grey adjusted the hem of a black leather glove, which to his mind didn't sit quite right. "Well, enough said," he continued, moving swiftly up the gravel path toward White Lodge. "Perhaps this is not the time and place for a history lesson."

Grey knocked on the door. Somewhere beyond the house a dog barked, chickens squawked. "I have it on good authority that today we will at last find the wayward brother in. A whole day absent after your brother is murdered? Doesn't look too good, does it?"

Hatton followed Grey into the house, where Sorcha McCarthy was waiting for them in the drawing room. The room was bursting with sunshine, dappling the celadon walls with shadows cast from a little copse of birch and willow in the garden.

Someone had opened the French windows and drawn back the shutters.

Sorcha McCarthy must have seen something telling on Hatton's face, because she spoke directly to him, saying, "It's not normal practice, Professor, but I cannot bear to have Gabriel laid out in the dark."

A young man with red hair whom Hatton didn't know laid his hand upon her arm. He was clearly Gabriel's brother.

Hatton gestured toward a low trestle table. "Is this where you would like us to put your husband, madam?" The widow didn't answer, instead looked at her brother-in-law to speak, but the young man put his fist in his mouth and turned his back on the room. Hatton could tell there was real loss here. Since the death of his father, it was a feeling he understood the truth of.

But Hatton was not here as a funeral parlor man, to fawn and cry crocodile tears. He had a job to do, and so he called Patrice in from the hallway to help with the coffin. Quietly and inconspicuously, they laid the coffin on the trestle table, which was prepared with a cloth of pure white linen, and quietly eased back the lid.

And it was at that moment that Mrs. McCarthy cried out and would have swooned to the floor, but Hatton managed to catch her in his arms. She looked up at him, as if she didn't know who he was, her eyes quickly flickering toward the trestle table and then to the door. Damien McCarthy rushed to her side, and Hatton reassured him that he was a doctor, before turning to Patrice saying, "Be quick and get some porter, smelling salts . . . hurry!"

Mrs. McCarthy squeezed Hatton's hand, "Who's that you're speaking to? I don't want any more strangers here."

"He's no one that you should worry about, Mrs. McCarthy. The boy works for me at the morgue. Here, let me help you to your feet."

"Please, forgive me," she said, the color returning to her face a little, and taking the arm of Hatton first and then her brother-in-law's. "It's the heat, this desperate heat and seeing my poor dead husband, as if he's not dead at all, but just asleep and he might wake at any minute, rise, speak and . . ."

Inspector Grey, standing aside from the others, nodded curtly to Hatton that he'd done well to intervene, as Hatton continued, "Here now, Mrs. McCarthy, a sniff of the salts . . ." He stepped away, under the watchful gaze of the brother-in-law. Hatton gestured politely toward the body. "You may want to have your husband laid out again before the funeral?"

The widow revived, stood up from the chair and ran her fingertips pensively along the edge of her dead husband's coffin, "To lay his body out again? I hadn't even thought on it." She bent down, kissed her dead husband, a mere touch of the lips to his marble skin, the quietest of moments, then turned back to Hatton, "And his beads? Are they to be returned?"

"Beads, madam? I'm not sure what you mean. What beads are these?" Hatton looked at Inspector Grey for help, who only shook his head.

At this Damien McCarthy turned back to face the room, his face like thunder, saying, "His rosary beads, damn you. Gabriel was never without them. They were simple things, wooden with a silver cross, given to him by an old acquaintance he'd recently met, who'd had them blessed in Rome. The beads must be returned and buried with Gabriel. Someone's damn well taken them."

Hatton was taken aback by this sudden effrontery, but answered, "With respect, we found no beads, Mr. McCarthy. The clothes he died in are being kept at St. Bart's and . . . well, I don't want to cause further upset, but after a death such as his, they were in no fit state to return."

"Yes, yes, Professor," said Damien McCarthy. "We're not simple people. You don't have to labor the point for the Irish among you. The rosary beads would have been in his pocket. If they've been lost or stolen through your negligence, you'll answer for it. My brother was never without the sign of his faith."

The inspector made a note. "I see. But surely your brother was Church of Ireland? To uphold the Union, he must have been a Protestant."

McCarthy laughed. "Do you seriously think my brother didn't have a mind of his own? That he was obedience itself, as all the British papers claimed he was? Well, perhaps he was in politics, but not where religion was concerned. He lost his faith for years but in the end returned to the One True Faith, and merely attended the Church of Ireland for show. Because your people insisted on it. Or maybe I shouldn't say *your people.* You're Welsh, I presume a Methodist and thus a dissenter yourself, am I right, Inspector?"

Hatton watched a flicker of pain pass across Grey's face for a split second, unsure of himself, as he mumbled, "My religious beliefs are no concern of yours and neither are they relevant to this murder inquiry."

McCarthy was goading him because Britain—its government, the Establishment, Scotland Yard—was still run by the Old School of diehard English Protestants and Grey was on the outside, just as much as any Catholic.

The younger McCarthy continued, "He had refound the true faith, and it was perhaps his one saving grace. His beads were a gift from a friend from the old county. Ask Mrs. McCarthy here if you don't believe me. She's also very devout and can't tell a lie, never mind live one. Can you, Sorcha, my dear?"

"Be quiet, Damien. For heaven's sake, what does all this matter now? My husband is dead, your brother, sir, and please, for pity's sake, don't drag all of that into this . . ."

"All of what? You married all of that. Do you not understand this yet?"

The brother's tone with the widow was rude and abrupt, and Hatton had no liking for this upstart man who seemed to threaten the peace of the room, and more important, threaten her, because he was holding Mrs. McCarthy's arm in a manner which no gentleman would do.

"Mr. McCarthy," said Inspector Grey firmly. "Take your hands off your sister-in-law immediately. Where have you been, anyway? You've been absent, two nights on the trot, since your brother died. To that point, I'll need to know your precise movements from the morning of July 9 until now. We need to speak about your brother's death, at length, and also I'd like to ask some questions of another death that's come to light."

"Another death? I'm not sure I follow you."

Grey closed his notebook and put it in his pocket. He crossed his arms. "A man we found last night. Name of Gregory Mahoney? A gombeen man, bloodsucker, call him what you will, who was working in the rookeries of St. Giles. Heard of him, perhaps?"

"No, I've never heard of him, and I've no wish to speak to you today, Inspector. You've only just returned my poor brother's body. We're a house in mourning, sir. I have been busy on business for the last day or so and I have plenty that will vouch for me, but first of all, before I answer any of your impudent questions, show some damn respect."

The inspector stepped forward. "This is a police inquiry, Mr. McCarthy. I can talk to you here, or you can accompany me to The Yard, if you prefer. Perhaps now would be a good time for me to tell you, as Mrs. McCarthy already knows, your brother was known to me. On that point alone, I think we need to talk."

"Known to you?" Damien McCarthy grew pale.

Inspector Grey deftly hooked his arm through McCarthy's and steered him out into the garden without another word, where the two men quickly melded with trees, the high grass, and the tumbling roses.

How strange, thought Hatton, that Gabriel McCarthy had been known to Inspector Grey? If that was the case, why on earth hadn't he said anything of it before? Hatton knew Scotland Yard hobnobbed with politicians, especially someone as ambitious as Grey, but as to the precise nature of this relationship? Why was the inspector being so circumspect? If they went to the

same clubs, ate in the same fancy restaurants, met at some Westminster shindig, what of it? Well, thought Hatton, he wasn't
going to be brushed off so easily, as if he was just an adjunct to
this case. He needed to know more of this relationship and
would ask the inspector when the opportunity arose.

Meanwhile, Hatton remained where he was, watching Sorcha McCarthy who stood at the window. Her face had a chill
about it, and it was all that Hatton could do to stop himself
reaching out to her to offer her some comfort. Instead he said
brusquely, "Should I leave you for a moment, Mrs. McCarthy?"

She shook her head. "No, Professor, but there's something
troubling me." She asked him to shut the door. "Call it a woman's intuition," she said. "But I think you're hiding something. I
know Gabriel's death was no accident, but I have solemnly
sworn that I will say nothing more on the matter for the time
being, at least. I understand the sensitive balance of feelings in
this country, in relation to my people. I see the banners in the
streets. I've been at mass, when rocks are hurled and heard the
cries of 'Death to all Catholics.' But as I told the Inspector, I'm
sick to death of politics."

She fell silent until the two men were completely out of view
and then asked, with a narrowing of her eyes, "And why make
mention of this other killing? A gombeen man in the rookeries,
he said?"

"The man who died last night came from Ardara, Mrs.
McCarthy. The very same place where I believe you and your
late husband are from? It's just to our mind, mine especially, this
seems rather a coincidence. Ardara is a small place surely, for
I've never heard of it?"

She put her hand on the mantel. "Forgive me, Professor, but
you are English. I'd never heard of Highgate till my husband
brought me here, and why should I? It was nothing to me, a
foreign land, as Ireland is to you, but I can tell you this. Ardara
was devastated. Left empty. Tumbled, we called it. Many people
left and came to London or traveled farther afield. They had

little choice. They were starving, Professor. The fact that this man came from the same place as us isn't so unusual." Her voice was strained, and despite the heat, she shivered as if she had a fever upon her.

"I'm sorry," said Hatton. "It clearly pains you to speak of this."

She shook her head. "I was one of the lucky ones, but I'm telling you, these two deaths are not connected and we rarely set foot in St. Giles except for Latin mass. If there was a Holy Day or something special, our carriage would deliver us to the steps of the Sacred Heart, then promptly take us home again. The congregation was welcoming enough, but that priest, Father O'Brian, is a firebrand. Sure, he does good work with the poor and at Christmas, Easter, Holy Days, and so forth, and like any good Catholic, I must do what the Father says."

"Which is what?" asked Hatton, genuinely curious.

"Why, visit the odd sick or lonely parishioner, of course, but I don't care for him and he was no friend to my husband. You encourage me to speak freely but I want to hear from you. I know you're hiding something. What is it?"

Hatton was taken aback, because this young woman was bold, just like Mary had been. Perhaps it was an Irish thing. "Well, there was something," he admitted, but the minute it was out of his mouth, Hatton regretted it; her boldness had put him off his guard.

"I knew it."

"But you cannot speak of it, Mrs. McCarthy. I have given the inspector, my word."

She spun around, directly facing him; her hand gripped his arm. Her eyes were burning, "My husband is dead, murdered. You must tell me."

"A ribbon was found in his mouth."

Her hand fell away.

"But you mustn't speak of it. I shouldn't have told you."

"And the ribbon?" She paused. "Was it green?"

Hatton nodded.

"*Fenians.*" She was visibly shaking. "Do you know who these people are? They're killers. They attack anyone they think is standing in the way of liberty. My husband was prepared to wait and to win freedom, through peaceful means. But the Fenians know nothing of this. They are little more than thugs. They will break the Union even if it means murdering innocent people, their own kith and kin. You don't know what they're capable of . . ."

"Please, madam. Calm yourself," Hatton said, steering her toward a chair, knowing that women, when they were roused like this, should be treated with tenderness and care.

She was grief-stricken, more than a little wild, but she looked at Hatton with sudden daggers. "I'll not calm myself. I may be only twenty, but I have lived twice that life. All Irish women have." She sat down, despite herself, and clasped her hands, leaned forward toward him, her voice growing softer. "When I was a little girl, I watched from behind my mother's skirt, terrified. They would come down from the glen of Croaghanmoira and rampage through our village, armed with cudgels, pikes, whips. It wasn't the English landowners they came to teach a lesson, but us, Professor—their own people. They called themselves Ribbonmen and now they call themselves this Gaelic word, Fenians. There's graffiti in the rookeries, *Tiocfaidh ár lá*. Have you seen it?"

"I try not to venture into the rookeries, madam."

"You are wise. It means 'Our day will come.' There's revolution in the air, can't you feel it? And like the French who wore the *tricolore* cockades, the Fenians believe you're either with them or against them." She bit her lips, damson red again, and her hands were trembling. Hatton reached out and steadied them. Her hands were soft. She left her hands in his and looked into his eyes again, more beguiling than ever. "Please, Professor, you have to help me. I need Gabriel's rosary beads. To lose them will bring bad luck, and it's not right that my husband should be buried without the sign of his faith. The killer has taken them to mock us. But if you find them, they could be evidence, couldn't they? If the killer has left a trace upon them? A smudge of dirt? Blood?"

She released her hand from his. "My husband's killer is out there, somewhere, right now, I am sure of it, but you can surely help me find him? You see, I know a little of your work, Professor Hatton. I was a ward of the Arada Estate before I married, and was well educated. My husband's father took me in. I stood in rags, had lost my family, I had nothing. They fed me, clothed me, and taught me not just to read and write but history, geology, the constellations, the glories of science, Professor Hatton."

She sighed and went over to one of the many bookshelves. "The Irish gentry, such as it is, has a heritage stretching back to the Normans and are firm believers in educating women. I speak a little Latin, did you know that?" A faint smile came upon her lips but there was sorrow underneath. "And I have even read *The Lancet*. My husband bought the periodically every month and would read little snippets to me. I shall miss him and I shall miss his counsel." She held Hatton's eyes for the briefest second, as she continued, "My husband taught me so much and he spoke so highly of science. How blood circulates the body, how time of death can be measured. Is that right, Professor Hatton? And that *you* are some kind of expert?"

Hatton was flattered. He made a curt bow and gestured her back to the easy chair. She sat, like an eager student or a lady determined on self-improvement, and looked up at him. "Well?"

"It's true," he said. "Gone are the days when the testament of a witness is enough to send a man to the gallows, and the missing beads might offer us a clue and set us on a trail. But it's not clear to me why anyone would take them, unless they are incriminating in some way. I presume they are of little intrinsic value?"

"They were of great personal value. Are you a man of faith, Professor?"

What could he say? He couldn't lie to her, so said nothing.

She didn't seem to notice but only continued, "I have heard that you do tricks with mirrors and use thermometers to tell the nature of death. That you read a cadaver like a map and can run your hand along a dead man's skull and say if he murdered another. That you can slice a man open and see his last supper? Am I right? Can all this be possible?"

Hatton shook his head, "It's a little more complicated than that, Madam."

She became a little more insistent. "But this is what people say you do, Professor. And that you're the only man in London who carries out this science, which is, I must confess, partly why I sought you out."

"You sought me out?" He was taken back, because few sought him out, especially beautiful women.

"Of course," she insisted.

"You see, as soon as I saw the body, I knew it wasn't right. I was brought up in Ireland during terrible times, and as a child saw umpteen bodies racked by the blackness of cholera. So even in the first awful moment of discovery, I admit, though I am not proud to say so, I was afraid for myself. Death stalks each and every one of us, Professor, and if Fenians have killed my husband, then who next? I married him. My voice is strong, but my body is weak. I need protection." She looked across the garden. "But I'm not so sure about Scotland Yard and this strange Inspector Grey. What do you know of him? Is he any good, would you say?"

Hatton was surprised. "But madam, your husband knew him. Why don't *you* tell me."

She stood up from her chair and brushed her skirt down. "Yes, they knew each other, I believe, but my husband knew many people. He was a politician and Grey is a policeman. Sure," she said, "it seems to me in this country they are practically the same thing. But what do I know? I am a foreigner in this land and a woman."

"Do you miss Ireland, Mrs. McCarthy?"

Her face, her whole body seemed to melt. She leaned against

the drawing room wall and briefly closed her eyes. "England is not my home."

"I've heard it's very beautiful . . ."

"It is." She came alive. "Here, come with me and let me show you . . ."

She left the room, bidding him to follow her. They went down the corridor and into the music room. She closed the door behind her firmly and turning to him said, "Forgive me for saying this, but it's good to be away from death, if only for a moment." She took a deep breath and, despite her black silks and mourning veil, suddenly appeared to Hatton not as a widow, old before her time, but a vibrant, eager twenty-year-old woman. She pointed to a small oil on the wall beside her which was positioned above the piano. "It was my husband's favorite . . ."

It was wonderful, he thought, subtle with the delicate line and the precision of a serious painter. He said so. She inclined her head to thank him. "I painted it before we left Ardara. Most of the region is little more than bog, high mountains, but it's a magical place, full of legends, ancient customs, huge, gushing rivers . . ."

"And the sea . . ." said Hatton looking at the waves crashing onto a windswept beach.

"You are from the city, Professor?"

Hatton smiled. "I'm a nature child, like yourself, madam. I am cut from the land."

"But you do not farm?"

"My father's farm earns little and now he's gone and there's no one to manage it. And I am very busy."

She sighed, "But you own the land, still?"

He nodded, throwing off the guilt which haunted him. He hadn't been back to the farmstead since his father died. Lucy had written pleading with him to *do something*, anything. Sell it off in its entirety, rent it to someone who would tend to it—there were hops fields, she'd said, strawberries they could grow—but the thought of returning to the burden of those damp walls, the broken roof, and all those echoing ghosts made him shudder. Every day he thought of it, and yet he did nothing. The widow must have seen something telling on his face because she asked, "Did someone die there? Someone close to you, Professor?"

He didn't wish to speak of this now. Not speak of his mother who worked herself to death, out in the rain, her teeth gritted against the elements, her hands red raw, herding pigs through Hampshire mud to catch a chill, they said. A chill? He was eight years old when she died. And he would not speak of his father, nor would he speak of Mary.

"Yes, people died there, but this painting," he said, quickly changing the subject back to something pleasant again. "It's wild, open country. What about the estate?"

"As yes, the estate," she sighed. "There's a large oil in my husband's bedroom, a few more along the corridor as you came in and . . ." She opened a drawer and took out a black-and-white etching of a sprawling country house. "As you can see, the place I was raised from the age of ten was a solid house with very grand proportions. The McCarthys are what others call West Brits, Professor. My husband's family were fair landlords, but their management of Ardara was imposed upon the people by the British. Ordinary Irish cannot own land, as your family did. They may labor upon it, but they cannot buy it. The McCarthys were middlemen but my husband's family were good landlords. They did the best they could."

"But it's a terrible system."

"Yes, Professor. *It is.* The common Irish are no better than slaves. You see the cottage in the foreground?"

Hatton leaned a little closer to the picture to see a forlorn, run-down sort of place, a primitive hut.

"Sure, it's quaint to an artist's eye," she said, "but this is all we are allowed, even today. Nothing's changed. The West Brits live in the big house, while most Irish languish in a mud hut, with a grass roof, not even windows, just a hole to let the smoke out. If the tenant improves his property, the rents are increased.

Do you see, now? Do you see why there's so much anger on the streets, here in London? It runs deep, Professor."

Her face was flushed, she sighed, pushed a lock of jet black hair back from her face, and stood very close to him as she said, "But these are miserable things to talk of and I would rather forget them. I am just very glad you like my painting, but I shouldn't smile, should I? Nor should I profess pleasure in this time of mourning, for I've just lost my husband. I'm young, Professor Hatton, and you are most attentive. May I ask? Are you married?"

Hatton felt himself redden but said firmly, "No, madam."

She looked surprised, then said, "Marriage is a state of grace and one I hope you find. You see, my life was blessed when I met Gabriel. He was so much older, but he saved me, did everything for me. Loved me, taught me, even put me on a pedestal, but now he's gone."

He said it, before he could stop himself, as he turned to her. "I can see why he did so, you are so very—"

"Professor Hatton, you shouldn't . . ."

"No, madam, I shouldn't, but . . ."

Before he could say another word, a sharp knock interrupted. It was Florrie at the door, and if Hatton was not much mistaken, the slightly older woman gave the younger, prettier one, a sharp look. "We wondered where you'd gone to, madam, and the music room, of all places. Tea, Professor Hatton?"

Hatton coughed. "Tea would be most agreeable."

The widow rustled out ahead of him, her silk a whisper on the parquet floor, but her voice firm, "Lemon verbena, Florrie, and serve it in the parlor, please. Nothing to eat. It's far too hot and I hate to see food wasted. Professor Hatton . . ."

Hatton went to follow but as he did—"Urgggh . . ."—he physically collided with a skulking adolescent. Patrice, who must have been loitering all this time, lowered his head, his cheeks red with sunburn, cap in hand, his usual deferential self. "*Excusez-moi,* Professor?"

"Yes, Patrice. *What is it?* You trod on my foot, you dolt."

"Begging your pardon, monsieur. Should I stay here in the corridor or outside near the body wagon? Or I can go to the servant's quarters, if you prefer? That's what the maid has suggested. Oh, and Monsieur Roumande is here."

"Monsieur Roumande? Already?"

Florrie cocked her head. "Oh yes. Should have said so, sir. A big, burly man arrived ten minutes ago. He's got all sorts of tricks up his sleeve and making a right old mess in my master's study what with the flypaper, the blotting paper, the charcoal, and that Welsh dandy draped all over my master's chair and smoking cigarellos. It isn't right, so soon after the master's death . . ."

Hatton ignored the flustered maid and only hissed at the boy, "While I've got your attention, Patrice, did you find any rosary beads on Gabriel McCarthy's body? In the pockets, perhaps? Did you double-check everything, thoroughly? The mistress of this house is quite beside herself and says they are lost. Perhaps even taken."

The boy scratched his head. "There were no beads, sir. I'm sure of it. Monsieur Roumande is most particular. He has a system, a file and a selection of calico bags which . . ."

"Yes, yes, Patrice. I know the system."

Hatton turned around to see the maid who in a trice was back again laden down with a huge pile of sandwiches, cakes, buns, soda bread, glistening golden butter, porter, and other refreshments, quietly standing behind him.

"Excuse me, sir," she said. "Madam knows nothing of men's appetites. So, please, gentlemen, would you be so kind as to follow me?" Who the devil did that woman just wink at? Was it him or another? Hatton turned to see Patrice was standing directly behind him, grinning. *Hmmph* . . . thought Hatton. Roumande was right about that one. Lock up your daughters' time.

The maid ushered the two of them into the morning room and continued to talk, ten to a dozen. Hatton had no choice but to stand there and listen as she said, "Mr. McCarthy's body was supposed to be shipped back to Donegal tomorrow, but now they've changed their minds. The young master is very upset and has been shouting this morning, since the sun came up. But it's to be expected, of course, for he has just lost his brother. I wasn't afraid, no, not for me, but for Mrs. McCarthy. I worry a great deal about my mistress . . ." and on she prattled, making adjustments to the curtains in the room they now occupied, which was a smaller and duller affair than the one he'd left. But where was she? Sorcha McCarthy had gone off somewhere. The prattling was annoying, especially in this insufferable heat, and Hatton couldn't help but notice that it wasn't he she addressed anyway, because the maid's eyes were fixed upon another. Patrice smiled at her, and when he did so caused such a deepening crimson to her cheeks, Hatton thought the maid might drop the tray of cups and saucers, and so he took the whole lot from her with a grunt of disapproval.

She made a curtsy, lower than was required, and Hatton looked at the pair of them. She all red gold hair and freckles and Patrice, sallow-skinned, dark-eyed, Latin. But Hatton could see what she saw in him. The lad's face was fetching enough. He had a real gypsy look about him. And Hatton watched with creeping amusement as Patrice said "*Merci*" to the thicker slice of bread and butter and the more generous glass of lemonade.

But barely a sip was taken before the inspector popped his head around the corner and announced, "Roumande is a genius. I say bravo to the French and your strange modus operandi of forensics. Come quickly, Hatton. He has a print . . ."

Roumande was crouched on the ground in the study and Sorcha McCarthy was standing to the side of him, very pale, watching, a disk of sunlight blanching her skin to nothing.

"What have you got there, Albert?"

"I'm not sure, Professor. I left the gombeen man back at the mortuary and came as quick as I could. I've lifted something from one of the floorboards, which I think may be a fingerprint."

It was bright daylight outside. Too bright. Blinding. "Shut the curtains someone and turn on a gas lamp. Bring it over here . . ." Hatton was quick to the desk and Roumande was quick to his side with, "I need a word with you when we're out of earshot of that Taffy over there."

"Grey? What's he done now? He's been here with me all the time, Albert."

Roumande pursed his lips, shook his head, "Not now, Adolphus. Later."

"What's that?" Grey's voice bounced across the room. "No whispering in the classroom. If you have anything to say, you two, share it. So, can you make anything of it, Hatton?"

Hatton took his eyeglass from his medical bag. "Albert's done an excellent job to lift anything at all. This is the first time we've even attempted such a thing, but here . . . look for yourself, Inspector. It's a fingerprint mark all right, despite the maid and her scrubbing. Lifted by sprinkling charcoal and making an impression on the paper. *Almost* a perfect replica, but not quite. You can still see the whorls and troughs, but it's smudged. It's not good enough. But as you can see, it's from a smallish digit . . ."

The inspector turned to the widow. "But there are no children in the house?"

"Of course not." She stepped out of the disk of sunlight, her face suddenly world-weary, disappointed by whatever she saw or thought she saw. "You cannot read it, then?" she said flatly. Hatton shook his head, as disappointed as she.

"No, madam," he smiled at her. She inclined her head to the side, as inquisitive as ever. "You cannot use it, then?"

"Science is step by step, Mrs. McCarthy. An empirical endeavor. We make mistakes, yes, but we start again. It can take decades to perfect a scientific method or a theory."

"And you look for fingerprints, but why?"

"Because." He glanced at her hands. "If I may? It's easier to show you, by taking your fingertip, thus?" He reached out to hear her sharp intake of breath, but she gave her finger just the same. "Your finger pattern is unique, and as a forensic pathologist, it's my job to search for traces at a crime scene. Alien traces. A drop of blood, a hair, or a print which may lead me to the killer. I need a physical thing . . ." A hush fell on the room; as the other men watched, Hatton took her hand, pressing her finger onto the ink pad, then moving it to the paper, rolling it slowly, carefully, and then gently lifting her finger and releasing her. She bent forward to look. "Do you see?" said Hatton with a smile. Her print was perfect. "Those whorls and troughs of your index finger are completely unique. They are *you*, madam. They are very special indeed."

Her mouth made a little O shape in surprise, and then she said, "How I wish that I were a man so I could study such things. You are just like Mr. Darwin on your scientific journey, Professor Hatton. And from what my husband told me, just days before he died, Mr. Darwin has taken twenty years to perfect his ideas."

Hatton was impressed that she knew of these discussions already. How wonderful to meet a woman whose mind was so alert. He wanted to continue talking like this to her forever, but Grey snapped the curtain back and let light flood in. "Well, you haven't got that long, Hatton. Do you remember what I said to you? This is a test case, and I cannot continue to fund a method which doesn't get results. You'll have to do far better than a smudge." He turned to Mrs. McCarthy and bowed curtly. "I'm afraid I must leave for dockside. My condolences, madam. You will bury your husband, when?"

She lowered her eyes to the floor, but not before Hatton saw tears on her lashes. "Tomorrow, Inspector. Damien says it will take too long to ship the body home, so he shall be buried in the dissenter's catacomb in Highgate. It was not what Gabriel would have wanted, and I'm sorry for it, but Damien is insistent, saying it is hot, that's everything's prepared, and that he's the master now and I must obey him."

———

"So," said the inspector, as the men stood on the pavement. "What an interesting garden saunter I had. Damien McCarthy is all bark and no bite, although he insisted on boring me with his own version of Irish history. I let him blather on and called his bluff by presenting him with the death as one of either suicide or accidental death. I left the detail of the ribbon out."

"But we can't keep it quiet forever, Inspector. The Irish are as thick as thieves, and if it's a lesson in betrayal that's being meted out within their own community . . ."

Grey sighed, rustled in his pocket and, finding a topaz-colored bonbon, popped it in his mouth. "Want one?" Hatton shook his head because he liked to keep his senses sharp, not dulled by the stupidity of candied opium. "Watch and learn, Hatton," continued the inspector, crunching his sweet. "I asked him a number of leading questions. How often and where they went to mass? Who he knew in the rookeries? If his brother had debts, was melancholic and inclined to take a draught? I stressed that if that was the case, he couldn't possibly be buried in consecrated ground. I wanted to see how spontaneous his reaction was at my suggestion of suicide."

Hatton was intrigued. "And . . . ?"

"Pretty convincing, if he's lying. The poor man broke down and begged that a verdict of suicide was not acceptable. That his family name would be ruined forever, so I agreed, reluctantly, that under the circumstances I was prepared to be charitable. But I left it open, mind. Said I still had other lines of inquiry to follow which might yet point to suicide or, perhaps, even murder. But before I left him, I said a death certificate stating 'natural causes' would be the best solution, for the time being at least."

"And you mentioned nothing of the ribbon, to the brother or the wife?" Hatton wanted to be sure. He didn't mention that he had already told the widow. Let sleeping dogs lie, he thought.

"Now look here, Hatton. You have a headache, am I right? You need to get out of the sun because it's interfering with your logic. I have Damien McCarthy on the hop. There was no love lost between those brothers. The ribbon could simply be to cover Damien McCarthy's steps, setting us on a different trail."

"You think he may have killed his brother, then?"

"He's a suspect, of course. He has a motive. The estate, a seat in Parliament, quite possibly the wife. It would have been easy for him. The ribbon perhaps merely a thumb bite at his brother's Unionist politics."

"And the gombeen man? Did you press him on that?"

"My dear Adolphus, you heard me in the drawing room. He denies all knowledge of Mahoney, but I'm not without my informants in the rookeries. I'll get there, although I fear the clock is against us."

"You think there could be more punishments to come?"

"If these deaths *are* punishments. What about the glitter stuff?"

"I'm working on it."

"Well, let's give him the death certificate he wants and put him off his guard. He's either killed his brother for a personal reason or maybe these two killings are linked to something bigger, something political. But if that's the case, an upstart like that won't be the ring leader—they'll have bigger fish to fry. Maybe some of his friends will come to the wake. Who knows? Maybe he'll go visit them, and if he does . . . watch and learn, Hatton."

But this didn't excuse lying. Hatton stuck to his guns. "So I am right to think you want me to write a false death certificate to put him off our tracks? Is that what you are saying, Inspector? I am to practice subterfuge? Potentially lose my job, my reputation by lying for The Yard?"

"I've told you of my strategy. Enough, I say."

Roumande and Patrice were by now standing a yard or so away, chatting to each other casually by the empty body cart. Grey took his opportunity. "Let me give you a word of advice, Hatton. You, sir, should pay attention to your *superiors,*" and for the second time in so many days, Hatton felt the hands of Grey upon him, this time pressed firmly to his larynx.

Hatton couldn't breathe or call for help, Grey's face now less than an inch from the professor's. "As to what these killings mean, I am well attuned to the Irish and their little gangs of thugs, but that's for me to investigate. Forensics is nothing more than my backup. Do you understand me, Professor?"

He released his grip. "I didn't have to give you the gombeen man, by the way, but I knew you wanted that particular cadaver very badly, and not just for the sake of the autopsy. Let's call it a favor, from one gentleman to another. I know you have a taste for veal . . ."

Hatton took a step back, still spluttering from the policeman's ironlike grip. How on earth did Grey know the term that Albert and he used as code, known only to each other?

"I see I surprise you, Professor. *Veal* . . . isn't that what you anatomists call gross deformities? Tender meat, as opposed to the normal run of beef or pork? It's not strictly legal to be hoarding abnormalities. In fact, I think under the 1839 Human Remains Protection Act it's completely illegal, but on that particular issue I shall say no more, our little secret, eh, Professor Hatton? You see, I know all about your basement." He tapped the side of his nose again. "Little bird told me, but if word got out you were up to all sorts of ungodly experiments with poor, dead, Christian souls, St. Bart's reputation would be . . . My God, it doesn't bear thinking on it, does it?"

And with that, Grey turned on his heels, jumped into his barouche, shouting at his driver, "Hecker's Flour Mill, Salmon Lane, Limehouse, quickly—" and in a rise of yellowing dust was gone.

Hatton shook his head in disbelief. Was nothing sacred anymore? He turned toward White Lodge in the vain hope that he might catch one more glimpse of her, to lift his spirits a little. But instead he saw Damien McCarthy standing at the study window with nothing but contempt on his lips. Was it contempt? Hatton couldn't be sure, but he was certain that this young man with his red hair and fiery temperament should be watched, very closely, whatever might have happened.

The professor got into the carriage with Roumande, but no sooner were they settled, than—

"We have a problem, Professor."

"What sort of problem, Albert?"

"The gombeen man."

"You got him, didn't you?"

"Not quite."

"What do you mean not quite?"

"Most of him."

"Most of him or all of him?"

"All the body parts."

"I don't follow." God, his head was splitting.

"Mr. Tescalini was there . . ."

"And?"

"I didn't fancy my chances, Adolphus. I'm a family man."

"You're speaking in riddles, Albert. We have the corpse, the delivery note, permission to cut?"

"When I got to the Dials, he'd changed somewhat. I pressed Mr. Tescalini on it but he told me, in his own special way, to mind my own damn business. Anyway, I'd already noticed by then that the mouth was like this—" Roumande leaned back in the carriage, lifted his chin and opened his mouth, wide like a frog.

He shut it again and said, "Remind you of anyone? Because rigor mortis had set in. His mouth should have been clamped down like a London oyster, but it had been yanked wide open, Adolphus. They'd left a thread that I detected with an eyeglass, peering down the cadaver's gullet on the way back to the morgue. Vibrant green it was, but the rest of the ribbon had vanished into thin air, just like that poor Monsieur Pomeroy fellow."

"Damn," said Hatton, thumping the side of the carriage door with his fist. "Damn that man. But don't worry, for I've a plan already. You go to St. Bart's and start cutting without me, Albert. I'm heading for Whitehall."

13

PICCADILLY

Inside the carriage, O'Rourke's eyes scoured the estates involved in the Gregory Clause. "And Ardara was one of them, as I've long suspected. A deal was struck, leaving the McCarthy family rich, acting as land managers for the British in Donegal, which begs the question as to our future involvement with Damien? Before Gabriel's death, he could act the black sheep, but now?" O'Rourke paused, looking at the priest's face for a second, and then continued, "We might have to sever him, Father."

They had reached the corner of Piccadilly Circus as the priest shook his head and said, "I made up my mind about Damien long ago. This is a war we're fighting, and besides, The Yard will be watching his every move. He's too big a risk for us now, so you're right, we need to sever him."

The two men slipped through the crowds and into the arcade that ran along a covered hall decorated with metal hanging lamps and, soaring high above, a cathedral of glittering skylights. Un-rolling the map, O'Rourke quickly found ten shops down on the right. Dawson's, Purveyor of Fine Jewels and Clocks. In the window of Dawson's a display had been created with a hundred different clocks, so as they stepped into the shop, the pinging began, a reverberating sound of one clock chasing another clock. Looking to his right, O'Rourke caught sight of a timepiece which was embellished with flowers, a spray of feathery blue.

"The mantel is by Asprey's," said the horologist, as he came out to greet them, his eyepiece in, his halitosis unmistakable. "The movement is Swiss," he breathed. "The craftsmanship is second to none. Perhaps you're viewing for your wife, sir? It's a lady's clock, you see."

O'Rourke answered quickly, pulling out his pocket watch, "We're just here for some mending, Mr. Dawson. It was my father's and once kept excellent time, but it now seems to be dragging a little."

The horologist nodded, taking the watch and turning the face toward him before flipping it over and taking a tiny pair of tweezers, opening the back and examining it, saying, "It's veritably clogged. A good clean would see the watch back in perfect working order, and I could have it ready in a few days' time, at a price of two and six?"

"What about tomorrow? We're in a bit of a hurry, you see."

"Hmmm . . . tomorrow is certainly possible . . ."

The horologist looked over at the priest, who appeared to be inspecting a grandfather clock, opening and shutting the front.

"It's magnificent, isn't it, sir?" he said.

The priest patted the clock and said in a perfect English accent, "Just window shopping today, but tell me, are you are losing customers due to this great stink? The arcade seems a little quiet today."

The horologist smiled. "Stinks don't bother me, and by late afternoon we'll be jammed to the gills with courting couples, trippers, you name it, honking river or not."

"I see," said the priest, shutting the door of the huge mahogany clock behind him, his back pressed flat to it, before continuing, "Well, we don't want to take up too much of your time."

"Yes, just the mending, please," added O'Rourke, catching the priest's eye.

"Your name please?" asked the horologist, his pencil at the ready.

"My name?" said O'Rourke. "Mr. Jones. Mr. Edward Jones."

"It will be ready tomorrow at opening time, Mr. Jones. It's a very nice watch," the horologist said, against the incessant *ticktock, ticktock, ticktock, ticktock.*

14

WHITEHALL

At Scotland Yard, the brass plate announced *Metropolitan Police: Criminal Investigation Department.* The room was large, sunlit with a sense of men just vanished, with its overflowing desks, ashtrays, bottles of spent whiskey. It smelled of sweat, toil, and trouble but there was no one about to ask, so Hatton simply plonked himself down where he needed to be, grabbed a piece of paper, wrote *"Dear Inspector Grey,"* then scrubbed out the *"Dear"* and started again with *"For the attention of: Inspector Grey. Urgently require discussion on Ribbon Murders case,"* but that wasn't right either. *How can people work like this?* he asked himself, as he tried to find a space amidst a cacophony of files, multicolored inkwells, postcards from Morocco, and a huge number of recipe cards illustrated with little scenes—ladies having a picnic, a man serving soup. Hatton glanced down at their titles, *"Drink and Be Merry," "A Christmas Celebration," "Parlors and Tea Parties," "Sugared Dainties—A Home Cook Book,"* and noticed at the bottom: *Recipes courtesy of Monsieur Gustave Pomeroy, Chef of Verrey's Restaurant. London.*

Gustave Pomeroy? It beggared belief. Hatton pushed the

leaflets away with distaste and took the quill again, "*For The Urgent Attention of Inspector Grey. RE: Ribbon Murders. New forensic evidence relocated to St. Bart's. Yours in faith, Professor Adolphus Hatton.*"

This was where their attention should be, not gadding about eating free suppers in London's best restaurants. Why, everyone knew that all chefs were a histrionic breed, and no doubt this Pomeroy chap was drunk as a lord in some bordello. What a waste of precious police time. Unless?

Hatton looked again. Recipe cards? Inspector Grey had mentioned recipe cards only this morning. Could they somehow be connected to the McCarthy case? But these weren't recipe cards for cooking corn. He sighed, opening the drawers then shutting them again. Nothing. So where was the ribbon, then?

Hatton left the detectives' room and, slipping down the hallway, pushed open a door and quickly found the jacket Grey had worn last night. How obvious the inspector was. If they were going to tamper with evidence, they should at least have a foolproof system. *Dullards*, he thought to himself as pulled the little bag out, clearly labeled *Evidence. Item 1: Silk Ribbon, Mr. Gregory Mahoney. July 10, 1858. Deceased.*

So it simply had to be the Ribbonmen, didn't it? This idea of Grey's that it could be elaborate subterfuge by the McCarthy brother seemed too far-fetched. Hatton could see the young man had a motive to kill his brother. That he was brutish, ill-tempered, a radical to boot, but why kill a rent collector? It didn't make sense. Mob rule and gang punishment seemed the simplest explanation. On the one hand, an Irish MP who stood in opposition to repeal, and on the other, a gombeen man who bled the people dry. Both worked for the English. Both are duly punished on the eve of Drogheda. But, thought Hatton, both from a place called—"Ardara," he said, under his breath, but where exactly was this place? And why was it so important? What had Sorcha said? A sweeping place battered by Nature, a painter's world of sunbursts, fields of emerald green. This place was God's Own Country, yes, but what else? Was there a secret hidden in Ardara that was dark enough to kill for?

Hatton's thoughts were interrupted by footsteps coming down the hall, a click, and then steps heading back down the corridor. And it suddenly occurred to him, what on earth was he doing? Holed up in the inspector's store cupboard, a man in his position? He'd had enough. He would walk out, and if anyone tried to stop him . . . Hatton made up his mind there and then that he would shove the ribbon in their faces—saliva, blood clots, and all. For it was *his case, his evidence,* and if Scotland Yard wasn't going to pursue the matter properly, well . . . Hatton turned the door handle. "Damn, someone has locked me in," he muttered to himself, as he sat down on his haunches and nestled his face into the soft caress of a smoking jacket. *Jesus, I could be here for hours,* he thought, and so for the hell of it, and with nothing else to do, he rustled in a couple more pockets, taking out a bundle of things which felt odd in the dark. *Paper,* he was sure of it, a rattling tin of something, maybe peppermints. He popped one into his mouth, yes, peppermints, and something perfectly smooth on one side, on the other a raised elaborate pattern. A cigarette case, perhaps?

"For heaven's sake, get me a new tie and a clean shirt. I am covered in the stuff. Drenched in it. Three changes in one day. It's a record! Hurry up. *Veloce, veloce . . .*"

The closet door opened, but rather than diving out, for some reason Hatton chose to stay hidden, watching carefully as Mr. Tescalini selected a jacket from the cupboard, a starched white shirt, a paisley tie. The Italian left, leaving the door ajar, and went off whistling somewhere. And Hatton was out, not looking back for even a second, but keeping up a pace until he turned the corner into Pall Mall, and hailing a hackney, thundered back to St. Bart's, despite all that had happened, ahead of himself.

There was a loud noise emanating from the mortuary room. The sound of hacking, indicating that Monsieur Roumande was already sleeves rolled up, bespattered in gore, and organizing some sort of lobotomy or a partitioning of bones. Flies were already thick in the air, the oilcloth on the floor swimming with guts, as Hatton reached the dissection slab where the new cadaver lay. Roumande looked like he had been in a fight with a bear. Taking a cloth, Hatton said, "Here, Albert. I can't have a conversation, until I can see you better!"

Roumande did his best to get the bits of gristle out of his stubble. "Well, did you get it?"

Hatton put the ribbon down and smoothed it across the table, "PC Plodders, the lot of them. It was only in Grey's dinner jacket, hanging in that ridiculous store cupboard he has . . ."

"Well done, Professor. I'll put it with the other one. The deaths are definitely connected, then?"

"Most certainly, but please, Albert . . ." said Hatton, looking around him at the organs, the bones, the floor awash with blood. "This is too much for one man alone, even if the man is you. Where the devil's Patrice? Why isn't he here helping you?"

"Patrice is in the South Wing with Dr. Buchanan, earning us money. Ten guineas a throw, remember? The light at this time in the afternoon is excellent, according to our resident artist. As soon as we got back from Highgate there was a message demanding a sitting, for Dr. Buchanan's portrait . . ." Roumande trailed off, distracted, flapping his hands in the air, "I'm worried these flies will lay eggs in our cadavers, although I have been toying with the idea of letting them anyway. Empirical research, Professor?"

"Hmmmm . . ." said Hatton.

"We could watch what they do. Just go ahead and let them. What do you think, Professor?"

Hatton allowed himself a smile, relieved to be back where he belonged. In the morgue, questioning the known parameters of science. "Measuring decomposition? Why the devil not. There've been a number of cases where time of death has been pinpointed, more or less, despite advanced decay, by looking at the mites in a cadaver."

"I read that article, too. The missing milkmaid? She'd been raped, butchered, then hammered under a doorstep and left for years, only unearthed when the new owners of the house were having some work done. The April issue of *The Medical Journal*, I believe. Is that the case you refer to?"

"The very same, Albert." Hatton pointed at his friend's chin and Roumande scrubbed a little harder with the gum-pink soap. The head of Mahoney had already been decapitated and sat, yellow leather on a blood-smeared plate.

Roumande walked around the slab where the rest of the cadaver lay. "One Gregory Mahoney, aged sixty or thereabouts, native of Donegal, resident of St. Giles, London, now deceased. There was so little keeping him together by the time I took the spade out, it was easier just to finish the job, and then by the time I did that, well, I didn't want to step on your toes, but . . ." Hatton nodded, keep going. "His testicles were cut with a sharp knife, not scissors as you initially supposed, Professor, and as to *the veal*? Now that's the really interesting bit, because . . ."

A rap at the door interrupted them. "Come," Hatton said impatiently, as a hospital porter, with huge ears and a broom in his hand, barged in and went directly over to Roumande. "Dr. Buchanan says he wants your lad for the rest of the afternoon, monsieur."

Instantly, Hatton sprang over with, "No, no. Sorry, he's had an hour. There's a mountain of work here in the morgue, and Infectious Diseases is swimming in people."

"Dr. Buchanan was most insistent, Professor," the porter continued, his huge ears casting batlike shadows on the wall. "Bloody hell," he gasped. "Is that a man's hand?"

"It's a limb, of course, but what do you expect here?" Hatton answered stiffly. "We're surrounded by them," *you imbecile*, he thought as he continued, "But I'm sure I don't have the time to discuss the aesthetics of the mortuary with the likes of you. Now go back to Dr. Buchanan and tell him I cannot spare Patrice a second longer."

But then Roumande did something he rarely did. He interrupted Hatton with, "Ah, there's a slight problem with that, Professor. You see, the hospital director's now paying for a whole set of new illustrations for St. Bart's. You weren't here when this larger project was discussed and so, as we are a little hard up with the possible risk of closure . . . In France we say *un petit service en vaut un autre.*"

"By which, I think you mean, Albert, quid pro quo."

"Exactly, Professor."

"And he's paying more than just ten guineas, then?"

"A hundred guineas, Adolphus, which, by my estimation, will pay for the beginnings of our work on fingerprinting, your acid tests, phrenology, a part-time chemist, and all those things we've been dreaming of."

Hatton sighed, "Very well, but enough interruptions. Back to the case in hand."

"The hand? Ah yes, very droll, Professor, and after the fingers, I've a little something else to show you." He tapped the side of his Roman nose and winked at the professor. "*J'ai tenté le coup! Un petit détail médico-légal, pour toi.*"

"Indeed." Hatton was intrigued, as he walked back over to the trestle table. The gombeen man's hand looked like a crab, which might at any moment move to the end of the trestle table in a crustaceous sort of way, throw itself off, and scuttle out of the morgue.

"Shall I turn it over for you?" Using a pair of pinchers, Roumande lifted the hand up and placed it back down the other way, so they could see the palm clearly.

"You were right about the veal. Just look at the fingernail."

The nail in question was possibly three inches long and sharp like a knife.

"He played the fiddle, perhaps?" suggested Roumande.

"That thing would cut the strings to any bow. I'm not sure what to make of it. But this nail's most definitely veal." Using the end of a scalpel, Hatton lifted the nail slightly. "So, Albert, what do you think of our medical colleagues who suggest that our body parts continue to grow, postmortem?" Hatton locked eyes with his friend with a half smile, interested in seeing what Roumande made of this debate.

"I think those quacks who think such things haven't cut up as many cadavers as us."

Hatton popped the scalpel back into his top pocket, glad that Roumande agreed, because he'd had this very argument with Dr. Buchanan only a month ago, but then Buchanan was only an ignorant physician and didn't fully understand the secrets of the dead, the intimacies of a cadaver, its cavities and smell, as a pathologist must.

"*Excusez- moi.*"

It was their apprentice, back again.

"I thought you'd another hour at least with Dr. Buchanan, Patrice?"

"*Non, non, monsieur.* The light was slipping and casting deathly shadows over his face . . ." The lad stepped forward and peered at the finger saying, "*Mais le doigt. J'ai déjà vu un ongle comme ça!*"

Roumande beamed at the lad. "You've seen a finger like this before? Excellent, so, Patrice, tell us what you think. Here's the delivery note. You read English, don't you? Out loud, please . . ."

"Is that an *M*? Ma . . . ho . . . ney? *Oui.* I know this, too. It's an Irish name." His face was solemn, as he said, "These people were starving once. They had nothing, not even knives by the end, monsieur. They lived in bog holes, ate grass, berries, anything they could lay their hands on. Some even grew their nails long enough to peel the blighted potatoes by. Or that's what my old gangmaster said. Slit your neck to the bone as soon as look at you, those Paddies, or that's what he said, monsieur."

"A charming story, I'm sure," said Hatton, but quickly realized Roumande was in agreement with the boy.

"You believe that fanciful nonsense?" Hatton was aghast.

"I've heard similar tales of St. Giles, but come on now, Patrice, there's work for you to do. I've something else to show the professor, which doesn't concern you."

But the boy just stood there, his hands in his pockets, a pencil behind his ears, looking a little insolent, thought Hatton, not going anywhere at all.

"Are you listening, Patrice? Get on with your work, I said," repeated Roumande.

The lad went from sullen to suitably embarrassed, saying quickly, "*Oui,* monsieur. Straight away, monsieur . . ." and at once began brushing the floor vigorously while Roumande tutted and then disappeared, telling Hatton he would just be a moment, then reemerged from the back of the morgue with a tiny square of laboratory glass. He put it carefully under the Zeiss.

"I took the liberty of taking a couple more skin samples before I embalmed Mr. McCarthy, as is our normal procedure with murders. And you will remember, Professor, that there was a great deal of bruising, which is to be expected when a man has consumed poison, for we crash and we bang." Roumande swayed as he said this, to add a little drama to the proceedings. "And so he did this," he crashed into the side of a table, "and then perhaps that," the chief diener knocked over one of the chairs. "And finally, he would have . . ." Roumande put his hands around his own throat and, making a choking sound, fell to the ground.

"Albert, please. The floor is mightily bloody, but I follow your meaning." Hatton hated it when Roumande did this, but he had to confess it was sometimes useful to reconstruct the crime.

Roumande jumped up, as if he were a far less bulky man, and lit the gas lamp that was positioned over the table where the Zeiss was sitting, continuing, "In my humble opinion, a German microscope is better for tissue samples, Professor, than the American. The Zeiss is cleaner, brighter, more dazzling in its display. I've tried both, and the difference is quite noticeable."

Hatton wasn't going to argue with his friend, although he knew Albert was wrong, but instead, Hatton looked down the viewing columns, twisting the little handles of the Zeiss. The tissue cells swirled as they splurged into globules before contracting again into a sea of cosmic creatures with wills of their own. "Hmmm," he said. "Interesting. Where did you say the skin came from?"

"From Mr. McCarthy," Roumande answered rather unhelpfully.

"Yes, Albert. But exactly where on Mr. McCarthy?"

"From his arm, and that's the strange thing, Professor. This mark's not consistent with a knock."

"Something else, then?"

"A pinprick, a minute rupture, surrounded by blood vessels which have broken across the skin like a map, or that is my considered view, Professor. What do you think?"

Hatton kept his eyes pressed to the columns and twisted again to see the point of insertion surrounded by threaded violet and greening yellow. It could mean only one thing.

"So," said Hatton. "It appears that Mr. McCarthy didn't imbibe the poison as we thought, but was injected."

And out of nowhere, Monsieur Roumande lunged forward, grabbed Hatton, administering a sharp jab to the top of his arm with a sharpened pencil. The pain was excruciating. Albert had gone too far this time.

"Damn you, Albert. What the devil are you doing? Have you lost your wits, sir?"

"Excuse me, Adolphus, but I think Mr. McCarthy was attacked from behind," Roumande continued excitedly. "A needle was pushed into his arm with the poison upon it, straight into the bloodstream. The impact would have been instant. We know he took laudanum to sleep, there were copious amounts in his body, so he would already have been woozy. He was a heavy user, it seems. The strychnine would have closed his throat, he would have collapsed as I demonstrated, and that, Professor, would have been that."

Roumande was right. It would have been easy on a summer's night with all the windows open. Anyone could have entered the house, and although Hatton didn't approve of such theatrics in the mortuary, he was chastened by Albert's performance, hammy or not, because creative thinking was supposed to be his work.

But he added, "He wasn't attacked from behind. There were two sherry glasses, Albert. And the maid said he never drank the stuff except when he had important visitors. There were two mugs at the gombeen man's house. No sign of forced entry there, either. So both men had a visitor. A friend, someone they spoke to, someone they trusted, someone they let in their home, willingly. Perhaps . . ."

"Go on . . ." said Roumande.

"I'll have to think a little more, Albert. If the killer is a Fenian, he didn't come with a cudgel in his hand. The ribbon was hidden somewhere, out of view, to be pushed into the victims' mouths postmortem, or at the very moment of death, but what is this telling us? It's saying whoever this visitor was, these men knew their killer. I'm sure of it, but, God, it's hard with this damned throbbing in my arm."

The door was kicked open with a bang. Inspector Grey had decided to join them. "Bad arm, eh? Could be a lot worse, Hatton, by the time I finish with you. Been rustling around in my store cupboard, have you?"

Tweedle Dee and Tweedle Dum, thought Hatton, not turning around at all. Roumande could deal with these fraudsters, for he would not, could not. Instead, Hatton continued with his work, placing the ribbon under the microscope and making a miniscule note.

"The least you can do is be civil and turn around and face me, Professor." Grey's voice pierced the room. "You have the other ribbon, I see."

Hatton carried on writing, *Item 1: Green ribbon, Fenian green, stuffed in the mouth, silk.*

Grey continued, "I'm quite happy to share my latest news on the Irish situation with Roumande and leave you out of it altogether, Professor. Is that what you want? And while I'm about it, perhaps Dr. Buchanan would be interested to know that one of his most senior doctors is helping himself to police evidence."

Adding a full stop, Hatton put the quill down. "Inspector Grey. Good afternoon. How good of you to come. I was a little perturbed that you didn't send the cadaver in its entirety, and so yes, I had to extract the ribbon myself. Roumande saw a telltale thread in the dead man's gullet and was somewhat shocked that the rest of it had gone. Well, despite your threats and bribes, we're not prepared—" he stopped here and beckoned to Roumande to close the door behind them so they could have some privacy. "The tampering or withholding of evidence, for whatever reason, is a crime, Inspector. But tell me something, why hide the ribbon at all?"

The inspector stood firm. "You found the ribbon in my dinner jacket, bagged and labeled, didn't you? Hardly tampering, then? I was going to hand it over as soon as I was ready and you're welcome to it. For both our sakes, and to find this killer, let's keep the real enemy in sight. To that point, have you ever been to Limehouse, Professor?"

Hatton's focus was still on the ribbon.

The inspector continued, readjusting his cuff links. "It's a rank place and fairly takes a man's breath away. Why, the vapors from the lime kilns are so noxious as to burn a man's nostril hair. I thought by now you might have heard, because the news is out already. Mr. Tescalini and I have been to quite a party there, haven't we? *E stata una bella scenetta.*"

Mr. Tescalini for his part only cracked his knuckles together.

"I had to wash from head to toe when I returned," said Grey. "They're gangs of Irish navvies outside Hecker's flour mill, rioting on the streets and bombarding anyone they think is a toff or an industrialist with clods of horse shit, cabbage leaves, sticks, whatever they can lay their hands on."

"I thought you investigated murder, Inspector, not public disturbances."

Grey smirked. "As of today I've taken it upon myself to extend my own brief. Henceforth sedition is something I shall seek out and crush. It's quite an obsession with the commissioner, and it won't do me any harm to be seen to be taking a lead. Either way, we were unprepared for such a battering, but I have since organized a little *tête-à-tête* for those thugs down at the factory gates that they'll never forget."

"And what *tête-à-tête* would that be?"

"A *tête-à-tête* with the boys in brown, Hatton, because it's the only language the Irish understand."

Roumande caught Hatton's eye and the professor's heart sank—they both knew what this meant. Roumande immediately began packing a surgical bag with morphine, crepe, iodine, splints. "They will need as much help as they can get, Professor. I'm coming with you . . ."

Grey shook a trouser leg, to realign the crease. "There was no one dead when we left, so no need to panic. But yes, a few bandages might not be a bad idea. Mr. Hecker, who I had an appointment with, ironically, is stuck inside the mill. No one can get in or out of the factory, for love nor money. You can see your Ribbonmen in action there, Professor, for sure as eggs are eggs, they're behind this."

"Take the other road," shouted Inspector Grey, but the coach driver was already pulling his horses up, begging to differ, refusing to go any further. But Grey was out, and moving like a bullet along the wharfside. "Can you hear the shouting up ahead? It's not as bad as it was . . ."

The roar ricocheted toward them and slammed into a nearby building. Hatton threw himself to the ground, then jumped back up, smothered in dust and shards of glass, to see the inspector sprawled in the dirt. Roumande was ahead of him, spread-eagled.

"In God's name, what the devil . . ." *Wham.* Hatton headed to the floor again as windows shattered, a wall collapsed, roof tiles smashed, a chimney came hurtling to the ground, thinking, *Don't let me die, here . . . not yet, not now . . . not until . . .*

"A fucking cannon ball. What the devil are those boys doing? Get up, Hatton, you're right in the line of fire," said Grey, and before Hatton knew it, he was being hauled up and shunted elsewhere. "You as well, monsieur . . ."

Roumande belted across the street, his face covered in black grit, glints of glass. Hatton went straight to him, grabbing tweezers from his medical bag, iodine. "Keep still, Albert. There's a shard right near your eye . . ."

"Keep your fucking heads down. There's glass flying everywhere. Welcome to Limehouse, Adolphus." The inspector was enjoying himself; he was laughing like a madman.

"Leave him," said Roumande, and if Hatton hadn't been otherwise detained, he would have grabbed the detective, his hands around his scrawny neck, and pummeled his face to nothing. Instead, he said, "You're bleeding, Albert. But they're surface wounds, nothing more, but no thanks to him." The two friends locked eyes with each other then crouched down, hands over their heads, shielding each other till the pounding stopped and the screaming started. Checking his doctor's bag, Hatton knew there was nothing else for it.

"Come back, Professor. We're not clear yet," cried Grey, but

Hatton didn't heed the inspector's warning. His legs were carrying him forward. He could hear Roumande's heavy breathing coming up behind him. Hatton didn't dare look back but headed around the corner to see the river ahead, then at least eight army officers, muskets at the ready. *Jesus. Is that a cannon?*

"I'll head up Commercial Road, Adolphus. There's people dying up there, but I'll do what I can—"

Hatton had stopped in his tracks. He looked three feet ahead of him to see half of the brain was gone, the child barely nine. The rest of the carcass was ten feet away. The boy had breeches on, and next to where he lay was a slice of pie and an apple. The boy hadn't eaten a bite when the guards had blown him to kingdom come. *Kingdom come?* thought Hatton. *Would it? For this child?*

Hatton shut his eyes, sick to the stomach, and said something like a prayer, but knowing what he should have done was stand there, among that bloody carnage, raised his arms to heaven, and screamed for God's mercy. Instead, being the good doctor that he was, he turned his attention reluctantly away from the dead, to the living.

The boy wasn't the only decapitation. An arm had been severed and been blasted across the street from the rest of a man, so that all that remained was a trunk and a hand clutching a sign about *Liberty* and *The Rights of Man.* Groaning, moaning, and soft, soft crying and a yelling of "Stand back, boys" in an English accent, and prayers uttered in a foreign language and calls for God.

Bending down, ignoring the limbs littered around him, Hatton lifted the head of a man and saw half his guts were gone. Hatton told the man he was a doctor, as he jabbed the morphine in. "Close your eyes. You can hold my hand . . . that's right . . . squeeze a little . . . gently now . . . ." Four dead, he thought, by anyone's counting.

"Move out," came an ugly cry from behind him. All around,

the galloping of horses, the smack of truncheons. Gunfire as Hatton headed up a lane, toward the factory where the rioters had tried to level the gates, but failed. A great monster padlock had seemingly stopped them but now it was bent and hanging at an angle. The rioters had already gone. Just a tilted sign, flapping in a lifting breeze. It must have been the last two words that did it: SITUATIONS VACANT: *NO IRISH.*

Turning back to look at the carnage, Hatton suddenly caught sight of a redheaded man crawling away from the river. Hatton rushed over to him, in time to hear him whisper, "Call a priest, Da, for I'm dying. And where's the priest, for I saw him here." Hatton bent down to the injured man, wrapping the terrible wounds, lifting him up but then slapping him hard around his ghostly face, to stop him from slipping away. "What's your name? For God's sake stay with me, tell me . . ." Hatton begged. "Seamus. My name's Seamus, but don't you know that, Da? Don't you know your own son? Or are you the priest? Are you Father O'Brian?"

"I'm whoever you want me to be, but just stay with me, Seamus, stay with me . . ." Hatton began to work quickly, pressing on the bloody wound to stem the flow. The next voice that spoke was a cold one. "That's Seamus O'Reilly, the factory floor steward. Make sure that one lives, Hatton. He's a well-known radical and an agitator. It's a bit more than a flesh wound, though, isn't it? And what was that about a priest? What the devil was he muttering?"

Not answering Inspector Grey, Hatton did what he could until two soldiers appeared with a stretcher. "If you move him, you'll surely kill him," Hatton yelled, but the soldiers were already running down the lane in the other direction, the man screaming in agony.

"So, if you've finished with your heroics and the saving of savages, let's try and find Mr. Hecker before it's too late, shall we?" Grey moved off toward the factory, and as he did passed under the stuffed feet of an effigy, which was swinging from a nearby lamppost. A grotesque figure dressed in a top hat and tails, with a loaf of bread in its hand and a sign around its neck: *An-iochdaire*. The face was on fire. But Hatton looked at another face he no longer recognized. Grey was smothered in other men's blood, his mouth opening, words coming out into a black void of what felt like hell, and he was, what? The devil?

Roumande was already waiting for them at the factory gates. Behind him, the yard was empty, the great water turbines of the mill still turning, slow sloshes of river water dripping down shuttles. The main building was attached to other outbuildings, linked together by little iron bridges. Running along the top of the factory were the words *Hecker's Flour and Machine Made Bread. Britain at Its Finest* The line of the sky was pewter with the threat of an oncoming storm, so the next rumble in the distance was Nature, not man.

"Quick, this way," said the inspector, gesturing the two men into the massive factory. "They're the mechanical roller mills," said Grey. "I've been here when the whole thing's working. You have to shout to make yourself heard. It's quite a sight. The other workers must have fled, though it would take something extraordinary to make Mr. Hecker stop the mills. Like a visit from the Queen or," the inspector laughed, "an exceptionally beautiful woman."

Grey seemed to know exactly where he was going, past a huge oil painting of a hurling sea, a windswept beach, heather-kissed mountains, which hung above the stairwell and was entitled *Home Sweet Home*. Hatton glanced at the painting, but then followed.

"He'll be up in his office under the table, if he has any sense, hiding from the mob," Grey shouted behind him, as he leapt up the flour sprinkled steps, two at a time, followed by Roumande.

"We need to find out who's been behind all this, aside from Seamus O'Reilly, of course."

"You don't even know if that man was involved in this, Inspector," said Hatton, trying to keep up. "A man is innocent until proven . . ."

Grey stopped in his tracks at the stop of the stairwell, turned around, "Yes, yes, and I'm a Dutchman. He was here, wasn't he? And is leader of their damned Worker's Association? O'Reilly was directly outside the gates, which is why he got a pummeling. There's no doubt in my mind how all of this started. A man has a right to choose his workforce. We don't have Johnny Foreigners at The Yard. It's all very well at St. Bart's, but there are limits to an Englishman's tolerance, and this is *food* we are talking of."

But you are Welsh, thought Hatton. The inspector's voice echoed, "Mr. Hecker? Are you here, sir?"

Upstairs, Mr. Hecker's office was just another floor of the warehouse, covered with bags of grain standing in corners, ropes and pulleys, little trolleys on wheels, barrows and crates, huge mechanical sifters. And to the back, a vast arched window, made silver by the sun, an oak desk and a huge leather chair on castors. On the desk were quills, ink, pencils, some half-eaten biscuits, morsels of cheese, and a couple of crystal glasses. The place was glittering. Was it sunlight? Fairy dust?

Roumande gestured toward the sheen. "Look, Professor . . . the dust . . . and he's definitely had a visitor . . ."

The inspector's voice reverberated around the empty building. "Mr. Hecker? Are you here?"

Only the gaping silence answered, a flurry of floury motes shimmering in the air.

"Well, he has to be here, somewhere . . ."

Hatton turned to Grey. "That painting . . . the one in the stairwell? It's exactly the same as . . ."

"Worth a bloody fortune, Hatton. It's a Mallais. An original, no less. Hecker had it commissioned a number of years ago. Very pretty I suppose, if you like that sort of thing. I prefer nudes."

"But it's called *Home Sweet Home*," said Hatton. "And it reminds me of a painting of Ireland. One I saw only yesterday at White Lodge . . ."

Grey bit the end of his thumb. "Well-spotted, Hatton, but there's a man's life at stake here. We'll come back to that painting, but right now, we need to split up to cover the ground and find Mr. Hecker. Hatton, you go to where the grain supply is kept, over the connecting bridges. Roumande, you take the biscuit section and I'll search elsewhere. Here . . ." The inspector rummaged in his pocket and pulled out two silver whistles. "Take these and mind yourselves. Some of those leprechauns might be waiting with a cudgel, so keep your eyes skinned and if anything should happen, just put your lips together and, well, you both know the drill."

Roumande sped to the right, his hand not on a whistle but on his pocket pistol. Hatton stood where he was for a brief second and looked upward. The bridges which linked the warehouses were vertiginous, but this was no time for fear, thought Hatton, as he left the other two and headed up wrought-iron stairs. Only once did he look down, grasping the metal railing to see Roumande disappearing into the biscuit section, and as he stepped outside onto a little platform saw a toy world below him. Little houses for miniscule people; cows the sizes of pinheads. At the best of times, Hatton had little head for heights, but he kept going. And the final bridge crossed, he found himself in the interior of an enormous brick silo, and toward the bottom, he could see the storage bins. Huge bullet-shaped metal containers, painted Cornish cream, with the words on the side emblazoned *T.W. Hecker 1855.*

"Mr. Hecker . . ." Hatton's voice bounced around the walls as he descended an iron staircase that hugged the inside of the redbrick wall. "Mr. Hecker." But there was no miller at the bottom of the silo, just piles of grains, old sacks, cloths, the scurrying of mice, and beyond the grain, a voice. Inspector Grey must have come around the back. He was still brandishing his pistol, as he stood under the lintel. "We're too late, I'm afraid, but I've found Mr. Hecker."

Hatton followed the inspector outside to see a delightful orchard full of sweet, black plums. His eyes scoured the abandoned millstones lying dead or supine in the high summer grasses, the old rusty machinery, interlaced with bright red poppies and golden buttercups cascading toward the river, under the darkening of storm clouds. And in the middle of it all, Hatton's gaze settled on a body that was nobody at all because the runner stone had been lowered upon the bed stone, and the contraption turned, grinding poor Mr. Hecker like grain among the burgeoning flowers. "Oh, the pain," thought Hatton. The terrible pain.

15

LIMEHOUSE

Roumande had just joined them, as Hatton crouched down on his haunches, his magnifying glass pressed to his eye, studying the crimson specks that feathered through the meadow grasses toward the river. But the attackers had vanished, leaving behind nothing except a shape in the air, their lust for unspeakable violence, an echo. There were no footprints, no scraps of cloth caught on bushes, no obvious fibers. Hatton took a soil sample, a grab of grasses, and one or two kernels which were scattered on the ground.

"They're hops, probably dropped by a bird," said Grey. "There's a huge swathe of hop fields beyond the Greenwich Marshes, which isn't so far from here, and plenty of breweries further along the river."

Hatton popped the hops into a calico pouch, thinking whoever did this—gang or no gang—would have been as strong as an ox to lever that stone. The man's body had been pulverized; his blood squeezed like HP Sauce from a bun. "Well, at least we can be clear about the motive, Inspector."

"The fucking ribbon? Well, we could hardly miss it," said

Grey, looking at the huge swathes of ribbon that were wrapped around the stone before pulling out his pocket watch, tutting at the broken links in its chain. "Cost me a pretty penny this. Must have snapped during the riot. Anyway, I don't need a watch to tell me Drogheda will soon be upon us and these murderers, whoever they are, will surely kill again. But *where*? And more important, *who*?" Grey wrinkled his nose against the cloying stink of Mr. Hecker. "But I can't think here. Back to the factory, gentlemen . . ."

The three men made their way quickly back to Hecker's office, where light streamed in from the window, a diamond sheen just visible on the windowsills. "Do you see it . . ." hissed Roumande.

"I see it," Hatton whispered back, but held his hand up to beg Roumande to let the inspector, who seemed to be grappling with something just beyond his reach, speak. Grey was preoccupied, as he ran a gloved finger along the edge of the oak desk, saying, "When he asked me to come and see him, I could sense Mr. Hecker was worried. He stood exactly where I stand now and had a signet ring on his finger and kept turning it. I remember the ring especially, for I admired it. He had excellent taste, Mr. Hecker, in all manner of things."

"A ring's a ring," said Roumande.

Grey tutted, "Not so. This ring was a delight, monsieur. A dear little ship, I remember. Gorgeous thing. Hecker pursued a number of different commercial ventures, shipping being one of them. But as I say, he was worried and stuttered every now and then, especially when I asked them how long he and Monsieur Pomeroy had known each other. Where and how they met? He only said that he was simply concerned for Pomeroy's safety, as a friend. That his disappearance was out of character."

Hatton was intrigued. "But he'd only been missing a week? Men can disappear for much longer before anyone turns a hair in this city."

The inspector sighed, "I wish I'd pressed him more, but their friendship seemed so obvious to me. Pomeroy had recently branched out and was selling recipe cards, each one recommending Hecker's Premium Flour. Two shillings for ten and flying off the shelves, by all account. They needed each other—one man a purveyor of fine flour, the other, his most valued customer—and Pomeroy was well connected in this city, especially with politicians. Before he became so celebrated, he cooked private dinners for Charles Trevelyan, I believe."

"Baronet Trevelyan?" Hatton was looking at the glitter along the windowsill, using a fine brush to sweep samples into a test tube, which he carefully placed back in his medical bag, under the close supervision of Roumande as he continued, "You mentioned the government work committees ran soup kitchens during the famine, Inspector? Wasn't Charles Trevelyan in charge at the time?"

Grey leaned against the desk, shut his eyes for a second, opened them again. "You're right, Hatton. Trevelyan was in charge of the emergency feeding program in Ireland, such as it was. Pomeroy would have been serving up the finest food at glittering tables, as the baronet and the other politicians discussed the famine. We already know Pomeroy was a religious man. That might have been hard to stomach, unless . . ."

Hatton added, "Unless he offered his services in some way to appease his conscience. Perhaps Pomeroy, out of charity, went to Ireland to help, and we know he was deeply religious because his sous chef said so."

Grey nodded, curtly. "But if that's the case, then we need to go to Pomeroy's home in Fournier Street immediately. Perhaps he does have a connection with Ireland after all, as you suggest, and the Fenians are holding him, still? Perhaps they intend to ransom him? But if that was the case, they'd have left a note, wouldn't they?"

But Hatton was still intent upon the glitter. "I have to go somewhere, Inspector—sooner rather than later. A chemist, name of Dr. Meadows, who I think can help us with this glitter stuff and . . . err, Inspector, put the match away . . . I wouldn't have a cigarette in here, I really wouldn't . . ."

Hatton lunged but too late, the match was lit. But Grey, as cool as a cat, simply pursed his lips and blew it out. "Panic not. The chemical compound, if that's what it is, will have to wait. A man's life could be at stake. I thought you said it was just silver firmament, anyway?"

"And something else . . . a type of acid . . . but I'm not sure what."

"Well, talk to this Meadow's chap if you think there's a forensic link, but that picture you mentioned? The one in the stairwell?" Grey licked the hot match with his tongue, popped it in a pocket and began rattling around in various drawers, looking in cluttered shelves, muttering, "Nothing . . . nothing at all." He slammed the drawers shut. "And the yet the title of the picture is *Home Sweet Home*? And you say it reminds you of Ireland and another picture you saw?"

Hatton nodded, moving toward the picture, looking again more carefully as he said, "It's similar to one Mrs. McCarthy showed me in the piano room. The frame of the mountains is almost identical and the curve of the beach, except here in the distance," Hatton pointed out. "There's a ship. But are you looking for something specific in the drawers, Inspector?"

"Deeds . . ."

"Deeds? Deeds of what?"

"Deeds of sale, Hatton. *Home Sweet Home*? There were umpteen sales of land during the famine. The land was going for practically nothing. But assuming Hecker bought land in Ireland, what did he want it for? And why buy in the West of all places, where Ardara is, being little more than bog and stones, and he couldn't have grown corn or anything profitable, so why be there at all, unless . . ."

"Unless what, Inspector?" asked Hatton.

Grey suddenly slumped on a nearby chair, as if someone had suddenly taken all the air out of him. He seemed to rise on the crest of a wave, only to suddenly dip again. "Buggered, if I know," he said. "It was just a hunch, that's all, that he may have had investment there, along the West coast. I knew Tobias Hecker and he was a man motivated by profit. But you can't grow corn on bog. And the West of Ireland is bog."

What had Sorcha said? Hatton asked himself again. That Ardara was a land of legends, gushing rivers, windswept beaches, the glorious Atlantic. The picture above the stairwell was so similar—malachite fields, refracted sunlight, thunderous skies, a swelling sea, a ship. Sailing west toward the horizon and beyond the horizon, west toward . . .

"You say Mr. Hecker wore a signet ring because he had interests in shipping? It might have survived. I want that millstone up."

"What, now? I'll need a posse of officers to lift it. Do you have something, Hatton?"

"The millstone, Inspector."

"You think you have something, don't you?"

That millstone weighed what? Twenty tonnes? And the compression on a signet ring would be, what? Double? Even if the gold was mixed with iron, it would hardly survive the impact of that tremendous weight unless, despite the drugs, Tobias Hecker being of farming stock, a big man, struggled and . . .

Hatton didn't wait for the posse, but rushed back to the orchard, lay on his stomach, slipping his hands under the cool of the millstone. His fingers were thin and sinewy; the fingers of a surgeon, adept at peeling back fat, the finest of membranes, tissues, threadlike veins, and . . . the grass under the millstone was moist as Hatton patted around in a crack of dark, flat, empty nothing. He grazed the top of his knuckle, reaching further, further, patting the ground and thinking nothing, nothing, nothing, nothing . . . until. "Got you," the cold of the gold on the tip of his fingers, a gift. "Not so clever, are you?" he muttered under his breath. "Well, a few more mistakes like that, whoever you are, and I'll have well and truly got you."

Two hours later, Hatton was back in the morgue, the inspector pacing the floor. At Fournier Street, the curtains had been drawn, the bed made, the tables polished, Pomeroy's private papers rifled through by Scotland Yard already, and as for forensic traces after more than ten days? Virtually nothing. Only a singular thread caught around the bottom of the door edge, noticed as they left.

"Well, Hatton?"

Taking a miniscule pair of tweezers, Hatton had popped the thread into an evidence bag, smothered as it was in a week's worth of London soot, but under the strength of his eyeglass, soot didn't cover the fact that the thread had once been vibrantly colored. Coincidence? Pomeroy was a religious man (there were icons all over the house) and entertained regular visits from Catholic priests and numerous feminine customers smothered in silk, keen to converse with the maestro about dinners and puddings, but did they wear green, he asked himself? Quite possibly, meaning the thread could have come from anywhere.

But here at St. Bart's, despite the greased-up windows of the morgue, the shut door, the interminable heat, the case seemed a little clearer, its burden a miniscule lighter. Step by step, link by link, a molecular chain was forming, thought Hatton to himself, as the inspector pressed again with, "Well, Hatton?"

"It's clearly a frigate. You can see the gun holes on the side."

"*Non, non,* Adolphus," said Roumande, peering over the piece of parchment where they had just made an indigo impression of a tiny sailing ship from Mr. Hecker's signet ring. "See the angle of its bow and the complicated rigging. It's clearly a brig, Professor."

Patrice was in the gallery, his illustrations for the hospital, in charcoal, laid out across a table. He pushed them to one side and quickly came to join them with a shy, "*Excusez-moi,* but I might be able to help you here." The other men stood back a little and made a space for him, as he traced the image with his finger. "There are many ships like this at the Isle of Dogs and in Marseille, I painted a few to make a little money." He leaned a little closer and nodded to himself. "It's a clipper. A trade ship, do you see? With its square build, its four masts, built for speed, whereas the brig has only two. And the square of its hull is for cargo. For tea, timber, slaves from Africa, and here"—he pointed to the deck—"it has a broad deck for passengers, who can sleep up there for practically nothing. The third-class berths are below."

The inspector nodded to himself. "Mr. Hecker had shipping interests, which is why he had the ring, as a sort of memento, I suppose. Ten years ago, Hecker had a whole fleet of ships for exporting corn from the East of Ireland, but not from the West. Why, any fool knows that it's the eastern plains of County Wicklow where the real money's made, not the rocks and bogs of Donegal, where a man can grow little. But the mill and the biscuits were his preferred ventures these days, and I believe most of Hecker's vessels were donated to the British government when the smallpox broke out among the sailors back in '52, as a sort of grand philanthropic gesture, and they remain moored somewhere along the river up near Greenwich."

Hatton knew these huge hospital ships, the *Dreadnought* and other frigates, which cast eerie shadows across the brackish waters of The Thames. However, the image on the ring didn't speak of typhus and disease but was jaunty, heraldic; almost musical in its impression. Hatton said so and added, "But what interests me, Inspector, is why hang the painting in such a prominent place at the mill? You've told us that the boggy land of Ardara is worth nothing, so why celebrate it by commissioning a Mallais, of all things?"

"Why celebrate it, indeed?" The inspector's eyes widened. "The title of the painting is *Home Sweet Home*? I suspect Mr. Hecker owned that land, which is why he had it painted and why I was looking for deeds of sale back at the mill." Something suddenly occurred to the inspector, a triumphant smile on his face. "Of course. He wasn't exporting *grain* from the West. Do you remember what I told you? He loved a quick profit and must have been there in Donegal during the famine, like so many other traders with vessels. There was a program at the time to help the people leave. To flee the famine and start a new life in America. That's why he was proud. He was making money and at the same time helping people survive. Shipowners offered those wretched peasants a lifeline, Hatton. Thousands more would have died if they hadn't sailed on these clippers to the New World because . . ."

A sharp knock at the door interrupted.

Mr. Tescalini was standing under the lintel, holding a scroll of paper and panting a little in the heat accompanied by words in rapid Italian, interspersed with something unintelligible about the back of a filing cabinet, but before he could finish with his broken English, the inspector lurched forward, grabbed the scroll, and shot a look at Hatton. "I knew it. Here, what did I tell you, Hatton? Read it, and for good measure take note of the signatures at the bottom left-hand corner."

The room melted to nothing, just a ticking of wall clock, the scurry of mice, the odd drop of blood—drip, drip, drip like an overflowing bath—into a brand-new tin bucket, as Hatton read:

Deeds of Sale . . . Four hundred and twenty acres . . . Sold on behalf of the Ardara Estate, by Land Manager, Mr. Gabriel McCarthy to Mr. Tobias Hecker Esquire. In the presence of "Witness to Sale," Monsieur Gustave Pomeroy. Sligo House, Ardara, Donegal, October 1, 1847.

Grey for once slapped his own thigh. "Bullseye! Hecker bought land from McCarthy and just look at the fucking price. Fifty damn guineas for a huge swathe of coastland. Maybe he'd plans to build there. A mill perhaps, or even a dock? Wish I'd known at the time because they practically gave it away, and see the name of the signatory witness? *Pomeroy.* But why was he there? And witness to a sale? He was just a chef, goddammit.

Hatton paced the room, muddled thoughts in his head, suddenly translucent. "Chefs helped the government, didn't they? You said so when we went to White Lodge."

The inspector gave a sharp nod.

"And Pomeroy cooked for Charles Trevelyan, who ran the overall emergency feeding program?"

A purse of the lips this time. The inspector's eyes became slits as he looked at Hatton, concentrating on every word said.

Hatton carried on, "We know Gabriel McCarthy was responsible for the tenants of Ardara, for their welfare during the famine. So it's conceivable that Pomeroy, encouraged by Trevelyan, volunteered to go the worst-affected area. Or perhaps just went to a place he'd already heard of, because his friend, Mr. Hecker, had interests out there. Maybe Pomeroy specifically requested to be stationed near a friend, so he didn't feel too out of his depth. It would have been difficult work, shocking even, and he was a foreigner in a strange land, so that connection makes sense to me. Although I didn't know the British ever reached Ardara and the West. I thought the Board of Works was in Dublin and thereabouts, and that the West had to fend for itself."

"The roads were terrible that far west, barely there at all, but I think you could be right, you know, Hatton. Either way, one thing's settled."

"They all knew each other," added Roumande. "Apart from the gombeen man, that is."

"But he lived there, didn't he? He came from Ardara so he's connected too," said Hatton, as he wandered over to his desk and took his favorite chisel blade out from a drawer, thinking Sorcha must have been, what in '47? A young girl with a curious mind and a foreigner in that remote part of Ireland would have been a source of wonderment, surely? Or idle gossip, certainly. He would ask her what she knew and he would seek her out tonight. Alone.

"Yes, they all knew each other, or as far as Mahoney's concerned, knew this place, Ardara," continued Grey. "And there's an outside chance that Pomeroy could still be alive. There's no ransom note, as I've already said, but perhaps they're just waiting for tomorrow, God help the man. It's odd, though, if I'm right about Pomeroy, that they should take a Frenchman of all people, because your two nations are as thick as thieves, aren't they, Roumande? What with the papist thing and your mutual hatred of the British? The French have always supported the Irish and their rebellious ways."

Roumande smiled. "The Wexford Rebellion was sixty years ago, Inspector. And the English crushed both forces. France has enough on her hands these days without involving herself in Ireland anymore. I think that's a leap too far, Inspector."

Grey's whole body seemed to tighten, as he said, "Not for the likes of Benjamin Disraeli, that Jew, it isn't. As a race, of course, they're obsessed with conspiracy. He sees it in everything. You should hear Disraeli in the House and his boss, our prime minister, Lord Stanley—who's just the same. Since the Sepoy Mutiny in India, they're both obsessed with the idea that there's a secretive international fifth column trying to topple the British government and destroy its hold on the colonies."

Roumande laughed out loud this time. "That's the stupidest thing I've heard all day . . ."

Grey's voice was strained, "Is it? Is it really, monsieur? Well, now that Mr. Hecker's dead, these are the men I must answer to. My masters. The leader of the House, a paranoid Jew, and the PM, a blustering, pony-riding Tory. But one day things might be a little bit different, when I get my way, when I reach commissioner and . . ." Grey seemed to lose his train of thought, as he looked away for a split second, but then he gathered himself. "But back to the facts, gentlemen. Customers the length and breadth of England bought Pomeroy's recipe cards. We need to look beyond the city. Someone must have seen something."

"Don't forget the hops we found, Inspector. They might offer us a clue. Narrow the search, a bit," offered Roumande.

"You're right, monsieur," said Grey who turned to Tescalini with, "Go to Greenwich, immediately. We found some hops beside the millstone and the hop fields of Essex lay south of the marshes. Find out if any of these men were seen anywhere in the area. And if they were, what they were bloody well doing there. *Veloce!*"

"*Ma non posso camminare veloce alla mia eta', ispettore. Mi farete venire un infarto.*"

"But that's precisely why I have bought you the Penny Farthing. To trim you down a little. To sort your fine figure of a figure out. What, still here? What are you waiting for, man?"

"So," said the inspector, turning back to Hatton and Roumande. "Speaking of clues, back to the corpse. There is so little left of Mr. Hecker, but can these lumps of gristle tell us something? Anything, Professor?"

Hatton looked at the main dissection slab and begged the inspector and the Italian, who hadn't yet left, to move a little to the right, so he could get on with the next stage of their work. Even without policemen under his feet, the mortuary was a cramped place at the best of times.

"Perhaps *someone* can find me a little morphine, while you get on with your cutting," sighed Grey, who, having roused himself briefly, seemed utterly drained again. Despite the need for the two men to work together for the sake of the case, Hatton hadn't forgiven the man for his appalling behavior at the factory, and if truth were known, he didn't really care what the inspector did or didn't do. He could, for all Hatton cared, drown himself in laudanum. And to make the point, he told Grey, "Be my guest . . . help yourself," pointing over to a large, industrial-sized bottle, thinking, anything to ameliorate this dreadful man.

Hatton dug into what was left of Mr. Hecker as the inspector kept talking, between copious swigs. "But not a word about the ribbons to the press. It would simply help the Fenians. They're raising money in America, getting organized, using sophisticated methods to break the Union and force repeal. Disraeli could be right. This could be the Sepoy Mutiny all over again, but this time not in India but Ireland—a mere spit away. Am I making myself clear?"

"Crystal," said Hatton as he tried to concentrate on what was left of a liver, knowing Mr. Hecker must surely have been drugged to get him onto the millstone, but also that an opiate like laudanum was practically tasteless. And just like the others, Mr. Hecker had a visitor before his demise. There had been two crystal glasses on Mr. Hecker's desk. The Zeiss would show up any grams of opium and Hatton could use his favored method of separation—the Metzger Mirror. Roumande stood quietly next to the Professor, as he carried on dissecting.

"So much blood, Albert," said Hatton, turning to his friend. "And yet not a single footstep near the mill or by the river? Whoever did this knows something of my work. The man wasn't cracked on the back of the head and dumped straight into the water to disappear downstream, which would have been the obvious thing. Instead, he was put on display and, I feel sure, there's something we're not yet seeing."

"Very well, but what?" asked the inspector, knocking back the bottle of laudanum. "Perhaps forensics will tell us? Either way, may I ask when you've finished to bag up Mr. Hecker, as best you can, and put him in one of your ebony caskets. The Yard will pay. It's the very least we can do because he was . . ." swig "quite simply like his flour, *Britain at Its Finest*."

Hatton was cutting, not listening as the inspector slurred, "Those fucking Tories at The Carlton might look down their noses at the likes of . . . but they're . . . half . . . yes, half . . . the man . . . he was."

The laudanum was taking effect, because the inspector began to sway and sniff a little. "I had humble beginnings myself, you know. My mother was a washerwoman, my father was a lay preacher, near the docks in Barry. A slice of toke, a cube of lard, a singular currant, and nothing else, only prayer to keep us going." Swig. "He was a violent man . . . but it was only a scarf . . . my mother's scarf . . . but it was the rouge what done it . . . a regular beating, he gave me, but I'll hunt these killers down . . ." He wrung his hands. "Make no mistake about it . . ."

Hatton was thinking he should have checked the bottle. The solution was clearly too strong. The inspector was suddenly overcome and buried his head in his hands, sobbing about "That brute of a man." Hatton sighed, picked up his dissection knife and started cutting muscle, separating sinew, but then put the knife back down again as the sobbing got louder.

"It's been a long day, Inspector," said Hatton.

"Quite so, Professor," answered Grey, who immediately seemed to recover himself, and after peering briefly at the autopsy notes, jumped up and said he really must be going, that he had other business to attend to, *police business.* "It's my belief they've got poor Monsieur Pomeroy prisoner somewhere, if he's still alive, that is. And I have my own tried and tested ways of securing information. But do you mind if I take the bottle?"

Hatton shook his head, gesturing for the opium back. "You've had quite enough, already." And taking a wild guess where the inspector was likely heading, high on laudanum. To a prison cell, most likely, which would probably hold Seamus O'Reilly, if he was still alive. But there was nothing else he could do for the factory steward, damned already.

The inspector gone, he washed himself down and dressed in a new white shirt and the cleanest of breeches, a bitter taste in his mouth. He sat on his chair by the unlit grate and thought of Sorcha. She seemed so afraid of something. And now another man was dead. Did the widow have reason to fear for her life? In the celadon drawing room she'd said that death stalked her, that death stalked all of them. But what was Hatton thinking? He had no hold on her.

"Shall I finish up here for you, Adolphus?" Roumande pulled up another chair beside him.

"Finish up? I don't see why not. And Hecker must have died last night and not this morning when the riot took place. A crime like this could only have been carried out under cover of darkness. That could be important when the case comes to trial, especially if Grey remains hell-bent on pinning the murders on anyone who seems to fit the bill, even if they're innocent."

"What do you mean, Adolphus?"

"I found that poor man, crawling along the lane from the factory gates. I did what I could to save his life, but what's the point? If they're holding him at The Yard by now, Inspector Grey will force a confession, evidence or not. But Hecker died last night. He was working late, perhaps? Or meeting someone? There were two glasses on his desk, do you remember?"

Roumande nodded yes, he remembered.

"And O'Reilly and the others stormed the factory this morning, because they thought Mr. Hecker was still alive. Otherwise, what was the point of a riot?" Hatton paused and then said, "I should go after the inspector, shouldn't I?"

"By your estimation," said Roumande, "this factory steward is entirely innocent of murder, and you know what they're like at The Yard. The steward is Irish, an agitator, and once in a cell, he's as good as hanged. One of us needs to go after the inspector. We might save O'Reilly's life."

Hatton didn't answer but rushed along the hospital corridors, but by the time he reached the wrought-iron gate the inspector was already gone. He looked at his pocket watch. Time was pressing. The sun would be setting in three hours and the morgue would already be thick with shifting shadows, making dissection work more difficult, less exacting. He grabbed one of the hospital beadles and, giving him a crown, begged him to take a message to The Yard, quickly scribbling down that Mr. Hecker had almost certainly died last night and therefore, O'Reilly couldn't be the killer. That the case continued and if the inspector needed to speak with him, he'd be at the morgue for a little while longer. The beadle spat on the coin and shook Hatton's hand, taking the note and saying, "Leave it to me, Professor. I won't let you down."

Hatton returned to the morgue, where Roumande and Patrice were busy on the other side of the room, taking it in turns to peer down the viewing columns of the Zeiss. "Back already?" asked Roumande.

"The inspector had already gone. I've sent a message with one of our more reliable beadles."

"Good," said Roumande. "Because we've got something to show you. While we were at the riot on dockside, I asked Patrice to take a closer look at the skin samples. See what he could see, and report back to me."

Hatton crossed his arms, slightly disapproving, "With no supervision, Albert? Is that entirely wise?"

Roumande shrugged, nonplussed. "Learning and erudition, Professor. On the job, as it were? No better way for the lad to get to grips with things, and he's come up trumps because, although there was nothing more telling on Mr. McCarthy's skin samples, it appears that the gombeen man had a smear." Roumande made the sign of the cross. "A smear of oil on his forehead."

Hatton was pensive, taking over at the Zeiss. "So he was anointed, Albert? But by whom? A priest? " Hatton looked at it under the viewing columns. "It's an odd color. Is it saffron? Isn't that what Catholics use?"

"Saffron is golden, Professor," added Patrice, who had stepped forward to help. "This seems more orangey in color."

"Hmm. Quite so. Orangey yellow, I'd say. Good thinking, but in forensics we need to be precise."

Hatton walked over to the adjoining door where they kept a few rudimentary botany books, to notice a new and delightful sketch clipped to the line in the gallery. It was an image he rarely saw in the mortuary. A depiction of beauty, tranquillity—peace. It was the girl they hadn't cut. The girl they'd buried. The slum girl. But in this picture, there was no shadow of cholera on her skin, just a sleeping alabaster angel, made modest by a shroud. The lad had followed Hatton into the gallery and said, "I have called her *Sleeping Beauty*, Professor. And she is, isn't she? She reminds me a little of my elder sister, Katherine . . ."

"You have a sister?" said Hatton, turning to him. "I've a sister, too. Her name's Lucy. Married a doctor, like me, would you believe?" He rubbed tired eyes, though it was only six o'clock in the evening. "A general practitioner, and they live north, in Derbyshire, and I must confess, I miss her." But then added in a brisker voice, "Albert, what do you say to hanging this picture above the sink, next to our *Perfect Specimens for an Exacting Science* sign?"

"Yes, why the devil not?" said Roumande, a touch of concern on his face, catching Hatton's eye, who was thinking perhaps he'd said the wrong thing, but nevertheless handed the youth a florin. "Get it framed, Patrice, and then with whatever's left, have some supper on us and an early night. You look tired and we have a huge amount of work tomorrow."

"Thank you, monsieur." The lad doffed his cap, sticking the pencil behind his ear, taking a few minutes to admire the picture himself, as Hatton took Roumande by the arm and whispered in his ear, "I know that look, Albert. Have I done something wrong?"

Roumande lowered his voice to a whisper. "He dines at Fleur de Lys tonight, remember? The girls and Madame Roumande are cooking a feast for him. They've been at it all day, as far as I know. You know what women are like, but it's the least we can do for one who's alone here in London, making the best of things. He hasn't seen his sister for years. So many rural children are vagabonds, magpies we call them, wandering village to village, desperately looking for any kind of work." He shrugged. "But I'm afraid, these days, it's normal in France. The country's gone to the dogs."

A little embarrassed about his earlier comment, Hatton did his best to smooth over it, saying to Patrice, with as much forced jollity as possible, "Well, don't let me keep you from dinner with Madame Roumande. I hear she's gone to a great deal of effort for you. Sylvie's an excellent cook and the girls an absolute delight, as you know. So go with a light heart, Patrice, and enjoy their excellent company." But Patrice didn't go. Instead, he stood, looking at Hatton, surprised at his dismissal and asked, with genuine concern,

"But shouldn't I organize a body wagon for Limehouse, Professor?"

Although slightly unnerved by the remark, Hatton couldn't blame the lad for this inquiry. It was only natural to ask. But the dead would be gone by now, gathered up by the families, blessed by priests, and under shrouds.

"The last place you should be is Limehouse. Stay away from the rookeries. It's a tinderbox out there."

The lad despatched, Hatton turned to Roumande.

"Sorry friend, but I'm finished for the day, and anyway, I need to think, not cut. I need a breath of fresh air, a long walk to blow away the cobwebs . . ." Hatton sighed, thinking of the long day which had unfolded, but one image above all stuck in his head. Not Mr. Hecker and the millstone, but that poor boy, lying in a pool of blood on the cobbled lane in Limehouse. The little cap on his boyish head, his severed trunk, and, looming in the distance, a heartless world that cared so little for children. The merciless river, the beaching docks, and another innocent lost, all in the name of what? A riot, because men wanted their jobs back, who had their own families to feed. Hatton shook his head and then stretched his hand out to Roumande—*good-bye, see you tomorrow, then*—in an absurd show of formality. And as he did so, felt Roumande's great arms around him, his eyes full of concern as he said, "You know we did our best today, Adolphus, and we can't do any more."

"But that child, Albert. I can't help thinking, if only we'd known. If only we'd got to Limehouse earlier, we might have been able to save him."

Roumande shook his head, "We did what we could. You heard what Grey said. These killers haven't finished, and this Pomeroy fellow might still be alive. Drogheda is tomorrow and we must focus on the living. Agreed?"

Hatton cast his eyes to the floor. "Yes, Albert. You're right, of course."

"We must see this Dr. Meadows first thing tomorrow, because that chemical compound was at both crime scenes. Somebody's brushed it off by accident. It's come off their clothes perhaps and might yet lead us to these killers, but as to the rest, you're tired, Adolphus, so leave the oil and the botany with me, for this evening."

Hatton was grateful to Roumande, but when it came to plants, Hatton was no amateur. Before he moved to Edinburgh to begin life as a pathologist, he'd spent some time at the Hunterian School in London. Scrimping and saving, he had footed the bill himself. A young man, eager to learn, he'd gained a solid grounding in all things anatomical, surgical, physiological, and botanical.

Years ago, at the school, the chief apothecary had stressed to Hatton that "A knowledge of buttercups can be just as useful when it comes to saving lives as any amputation knife. You're from the country, am I right? Well, sit yourself down, young Master Hatton, and let me show you something."

And here was a world where petals were moons, stamens swam, pollen had tails, became wormy like creatures that slithered. Hatton had gasped in amazement at this cellular universe. *Science*, he'd thought. *This is how a man should feel. Sick with excitement. Raw with energy. Captivated.*

"So," said the apothecary, "this flower is St. John's Wort and is used commonly for a melancholic state of mind. Are you the melancholic type, would you say, Mr. Hatton?"

Hatton had looked up from the microscope, with unadulterated wonder in his eyes.

"No," said the apothecary. "No, I don't think you are. You are more a man of passion."

Mister Smith, *Mr. Joshua Smith*, Hatton was sure he'd read in *The Lancet*, the man was now chief druggist for the Society of Apothecaries, based in a large classical building, a minute's walk from Dr. Meadows, the university chemist, who he would see at nine o'clock tomorrow. It would be an honor and a pleasure, he thought, to see him again.

"You carry on, Albert," he said. "I have ideas of my own."

"Mister Smith is dead, sir. Hung himself a month ago. But you can come in and look round the place, although he left nothing to nobody, just some old books and some pestles and mortars, but only the chipped ones are left. The others got nabbed pretty quickly by the druggists."

Hatton thanked the beadle, who opened the door to a dusty room, where it seemed nobody had ventured for years—a pile of botany books on an otherwise empty shelf, a lingering herby smell, cobwebs in corners.

"The old microscope's gone. But help yourself to the books. It's science the public wants now, not flowers. Sad state of affairs. Dead by fifty-two. How old did you say you are?"

Hatton looked at the beadle. "I didn't."

"Well, if I may say, you don't look a day over forty, sir. Anyway, help yourself. Poor man had fevers toward the end, saw visions, couldn't sleep. St. John's Wort and overwork was the root of it. Very easy to become a slave to both in the medical world, ain't it, sir?"

Forty, did he say? *Good God*, thought Hatton, *I am only thirty-five*, but also thinking poor, poor Mr. Smith. Hatton sat down and flicked through various books, every now and then having to blow away dust, dead wood lice, moths until he found what he was looking for. A simple tome—*British, European and New World Flora*—which he tucked under his arm to read later at home.

It wasn't the breakthrough he needed, thought Hatton, as he made his way toward his lodging rooms in Gower Street, not knowing if that's really where he wanted to be—after the day he'd had, he was in need of a drink. But to sup ale by his own, to talk to strangers or stare into dregs? He couldn't face it. Instead, Hatton turned off before he reached his road, and found himself in Bedford Square Gardens.

Sitting down on a bench, he watched chaperoned girls skip by and children with hoops making a nuisance of themselves. Across the square, a dowager lady took a swipe at a boy who was taunting her dog, and beyond her, a young couple walked arm in arm, nestling close and whispering sweet nothings, he supposed.

It was still hot, but a breeze was lifting and a current of air expired a tepid sigh on his skin as he shut his eyes. Voices melding into chatter, children laughing way off somewhere, and so close the zerring of a wasp, and all around the chirrups of London sparrows. Another breath of air as Hatton felt the stirring of the grass beneath his feet, the resonance of a wood pigeon cooing, or was it doves?

One thought drifted into another. Images popped into his head, fields of flowers formed but were they primroses, marigolds, or celandine? Unsure, Hatton opened his eyes again to see the two embracing lovers. Sweethearts, his sister would have called them. But Lucy had gone north to the smoke of Derbyshire. She was sitting somewhere now, a GP's wife under the shadow of those dark, satanic mills, and not drifting through the flotsam of London, as Hatton felt himself to be, unanchored by convention, respectability, a spouse.

But Lucy was not a woman to suffer a fool. He heard her voice in his head, insistent. "Gather yourself and less of the long face. You've work to do, so up, up I say. And you've the perfect excuse, haven't you, Addy? This secret of Ardara? And if you like her so much, no more moping, brother. For heaven's sake, just go and see her."

He looked at his pocket watch. It was gone seven o'clock,

midsummer bright as the storm clouds dissipated. He could walk there from Bloomsbury, instead of going home, and at a quick pace be there in thirty minutes or so. And with that thought, he put his best foot forward, remembering a tune he used to whistle along the lanes in Hampshire when his father was still alive, as they chatted amiably, past the hedgerows, up to their farmstead, with the scent of wild strawberries in the air.

But how on earth had he ended up here, in London, among cadavers, felons, and murderers? Hatton laughed despite himself, sticking his hands in his pockets, having entirely forgotten the wad of correspondence he'd taken from The Yard, the tin of peppermints, and the cold square thing, which initially appeared to be a cigarette case. Smooth on one side and the other? An embossed pattern which Hatton knew, as he looked at it now, was Indian hemp, better known as cannabis. *A drug case*, he thought, as Hatton opened it up to find a syringe, nestled in green velvet, which he tapped, then held up to the light, but it was completely empty.

He'd test it tomorrow in the morgue, but experience told him this syringe hadn't been used before. So why did Inspector Grey have an injection in his evening jacket, of all things? Was the inspector an addict? Hatton thought of the scene in the mortuary and the inspector's insistence on laudanum. And his behavior was certainly inclined to the erratic.

Hatton took one of the mints, popped it in his mouth, knowing that Gabriel McCarthy had been injected. But Hatton trusted his intuition on matters of murder, and Inspector Grey didn't seem the murdering kind. Too in love with himself, thought Hatton. The act of murder required something else, deep within the core of a man. A cause? Passion? Fear?

Grey displayed none of these emotions, only deep-rooted vanity and a certain kind of histrionics. Although he was definitely, in Hatton's opinion, a brazen liar.

16

ST. GILES

He took the pistol from the sacristy, the bullet rounds, the leather gloves, and shook the Father's hand.

"Don't take no for an answer," said the priest. "I want him dead or gone, understand? And I'm sure there's another mechanism somewhere, stashed away in White Lodge. Get it from him and make sure there's nothing else hanging around that the police can trace back to us."

O'Rourke said, "Very well," though he had a heavy heart. *Judas,* he thought. *I'm a fucking Judas . . .* But his loyalty was to Ireland, not Damien, and today had been a day from hell. The priest smeared in dying men's blood, whipping the crowd in Gaelic, goading the rioters on, whilst O'Rourke spewed out the story in green ink, as fast as the bullets were flying—*"Bloody Carnage in Limehouse." "Innocents murdered . . ." "Death to all British," "Tiocfaidh ár lá!"*

"The rest of London will be alight soon, go up like a fucking firecracker," O'Rourke muttered to himself as he entered an Irish tavern on Highgate Hill, spotting Damien McCarthy surrounded by heaps of leather-bound files, bills from the estate,

Points of Notice. He didn't look up, but seemed woebegone and preoccupied.

Did he know something? Did he sense what was coming?

O'Rourke stuck his hand deep into his pocket to feel the cold hard metal of the gun.

"All right?" said O'Rourke.

Damien stood up, got the round of porter in, and started talking of the terrible events in Limehouse and how he was desperate to be there but "O'Brian told me to stay away, and my responsibilities are many now, John." *I have to manage all of this*, his eyes said, as they flittered across the huge pile of papers he'd scattered across the tavern table. "I think I see my brother in the study, hear his voice, our arguments echoing through the drawing room, like a ghost. Do you know I called him a West Brit bastard the last time we spoke? And the next time I saw Gabriel he was dead. So I came here to try and concentrate, but Ardara is a heavy burden. How terrible, that it took my brother's death for me to understand that."

O'Rourke took a chair, lit a pipe, and let the other man speak. "After the famine, all the work committees left," Damien continued. "Not that they did much when they were there. But you're from Fermanagh, aren't you? So it wasn't so bad for you?"

O'Rourke spat a bit baccy out across the floor, "People died there, too."

"But at least you had the roads, John—the docks, the silver mines, and fisheries—and Donegal is not like the North. Our people were hard to reach and the hungry season is upon the cottiers again, so I'm starting to think perhaps my brother had a point."

So, thought O'Rourke, an ache in the pit of the belly, it's started, just like O'Brian said it would. With the single stroke of the pen, the last will and testament, Damien was the estate manager now, had a Seat in the House, responsibilities and all the trappings of a West Brit life. How long then would it be till this man, his friend, sitting in front of him, would buckle?

"Word is," said O'Rourke sipping his beer, "you were seen talking to that detective? That you even shook his hand?"

McCarthy grew pale. "What of it? He's investigating the death of my brother. He was giving me his condolences, nothing more than that."

"Father O'Brian sends his condolences, too, but"—O'Rourke leaned over the table, the veins down the side of his face jumping a little, his breath rank—"he wants to know are you doing a deal for clemency? Because if there's a whisper of a deal with the British . . ."

"Jesus," hissed Damien, looking over his shoulder. "Keep your voice down, and what the devil do you take me for anyhow? A deal with the British? I'd rather cut my own throat. How can you think so little of me?"

O'Rourke leaned back on his chair, tapped his pipe. "Ardara is a mountain of debts, and it's well known only British government money, dirty money, keeps the wolves from the door, am I right? Word is, your brother was feeding the government information."

Damien laughed. "Rubbish! You knew my brother. He wasn't a spy, for pity's sake. He was a liberal and a do-gooder who headed up those work committees and almost killed himself doing it. He thought what he was doing during the famine was *right*. Misguided, till his last sorry breath, but with a good heart."

O'Rourke said, "Answer the question, Damien? Has that Inspector Grey from The Yard offered you and that widow some sort of protection?"

Damien's face drained of color. "Protection? Protection from what? Protection from whom?" thinking, *My God, I'm out, I'm definitely out.* "Why did you really want me to meet you, John? Tonight of all nights? You know I bury my brother tomorrow," said Damien solemnly, but knowing that, at twenty-one, he was a man now, with responsibilities and he would face these people down. Already "these people" he thought. It had taken no time at all.

O'Rourke hesitated, moved a little closer, dropped his voice to a whisper, leaned forward, a dark-eyed messenger. "Father O'Brian thinks you should give it all away. All of it back where it belongs, to the people of Ireland. There's nothing but blood in that land. You know it, Gabriel. Give it away or it'll be the death of you."

The word caught in Damien's throat. "What did you call me?"

"I only think it could be the death of you."

"You called me Gabriel."

"Did I?"

Damien looked at O'Rourke, searching his eyes for the truth but only saying, "It's an easy mistake I suppose, though I'm not gray yet. That'll come I suppose with all of this." He pushed the bills, the letters, the parliamentary papers, the newspapers with a great whoosh off the tavern table. O'Rourke stood up, a great shadow across the bar, and in a second, the landlord had gone, the customers vanished but O'Rourke knew what he was going to do before he said it.

He put the gun on the table. "You must relinquish your Seat, go back to Ireland and take the widow with you, never to be seen again. And God forgive me, Damien. I didn't mean anything by calling you your dead brother's name. The heat plays games with our heads. Drives men mad and sure, did you hear in the rookeries that a man was cut in half with a spade? A ribbon stuffed in his mouth. Rumors are spreading like wildfire."

"A ribbon? A fucking ribbon? Jesus, Mary, and Joseph."

"Bury your brother, then leave. Tell the widow to pack her bags tonight. A vessel sails for Dublin tomorrow."

"I don't have a choice, do I?"

"I've given you a choice, so take it—go home."

Damien stood up and was about to leave the tavern when O'Rourke said, "One more thing. O'Brian's worried about incriminating evidence at the house."

Damien put his hand deep inside his frock coat pocket and

took out a huge iron key. "You know the safe in Gabriel's study? The one behind the landscape of the island, that Sorcha painted?"

O'Rourke nodded. He knew the picture. He'd been to the place once or twice, under cover of darkness, when the rest of the house was asleep. As a guttersnipe journalist, he'd been required from time to time to snoop around, to go to places uninvited, under the behest of Father O'Brian. He'd admired the oak desk, the crystal paperweights, the sixteenth-century maps of Ireland, and he remembered a burnished oil of a skiff, a tawny river, meadows of bright orange flowers and in the distance an ait, a river island. He'd poured himself a sherry, toasted Gabriel's health.

"First place, they looked," said Damien. "But I'd already put the timer in the crypt, never dreaming for one minute my brother would end up lying there. It's a dissenter's tomb, beyond the Egyptian passageway, three catacombs down on the left. But for God's sake, don't scale the railings or you'll be seen. Go round the back of the house; the tunnel starts at the bottom of White Lodge meadows. It's dark down there and the tunnel's full of rats but goes all the way to the crypt, and once you're inside, you'll see the timer there. Sure, my brother was more useful to us in death than life, wasn't he?"

17

HIGHGATE

She was sitting in the garden on a bench under the shadow of a willow tree, all tousled hair and girlish grace reading a book, her lips mouthing words which might have been a prayer. Hatton couldn't tell but what I wouldn't give, he thought. One night of bliss with a girl like her? Was it the languid air? The blackbirds calling each other across the garden, heady with desire? Or simply the rays bouncing off a brooch, clipped on her glistening mourning silks, so that as he walked up the long gravel path, he was blinded by her and his eyes rested where they shouldn't have.

There were long shadows in the lawn, the shifting shapes of a late summer evening. A coppery gray bird flitted at her feet and as he watched her, unnoticed, she took a handful of seeds from her pocket to feed it. He hesitated, because for just a second he wanted to stay like this. Watching her, hidden by an overgrown rose, but she must have heard the gate swing or the crunch of his boots on the gravel that snaked up to the door of White Lodge. She looked up from her book, blushed, a spreading color across milk-white cheeks. He stepped out from the bower of the roses and tipped his hat.

"Do you bring news of my husband?"

Hatton took his derby off, sweaty in his hands, slicked his hair back a little, but her clear voice—"Well, Professor?"—strengthening his resolve that he was right to come here. But that he must tread carefully. This was a murder case, after all. In any other situation, he would have wooed her, brought a little present, a spray of freesias, and not talk of death, as he knew he must. But death was what brought them together. An intimate space, which shifted between them.

"May I?" he gestured to the bench.

"Please," she said, tucking unruly locks back up into an unkempt chignon, composing herself. He didn't take his eyes off her for a minute.

"Lemonade?"

"Please, Mrs. McCarthy, don't put yourself to any trouble on my account."

But the widow was insistent and rang the servants' bell.

"So," she said with concern on her face.

He leaned down and opened his medical bag, catching a brief sight of ankles nestled in lace. She cleared her throat. So he shifted his eyes away from the sharp, jutting shape of her ankles and found his notebook. He deliberately sat at the far end of the bench.

"I'm sorry to be so blunt, Mrs. McCarthy, but I think, under the circumstances, straight talking is the only way. Another is dead, and we have reason to believe it was the same people who murdered your husband."

"But why hasn't the inspector called on me? He hasn't told me anything."

"There's been a riot in Limehouse, Irish agitators, a factory owner murdered and . . ."

"Yes," she said. "News travels fast and I'm truly sorry about the factory owner, God rest his soul, but I also heard that children were butchered like dogs and that the soldiers used cannons, guns, anything they could do to quell men armed with only placards and cudgels. Without the mill, those men will starve, Professor."

Hatton looked briefly to the ground, unable to offer an answer, because what words could express the butchery he'd witnessed.

"My God," she said "were you there? Did you actually see it?"

"A child was dead. Another man died in my arms. A third, I tried to save but all I had was some morphine, some splints . . ." He felt his eyes smart, he swallowed hard. She didn't take her eyes off him for one minute, as Hatton, determined, pressed on. "What happened today was a disgrace, but the man who was murdered at the mill today, a Mr. Hecker, bought land in Ardara and knew your husband, madam, and that is why I came."

"I see." She stood up and walked away from him toward a small, ornamental lily pond. He followed her with, "Well, Mrs. McCarthy?"

She turned. "Well what, Professor?" She had tears in her eyes.

"I'm sorry if this pains you, but the man who died bought four hundred acres of Donegal coastline from your late husband, back in '47. *The deed of sale* was witnessed by another man who's missing, possibly dead, name of Gustave Pomeroy. Did you know these men?"

She looked astonished. "As God is my witness, I've never heard these names before."

"Gustave Pomeroy lived in Spitalfields, has been missing ten days or more, and was like you, madam, a Catholic. He was known to politicians like your husband, and by all accounts was extremely devout. There's only one Catholic church of any note in this city and that's the Sacred Heart. Are you sure you haven't heard of him?"

She looked him straight in the eyes. "Believe me when I tell you, I never met him. The congregation in St. Giles is large, and like much of Soho, mainly foreign. Spanish traders, Italian entertainers, the French from Spitalfields, and my people, of course. When my husband refound his faith, he insisted on the Latin mass, which,

I'm sure you know, is only said at midnight. Chefs work late, don't they?"

"Very."

"Well, there's your answer. He probably went to mass in the morning and that's why I never met him. And if you want to know about the details of the estate, you must ask my brother-in-law. My late husband was twenty years older than me. He told me little on matters pertaining to business. My country was devastated. Land was cheap. All I know is my husband ran a work's committee, trying to build roads, giving handouts and selling off land, he only tried to help people."

"By selling off land? I'm not sure I follow."

She sighed, "It's complicated, truly it is."

She sat down on the edge of the lily pond.

Hatton stood next to her, looking at the orange petals on the surface of the water. "Why don't you tell me?"

She swished the petals away. "The estate is a creature with its own heart and its own lungs, Professor. My husband's family bequeathed its management way back when. Nobody really knows who owns the land. Some long-dead English nobleman? But Gabriel knew his duty. By selling off the land, he raised capital to try and help feed the starving tenants with imported Indian corn. These were desperate times and Gabriel did his best." She ran her hand through the glassy water.

Hatton sat next to her, the air thick and cloying. "Did he save people?" he asked, as she took her hand from the water glistening wet, her skin the color of a pearl, he thought. Without another word, he took a calico cloth from his medical bag. She gave him her hand as he dabbed, twisting her body around to face him. "Perhaps you've heard of Peel's Brimstone?" she said, with a strength of voice he hadn't heard before. She left her hand in his. "Bright yellow," she said. "Your old prime minister, Robert Peel, bought cheap Indian corn from America to try and placate the troublesome Irish. He bought too little, far too late, and anyway, it was rough, too rough for milling. People shattered their teeth on it, trying to make it into bread. The corn gave us bellyaches and worse than that, those babies that were fed it were poisoned. That's why we called it brimstone, for after the first few deaths, no one would touch it," her eyes suddenly full of tears again. "There were riots then, too. Women screaming for food they couldn't even eat, men wailing like animals driven mad by the hunger, having buried their entire families, but why am I telling you this? I don't even know you. But I think you love children? You saw a boy die. I can see in your face, you feel responsibility, don't you?"

"I'm a doctor. I took a Hippocratic oath to save lives, not be part of a bloodbath."

She shifted closer. "But I thought you only dealt with death?"

He looked deep in her eyes and saw that look, that look when a couple knows, and felt himself falling, but also, at the same time, angry, misjudged. If she asked such naive questions, then he would have to teach her. "Pathologists deal with life, madam. *Mortui vivos docent?* It means the dead teach the living. These last few months I have worked on nothing but cholera. I've chopped up countless bodies and it's a simple medical fact that we all have to die. But what makes me angry is when I see children who have had no life at all. The boy I saw at Limehouse was nine years old. No words can describe what I felt."

"I know of death, too. But it doesn't seem right to speak of these terrible things and call you *Professor*." She shifted closer still. "Tell me who you are, who you *really* are?"

"Adolphus," he said, feeling the warmth of her hand, now firmly in his. She hesitated, sighed, and then took her hand away with the merest press of her fingers. "My hand is dry. My tears, too. See?" She brushed her skirt down and stood up from the edge of the pond saying, "I was reading a book when you came. Happy tales told by one of my cousins, who now resides in Canada. Such wonderful stories of logs cabins, black bears, wolves, endless winters along the mighty Lawrence. It sounds like a harsh life but an honest one. To grow your own food, to till your own land, to have freedom?"

"Freedom? It's a nice word."

She smiled, "In Ireland we say *Saoirse*. It's something all Irish dream of. Have you traveled much, Adolphus?"

He shook his head, relieved to change the subject away from the dead but not a jot sorry for his outburst. People needed to know that only by studying death did truth unfold for the living.

"I studied in Scotland. I became a surgeon there and then a pathologist. And for reasons of my own, had an interest in crime, which led me to forensics, but tell me . . ." He hesitated. "That word you just said? I've heard it before . . . what does it *really* mean?"

She looked delighted to know something he didn't know. "*Saoirse*? It means freedom, as I said, but it can also mean, 'let go of me, give me liberty.' "

He laughed, of course. "That's why she had said the word over and over again. My God, all this time and now at last I know."

She inclined her head. "She? So who were you imprisoning?"

"A girl." He laughed.

She smiled. "A girl? A girl you captured?"

"I think I must have done."

"Was she your sweetheart? Do you think I'm very bold for asking?"

He reddened. "No, no. Not all all," wishing he could hold her hand again and was just about to tell her what an enigma she was, when the maid appeared with a tray, a cut-glass jug, and a curt, "Lemonade, madam?"

"Thank you, Florrie." But the maid didn't go away. "Are you all right, Florrie? You are terribly flushed."

Florrie kept looking over her shoulder. "No, I am not all right," said the maid, slightly hopping from one foot to the other. "I'm all of a thither, as you can see, madam, and the damn servant's privy is . . ."

"Florrie! I won't have such language . . ."

"Can't help it, madam. But if I tell the truth, I'll only go and ruin it."

"Ruin what? You speak in riddles. What is it?"

The maid blushed, twisted her foot in the gravel like a willful child. "Just . . ."

Hatton intervened. "Come along now, Florrie. Tell us."

"You'll laugh . . ."

"Nobody's going to laugh. Just say it."

"I'll not say it in front of the gentleman, madam . . ."

Sorcha tilted her head and said with an audible sigh, "Very well?" The maid duly whispered in her ear and Sorcha looked cross. "Stuff and nonsense. And on the eve of your master's funeral? Your head's away with them, Florrie, that's for sure. You need to rest, to sit down in the cool a little. Fairies? Really, Florrie!"

"Well, you can think what you like, madam, but I saw them. Maybe they're wood sprites come to see the master off, drifting on the air like pollen, and you'll be laughing on the other side of your face when the clock strikes midnight and the spooks come out of their graves in the Necropolis and . . ."

Hatton grabbed the maid. "Tell me what you saw? Precisely what you saw? And more to the point, *where*?"

Sorcha started to talk, but Hatton held his hand to the mistress to stop, as the maid said, "At first I thought they were dust motes, but I cleaned that privy. The servant's privy, sir, the one beyond the coppice of hazels? Light was steaming in through the slit window, the air full of spangles, so I says to myself, what's all this? For I was, excuse me, sir, squatting and looking up, but then, there was such flittering and I'm sure I heard one of them whisper and I was so overcome with excitement, well, I didn't even wipe myself . . ."

"Florrie!"

"Gentleman doesn't seem to mind. Sure look at his face, madam, he's lapping it up . . ."

"Stay right put! Both of you . . ." yelled Hatton as he ran toward the privy, spotlessly clean last time he saw it. The servants' privy doubling up as a kind of store cupboard for garden tools, rattraps, mothballs, seedlings.

"What is it?" The widow hadn't stayed put, but hovered directly behind him in the lime-washed privy. He turned to her, gesturing at his medical bag, which she quickly passed to him. "I'm not sure," he said, scraping up the tiniest trace of silver. "But who has keys for this place?"

"Florrie, of course, not that we ever lock it, and oh, yes, Damien. He keeps his tools here as you can see—the rattraps and fertilizer for the flowers." She put her hand to her throat, her fingers on the edge of the diamond brooch. "He's not in any trouble is he?" Her eyes were gray in this light, lunar like the moon, an odd sheen to her face, her voice strained.

"Tell me about your brother-in-law," demanded Hatton, his voice changed as well. Rock hard and jagged edged, which demanded the truth and no more nonsense from either of these women. "And where the devil is he anyway? And this, the eve before his brother's funeral. It's highly unusual. Shouldn't he be praying? Dealing with his dead brother's business, at the very least?"

She slunk against the wall and seemed to grow smaller, as she whispered, "I feared he might have gone to Limehouse today and got himself in trouble. I confess, he keeps bad company, but he's no murderer, if that's what you're thinking. You see this?" She touched her glittering brooch. "My husband was a busy man and I would have spent my days all alone if it wasn't for Damien. He helped me buy this little thing just a few days ago. How many men would take their sister-in-law shopping, willingly? He arranged the carriage to Regent Street, followed by my favorite, cake and tea at one of the coffeehouses. You do believe me, don't you? He's young, fiery, but a good man, a devout Catholic. You must believe me . . ."

Hatton hung his head, said he must be going, not sure what

he thought of these McCarthy people anymore. He bid the widow good evening and gave his condolences. She went to speak but he shook his head at her. *No more, nothing more between us, nothing at all, not till this business is finished with.*

She seemed to understand, to read his mind, a private language between them. Bolstered a little by that, he turned his back, saying he would be back tomorrow with the inspector. And thinking to himself, he was beguiled by her, yes, but not so much he didn't notice that there were orange petals floating in the lily pond. Marigolds? Celadine? Despite his botanical training, he wasn't sure about the flowers, not entirely, but he was sure of this. White Lodge was where the murders had begun. And that this brother-in-law kept bad company, but *where*, and more important *who*? Damien McCarthy had openly denied it, but did he know the gombeen man? Was he lying? Jealous? Trying to raise money? Killing off anyone who suspected him of . . . what? Murder? Double-dealing? Sedition? All of it?

And Sorcha had given herself away on another matter. What sort of husband would let his brother take his wife shopping? Hatton recalled the widow's words when they first met. She'd said that she had bid her husband good night at eight o'clock, that he was a good man, so much older than she and that he *never disturbed her.* That she *bid him* good night. She *bid* him? Not kissed him? This marriage was barely a marriage at all, he thought. She slept alone.

Breathless, his heart pounding, Damien McCarthy arrived back at the house, raced upstairs, and burst through the door to find Sorcha at her dressing table framed like a picture against a bay window, watching the light melt from an incandescent sky. She spun around but not before he lashed her with Gaelic, then said, "Yes, you heard me right. Gabriel will be buried at dawn. And I need you to pack. No questions. Just for once, Sorcha, do as you're told. There's a ship sailing tomorrow."

"I'm not coming with you, Damien."

"You'll do as I say. Don't you understand that your life's not your own and neither is mine. The house, the estate, I've inherited everything and a sorry bag of problems it's turning out to be. I can't explain everything now, but when we're back in Ireland, we can talk for as long as you like, forever if you want. That's up to you."

"What choice do I have?"

"You've no money of your own, have you? So how would you live without me? Gabriel's left you nothing and a ship sails at noon tomorrow for Dublin, so say your farewells if you must, and then, we're gone."

So much for *saoirse*, she thought, but after he'd gone, she put her fingers to the tips of her lips, thinking, *Now wait a minute*. She slipped down the corridor to hear voices downstairs. Damien speaking to Florrie in hushed tones, as she found the key to her husband's room where she'd left it on the top of the lintel, and with trembling hands turned the lock, thinking, *Don't make a noise, please, don't make any sound at all*. The door eased open, silent as death. She shut it behind her, her heart missing a beat, and for a second, listened. Nobody was coming. She sunk to her knees, then flattened herself and slipped under a tester bed. It was dark underneath, but with a gentle pat of her hands, she found the loose plank, lifted it.

Courage is flight, she thought. In her hands a wooden box, and opening the lid, dusty memories—a lucky farthing, a blackbird's feather, a hand-drawn map for pirate's treasure, and added to over the years, other little things which her husband had squirreled away. Sorcha smiled to herself to see a lock of her own black hair. She rummaged until she found what she was looking for. A check, for the princely sum of one hundred pounds, signed by Inspector Jeremiah Grey.

She put it to her nose and breathed it in, but it didn't smell of the blood of Irishmen. It smelled like the end, and the beginning of something. She shot back to her room and, opening the drawer of her dressing table, gazed at an eternity ring, a diamond neck-lace, a ruby pin for her hair. All still in their box with the labels on—*Dawsons, Purveyor of Fine Jewells and Clocks, The Burlington Arcade*. She made a little calculation before popping them into the jet bag with the gold clasp, adding the check and snapping it shut.

18

Hatton had risen at dawn and arrived at University College a good fifteen minutes early, eager to get on. But it was gone nine o'clock when Roumande finally jumped out of a four-wheel growler on the corner of Fitzroy Street, his hat pushed over his eyes, unshaven, saying, "I'm not late, am I?"

Hatton smiled, quickly checking that he had all the right samples in his medical bag. "Not much, Albert, and from the look of you, it was a good supper, last night?"

"Excellent." Roumande patted his domelike stomach. "But I need to watch my wife's cooking because, I'm telling you, these breeches barely fit me anymore, but yes, much fun was had at Fleur de Lys. Patrice is a very entertaining fellow. He did likenesses of all of us. Look, here's mine."

Roumande put his hand in his frock coat pocket, the one with the patches on, and pulled out a small sheet of paper. "Southern born but Parisian trained, eh? Hence that slightly refined accent which we all like to tease him for, but he rustled this one up in less than five minutes. Said when his family's farm failed, he left Marseilles and headed for Paris and made a little rhino, sketching ships on the Montmartre pavers, courting couples, rich men in top hats, courtesans. Pretty much anyone who'd pay to see what he could do. Look . . ."

The anatomical detail was incredible. The likeness was a miniature masterpiece of threaded veins, a large Roman nose, the broad face textured with creases, and if the eyes were the window to the soul, Patrice had caught Roumande exactly, because these eyes had spontaneity but at the same time, a permanent, almost geological intensity. These eyes spoke of intelligence and fairness.

And on that note, they reached a door with a brass plaque announcing *Dr. Andrew Meadows, BSc, MSc, PhD, Research Fellow, Material Physics and Chemistry, University College,* which swung open of its own accord, as a voice yelled, "Shut the door, damn you. Is that you, Professor Hatton? Well, put your hands over your head, whoever you are, count to three and . . . . duckkkkkkk . . ."

The explosion was more of a pink puff. The friends dived in different directions, Hatton thinking, "Mad Meadows," as they used to call him back in Edinburgh, never changed a jot. Roumande, meanwhile, was on the far side of the laboratory brushing himself down and in a gentle voice saying, "Come along now, boys. Calm yourselves. Settle down now." Roumande was looking through the bars of a cage and thinking to himself that animals should be petted and loved before they were locked in the dark, to be cut up in the name of science. But Dr. Meadows, being a chemist, had no such views, keeping his laboratory stuffed with doleful-looking puppies, tabby cats, white mice, and, for some inexplicable reason, a couple of scruffy-looking badgers.

"So," said Dr. Meadows, smelling strongly of sulphur and slightly frayed around edges. "What can I do for you gentlemen? A chemical puzzle, your apprentice said? That you were planning to bring me a test tube of unidentified glitter? Well?"

Hatton opened his medical bag.

On the table was a portable stove and next to that, an alembic used for separating gas from essential elements. Dr. Meadows lit the stove and the two friends watched the silver gas rise and smoke into vapors. "I can trap it with this," said Meadows, producing a kind of triangular test tube with a stopper, but not before dipping a piece of litmus paper into the right bulb containing the chemical fug, which he then took over to a huge Zeiss microscope, even bigger than the one they had at the morgue.

"Well, well, well . . ." said Dr. Meadows. "Very interesting." The litmus had turned a sapphire blue. "One of the chemicals is exactly what you thought it was."

"Silver nitrate, Andrew?"

Meadows nodded. "An element used for . . . hmm . . . all sorts of things—mirrors, leafing, candlestick making, and, watered down, an excellent healing material for sores and open wounds. And photography, of course. Helps get a clearer image, I'm told. The other gas is from nitric acid, used for all sorts, but as a farmer's son, Adolphus, you should know of course, that landowners add it to . . ."

"Manure?" offered Roumande.

Meadows nodded, displaying a full set of white pearly dentures and inexplicably pink gums, which were clearly not his own. "On the nose, monsieur. No flies on you. Nitric acid makes an excellent fertilizer. Very good for roses, but it's also used for making gelatine, and widely applied during the process of leather production. There's also some hydrochloric acid present, and this makes me both nervous and, I admit, a little excited."

Hatton stepped closer to the elaborate experiment. "It's all highly flammable then, as I suspected?"

Meadows pursed his lips, looked more closely at the litmus paper. "Add a few more things and it's highly explosive. And in the right, or I should say, wrong conditions, this little package could go off any moment, but you need to add a little charcoal and, possibly, some pyroxylin. Oh yes, and a timing mechanism, if you're not going to blow your own heads off. Where in hell's name did you get it from?"

Hatton explained.

"And these murders are connected to Ireland?" Meadows walked over to a shelf and taking a periodical handed it to Roumande. "You should read this, monsieur. It's an article by another foreigner. A man called Mr. Marx, a German, big beard, rather a sour-looking fellow who I occasionally bump into when I work in the museum in Bloomsbury. He says they're all at it, you know. Well, your lot did it all a while ago."

"Our lot did what?" said Roumande thinking he might take one of those poor little puppies home. He'd ask him in a minute. He'd ask for the smallest, with the saddest eyes.

"Romanians, Serbians, Ukrainians, Austro Germans, Poles, Czechs, Slovaks. Revolution, monsieur. Public disorder, anarchy using a strategy of organized riots, secret meetings, assignations, handbills, you name it. Oh, and public places are de rigueur among the anarchists at the moment . . ."

"De rigueur, for what?" said Hatton.

Meadows thumped the table. "Bomb blasts, gentlemen. Right in the center of European cities, preferably near to gathering politicians, popular restaurants, opera houses, or, even better, the moneyed and the bewildered."

"The bewildered? Can you be more specific, Andrew? You see, we don't have much time. Today is Drogheda and the inspector on the case has spoken of some kind of crescendo, which is likely to happen any minute now. And if you're right about this glitter, and the Fenians have a bomb, we need to find it. But think, Andrew, where the devil would they plant it? London's full of eateries, penny gaff shows, and what do you mean by the bewildered?"

Meadows laughed. "Thus speaks the confirmed bachelor, but monsieur," he said, turning to Roumande, "I see you wear a wedding ring, so I'll ask you a simple question, if I may? What does your wife like to do above all else in the world?"

Roumande scratched his chin. "She likes to visit the markets of Spitalfields, of course. Meet other women there for idle chat. Perhaps buy some fruit, a posy for her hair . . ."

"Exactly. The gentler sex love nothing better than going from place to place for no particular reason at all, other than the pursuit of silk, hankies, gossip, haber-bleeding-dasheries. Shopping, Adolphus, shopping . . ."

Hatton looked at his pocket watch. The shops opened in less than half an hour.

At Scotland Yard, the two men raced to the detective's room, one with a puppy under his arm wagging its tail furiously, only to be instantly sent on to another room up a winding, mahogany stairwell. Hatton knocked, catching sight of a distorted image of himself reflected back in a highly polished plate which had the word *Library* etched upon it.

"*Si, si. Entrare . . .*"

Mr. Tescalini was sitting on the edge of a chaise longue with his legs splayed, surrounded by books. The huge room had a wonderful view of the St. James's Park, dappled in sunlight. Tescalini grunted, putting his copy of *Volume Three: Procedures for Interrogating Suspects, Metropolitan Police Force, 1857* out of the way.

"Where's your boss?"

"*Per favore, ripeti?*"

"Your boss?"

"*Per favore?*"

"Oh for heaven's sake. What's the matter? You normally understand us, even if you can't speak . . ."

Roumande, being a little more patient, interjected, "Let me try, Professor," and taking a pen, drew a rather bad impression of a foppish-looking detective with a pencil-thin moustache, to which Mr. Tescalini slapped the middle of his forehead. "*È uscito a fare la spesa.*"

The two men then spoke rapidly in half French, half Italian accompanied by what looked like a particularly exuberant game of charades, which seemed to involve the puppy and a number of clocks, which were peppered around the library.

"A watchmaker in Regent Street, is that right? To get his timer fixed?"

"*Si, si.*"

Enough said.

The puppy left behind, the two men ran across the grass of St. James's, past the curving lake and basking pelicans till they reached the Eastern Gate of Green Park. Up ahead, a shopper's paradise of Piccadilly Circus, Regent's Street, Mayfair, The Burlington Arcade. "Does Grey know something already? Perhaps that's why he's come here and it's nothing to do with his watch. If you were a bomber, of all the places in London, where would you choose, Albert?"

Roumande looked around frantically for a clue, any kind of clue, as Hatton seemed hamstrung for a second, not knowing which way to go, surrounded by costers yelling, hawkers selling, dogs pissing up lampposts, paper boys screaming in the super-heated air, "Fifteen dead. Death toll rising in Limehouse . . . read all about it . . . read all about it . . ." and suddenly looking up, to see—ahead of him—a massive sign above a dome of glittering glass that must have been what, fifteen feet across: *London's Finest Shopping at the Burlington Arcade: No whistling, no singing, no playing of musical instruments, no running, no carrying of large parcels, no opening of umbrellas, and strictly no entry for baby's prams.*

Something told Hatton, deep in his gut, that this could be the place, and that if Damien McCarthy was involved, wouldn't he have to be here somewhere? But Hatton knew he'd be at his brother's funeral, four miles away on Highgate Hill.

"Mind where you go, damn you," he said crossly as two men—banking types—rushed past, practically knocking him sideways, and then, recovering his balance, Hatton said, "You go around the back, Albert. The other entrance is just up here." The two friends shook hands, split up, ran. Then Hatton remembered what the widow had said to him last night in the garden. Damien McCarthy had brought her here, just days ago.

Hatton ran into the Burlington Arcade thinking left or right? But then he spotted it. A watch shop with a huge queue outside. He could hear his own footsteps as he started to run toward it.

"Oi you, in the derby? Yes you, sir. Stop, I say. No running in here—"

But Hatton kept going, pushing through the crowds, past a small boy, a fine lady in Indian silk, a gaggle of girls admiring a window display of hats, and he could see toward the back of the Arcade, in a watch shop called Dawson's—like a miracle— the inspector through the glass, mouthing something to a horologist.

Inspector Grey was gesticulating wildly, blocking his view, but Hatton could just catch sight, behind the inspector, of another he knew—an iridescent hand, tipped with black lace, and beside her on a counter, a little jet bag which was open, with a myriad of precious jewels spilling out.

Had they arranged this? Were they meeting each other here, and if so, *why*? The inspector seemed to be leaning toward her, having some kind of argument. Was it an argument? Was she simply speaking? Or weeping? Was Grey, in fact, comforting her? Hatton couldn't tell, breathless and pressing his face against the window. No time to hesitate. He pushed through the crowd. "Get out of my way!" as the pinging began with a window display of one clock chasing another clock—a terrible reverberating sound. It was almost ten o'clock, as the widow turned around, a smile on her face. "Adolphus? What are you doing here?"

The inspector was holding up a watch chain. "Damn good job, Mr. Dawson. Ten and six, did you say?" Then he turned and said, "Hatton? What the devil?"

Boom, boom, boom went the grandfather clock behind Hatton. One thought in his head.

Get them out. Get them out—right now.

Hatton grabbed the inspector, who was nearest, first and pushed him through the door, yelling at the heaving crowd to run, and was about to turn around and grab Sorcha, to pull her away from the shop, his fingers just reaching hers, the look on her face, a smile morphing into fear, fingertips, so close, so near.

A vortex of molten air, as he felt himself being pulled back by a whirling sound, a incredible roar, the sky suddenly upside down, Hatton flying through white light against another noise, so low it shook the bowels of the earth, and then muffled screams, blackness, glass shattering. Hatton crashed to the ground, his heart pumping a thousand beats a minute, thinking, *Sorcha, please God, no.* He crawled, dragging himself to see—two feet away— Grey, lying in a pool of blood, charred flesh, brittle bone.

"Lie still, Inspector. Here, bear your teeth down on my sleeve. That's right. Hold fast."

The inspector's arm was as good as gone, but all he could say over and over again when he saw Hatton was, "You! So where's my watch? My fucking watch? Have you got it, you pathological bastard?"

"For pity's sake, hold still, Inspector. I'm trying to tie a tourniquet. Forget about the watch. Don't move, Inspector. I need to splint this . . ."

"Move? Are you fucking mad? Where's my fucking watch? I'm not going anywhere without it. Get it for me, you fucking imbecile." He was sobbing like a baby. "I want my watch . . ."

Hatton looked up and around him to see people running everywhere, a rush of blackened figures, their faces thick with blood, hair on fire, hot metal, screaming. Others were helping a girl who was leaning on an old man, staggering out of a shop.

Sorcha.

"Get back," Hatton shouted, as he ran full mettle and caught her, just before she hit the ground.

"Keep your palm as flat as you can against your cheek." Hatton watched a white hand trickle crimson. "Be brave, darling girl. You will live," he whispered, and he already had her up and cradled in his arms.

Roumande came of nowhere. "Mon dieu. What's *she* doing here?"

"No time for questions, Albert. Inspector Grey's over there. I've done my best and tried to rescue the arm, what's left of it, but time is of the essence or he'll bleed to death. There are at least two dead bodies in there . . ." He suddenly stopped in his tracks, catching sight of the debris behind him. The bomb had ripped apart three shops and destroyed the arched glass dome. Piles of brick dust lay everywhere and littered among the rubble—clock faces, battered hats, gloves, canes and flickers of sparkling diamonds, a lady's dance card, a baby's rattle.

"Take all the injured to St. Bart's," he cried, as he held Sorcha in his arms, her head nestled to his thumping heart, and once in the dark of a carriage, seeing the light slipping away from her eyes, her black lashes caked in blood, thinking, *Please God, not another one, I can't fail again.* But knowing he must wait—that everything must wait.

19

Out in the hospital courtyard, a loud cheer went up as the resident stonecutters, using a series of ropes and considerable muscle, hauled the marble fountain into place, against a rousing "Three cheers for Dr. Buchanan!" His speech finished, the portly hospital director took an unsteady bow as a band struck up slightly out of tune and business at St. Bart's continued as usual. But in the South Wing, Hatton stood alone, paler than ever. He was haggard, his cheeks hollow, having barely slept for a fortnight.

He ate when he could, worked if he had to, but otherwise, mainly prayed to some omnipotent presence he had no faith in. God? Fate? Anyone who would listen, he thought, and he was praying right now to some nebulous deity, when there was a light tap on his shoulder. Hatton looked up with expectation in his eyes, only disappointed to see it was just Inspector Grey, who'd somehow wrestled himself out of his bed and hobbled into the corridor, his stump hidden beneath a red smoking jacket with a gold tassel. "I'm discharging myself. Sitting around in a hospital only makes you sick, and besides," Grey winced, "I'm getting piles, bedsores. But give me your hand and let me call you friend. I am indebted to you, Hatton. But what the devil's that noise? Sounds like a farmyard out there."

At this point, the band had struck up even louder, dogs were yapping in reply, pauper boys were whistling from rooftops, babies crying. "Is that a duck, I hear?" said Grey, his eyes widening. "In a hospital? Well, whatever it is, I can't think in this place. I'm heading to The Yard, so give me a hand, Hatton, and get me out of here. Oh, and I want any forensics evidence you've found, on my desk no later than tomorrow."

"Of course, Inspector, if you're sure you're . . ."

"No delay. The case continues and now it's damn well personal, so there'll be no budget restrictions on anything that helps the inquiry. In other words, do what you like. By the way, have you been back to the bomb blast? Seems I've been rather delirious, in and out of a coma, I'm told, for a fortnight . . ."

"Inspector, forgive me, but you've been ill so I haven't bothered you . . ."

"Fiddle faddle." Grey's eyes were bloodshot, horribly so. "But you've been back, haven't you? Find anything useful there?"

Hatton looked at his boots. "I've been here all the time, Inspector. Since the blast, I've barely moved from this spot, but Monsieur Roumande has been numerous times. He's writing up the forensic report as we speak."

But what had he found?

Crouched low among a hundred sprung clock faces, Roumande had done what he could. Knowing with each passing minute, any forensic traces might disappear forever, so, leaving Hatton at the hospital with the wounded, he'd packed a bag, taken Patrice, and, together with The Yard, they'd sealed the whole area off. Picked their way like crows, through every broken brick, every shard of glass, slowly putting the puzzle together of how the whole place had gone up like Guy Fawkes Night.

"So that's all I know. The bomb blast was some sort of timed mechanism that must have been set off by hand. According to Roumande there was a large grandfather clock to the front of the shop, whose existence he discovered initially by piecing together its shattered face and a number of Roman numerals. Mr. Dawson, the shopowner, died in the blast, but a number of his customers verified that there was indeed a clock, to the right-hand side of the door."

"So the bomb was hidden inside a grandfather clock?"

"The perfect place, if you think about it."

"Fucking ingenious, Hatton. People say the Irish are stupid but I think they're a race of duplicitous intelligence and they've certainly applied it here. I didn't even know you could get chemicals to blow like that, on command, as it were."

"Roumande's done a bit of asking around Soho way, and says it's well known among the émigrés that a number of anarchists have tried to carry out similar atrocities in Italy, but none done with such perfect timing or accuracy."

"So, a force to be reckoned with. Any ribbons there?"

"No, Inspector."

"Anything else?"

"Traces of silver nitrate were found in the shop, but not as much as we thought there'd be and it doesn't match the other stuff. The explosion, when we studied it back at the morgue, seems to have been of a different nature. Mainly nitroglycerine, and gunpowder, but how they manage to set it off with a timer? Who knows? Nobody's managed before, so whoever did this job is a master of explosives, more so than even Dr. Meadows."

"Someone from the army, perhaps? A huge number of Irish were drummed into the Crimea by the British, so that doesn't narrow it much."

"Our report will tell you everything you need to know, Inspector, but as to our initial suspect, Damien McCarthy's hours are accounted for, to the very last minute. He went to White Lodge immediately after his brother's funeral, and the maid, Florrie, swears he never left her sight for a second. He was packing to leave, by all accounts. Others saw him there, too—local villagers, including a vicar—so he's in the clear, it seems."

"But you said you found chemicals at his house?"

"Not much, and as far as any court's concerned, what traces I did find would be deemed purely circumstantial. And the nitrate might have simply been from a fertilizer, which is what he claims."

"Hmmm," said the detective. "Well, we'll still keep a close watch on him. Just because he wasn't there doesn't mean he wasn't involved, though I doubt he'd choose to blow up his own sister-in-law, fine-looking filly that she is. But we'll talk of her in a minute. First, I need to know, did Roumande do any of that fingerprinting he's so enamored with?"

"The place was soot, Inspector. Broken glass and soot, so any prints were lost, but oddly, well, it's in the report and it may be nothing . . ."

"What?"

"A prayer book. We've kept it back at the morgue. Patrice found it just outside the entrance to Dawson's, barely touched by the blast . . ."

"A miracle?"

"I doubt it. A number of helpers ran straight to the scene of the blast within minutes, plus the usual gawpers. It might have been dropped by anyone. No inscription in the book but it's definitely Catholic. It has an ornate cover and, inside, a prayer dedicated to the Virgin Mary. Coincidence?"

"And the nearest Catholic church to the blast is the Sacred Heart, which is bang slap wallop in the middle . . . well, fuck me backward into a month of religious Sundays." Grey began to sway a little and grabbed Hatton's arm. "Bang slap wallop in the middle of *The Dials*, Hatton. Thirty pieces of silver?"

"And the gombeen man had been anointed, Inspector. With prayer oil?"

"And Pomeroy was religious. Gabriel McCarthy was covered in ash. Don't the Catholics do that?"

"Only on Ash Wednesday and I'm not sure that's relevant."

"What about that shop steward? I could have sworn when we were at Limehouse he was talking to you, Hatton. Did he make some sort of confession? He was muttering something about *a priest*?"

"The man was dying, Inspector. He was delirious and should have been taken to St. Bart's not to those butchers at St. Thomas's. He might have made it and not bled to death on a surgeon's slab."

"Either way, Mr. Hecker doesn't fit this line of thinking. He was a man who only worshipped money, but I still want to talk to that priest, O'Brian."

"Well, go ahead and do it, Inspector."

"It's not as easy as you think, Hatton. Disraeli's on the warpath again about the fragility of the Union and my superiors have warned me to tread extremely carefully. St. Giles is a city within a city, and O'Brian's commonly known among his parishioners as The Chief. One false step, and . . . well, I'm not here to create innocent martyrs for fanatical freaks. But we'll certainly question him—"

It came back to him. "Damien knew this priest, I'm sure that's what Sorcha McCarthy said."

"Indeed."

Hatton helped Inspector Grey struggle his good arm into a frock coat, knowing it would be ten more weeks till any prosthetic could be fitted, but the detective seemed determined that his time in the hospital was well and truly over. *It's now or never,* he thought. Hatton knew if he didn't ask the inspector why he was talking to the widow in Dawson's on that fateful day two weeks ago, he'd never know the truth.

"Before you go, Inspector, something has troubled me. I didn't know if you would live or die, but I feel now I must press you to tell me . . ."

"Spit it out, Professor."

Hatton plucked up the courage. "Very well, Inspector. I've been waiting for you to recover, but I simply must know to what purpose were you meeting Mrs. McCarthy at the jewelry shop? You see, I saw you through the window of Dawson's and she was crying, I think, and I need to know . . ."

"Say what you have to say and make it quick. I've an appointment to keep. Here, grab my good arm, Hatton. Lead the way!"

"It's just, that fateful morning, she looked distressed and, well, I simply must," *say it damn you*, said Hatton to himself as he steered the inspector like a drunk on a ship. "I simply must press you . . . in relation to the case . . ."

The inspector raised an eyebrow. "Distressed? No, I don't think she was distressed, other than she'd just buried her husband, but well, it's no secret. I was simply getting my watch fixed and, frankly, I was as surprised to see her there as you were."

Hatton's shock was palpable. "You hadn't arranged to meet her, then? When I saw you together, I thought perhaps, for some reason, you might have done."

The inspector raised his other eyebrow. "That day is still a little hazy, but London is a small place, practically a village, and Dawson's is well known. She was there it seems on some practical matter."

"But you were talking. You seemed to be together."

The inspector laughed. "Imagination is a fine thing if you have it, but no, sadly, she was merely intent on returning some rather beautiful jewels her husband had bought her, and being first and foremost, *a policeman*, I was suspicious. Odd sort of behavior, don't you think? So soon after her husband's demise? Selling off love tokens?" He looked at his pocket watch. "I know I wouldn't do it."

Hatton felt a wave of relief wash over him, as the inspector continued, "I challenged her, of course, and she grew a little agitated and declared that she was glad to bump into me because she had a delicate matter she wished to discuss. I think the term she used was *blood money*."

He laughed and shook his head as if the term was ridiculous.

"I'm not sure I follow you, Inspector."

"You're a man of the world, and she's bound to tell you anyway. Walls have ears, Professor, especially hospital walls. I have heard, of course, of your visits, the exotic fruits, the bouquets of flowers. " Hatton's face remained perfectly blank. "You see, Gabriel McCarthy was well connected with the Irish in this city and, it appears, the widow found a check I'd given to him. We did a little business, he and I. *Police business*. She had it in a little bag, along with her gems and rather theatrically tore it up, there and then, and if you must know, cursed me. Said I was a wicked man and that God would punish me." He laughed. "And I told her she'd better mind her manners, paid for the watch, and then, of course, you grabbed me out of that shop but not before I told her she was a sanctimonious little hussy."

Hatton was astonished. They were now outside on glistening London pavers, among a circle of pigeons pecking at bread, as Inspector Grey said, "My business with Gabriel McCarthy is no concern of yours, but so you know, he was supposed to help feed me information about possible flare-ups among the Irish. As it turned out, he was a fat lot of good, head in the skies, a do-gooder, completely useless, but she's another thing entirely. So, keep an eye on her, Hatton. She will be here at St. Bart's for how much longer would you say, Doctor *Amour*?"

This time the blank response was a crimson blush, as Hatton stuttered, "Another week at the most and . . ." *Is it so obvious? It must be obvious.* "Then it's her wish, I believe, that she wishes to recuperate in Highgate where the air is better." His color deepened to livid. "I've volunteered to look after her, in between my work at the morgue."

The inspector stood a little unsteadily, as they waited for his carriage to arrive. "Your duty, eh? Well, keep close, Hatton. Watch her every move. Don't let her out of your sight. And if you take her back to White Lodge, use your intuition. Use stealth and check the house again for ribbons or anything that seems relevant. I want to know exactly where the widow goes, who she sees, what she does, understand?"

"Surely you don't think—"

"All I think, Professor, is that you should stay close to Mrs. McCarthy as I shall stay close to the brother. No hardship, surely with a beauty like that? She's a little uppity for my taste but I think she trusts you, which suits me very well."

The carriage arrived.

"I have been told that I must at once to Clacton for sea air, but these gentlemen surgeons really have no understanding of my work. Still, I have Mr. Tescalini on the Pomeroy case. He's following a trail, which has taken him beyond Greenwich to the borders of Essex."

"The chef? You are still on the trail of the chef? You think he's still alive?"

"He's not officially dead. For that, I need a body and an autopsy from you, Hatton. I thought perhaps the body would be displayed for us somewhere on the anniversary of Drogheda, but it seems the Fenians had other things planned. Bigger things." He looked at his arm. "But I haven't given up on him, if that's what you're asking."

The carriage having arrived, Hatton opened the door to help the inspector in as he continued, "And I've learned a great deal about Gustave Pomeroy while I've been lounging round in bed. Like Mr. Hecker, his fame was based on philanthropy. He was in Ireland, Donegal specifically, and advised a couple of the work committees with a particular type of workhouse soup. Here . . ." Grey wrestled in his pocket. "Seems it wasn't a great success but at least the man tried, which is more than many others did." Hatton looked at the recipe which suggested a little mutton, two carrots, a lump of lard, two tablespoons of dripping, one dessert spoon of corn, a handful of barley, some salt, and thirty pints of water. Boil then serve. Hatton was no gourmand, but this looked utterly disgusting, and at the bottom of the page was the suggestion, signed again by Pomeroy, that this was enough to keep a family of ten going for a month. A month? It was barely enough to keep a fly alive, never mind malnourished children whose hungry stomachs would be descended, their bones as brittle as ice, riddled with disease like the flux, lice, typhus. They needed butter, bread, milk, eggs. They needed proper nourishment, not this muck.

"Seems when he got back to England, the ladies of London went berserk, thinking what a wonderful, noble man he was to help the Papist babies and off on his back, so to speak. He got invited to talk about his experience of the famine at all manner of places and it did his reputation—and his number of customers—no end of good. So how can a man like that disappear? Unless he wanted to? Or unless the person who abducted him he already knew, trusted even."

"Go on, Inspector."

Grey's face looked odd in the carriage light. Unnatural, ratlike, as he continued, "His wife died last year, and by all accounts he'd become lonely, a little melancholy, and talked to friends of having mystical visions. They thought he was hitting the absinthe again. Let me tell you, Hatton, I know a little about addiction and I suspect he'd become reliant on someone. Addicts reach out, take whatever they can get. Perhaps he leaned on a friend or even a woman?"

The inspector grimaced in pain.

"You will tire yourself out, Inspector. You must do as the surgeons tell you and rest."

Grey shut the door and pulled down the window. "If only the damned itching would stop, for all the time I feel that my hand has pins and needles and a throbbing ache, but there's nothing to scratch or rub. It's strange, isn't it, how the mind plays tricks on one?"

Despite their previous antagonism, Hatton felt sorry for the man and so tried to sound encouraging, as he said, "Your phantom limb, Inspector. All amputees have one, and it will serve you well when the prosthetic is added. Have you decided on what you would like?"

The inspector cheered a little at the question, thinking of a tropical hardwood and an ornate filigree hook. "My business with the McCarthys is far from finished." Grey slammed the door to his elegant barouche and the carriage took off.

Hatton made his way back to the hospital. The same thought had run through his own mind. But Sorcha could have nothing to do with such an outrage, surely? And she'd been horribly injured herself. No word had yet come as to who had committed the crime, but as the days had passed, rumors had circulated that there was little doubt. *Fenians. Ribbonmen.* But was this the crescendo the inspector had feared or was there more to come? During the famine, three of the victims had sat on a works committee with McCarthy at the helm. They'd tried to build roads, feed the starving, help the hungry to a better world, she'd said. But they must have done something else that someone didn't like. But what? And could there be other victims to come?

Since the bomb blast two weeks ago, Damien McCarthy had been questioned on the work committees at length, but simply answered that Ireland was in chaos at that time—Donegal being no exception. According to his witness statement, he thought there might have been fifty men or more on the committees, so half of them were surely dead by now, the others scattered to the wind, and that no one scribed the conversations anyway, that decisions were made on the hoof. And he made mention that the committees had nothing to do with land sold to Mr. Hecker, which was well known to be bog. He went on record that he thought the British police to be "Peculiarly stupid, for sure, didn't you know that? We couldn't even bury our own people in it, such were the sodden turf and the rocks." And that Hecker had probably bought the land for that peculiar English quality which Damien called "Colonial vanity. His little piece of Ireland which is so much cheaper and nearer than India. It's rape of the land, nothing more." He then, apparently, folded his arms, sat back in his chair, and flatly refused to cooperate with The Yard anymore, mentioning he had alibi's at the time of all the victims' murders, had friends in high places and, his lawyer pointed out, was entirely free to go.

Hatton didn't know any more than this, but perhaps this priest, Father O'Brian, did, he thought, as he took his little detour which, since the bomb, Hatton had made each morning, twice in the afternoon and once in the evening, sitting at her bedside till the sun set. And if for any reason, he was delayed a little, Patrice had nobly stepped to the fore and volunteered to run any errands required, to be at the widow's beck and call. But only on the professor's say-so. A little fund had bought flowers, chocolates, French cologne, a fan, a silk coverlet, lace doilies for her side table and, a couple of days ago, this encounter—

"What have you got there, Patrice?"

"The prayer book we found at the scene of the blast, monsieur. Madam requested a Catholic one. I took it from the morgue and . . ."

"No, no," said Hatton, rifling in his pocket and handing over some money. "You can't give her that one, Patrice, because it's evidence. Here's a few shillings, go buy her another one. I'm on my way to the ward right now. I'll explain to her."

Patrice had tipped his forelock, slipping back into the shadows of the hospital.

And two weeks ago, on the morning of the blast, as the injured were rushed to the surgical room, the poor lad, ashen, had asked in a whisper, "Her face, Professor? Will it mend, do you think?"

Hatton was ashen himself, sick to the stomach. "I'm not sure. The idea of a skin graft is experimental. We shall just have to wait."

They were standing a hairbreadth from the hospital chapel. Patrice looked toward St. Bart's The Lesser and asked almost of the church, "And pray, Professor?"

Hatton nodded. "We're not out of the woods, but Mrs. Mc-Carthy is young, strong, and yet, yes, we must pray. Pray very hard, Patrice."

And that very evening, as a pink sky melted into red, Hatton had caught a glimpse of Patrice bent in prayer, his rosary beads to hand, thinking later that someone, somewhere must have listened to that boy.

For here she was today, sitting up, her dark hair across a pillow, able to speak but only a little. Her face wrapped in bandages, but under the dressing, a myriad of stitches running gridlike across the skin graft that had been used to cover the sheared-off muscle. But considering all that she had been through, to Hatton's mind at least, Sorcha McCarthy was still beautiful.

"And how's my delightful patient today?" Hatton asked, sitting himself down at the side of her bed and pouring her a glass of cordial. He had a little paper straw in his pocket and, making sure it was absolutely spotless, pressed it lightly into her mouth.

"Try, Sorcha. Just a little?" She leaned forward with a faint smile as he whispered in her ear, *my darling.*

She struggled to speak, but finding it too painful, pressed his hand. Hatton turned to the ward sister, "Has Mrs. McCarthy's dressing been changed today?" The nurse arched a brow at him. It was the second time he'd asked and she had given this unwanted visitor short shrift earlier. "Please do what your eminent Miss Nightingale bids, and open the window, sister. Mrs. McCarthy needs air." The nurse scowled, but Patrice who was also hovering near the bedside rushed forward, climbed up a tottering ladder, did the job himself, came down, doffed his cap, and with an embarrassed smile, excused himself.

Alone at last, Hatton turned to Sorcha. "And your brother-in-law? Is he coming today?"

Her eyes said yes. She pressed his hand again, *forgive me*. He tried to smile, overwhelmed by her. "So, I hear from Dr. Buchanan it won't be so long before they let you go home to Highgate? It will do you the world of good, and if you will allow it, I shall take you myself. As your very dedicated doctor."

Sorcha beckoned Hatton to bring a quill and a sheet of paper, as had become their habit. The sentence she wrote was, *"I long to leave this place and I dream of* saoirse. *Do you remember?"*

She looked away, perhaps thought Hatton thinking of another place, because he'd brought her a picture book of Canada, and as she had grown a little stronger, he'd talked of where he might take her for a little fishing, a picnic, bear hunting. He'd begged her not to laugh at such ideas and she had patted him playfully on the arm, whispering foolish things to him, about how if only her life could be that way. Simple. But not all his encounters were so innocent and charming, because, once in the night, her eyes had fluttered in an uneasy dream. Hatton had pulled his chair up close to her bone-colored skin, plum silk and Irish lace falling from a turning shoulder, delirious as she'd pulled him toward her and, drenched in sweat, muttered of danger, imminent danger and of a beach on an island, so quiet he had to put his mouth to her lips, a whisper melting into a kiss.

But it was daylight now and he adjusted her bed linen fussily, and promised her he would be back again on the ward as soon as he could. That she must get some rest. And thinking, whatever she did or didn't do, he would make it his business to keep Inspector Grey away from her, as long as he could.

"Have you finished your ward round, Professor?"

"I had to see Inspector Grey off the premises, Albert. To

make sure he actually left, you understand, and is not still somewhere in the hospital, lurking."

"It wasn't the inspector I was speaking of. You cannot hide
your ardor from me, Adolphus. I think Mrs. McCarthy has your
attention, and it's high time we had a little romance in the
morgue. As a Frenchman, I'm all for it."

"I don't know what you are talking about, Albert. My interest is strictly professional." Hatton was keen to change the subject. "But you seem very well occupied with a new cadaver? Is it
of interest?"

"Not especially. Five witnesses saw her do it and such is the
shame on the family, they left the body to float. This woman was
an opium smoker. She also used these." Roumande held up a rusty,
metal needle. "On her uppers, like so many, it seems. Well, she's
paying for it now, for it's not so often we get to measure fluid in
lungs as big as these. She was an opera singer. Would you like to
have a delve and see for yourself the extent of the opiate damage?"

"No, no. You carry on. I have an appointment with
Dr. Buchanan. But that needle, Albert, where do these people
get them from? And did you test that one I found before the
bomb blast? I'm sorry, Albert. I should have done it myself, but
I've been so preoccupied."

Roumande nodded, tossing the syringe in a tray with a rattle.
"In answer to your first question, they pilfer them, Adolphus.
Druggists, hospitals—anywhere they can get them. This syringe
had never been used, but the inspector's has no bearing on the
case, does it? You seem a little troubled, Professor? He's an
opium user, too, I suppose, but what of it? Half of London is."
Roumande's hands were now deep under the rib cage of the
practice cadaver, squelching around the lungs. Hatton shrugged—
What of it, indeed—and set off again, this time not to the wards,
but to Dr. Buchanan's office.

"Dr. Buchanan? A word, please, if this is a convenient moment?"

Professor Hatton was shocked to see how drawn Dr. Buchanan seemed, but then he was not young, nearly sixty, and today Buchanan looked every year of it. His skin was sallow and he was coughing. Bizarrely, in the corner of his office, in a little tin bath, was a brownish duck.

"Damned hay fever, and what with the opening of the fountain, the speech-making didn't help, but at least the band's stopped. Are you a sufferer, Professor Hatton? I am, and all my children, especially the girls, though they are all now safely near the South Coast with their mother, which is shortly where this little lady shall go."

Quack, quack, quack. The duck ruffled its tawny feathers.

"Somebody left her for me. Isn't she delightful? And very rare, you know. A present from an anonymous but very grateful patient, the gift tag said. Although she doesn't have the best, shall I say, toilette? I have called her Albertine, the duck being so very loyal and intelligent, just like Monsieur Roumande. She's American, a wigeon, I am told by those that know these things. "

Quack, quack, quack.

"Give her a toke, Hatton. I think she likes you!"

Buchanan continued, "My throat's on fire and I'm losing my voice, I fear. It's the damn pollen and the coal dust in the air. The Board of Works really ought to do something. This is the worst summer yet, don't you think, Professor Hatton?"

"Your family are in Sussex, then?" Hatton was happy to make small talk for a while. Dr. Buchanan responded by ordering a minion to fetch them both coffee.

"Or would you prefer tea, Adolphus? I'm in need of something a little kinder today. Mind and body ail, as we get older. I sleep only a little in this feverish heat. But on the positive side, last night I took part in a most erudite gathering and gave a keynote speech to a room full of cholera experts, including many who hail from the New World. I have the speech here somewhere." He rustled in his bag.

"You would be welcome to read it, Adolphus. And after last

night's effort, I've been promised a four-page feature in *The Lancet* for the October edition."

Hatton smiled, which gave all the encouragement needed.

Buchanan continued, grateful for the attention. "It covers all my most groundbreaking moments, from the very early days, as a young man sleeves rolled up and investigating typhus along the coast, to my latest and most important crusade, which as you know is the smallpox inoculation program for workhouse children."

Hatton thought it wise to be indulgent. "Well, that's wonderful, Dr. Buchanan. It really is. I shall read it when I find a moment."

"Yes, yes," said the physician, with a smile. "But enough of me. How can I help you, Professor?"

"Well, sir," said Hatton, stuffing the speech into his surgical bag, and trying to ignore the quacking. "With all that has happened, I failed to hand in everything we had on the cholera victims." Hatton handed Buchanan a thick file which was mainly diagrams, graphs, and a few of Patrice's drawings. Buchanan put it on his desk in a tray marked "Pending" and continued to cough.

"Well, I won't be able to give it my full attention until next week at the earliest, as the American typhus doctors need taking care of before they return home which, as the director of St. Bart's, is a duty which falls to"—he pulled a face, not unlike a duck himself—"yours truly, but I'm sure the work is, as usual, excellent."

Buchanan looked gray around the gills but continued, "Mr. William Farr is a good friend to this hospital and will be most grateful with your findings, as I am. Although I fear sometimes I don't say it enough, but believe me, Professor, pathology is an important part of this great institution's future, as is the science of forensics. Sometimes I think you feel a little left out of things, here at St. Bart's such is our focus on keeping people living. Am I right, Hatton?"

Hatton could see the director was sick, so he simply said, "So, my budget won't be cut then, as I heard?"

"Not at all, Hatton."

"Well, in that case, sir, we are all quite happy in the morgue."

Dr. Buchanan sipped his coffee, pushing the biscuit plate toward the professor and gesturing at the pathologist to dig in.

"Please, I insist. I've no appetite today and, talking of biscuits, is there any news yet concerning the death of poor Mr. Hecker? A terrible tragedy. Inspector Grey put me in the picture and reiterated the important role medical jurisprudence would play in determining this case when it comes to court, along with these other Fenian atrocities, though you found no ribbon at the blast, I fear."

Hatton shook his head, though he was sure the blast and murders were connected.

"But I hear a ribbon was found in that rent collector's mouth, though this is all old news, I know. I am sixty and not on the cusp of things, as I used to be."

Hatton reddened, but quickly realized that all had been forgotten about the illicit retrieval of the ribbon from The Yard, as Dr. Buchanan continued, "And on this particular point, there's to be some sort of announcement today, and if it's agreeable with you, Professor, I might catch up with Jeremiah Grey, who I understand has discharged himself and is planning a press conference."

Hatton was taken by surprise. "He said nothing to me about any press conference, and I've only just left him."

"Well, this is what I've heard. I won't get drawn on details of forensics, of course, but I think it's important for us to be there. We are, after all, an intrinsic part of the Criminal Investigation Department's work. I understand that The Yard is ready to announce a breakthrough in the case. I don't wish to step on your toes, Professor . . ."

"Of course, Dr. Buchanan. I'm happy to let you speak," Hatton lied, biting down on a biscuit, which was a square-shaped thing, full of dried fruit, not wholly pleasant.

"They're better if you dunk them, Adolphus. They're quite

the fashion on the Continent and named after that dreadful man, Giuseppe Garibaldi. So, was there anything else you needed to talk to me about?"

Hatton shook his head, thinking to himself, "*A break-through?*" Grey hadn't mention any of this, but he was quite determined that he would find out. Perhaps it was just the prayer book they'd found, and a possible link to this O'Brian fellow. But surely, given what Disraeli had said, Grey wouldn't announce anything to a crowd of hacks, unless he had hard evidence.

"Are you quite sure you want to go to Whitehall? Perhaps I should go with you, Dr. Buchanan?"

"Well, that would be kind, for I'm not feeling myself. They were serving salmon last night at the symposium dinner and it's not a dish to serve up in this temperature. You must excuse me . . ." and suddenly the poor man ran out of the office, his hand over his mouth, before returning a few moments later, sweating and grayer than ever.

He smiled a little weakly. "There is clearly something on your mind. Do not mind the duck. Speak freely."

"Well, there is one thing. Have we had any surgical instruments go missing, say over the last month or so?"

Dr. Buchanan opened the hospital ledger book, put some glasses on. "Just the usual things. Plenty gets pocketed. You know what physicians are like, also the nurses and as for the porters? Let me see." Buchanan flicked through the pages. "Last month alone, for example, six bottles of opium, ten rolls of crepe, eighteen rolls of flypaper," the director stopped, looked at the list again. "My God, eighteen rolls. Well, it must be the weather, oh, and sixteen syringes. As I say, nothing unusual." Dr. Buchanan shut the book. "Would you be a good fellow and call me a carriage. The press briefing is in an hour, Professor."

Hatton did as he was told, helping Buchanan to the front entrance of St. Bart's and into a coach, and as he did, the hospital director seemed quite cheery and said that he felt a little better. Hatton said nothing, for he felt the reverse seemed true and, seeing the pallid face in front of him, decided that he couldn't let the man travel alone.

"Let me come with you, Dr. Buchanan. I can be on hand to answer any technical questions, and if I may say so, you look like you need a younger man to lean on, sir."

The hospital director slumped back in the carriage, the relief palpable. "You're right, Professor. I don't feel too well.

When they arrived at Whitehall, it was three o'clock and the Scotland Yard library was fit to bursting, the press conference in full swing.

"Good morning, gentlemen, and thank you all for coming." Inspector Grey had a piece of paper that he was flapping, as he continued. "I have brought you here today, gentlemen, to reassure the country that we shall not rest until each and every Irish savage involved in this campaign of terror is brought to justice. On this paper, I have a list of suspects which, at this point, cannot be revealed."

The scribblers rose to their feet in applause, at the same time trying to jot down the inspector's words, adding a few embellishments of their own, such as "fearless," "lionesque," "Top Taffy."

"Five minutes only" was the note in exaggerated handwriting slipped from Mr. Tescalini to Buchanan, who was up next, but upon seeing the note and the sea of journalists, croaked into Hatton's ears, "I'm sorry, Professor. I'm too ill," before swiftly rushing out of the room, toward the water closet.

"So may I introduce, err, well, it was to be Dr. Buchanan of St. Bart's," said the inspector, "but it seems we have the man himself. May I introduce you all to London's most eminent medical jurisprudence expert, Professor Adolphus Hatton."

Hatton found himself immediately answering questions about the Fenian atrocities, the murders and the Irish woman who had been taken to St. Bart's, her innocence or otherwise. Hatton answered all of the points, and as the proceedings drew to a close, looked over at Inspector Grey, who was hastily folding up the note, which he'd just claimed listed a number of suspects. From where he stood, however, Hatton could see quite clearly that the sheet of paper was blank.

"Are you going to share the names of your suspects with me, Inspector?"

The inspector smiled, taking Hatton aside. "Ah," he murmured so that only Hatton could hear him. "Caught me out, already? Nothing escapes you, does it? The piece of paper," he whispered, "is a necessary piece of theater to keep these hacks happy so I can get on with my work, unimpaired with the demands of Fleet Street. Keep the wolves at bay for a bit, for I have my political masters champing at the bit as well, now they know I'm up and about. No peace for the wicked, eh? But where on earth is Dr. Buchanan?"

A loud groan emitted from the corridor.

"He's ill and I should go to him at once," said Hatton. "But before I go, this works committee in Ardara?"

"What of it?"

"Three of our victims were part of it. You have contacts in Westminster? Disraeli? Lord Stanley? The commissioner?"

Grey nodded. "Your point, Professor?"

"My point being, wouldn't they know who else was on it, even though it was ten years ago? My fear is the Fenians might be picking the committee members off one by one, and now they've the blast out the way, this could be the next stop. There must be a file on the famine relief effort in Donegal somewhere? Tell us what happened, precisely? And if there were other men involved, where are they now? What were the committee's successes or, more important, its failures?"

"What are you driving at Hatton?"

Hatton's mind was racing. "I'm a scientist and I recognize facts. And it's unpleasant fact that at least two men made a profit from doing so-called good works during the famine? Hecker exported corn in and out of Ireland, gave people a safe passage to America, bought cheap land, and made money. Pomeroy came back to London and established a whole career upon his good works. We don't know about this Mahoney man, but was he involved in something. He just had to be? And as for McCarthy, all I hear was how good he was, but there's no smoke without fire. He ran the damn thing and nobody recorded a single detail? I simply don't believe it."

"That's supposition, Hatton, not fact . . ."

Hatton leaned forward, a sharp light in his eyes, "But I'm right, aren't I?"

Grey gestured at his pocket for a cigarillo and match. "I believe you are. Let's try and speak to this priest. But I need to get agreement first from the 'powers that be' before I storm into the rookeries, because as you very well know, the Union is fragile . . ."

Another groan interrupted, louder this time, of an old man in terrible pain. Hatton took one more glance at Grey, then rushed outside to see Dr. Buchanan, who hadn't made it to the washroom, but lay amidst a pool of vomit.

"It was the salmon. I have been poisoned by those damn typhus doctors. This is a most violent food poisoning. Please, Adolphus, help me . . ." The doctor retched again as Hatton grabbed a bucket and, that done, bundled the physician out of The Yard and into a waiting carriage.

At Number 9, Seamore Place, Hatton hammered on the door until a butler came. Dr. Buchanan was barely able to walk, never mind speak, as Hatton helped the man upstairs, catching sight of his own reflection in an arrangement of sparkling mirrors that had been positioned along the second-floor corridor. Hatton looked lost, bereft, haunted as he wrestled Dr. Buchanan into his four-poster bed. Buchanan was feverish, as Hatton yelled, knowing time was of the essence, "Cool compresses, bed-pans, emetics. For pity's sake, hurry."

"Don't leave me," Buchanan sobbed.

Hatton squeezed the old man's hand, and smelled the rank-ness of his breath "You're running a fever, Dr. Buchanan, but we'll get it down, I promise you . . ." Hatton took Buchanan's palm and stroked it gently, whispering, "Shhh now. Please, sir. Shut your eyes. Rest a little. I won't leave you. You have my word . . ."

A year had passed since he'd held another old man's hand. Not among such décor, it was true, because when his father died there had been no sumptuous wallpaper or pendant chandelier, no liveried servants, no gilt and mirrors. They had kept the cur-tains shut because the glare had hurt his father's eyes. All of it crept back, a bitter memory. The sourness of the air, the ticking clock, which, when the time came, didn't stop as life had, but car-ried on with its incessant *ticktock* as if nothing that had gone, had mattered. That life was of no consequence at all. Hatton shut his eyes, dog tired, so desperately tired; a deeper resonating chime came from somewhere down the hall as Hatton watched the world around him flicker.

Who are you? What the devil do you want?

A man, his mouth rammed to the brim with green silk rib-bons, was walking toward him in a darkening room, saying nothing, and Hatton wanted to run away, wanted to hide, but he couldn't.

"No!"

"Help me . . . for pity's sake!"

No scream, no noise coming out to save him, and sensing far below, in another room, another country, another world away, people were stuffing seven courses of chocolate cake, and drink-ing toasts to gluttony. *Huzzah!* But they weren't coming to help, as he felt a rip in his chest and looked down to see his own heart—an exquisitely presented pumping machine, which was glistening, *A* to *P* in calligraphy.

"Help me . . ."

"Professor Hatton." A servant was peering in his face, as the clock chimed seven. "You were having a nightmare. I've brought you some coffee and the morning paper. You've performed a miracle, Professor Hatton. Your patient is up before you. Aren't you, Dr. Buchanan, sir?"

20

WHITEHALL

Leaving Dr. Buchanan to fully recover, Hatton had gone straight to the morgue, only to find two Specials waiting to deliver him promptly to where he stood now—inside the library of Scotland Yard. The inspector was on the chaise longue, his stocking feet stretched out before him. With some effort, Grey hurled a rolled-up newspaper across the room, which Hatton caught with the hand of an ace cricketer.

"Well, they didn't wait long before the next outrage. They must have heard I was up and about and timed it for that—to goad me—but don't worry, I'm on a mission now. I'll get them."

"What outrage?"

"It's a summary, rather than the actual document, but if you run your finger down to the end you will see that several of our most senior politicians are cited as privy to this policy."

"Policy?" asked Hatton, ruffling open the Irish newspaper.

Grey pulled himself up to a seated position. "Ten years ago some of our most senior politicians used the famine as a way of clearing tenants off the land. I've heard this scurrilous argument before but here it is naming names, quoting great chunks of a confidential document, and reproducing minutes of a private conversation with the then prime minister, Lord Russell himself. Thus proving the government knowingly and deliberately prolonged the famine." The inspector wiped his face with a silk kerchief.

"Since the blast, English Protestants have been marching in the towns of Londonderry, Liverpool, Glasgow, and this article is intended to incite them. It'll be in the second edition of *The Times* by two o'clock today and *The Daily Post* tomorrow. Need I say more? Murder, terrorism, and now, propaganda. Perhaps they *are* being helped by some European types, because Disraeli certainly thinks so. He had me in his office at six o'clock this morning. My ears are still ringing. But as I pointed out to our Honorable Member for Maidstone, this time they haven't been so clever." Grey gestured with his hand to his assistant. "Mr. Tescalini? Be so kind as to fetch Mr. Amersham of Her Majesty's Home Office."

Tescalini left the room and then immediately brought back a middle-aged man wearing the black frock coat, high stiff collar, and waxy, never-seen-the-sun pallor of a government clerk.

"Please, Mr. Amersham, sit down and explain to us how this sensitive document might have fallen into enemy hands?" Grey had moved toward the window and stood with his back to the room.

Mr. Amersham spoke quickly. "Foolishly, I bestowed the contract on a family firm in Clapham. The file quoted in this morning's issue of *The Nation* . . . I have the details here . . . File Number Seventy-eight . . . was definitely among the documents which went to Tooley and Sons. In my defense, they are bookbinders to Her Majesty the Queen. I had no reason not to trust them. I read the scurrilous article first thing this morning and, well, I can only say I feel horribly responsible, Inspector."

"No one is blaming you, sir, and in some ways this reckless act has done us a favor. This is the first proper breakthrough we've had in three weeks. Of course, the commissioner is spitting blood, Whitehall, too, but if it means we've hard evidence of sedition then it might be worth a little earache. And this bindery's in Clapham, you say? But isn't Tooley an Irish name? Is there, in fact, an O' in it?"

Amersham rubbed his hands together nervously. "Mr. Tooley came highly recommended, but I have no doubt as to the source of these articles. File Number Seventy-eight was most definitely in the pile we gave to him."

Hatton shifted on his feet, desperate to ask and interjected with, "May I?"

"Be my guest," said Grey, still looking out at St. James's Park.

Hatton turned to Mr. Amersham. "The victims of the ribbon murders knew each other, and we think they're in some way connected to the blast. It seems the men killed were all involved in the emergency works program in a place called Ardara, Donegal. I'm presuming, as a long-standing member of the Home Office, you would have played your part during the famine? The names of the dead are Tobias Hecker, as you know . . ."

"And Gabriel McCarthy, yes, yes . . . I know this . . ."

"And another—a gombeen man name of Gregory Mahoney? He came from the same place, did odd jobs for Mr. Hecker, and was, by all accounts, an outcast, a moneylender, a swindler, hated by others in the community. Rumor has it, he was even excommunicated by his own priest. What could he have possibly done that could have been so terrible?"

"Well," said Mr. Amersham, "you've answered your own question, Professor. He must have committed a mortal sin."

"Mortal, being what? Murder?"

"Not necessarily. There are many sins considered far worse by the Catholic Church. For example, fornication, abortion, masturbation . . ."

"They cut off his testicles, Mr. Amersham."

"Seems a high price."

"Yes, but we're going off the point. What happened in Ardara, sir?"

Amersham put his head in his hands. "After the blight, tenants had nothing to eat or sell. Unscrupulous landowners decided to raise the rent, driving unwanted people off the land, you see. The people begged for help. The government did its best and embarked on a series of food for work programs. As far as I know, Gabriel McCarthy was one of the good men, kept the rents low, did what he could—so why choose him as a Fenian whipping boy? There were many others they could have chosen who were far worse. Unless there was some other reason, something he was involved in . . ."

Grey turned around from looking out of the window. "Go on . . ."

"I'm not a policeman, but I can tell you this. The idea to force, what the Irish called the tumbling, driving tenants off their land, was used as a last resort. Not to prolong the famine, as this article suggests, but to end it. By driving people off bad land, it meant they were given no choice—they had to leave poverty behind and start a better life in America. They were offered cheap cabins on the clippers, land when they reached the New World. There was a certain logic to it."

Hatton was aghast. "Forcing people from their homes? Devastating families? The roofs were torn down, cottages burned, women and children fleeing for their lives, the land sold for a pittance to people like Mr. Hecker . . ."

"I don't know about that," said Mr. Amersham, a sudden hardness in his eyes. "But it was chaos and we were there to do a job. Save lives, any way we could. Work committees were set up all over Ireland, building roads, digging ditches, running soup kitchens—that sort of thing—but as to your victims, they're just the tip of the iceberg. Hundreds of men took part in the effort to ease the famine. Chemists came from London to try and solve the blight, chefs to help with the nutrition, mill owners to grind the grain we exported to the Irish at a pittance, shipowners, men of the cloth, Quakers . . ."

"But there were no millstones in Ireland, they didn't even

know how to cook it, and the West was neglected, wasn't it? Did the corn even reach that far?"

Amersham looked at the creases on his hands. "It's true many couldn't be reached. There's a place called Skibberdeen that I can never forget no matter how I try . . ."

"You were there?

Mr. Amersham grew pale. "Yes, I was there, Professor Hatton. So perhaps these men should kill me, whoever they are. Half of Whitehall's guilty of murder, if that's what they think. But there's not a single night that I don't remember . . ."

The room fell silent, just a light breeze snaking through a half-opened window, but mainly silence, an ominous silence as he said—

"I was part of a works committee for Kerry. Had never been to Ireland before, couldn't speak the language, and to my shame I've never been back. But in my first week, we came upon a farm, less than a mile from the town of Skibbereen, where a man still lived, but too weak to rise from his bed, lay next to his dead wife, his three dead children, and a dead babe being eaten by a cat. This is a fact. We shot dogs to keep them from the piled-up bodies, we dealt with lists and lists of people we knew to be starving, but these parishioners had been hunted from the land, lived in burned-out ruins, bog holes halfway up mountains—scalpeens, they called them—literally holes in the turf. Thousands were racked with the bloody flux and Ireland was an apocalypse. To allow them to leave, to help these people escape, was that a crime, gentlemen?"

"Enough said," said Grey, looking at his pocket watch. "It's time we went to Clapham. Professor Hatton? Mr. Tescalini, you, too, sir."

No swirling or lassoing this time, but instead, the Italian was quickly at the inspector's side and, using his finger and thumb, tweaked the gold watch back into the detective's fob pocket for him. Grey patted his pocket. "It's new and unpatriotically Swiss. But nevertheless, Mr. Tescalini has kindly had my initials engraved upon the back, haven't you, friend?"

Mr. Tescalini smiled, a disposition not entirely suited to him, and said, "*Si. E il nostro piccolo motto, Tempis Fugit.*"

"Indeed it does, and for the time being, that priest will have to wait," said the inspector. "Clapham first."

In the carriage, Inspector Grey said, "By the way, look at this . . ." It was a recipe card. "Thank heavens for the penny farthing because only yesterday a lead took Mr. Tescalini to a baker's shop in a village in Essex, near the River Thames." The card was entitled, *The Je Ne Sais Quoi of French Cooking.* "According to the chef's editor, this hasn't been published yet. It's an unfinished manuscript, which means Pomeroy was likely working on it the very day he disappeared. He's been gone three weeks now, but do you think he could still be alive? If the killers have abandoned him somewhere or imprisoned him, how long does it take if a man's been tortured? Tormented? Starved?"

How long is a piece of string, thought Hatton. Because a tortured man could live forever, but denied, food, water, hope? "It would depend as much upon the strength of his mind as that of his body. Without food, for the average man, perhaps six to eight weeks. Without water, in these temperatures? A man could sweat to death. Seven days, at the most."

"Well we can't give up hope, Hatton. I think Essex is the place and I want him found—dead or alive. I've Specials hunting all over the county, but so far nothing apart from this." He flapped the card. "But it's my bet, those hops we found at the flour mill weren't dropped by a bird, after all. Could they have been stuck on a coat and brushed off in the grasses as the killer made his escape?"

"It's possible."

"I tried to reach you last night at Gower Street to discuss this possible clue, because it could be important, couldn't it? But where were you last night, Hatton? It's not like you to be away from the morgue."

"I was indisposed, Inspector. Dr. Buchanan was taken very ill during the press conference, but he's better now, thank heavens."

"Glad to hear it, and your other patient? How fares the pretty one?"

"I didn't see Mrs, McCarthy last night, if that's who you mean."

The inspector became grave and leaned forward in the carriage as it hurtled across the river. "I can see the pain etched on your face, Professor, but let me give you a piece of advice, because the same thing happened to me once during a case. She was a lovely girl from Barry. A professional wrestler by day, with such thighs as could crush a man. But at night, well, she was a different thing altogether. A little rouge, a lace petticoat, a ruby dress, an ostrich fan, a little show of ankle, a shimmy, and she was a pearl. A ravishing pearl. But my desire led me to a dark and dangerous place. An evil place and even to talk of it now, it fills me with nothing but shame."

"And your point is what exactly, Inspector?" asked Hatton, at the same time not able to quite join up the image of a girl, a professional wrestler, and the docksides of Barry, although he knew they were a strange lot in Wales.

"Beauty blinds a man and Mrs. McCarthy's charms are obvious. But let me tell you that she's not to be trusted. Keep her close, make a friend of her, but don't fall in love with her, Professor, because, to put it succinctly, she's a suspect."

Hatton's face burned.

"A suspect? I hardly think so. She couldn't have moved that millstone or severed a man with a spade. And the idea that I'm in love with her is utter nonsense. It's a purely professional arrangement."

"Really?"

"Yes, really."

"Really?"

"Oh for heaven's sake, yes, Inspector, really, and I can tell you, she's no killer."

"Maybe not, but she's definitely a liar."

Takes one to know one, I suppose, thought Hatton, but he simply pulled a face and said, "How so, Inspector?"

"Do you recall my conversation with Mrs. McCarthy, when you asked if anyone had been weeding the garden and she said she supposed so because the garden was full of daisies? Daisies? I ask you! Daisies are well over by July, especially in this heat. And the morning she discovered her husband's body, she presented him so calmly. She was pale, yes, and in tears, but women so often are, and do you know, she asked for both of us to be involved in the case? From the outset, she claimed she suspected foul play. Quite a leap for the mind of a twenty-year-old woman, wouldn't you say?"

"But if you are suggesting she's a killer, then why would she involve the very people who might point the finger at her?"

"A double bluff, Professor. It's a strategy often engaged by the most cold-blooded killers."

"And the gombeen man? The spade? The millstone? She's the size of a London sparrow. No woman could commit such acts. Poison yes, but the rest?"

"I don't like her sanctimonious act. She tore up a hundred-pound check at the jeweler's shop as if to punish me and . . ."

But the conversation had to lie fallow because they'd arrived at their destination. A redbrick house on Clapham Common.

"So this is the place?" said Grey. "Pay the man please, Mr. Tescalini. And then give me the bottle." Hatton watched as the inspector used his teeth to wrench a cork out of a tiny blue bottle containing what Mr. Tescalini called "*oppiato.*" Still swigging, the inspector shot up the stairs and banged a large brass knocker designed in the shape of a bookend. No answer came.

A soft breeze sighed across The Common. Birds sang. A man threw a stick for a dog.

"Perhaps there's a side door to the bindery?" Hatton gestured the other two to follow him, around the house where stone steps led down to some spectacular hammering. Through a greased-up

window, rubbing with his sleeve, Hatton could see men wearing
bowler hats engaged in a variety of stages of bookbinding. Hot
stamps for the gold leafing, someone altering the French press
to make a Bible flat. And once inside, mirroring heat all around
from two vast furnaces, as the detective announced, "Inspector
Jeremiah Grey of Scotland Yard. Somebody fetch Mr. Tooley."

A man with a beard in an apron stuttered, "M . . . m . . .
mr. T . . . t . . . Tooley is s . . . s . . . s . . . seeing ccc . . . cccc . . .
cccc . . . customers, sir." Another chipped in, "Save your tongue,
Brian. I'll take it from here. Is it a contract you've come about?"

Outside light spidered through ancient sycamores, church
bells rang, as Grey put his hand to his forehead. "Down tools,
please, gentlemen, at once, because I'm here on government business. One of your files has fallen into enemy hands. Irish hands.
So, no Mr. Tooley then?"

A young man of about seventeen, answered, "He's in Pater-
noster Row, but he'll be back in an hour or so."

"Well, I can't wait in this furnace," said Grey. "Can we get
back to the main house from here?"

A woman who'd been bent down sewing pages into a book
stood up and said, "Forgive me, I'm Mrs. Tooley. You can wait
for Mr. Tooley in the parlor. Please, gentlemen, follow me."

At the back of the overheated room was a smaller flight of
steps leading to a leather-backed door. Professor Hatton followed while Mr. Tescalini stayed behind in the bindery.

The parlor was of the plainest style. No ornament, save a
washed-out pastel of weather-beaten countryside. "The picture
is of my father's land in Mayo. We left before the famine took
hold. I was very young when I married, but it's a good life and
I have five fine sons." Her face was smeared with sweat. She
wiped her hands down the front of her work apron. "One of
them was at the work top. Did you see him? He's almost seventeen, named Luke. Another is resting while the babes are asleep.
Shall I bring you both tea or perhaps a drop of something?"

Grey smiled. "Tea would be delightful, Mrs. Tooley. So, was

the lad I saw in the bindery the very same lad who went to the Home Office with your husband?"

"No, that was the middle child. Mr. Tooley considers himself to be English now, you understand, so we've given our sons Anglican names. It's better in the long run that we assimilate. Blend in, Inspector. The middle child is Jasper and he's a cripple. Terrible rickets as a child, so I indulge him a little."

Hatton looked at Mrs. Tooley, who wasn't old, but beyond the bloom of youth. She still had her thimble on and there were little shreds of multicolored linen thread stuck to her dress and shavings of marbled paper scattered about her hair, most of which was loosely pushed up into her work cap.

"I should like to meet your other son. He's not ill, I hope?"

A mantel clock ticked.

"No, no. But these last two weeks he's had the most terrible nightmares." She shook her head. "He's been screaming in the night, and waking up in the most wretched state, and the boy looked so very tired this morning, I felt it best he took a little nap. He's not in any trouble is he?"

"Just fetch your son, please. There's nothing to fear. In fact, to make things a little quicker, I'll come with you, shall I? Why don't you stay here, Hatton. I shan't be long."

Hatton shrugged, quite happy being left alone to think. Parlor rooms were meant for hospitality and frivolity, for light entertainment, but this sad affair was bereft of any charm. Hatton wandered over to the window to glimpse Mr. Tescalini outside on the pavers, gesticulating at the bindery workers, who were shaking their heads, and then watched, with some curiosity, the Italian gesturing at a policeman, who sauntered toward them. Hatton watched, as the policeman led the binders away from the house, toward The Common, and Mr. Tescalini headed back to the house.

Minutes went by when suddenly, up above him, Hatton heard a door slam and then something which sounded like a sack of potatoes being dragged across the floorboards, then whispers, scurrying. Maybe ten minutes passed before the professor, tired of waiting, went to the door to the parlor room and twisted the handle to find it was jammed. *What now?* He shook the door to no avail, put his boot against the skirting board, pulled, still no luck. *For God's sake.* He kicked the bottom, wrenched the handle again, heard what sounded like a muffled scream. Rushed to the window, to find it was also locked and then hurled himself forward, but as he headed for impact, the door suddenly opened. The inspector, who was standing on the other side, said, "I was just coming to get you. Come down to the basement, please. We're in dire need of a doctor."

"Somebody locked the door," said Hatton, to immediately see that Grey was drenched in sweat. "Are you all right, Inspector?"

"Couldn't be better, but there's a bit of a mess downstairs . . ."

"What sort of mess?"

But the inspector was already gone, back toward the basement and the sound of whimpering, like a wounded cat.

"The mother was dealt with swiftly and I've tried to get a signed confession, but he's being very difficult, and now it seems he's about to pass out. I need him up, alert. I've got more questions about what else was in the file, maybe a list of potential victims, so do me a favor, Hatton, would you, and deal with him?"

The door to the bindery swung open, to reveal a boy crouching in a corner, crumpled like a ball, and Mr. Tescalini towering over him, holding a claw hammer dripping with blood.

"No, please, God. Tell me you didn't, Inspector? You couldn't have?"

"Remember the rosary beads discussed in Highgate? McCarthy's beads? Well, take a guess where I found them—stuffed deep in a pocket! How did you find these, I asked him, because they belong to a dead man who lives five miles from here."

"Please, sir, I told the copper." Despite the pain, the boy seemed to have roused himself and cried out, toward Hatton. "I told him over and over again but he won't listen, sir. I found them in St. Giles. They'd been thrown on a rubbish tip. I'm always picking things up, regular magpie my da calls me . . ."

Grey kept his eyes on Hatton, ignoring the boy. "Likely story. Beads tipped with a solid silver figure, just thrown away in tip? As if . . . and do you recognize them, Hatton?" The inspector shoved the beads into Hatton's face. "Very plain, blessed in Rome and wooden, with a simple cross. Papist beads, from a boy who claims he's protestant, but he's nothing of the sort. And guess where he worships? Soho Square. Your mammy sends you there for catechism, doesn't she? And says you've been having night-mares for two weeks. Two weeks? Well, there's a coincidence because there was a bomb blast two weeks ago. Where you there, with The Chief? Isn't that what you Catholics call him?"

"I haven't seen Father O'Brian for over a year."

"Liar. Damn impudent liar. Mr. Tescalini—try another hammer . . ."

"I swear to God. I was just the lookout. Stand on Piccadilly they said and keep a lookout. A lookout for beaks, Specials, bluebottles, pigs, crushers, coppers, or general busybodies, but looking out, sir, that's all I did. I didn't kill anyone, I swear . . ."

"You'll do more than looking out by the time I've finished with you."

"Stop it," said Hatton. "Leave the boy, you'll get nothing by torturing him and if you touch one more hair on his head, as God is my witness, I'll—"

Panting, the inspector reeled back from Hatton's clenched fist. "You'll what? You'll do nothing. You work for *me* . . ."

But Hatton was cradling the boy. "Shhh, shhh now. Quiet now . . ."

"Keep him away from me, sir. The Taffy will kill me."

"Shhh now," said Hatton taking his doctor's bag, holding the boy gently, giving him morphine, stroking his head. Then turn-ing to Grey, daggers in his eyes. "You'll pay for this, Grey. If it's the last thing I do, you'll pay for this."

21

SMITHFIELD

"They'd crushed most of the metacarpal bones but his phalanges were still intact and he's young. The pain must have been excruciating but the boy gritted his teeth and bore it. He was brave, Albert. Braver than I would have been." Hatton tossed some calico bags in Roumande's direction. "These are the bags of so-called evidence. There were some ribbons in the bindery but they weren't the right color, but still Grey insists that he wants us to find an indisputable match, so he can wrap it all up. The bomb, the ribbon murders, the whole damn lot."

Hatton was outside in the yard and, for the first time in his life, lit a penny smoke. "He's a man gone mad, Albert. He'll break the boy and get a confession."

"He's a man turned criminal from what you've said, Professor. I cannot believe they would torture a child."

"I'm afraid they are capable of anything. I'll testify in court if it comes to it, because any confession Grey gets from that boy won't be worth the paper it's written on."

"I'm sure you did all that you could, Adolphus. Is the tobacco helping?"

"Not much. It's making my head light whereas I need clarity." A peevish impatience crept up on Hatton, "But where the devil's Patrice? Why's the lad never at his station when he's needed?"

"He's on an errand for me. We're running short of practice cadavers and there was a hanging at Newgate, but whether he'll get there in time for the spoils I'm not so sure. I told him I needed him back no later than two, but it's past that now."

"You're too used to working on your own, Albert. You need to keep a better charge of that lad. The mortuary is a mess. Whenever I see him, all he's doing is drawing or having cups of tea with Dr. Buchanan. Who washes the floors these days? Who sharpens our knives? *Perfect Specimens for an Exacting Science?* I hardly think so." Hatton sucked the bitter weed into his lungs, and Roumande, not caring for this pointless talk anymore, left him to it and went back into the morgue.

Hatton sat for a while with his own dark thoughts, knowing he'd done nothing for that child. He'd dressed his hand, but what of it? He could feel himself aging a thousand years as he sat in a mire of his own despondency watching the cigarette burn to his fingertips. In the distance he could hear the body cart. The rumbling got louder before the bulky shadow of their old nag, Snowdrop, loomed up against the mortuary wall, and then Patrice appeared, giving the horse a pat before coming across the yard with, "Are you feeling unwell, Professor?"

Hatton shook his head—*please, just go away*—as Roumande put his head around the mortuary door saying, "You're back, at last. What the devil kept you so long? Get the cadaver into the mortuary or it will begin to boil in this heat, and then you're wanted at Dr. Buchanan's office after I've finished with you. He's very delicate today and our department needs the money, so hurry yourself." Roumande clapped his hands with impatience.

Hatton took another puff, not entirely surprised that the honeymoon period was over for their apprentice. It was always the same. When they arrived, Roumande saw only the good in them, but as the weeks passed, it was a different story. Hatton kept his eyes to the ground as he said, "I can hardly believe Dr. Buchanan is here at all, after last night. Was anyone else taken ill from the symposium?"

"Nobody else that I know of. But you're quite the general practitioner, as he was back at his desk by noon today. The director said something to me as I went past his office, about what a gifted doctor you are."

"But I'm a better pathologist."

"And forensics await you, friend. I know we should hasten to the details of the case." Roumande put on a pleading face. "But if I could only make this fingerprinting work properly, it might just give us the breakthrough we need—and there are three of us here all together for once, but only with your say-so, of course, Professor."

"You're right." Hatton stamped the penny smoke under this thick-soled boot. "Work, Albert. Work is what we need to do."

Needing little encouragement, Roumande gathered up some fly paper, charcoal, a fine brush, and said, "As luck would have it, Sir William Herschel is back briefly from India. I bumped into him outside the Colonial Office and took the opportunity to ask him what he thought about our work and . . ."

"Sir William Herschel? The Raj connection? The one who uses this method on his Indian workers?"

"The very same, and he had a number of suggestions about the amount of ink I've been using, Adolphus, and also the powder. So I've cut it down a little on both. So let's see if this works," Roumande said, rolling his sleeve back and pressing his finger into the ink. He rolled his finger from side to side and, taking a quill, wrote his name against the print. "You can see my whorl is spiral and sits a little to the right, which suggests a propensity for tidiness. Which is true, isn't it? You next please, Professor."

Hatton did as he was told, as Roumande said, "Not too hard, gently does it, now roll it from side to side, lift, and, hey, presto."

Hatton was cynical. "And mine, Albert? What does mine tell you?"

"I would say your mark denotes a man with romantic inclinations. See, the loop is a single one and the whorl arches to the left. In fact, I believe it suggests a man who takes the weight of the world upon his shoulders. Am I close?"

"It's nonsense, Albert, and you know it. So, Patrice, you're next."

The lad shrunk back.

Roumande interjected, "Come now. We need all three of us."

"But you will not keep them, will you, monsieur? I have no wish to have my liberty threatened."

Roumande laughed. "Thus speaks a true Frenchman."

But Hatton shook his head, looking at his watch, impatiently. "Yes, well, we're in England now and we're investigating murders here, so come along now, hurry."

The assistant reluctantly offered a finger, as Roumande said, "Two double loops, a tented arch and a whorl which almost falls off the tip of the finger, denoting an artistic temperament, loyalty, and passion. Do you see?"

Patrice inclined his head. "*Oui,* monsieur, but what should we do next? How do we lift them?"

"Good question. Sir Herschel says he feathers the layer of ink with only a hint of powder using the tiniest fingerprinting brush, like this . . . and then lays something sticky upon it." Roumande leaned across the table. "If I keep it really flat, press down evenly, Herschel says the flypaper should work . . ." He looked at their apprentice. "This is the last sheet, by the way. We seem to be eating the stuff. Steady with those orders, Patrice, or Buchanan will have my guts for garters. Eighteen rolls, he claims have been used up by this department alone in the month of July."

"But the flies, monsieur?"

Roumande shrugged, "Well, use a flyswatter, as well." He rubbed his chin as he returned to the print and said, "It's not a perfect likeness, granted, but with a few more weeks of empirical research, Adolphus . . ."

"I'm as keen as you are for this method to work, but I fear

we don't have a few weeks, because if Grey's wrong, if the boy's information turns out to be misleading, we have days, hours, minutes before the next murder. Have we anything else to go on which might point to something? Anything?"

"There's still the oil, monsieur?"

Hatton turned to Patrice. "The oil?"

"*Oui*, the oil, do you remember? And oil suggests a priest, and the inspector, he has gone to arrest a priest, *n'est ce pas*? So the puzzle, Professor? Perhaps, it's coming together at last?"

But Hatton's job was to doubt. Always to doubt. "I'm not sure. The oil was only found on one man's forehead. A man who had been ex-communicated by Father O'Brian in the rookeries. But if *he* murdered Gregory Mahoney, why bless him at all? It seems strange and flies in the face of what he'd previously done. To be ex-communicated means your soul is dead, so there's nothing to bless at all. And whoever killed our victims has been careful to leave few clues. Just the glitter chemical, leading to the bomb. Anything else?"

"The ash on Monsieur McCarthy?" offered Patrice.

"We've dealt with that. Move on."

"The ribbons?"

"Thus telling us it's Fenians. We already know this. Anything else? Any other traces under their fingernails, in the hems of their trousers, any unusual splatters, footprints?"

"No," said Roumande, emphatically.

"Thirty pieces of silver," suggested Patrice.

Hatton's eyes narrowed, "A religious message, pure and simple. But half the bloody rookeries thought Mahoney was a Judas."

"More than half," added Roumande with a weary sigh.

Hatton sat down on his chair, bit the top of his thumbnail. "All the victims are connected. We know this, but maybe it's more than that. Maybe all these men did something, together. Something terrible, and yet everyone we've spoken to says during the famine—apart from Mahoney—these other men

tried. Made a bad job of it but still *tried*. According to Mr. Amersham at the Home Office, hundreds sat on these work committees, so there's nothing special in that, and we know the land
Hecker bought is worthless. And yet, so many things connected
to these killings point to a priest. And that's what's troubling me.
They *point*—as if they might have been put there."

"Like a trap, Adolphus?"

"Or a message, Albert, and we're simply not reading it. This
killer wants us to know something, but what?" Hatton found his
chisel blade and dug the tip deep into his desk, then twisted it.
"For example, the oil? So theatrically done, so how did I miss it?"

"You were drunk, monsieur?"

Hatton smiled. "Thank you, Patrice, and you're right, of
course, I *was* drunk the first time I saw him, very drunk, and the
next day paying for it with a wretched headache, but Albert—
not to accuse anyone—you were there, too, sober as a judge,
and the next day decapitated the corpse?"

Roumande was circumspect and shrugged. "There was so
much blood initially, and the next day . . ." another shrug that
said *Well, that could happen to anyone. Overwork. Too much to
do. A slip, nothing more.*

"Either way," continued Hatton, twisting the blade again. "I
suppose it would do no harm to check the oil again. That reminds me, those orange petals I scooped up from the lily pond
at the McCarthy place? Did they match?"

Roumande shook his head because he'd already checked that.
They were marigolds.

"So," Hatton said, looking down the viewing columns of the
Zeiss, "this orangey hue? It's a plant of some kind. A plant deriva-
tive mixed in prayer oil. Have you any ideas, before I tell you
mine?"

"The oil is olive, Adolphus, without question, but as to these
flower specs? Perhaps it's some kind of pollen, but I've been
through all the books we have in the mortuary. Nothing."

Hatton had his eye pressed close to the microscope. "I don't need a book to tell me it's not pollen. Pollen has a spherical shape whereas these flecks are tapering. These are petal strips, crushed then stirred into oil. It's a flower, but is it Welsh poppies or dandelions? From my research, I think this molecular structure is close to dandelions. Have you looked at the new book? The one that I got from the School of Apothecaries?"

"Not yet, but dandelions are mostly yellow, Professor. Our file for spices and other flora samples isn't all it could be. But if it's prayer oil, it definitely points to a priest."

"It doesn't have to be a priest. Anyone could have done this. Oil is easy enough to come by, as are petals, even in the city. We must ask ourselves a simple question. What are these marks telling us? What does an anointment mean?"

"Forgiveness, Adolphus?"

"Or a closeness to God? Purity?"

"Healing from a sickness?"

"Or simply to mark death, Albert. A full stop."

Patrice was away on the other side of the morgue by now, but hovering, waiting for his dismissal, having gathered up his sketch paper and pencils in readiness for Dr. Buchanan. Roumande asked him what was he still waiting for, then catching Hatton's eye as the boy left, added, "He has a real skill, Adolphus. He listens, is keen, and he has a great knowledge of herbs, which is useful when embalming. All of this combined together with a drive for self-improvement makes for a real possibility. In short, he's worth my attention and I can forgive a couple of foibles. His timekeeping is not the best. But he's young and I think, perhaps, has a sweetheart who's distracting him from the morgue."

"Mrs. McCarthy's maid, I suspect. I noticed a little romance when I was at the widow's house."

"Really, Professor? He's said nothing to me."

"Well, it didn't go unnoticed that Patrice fared far better than me at White Lodge. His slice of soda bread was definitely the thicker."

Roumande shook his head in sympathy. "Women, Adolphus.

They're all the same. But there's no arguing with Patrice's obvious charms. Everyone loves a handsome face."

Outside the mortuary, a fight had broken out. Glasses were being smashed and someone was shouting, "She ain't dead yet, I tell you! Not till I've finished with 'er!"

Hatton ignored the fracas. *Nothing to do with me*, he thought, and went over to his desk and poured himself a glass of porter, which he knocked back because it pained him to think the word, less so say it. Despite the work the surgeons had done, he knew another's beauty was . . . no, he couldn't say the word the surgeons used. He couldn't say "ruined."

"A penny for your thoughts, Adolphus?"

"My thoughts?" Hatton answered.

"You seemed far away. Were you thinking on a romance of your own, perhaps?"

"Nothing of the kind, I can assure you."

Changing the subject as delicately as he could, Roumande asked, "How long do you think it will be before they force a confession?"

Hatton shrugged. "All I know is there's nothing I can do for that boy, is there?"

"No, Adolphus. A broken hand is not a pretty sight, but it will be nothing compared to what will happen to him if the boy is guilty of either murder or sedition."

Hatton knew what murder meant. *Hanging. The hanging of a twelve-year-old boy.* It didn't bare thinking of. The law was an arse when it came to the punishment of children and the authorities disgusted him. But he kept this thought to himself, as he said, "Let's finish off here," his eyes hot, stinging as he continued. "The evidence bags contain some rosary beads which Inspector Grey believes belonged to the first deceased. Another contains some ribbons, found in the bindery."

"Gabriel McCarthy's rosary beads? But Professor, why didn't you say so in the first place?"

"They're significant to the case, Albert, but after almost three weeks, their forensic worth will be negligible. But I want to examine them carefully. There might just be something—" He turned the viewing rods. "I can clearly see smudges of something, which appears to be . . . glue." Another twist. "Yes, glue. There's plenty in a bindery, of course."

Hatton knew no Latin prayers, nor did he want to, but that didn't mean he couldn't admire the polished mahogany. But the silver cross was tarnished and the figure of Christ seemed anguished to him. "There's no mucus, no spittle, no poison or blood. There's nothing that would prove this item was linked to the murder in a court of law. Perhaps the boy's telling the truth and just found them as he said he had, but Sorcha said her husband rarely went to St. Giles except . . ."

"Except what, Adolphus?"

"To pray . . . she said they sometimes went to pray at Father O'Brian's church. So Gabriel McCarthy could, conceivably, have dropped them. We know he was a man under strain, overworked, took laudanum, and absentmindfulness is a curse of being middle aged and McCarthy was forty-five. On his way to senility."

Roumande laughed. "Thank you very much, Adolphus, for I am forty-five, but," the Frenchman displayed his chipped and yellowing enamel, "I still have my own teeth, monsieur *le Professeur*."

"*Touché.*"

"My pleasure, but for a case like this, the jury will be under pressure to convict someone, anyone in fact who fits the bill, and the boy practically had it in his hands. The beads alone will convict him."

"But it's shaky evidence and purely circumstantial. I could argue, if it comes to it, that the lack of any trace of poison or bodily fluids points to the boy's innocence. But I'm clutching at straws. I'll write up the conclusions anyway, as quickly as I can. After the case is finally closed, I have promised to give them back to Mrs. McCarthy. She's eager to see them and have them blessed again, before she has them put in the crypt with her dead husband. But perhaps I'll show them to her anyway. The sight of her husband's treasured beads might restore her a little and give her comfort that we will find the killer."

Roumande was about to say that was an excellent idea but there was a tap, tap, tap at the door.

"Can I interrupt you please, my dear Adolphus? It's your miraculously cured and very grateful patient."

Hatton rushed toward him and steered the elder man to a chair with "Good afternoon, Dr. Buchanan, sir."

"Well, I just wanted to thank you for the work Patrice has done on all the pictures. And to show you the results, so far. He's an excellent illustrator and delightful company. We've had some rare old jokes, he and I, about the dunking of those Garibaldi biscuits. It's so nice to have a little youth about the place and someone to chat with. Oh, and by the way, Grey's waiting for you in the Great Hall. I left him looking at our other paintings. The Hogarths and the Reynoldses? Dear oh dear. I'm rambling a little . . ."

"Not at all, Dr. Buchanan, but let me get you something. A cup of tea, or a drop of porter, perhaps?"

"No, no. I only dropped by to show you this."

Dr. Buchanan fumbled with a little leaflet and handed it to Hatton. "There's another symposium tomorrow with countless guests arriving from the New World, again." He rubbed his belly. "But I will be most particular when it comes to dinner, I can tell you. So, Professor, can I leave you to deal with Scotland Yard?"

Out of the corner of his eyes Hatton could see Roumande on the far side of the mortuary, legs crossed, reading glasses on, and flicking through the pages of one of the botany books—the new one they'd got—the tome called *British, European and New World Flora*.

"I'll see to it directly, Dr. Buchanan, and Godspeed to you, sir. A simple supper, an early night will soon see you firmly on your feet again, and more than able to deal with our American colleagues."

"They are mainly Canadian," answered Buchanan. "But they all sound the same don't they? Brutalizing our mother tongue with their sloppy vowels and swallowed adjectives? Still, they are keen on funding typhus work, so I must be charm itself and enunciate on their behalf." A sudden thought struck him. "Perhaps, Professor, you might even be able to join us? For the dinner, I mean. They are nearly all cholera experts from the Nun's Hospital in Montreal, and would enjoy a chat on the statistical data you've gathered. Mr. Farr will also be there. You could sit next to him."

Hatton couldn't believe his luck. To sit next to Mr. Farr, at dinner? He felt suddenly galvanized and so thanked Buchanan profusely and, taking the beads, quickly rushed to the ward to see Sorcha who was half asleep, half awake. He lay his hand gently on hers, as her fingers responded, knowing it was him. Her eyes fluttered open and widened, as she saw her husband's beads.

"Look, Sorcha. Look what we've found."

She murmured something, as Hatton helped her sit up a little. She took the beads, shut her eyes, whispered what must have been a prayer, before clasping the beads tight to her breast, "How can I ever thank you? But where on earth did you find them, because I looked everywhere. Literally, everywhere."

"A boy had them, said he found them in St. Giles . . ."

"St. Giles? He found them in St. Giles? So they were dropped then, or discarded by someone. So the killer must live in the rookeries?"

Hatton tucked a loose lock of her hair behind her ear, kissed her lightly on the cheek. "You're tired, you must rest, and the beads are evidence, so I can't let you keep them yet . . . I just wanted you to know that you will be able to bury them soon. It won't be long now, I promise you."

"So you think you are closing the case? You have the killers in sight?"

He couldn't promise her, so he just said, "We're doing everything we possibly can, and for some reason, I feel, yes, we're getting close."

She smiled. "But can I keep them for a day, at least? They're all I have left of my husband."

Hatton shook his head. "I'm so sorry, Sorcha. If it was solely up to me, of course, but they're police property and must be returned to the morgue immediately. We need to keep studying these beads, look and look again. That is the nature of forensics. The beads are unique and sometimes what isn't obvious may suddenly—"

"Speak to you, Adolphus? Like my dead husband's voice, telling you something. *Mortui vivos docent*? The dead will teach the living." She smiled, pressed the cross to her lips, and gave the beads back to him.

Grey was standing with his hands on his hips, looking up at an enormous Hogarth—*The Pool of Bathsheba*—which hung in the spectacular entrance to the Great Hall of St. Bart's. Unimpressed by the lurid paint, the gilt baroque didacticism of this English Master, he simply pulled a face and turning said, "Professor Hatton. Where the devil have you been? I've been waiting for some full fifteen minutes in this place. So, have you made any progress on the evidence I gave you?"

"I'm sorry, but the ribbons you found in the bindery are not the same. They are his mother's perhaps, or have been dropped by one of the sewing women? And apart from a little binding glue, the beads are clean and, forensically speaking, found such a long time after the murder was committed as to be almost worthless."

"And what about this fingerprinting thing?"

"Roumande has tried and tried again, but we need to be sure of the method before we can apply it in court. It's tricky to get right and not yet accurate enough."

"Well, keep at it," said Grey. "I was just passing, on my way to make an arrest. The boy has croaked, but only about the bomb. Seems it was a gang thing, as I thought, but he's adamant that the ribbon murders are nothing to do with them."

"*Them,* Inspector?"

"Ribbonmen, of course. Three, to be precise—Father O'Brian, which we suspected, Damien McCarthy, whatever he says to the contrary, and a hack called John O'Rourke who lives somewhere in the rookeries."

"A man called O'Rourke? So, does he know Hecker? Gabriel McCarthy? Is he from Ardara, as well?"

"Not sure, although I've since found out that O'Brian is from the far south. But if I could spare the details, right now, for I'm in desperate need of morphine. My arm is giving me terrible gyp. Have you any, Hatton?"

Hatton's lip curled. "First of all, when can I see the boy?"

"The prisoner, you mean? I feel he will be a considerable as-set over the next few hours. But perhaps it's his medical condition you're asking about?"

Hatton lowered his voice and stepped forward, face-to-face with the inspector. "I still can't believe what I saw. I'll make you pay for what you did to that child, whether he's guilty or not."

Grey's face was stony. "You're a fool, Hatton, but I put my country before the hand of a bomber. And I don't have to justify myself to you because what are you, after all? One small step up from a butcher?"

"I'd rather be a butcher than a torturer."

"Perhaps you would have preferred if I had gone up in the blast?"

"No, Inspector. I believe in mercy."

"Mercy? Yes, well, it's a noble idea," said Grey. "Well, per-haps the judge will show some when it comes to court. Send the boy to Australia instead of the gallows. Anyway, which way to get the morphine, did you say? And I need a new syringe. I ap-pear to have lost mine. Fingersmith's been in The Yard, again. Nice silver case? You haven't see it, have you, Hatton?"

But Hatton had already started to walk away, as he heard the inspector shouting after him, "Very well. You win. You want to see the boy? He's in the wagon outside waiting for the others to join him. So, are you coming, Hatton? Or are you just going to do what you usually do and sulk?"

22

SOHO

Father O'Brian knew his time in London was drawing to a close. His bag was already packed, hidden under a half tester bed and containing a few soiled shirts, a prayer book, a purple chasuble, a pouch of gunpowder. To his right, a note on a side table, inviting him to join a Mission in Newfoundland, where word was there'd been another cholera outbreak in some god-awful place called the Avalon Peninsula. *Canada*, he told himself, *will do for now.* He fumbled inside his pocket, checking he still had the ticket for his escape—a third-class berth on a clipper that was leaving from the Isle of Dogs tomorrow.

Taking his rosary beads, he left the house and went out into the church, where a thin line of light streamed in through a window, illuminating the nave in a pattern of burnt orange, pale blue, and hazy yellow. All was quiet, empty, as the priest moved toward the altar and knelt in prayer, then briefly looked over his shoulder as he heard, *nearer and nearer,* the thundering of horses, men shouting, the blowing of whistles. No time to waste, he was off his knees and out. No bag grabbed, just into the rookeries, turning right, turning left, turning right. His face, a pool of sweat as a woman pulled him into an alleyway and whispered, "This way, Father."

Out the back of the reeking tenancy block, jumping over rubbish, dead cats, upturned dogs and moving south toward the river where a sympathetic boatman, loyal to the cause, was ready to take the priest away. The backup plan in case things went belly up, as they clearly had. A quick push of the skiff and they were off.

"Put your back into it. Hurry up, man. My life's at stake here."

"Keep your head down till we're just past Limehouse, then another will take you to Folkestone and then to the open sea, Father. It's all arranged. We've been waiting for you."

"Too obvious. Take me to the border of Essex and I'll travel by foot from there. And in case Mr. O'Rourke sends word, just tell him I'm heading north till the land runs out."

"Always your obedient servant, so I am, Father."

The priest lay sweating under a thin layer of tarpaulin, listening to the river sounds. Far off, the harsh yell of a waterman. Above him, soaring gulls, squabbling over a scrap of something. Beneath the skiff, a river swell gently rocking him and then a great wash from side to side as the boat hit flotsam.

When the three men arrived at the Sacred Heart, the place was already empty. A vast echoing church, bereft of all life, except a white veil of light streaming through an ornate window from the bustling world outside.

"The priest's flown, but we'll nab the next one, I promise you that," said Grey after searching in the nave, the confessional box, the sacristy and coming out, brandishing a Crimean pistol and a torn handbill—"*Down with the British—Tiocfaidh ár lá . . .*"

"So they were at the riot?" said Hatton, from where he was crouched with Roumande.

"Looks that way, doesn't it? Likely, they were behind it," answered Grey, looking down the barrel of the gun.

But there was no silver nitrate anywhere in the church or the priest's cottage, his potting shed, the privy—just an old stop-watch wrapped in a worn piece of calico which they found under a bed.

"Are you taking prints, then?" asked the inspector.

Hatton looked up from underneath one of the benches, because it was his turn to try the method. But this technique required time, precision, tenaciousness, and Roumande nudged him to say the clock was ticking.

"Just leave it. Come on," yelled Grey, taking a sharp right out of the church, then charging toward Monmouth Street, where the boy had said they'd find the journalist, pushing through the crowds with his good arm, the other two behind him, to reach the main throng of the Dials—a wilderness of alleyways. "A printers somewhere off Neal Street, the Tooley boy said. O'Rourke's there, most afternoons, apparently. He'd better be right or he'll hang for that as well."

The three men stopped, lost for a second, at the seven-point crossing of the Dials, where malodorous roads and threadbare people jostled with each other, but not more than a stone's throw from the Sacred Heart, as Grey jabbed a kid-gloved finger. "Mark my words, I'll have every house in the rookeries flattened if necessary. Don't worry, I'll find that priest. Meanwhile, down here I think . . ."

The beginning of St. Giles—the rookeries—a city within a city of herb sellers, organ grinders, crossing-sweepers, parrot dealers, leather makers, knife throwers, hawkers of stolen goods, diviners, soothsayers, table tappers, notorious Quacks, Papists, paupers, beggars, and even the odd Italian opera singer, but mainly Irish and seeds of revolution in the air.

At the end of what appeared to be an alleyway was a broken-down tavern. Under a wormy lintel, pistols at the ready, the men looked about them to see through the blue fug of tobacco smoke, a metal-topped bar to the right, a pox-faced landlord spitting on a glass, a small room stuffed to the gills with Irish, growls of Gaelic in the air, and beyond this, to the back, along a small corridor, as promised, the deafening noise of a printing press.

No stopping now.

"Police! Stand back. John O'Rourke . . . we know you're here . . . give yourself up, man . . ." Inspector Grey shouted above the roar, and without a gun to defend himself, O'Rourke, hearing his name, dived for the floor and tried to crawl underneath the printing machinery, but as he did, Hatton saw a massive boot come down. Somehow, someway, Tescalini had got here before them. But in the fray, O'Rourke wrenched himself free and, swooping past Hatton with a hard shove, made a dash for it.

"Don't let him get away. Shoot him in the back if necessary," yelled Grey.

Whistles blew, but O'Rourke was running as fast as he could away from "Stop that man!" Hatton turned on his heels and raced after him and up ahead could see copious stalls overflowing with crates of oranges and apples, as O'Rourke leapt over the fruit.

"Oi! What the devil!"

"Mind my bananas, you fool."

But the inspector was clever—very—having herded the journalist toward a blind alley and—twelve hours from now, maybe less—death by hanging.

They'd left the prisoners in a meat wagon, Hatton having done what he could for the boy, checking the wound, smoothing his hair, saying, "Shhh. Settle down now . . ." as the child begged, "You will come back, won't you, sir? Or they'll hang me, won't they, sir?" Hatton hung his head, feeling nothing but shame as he peeled the sobbing boy from his arms, with Roumande looking on, but knowing they could promise the boy nothing. The image of the boy's pale face pressed to the grill begging for mercy, and Mr. Tescalini with the reins in his hand, primed for a full gallop to Newgate, cracking the whip. An image that stayed with Hatton now, in the porch of White Lodge, and Grey said, "It's not pretty, granted, but I wanted to show you that my means have an end. Let's not forget that I'm pursuing the men who probably cost Mrs. McCarthy's face, as well as my arm."

Roumande turned away muttering a curse, as Hatton gazed for a second at the swifts as they curled overhead in aerial arches, flipping through the trails of cirrus which feathered the sky. The birds were scarcely visible but their cries hurtled over the rooftops, circled the hill and below Swain's Lane, whistled over the Necropolis. Hatton felt Roumande's hand on his arm. "We'll write for clemency, and there are others, Adolphus, many who won't let a twelve-year-old boy hang no matter what he has or hasn't done. We'll get a petition going. There's Harriet Martineau, Mr. Dickens, Mr. Gladstone . . ."

They were nice words, thought Hatton, as he watched the circling birds, but words were sometimes hard to visualize on a day like this, even harder to believe in.

Less than a minute and the inspector was back again. "It seems another of our birds has flown the nest, gentlemen. Someone must have tipped him off, but Damien McCarthy can't have gone far."

Hatton turned to him with, "There was nobody in the house, then?"

"The house is empty, but there are luggage bags in the hall, which points to flight and flight is guilt. According to that Tooley boy, there's a tunnel that runs from the bottom of the garden, toward the east gate of the Necropolis, which Damien used to hide maps, bomb-making stuff."

The three moved swiftly to the bottom of the garden, where the grasses were waist high and the air was filled with the whir of insects. The inspector strode through the parched garden talking to himself, "Spreading oak tree to the right, a dell of ash to the left, and then passing a bed of orange marigolds take fifteen paces forward, due north. One, two, three, four . . ." Then he stamped his foot near a sod of grass which seemed slightly flatter than the rest. "This is the place. It's just as the boy said it would be. There'll be a shaft below with a rope ladder. The tunnel begins here."

But as Hatton and Roumande stood at the opening of the shaft, there was something they could sense—something ethereal, something intangible but omnipresent—a life ebbing away or something dead already.

Peering down into a black bowel of a vertical shaft, Hatton pulled, but the rope, made of chord and plaited green silk, kept slipping out of his hands, giving him burn marks. Roumande helped but the weight at the end was swinging, heavy like a rock, hitting the shaft from side to side, sending pebbles, clods of earth flying. "Put your back into it, gentlemen," came a terse voice from behind. Hatton kept pulling, Roumande, too, and emerging into the light came what they already knew—Damien McCarthy, hung, his dead eyes swimming in blood, his face colorless, lifeless. Deep ligature marks on the neck, telling at once of the struggle before he was thrown down the shaft and hung.

Hauling the body onto the grass, Hatton knelt down to see black blood around the mouth. The victim had bitten his tongue, but as Hatton peered closer, a salty taste in his mouth of dread, something telling—was it forgiveness, the last rites, a full stop, the end coming?

Roumande said, "It's a cross. The sign of the cross, Adolphus. This one's been anointed, too, but why?"

But this smear of oil was obvious and pressed on the oil, for all the world to see, not a hint or a hue or a faint suggestion, but strands of orange petals, incandescent bursts of sunlight. Hatton put his ear to the man's lips to hear, with shock, the quietest gasp.

"Is he still alive?" asked Roumande.

"Only just, Albert," Hatton said as he pushed hard down on Damien's chest to grab him back to life. "Breathe for pity's sake, breathe." But it was wasted effort because Hatton knew already, *He's as good as gone*, but then a twitch at the corner of his blood-smeared mouth and a sound of *Sssshhhhh*.

"What's he saying? Is he saying something? And what the devil's he covered in?"

"I can barely hear him, Inspector. He's dying."

Grey pushed forward, pulling Roumande out of the way. "Let me speak to him. What's that?" Inspector Grey was shaking the man. "What are you saying, *Fffff*? *F* for Fenian? Or is it, Shhhhh? Are you saying a name? A place? What are you damn well saying?"

"He's gone, Inspector."

"Gone? My master's gone?"

But this was a woman's voice speaking, not the inspector's, and Hatton turned around to see the maid, Florrie, who'd stepped out of nowhere. "But what have they covered him in?" she asked, her eyes wide.

Hatton took a pair of tweezers and peeled a little bright sunset from the dusky pallor of the dead man. "They're petals. He's been decorated."

"And there's a bed of marigolds, here," said the inspector.

Hatton shook his head, rubbing one of the petals between finger and thumb. "No, these are a much bolder color." Hatton crouched down again by the body. "Whoever did this was mocking him because orange is a Protestant color. It's another religious symbol but telling us what?"

Florrie shook her head, biting her lip, as pale as death herself.

Grey said, "Have you something to tell us, Missy?"

Her hand back to her mouth to stifle a sob, she said, "I was at the top of the house when you came. I heard the knock and came to the front door only to see you. Yes, it must have been you, Inspector, disappearing into the garden. I hesitated for I wasn't sure I'd seen you at all. The mind plays tricks in this heat. Only a little while ago, I could have sworn I saw someone else moving toward the Necropolis, while I was hanging out the washing. But in a blink, the figure was gone."

"When was this?"

"Maybe ten minutes before you came. I swear the Necropolis is haunted and I had a mind that it was a spirit. I could feel something drawing me toward it, which is why I hid at the top of the house. My mistress was always talking about how someone was watching her. Watching over me, she said. She was mad in the heat, all cooped up, dreaming, talking to herself, saying she was suffocating, pacing the rooms, so very agitated. I think she was homesick, and she was definitely lonesome with her husband always at work. That's why the master encouraged her, you see."

"Encouraged her?"

Her voice came rapidly, as she was telling a secret, borne too long. "In her celebration of nature, sir. Why, didn't you know that madam loved to paint? Those flowers, they're not flowers at all. My mistress sketched a little scene which is hanging in the drawing room. She has them in the foreground. There's plenty more in the outhouse and we had a little laugh about the name when she finished them."

The rustic outhouse. The flowers that look a little like dandelions. Of course, thought Hatton.

The inspector was incredulous. "Your mistress painted these flowers?"

She bit her lip again. "Madam went on so many walks before the heat took hold. She'd come back covered in dust, cleavers stuck in her hair and only last month smeared in a rash of stingy nettles liked she'd gone tumbling in the meadows. She was a terrible sight and I asked her, madam, where have you been to be looking like that? 'Essex,' she said. 'Florrie. I've only been to Essex.' But she swore to me she was never alone, not for a minute. That she had a chaperone. That it was all perfectly proper, he was a visitor from the New World, but I wasn't to tell anyone."

"A chaperone? From the New World?"

Her lip curled. "At first she told me it was young Master Damien, but it wasn't. It was someone else, I knew it so I pressed her on it, but she wouldn't give me a name. She said it was none of my business."

"Just someone else, she said?"

She shrugged. "It can't have been Master Damien. He promised me he didn't. Swore to me he wouldn't." And as she said so, she was clearly about to cry.

"Come now," said the inspector. "Your master's gone and I'm sorry for it, but there's another man's life at stake, name of Gustave Pomeroy, if he's still alive, that is. You need to tell us about the flowers, missy."

She looked surprised at the question, as if the inspector was a fool not to know. "In Ireland we call them the Devil's Paintbrush because they grow like weeds." *Hawkweed,* thought Hatton. *The flowers are hawkweed. Of course.* "And to cover my poor master's face in them? It doesn't make sense to me. Now if you would please, ask me no more questions and step out of my way, sir."

And without a second glance at either of them, she lay bodily upon the dead man as if they were sweethearts, stroking his hair, kissing his face, his cheek, his lips as her sobs came low; a terrible, visceral gulping of "My poor, poor baby. My poor, poor angel. What the devil were they thinking of?" Tearstained, smoothing back his hair, she said, "Essex was where she went. I even know the village. Just beyond Greenwich, so not so far from here. This American had a skiff by all accounts and she threatened me that if I told anyone where she went or what she did, she would tell the whole village about me and the young master, here. Then sack me to boot and I'd lose my reputation as a good girl and never work again. So I bit my tongue. Told me to tidy up the room she did, after her husband died. Well, it's not right, is it?"

23

Hatton stood on the bend of a glorious river, bordered on one side by wavering hop fields scattered with hawkweed, and on the other side, across the water, the thickest of English woodland. But before that, an island—a hump of river sand covered in thickets of summer grasses, briars, cleavers, and the roots of ancient willows. Her image had clouded his mind, and for the last two weeks had clouded his judgment as well, so Hatton pushed her away. Whatever she'd done, he still loved her, if this sick awful feeling was love. He knew it was love of a kind, but was it drawing away. Horribly drawing away, like a tide on a beach. Love was slipping away from him, minute by minute.

In Highgate, before they'd called a carriage to leave, they'd looked high and low in the cemetery for a shadowy figure, but found nothing, just a feeling they were finally on a trail, an invisible trail of something ethereal, a shape in the air, a trace of something which had led them here.

Death stalked her, Sorcha had said. And now it stalked Hatton. It was calling him across the river.

Damien McCarthy's dying word began with *F. F* for Fenien?

Or was it *Sh*? *Sh* for ship, but the other word Hatton pushed away, like a bad penny. Because it couldn't be, could it? It couldn't be Sorcha, but the way Roumande had looked at him had said one word: guilty.

But what was she guilty of, he asked himself, because if she was a killer, she couldn't have murdered those men alone. It didn't make sense. But nothing made sense anymore, except to do what he always did when his back was against the wall—keep his nose to the grindstone and work. But as Hatton stood looking across the water, the shadow looming before him wasn't from the sun dripping the last drops of amber into the ripples of the river, but doubt. Black doubt, and Hatton knew that this was a time for action, not self-pity.

"Over here," said Hatton.

"I'll get the inspector," said Roumande in reply, heading up the beach to grab Inspector Grey, who appeared to be examining flowers near a hedgerow and picking the petals, one by one like a silly girl might do—*he loves me, he loves me not*. The inspector stopped picking the petals on seeing Roumande, stood up and said in a manly voice, "Do you think these petals might be evidence, monsieur?"

"This way," said Roumande.

Together, the three men uncovered a little rowing boat, which had been covered in branches, bracken, a sheet of tarpaulin. Hatton pushed the skiff into the topaz water.

Rain threatened and thunder stalked the sky, as the inspector leaned back in the skiff and said, "What on earth was she doing here? A respectable, married woman? Well," he corrected himself. "Hardly respectable, I fear . . ."

Yes, but why, thought Hatton? And who was this chaperone? There were American doctors who'd arrived only days ago to see Dr. Buchanan. Could there have been earlier guests? And hadn't Grey said, "*They're raising money in America, now.*" But a rebellion orchestrated by a twenty-year-old girl? It was too incredible. She was educated, passionate, yes, but to be involved in underground politics she needed cunning, stealth, and above all money. So, was the husband in her way? Did he suspect something? And what was Hecker to her? Hatton recalled that the inspector had said that the mill never stopped, that the man kept working all day and all night long, unless he had—"*a visit from the Queen or an exceptionally beautiful woman.*" So was Pomeroy the same? Though she denied ever knowing him, hadn't she made mention of visiting parishioners? She said she didn't like O'Brian, but did the priest help her, ease the way? But if that was the case, why didn't the boy make mention of her? And, more to the point, what the devil did she do to entice them? Hatton thought of their moments together—in the outhouse, the piano room, the garden—but her tenderness had felt so real.

Damn her.

Damn her to hell.

All these men were like flies to a honey trap, *including me,* thought Hatton, *fool that I am.*

Was this thinking, mad? Was it insane? That Sorcha was some sort of political rebel? The cancer within the very heart of The Union? It just didn't sit well, because when women murdered, it was someone close to them, something personal—a husband, a lover. Not politics.

As he rowed, Hatton's mind raced around the possibilities, but not another word was said by anyone till the men reached the island to find another beach, the color of platinum, and a dusty path leading into a density of thickets, littered with mussel shells, crushed nettles, flattened grasses, and . . .

"Look up ahead, Professor."

Half in and out of the water, on the other side of the island, hidden from view at first, by the overgrown bracken, the high trees—a shipwreck.

There were no masts, there was no one on the rigging, no smell of turpentine or shanty songs singing, but this ship had definitely been a clipper once. Not a brig or a frigate, but *a clipper.*

And even though she was a washed-up thing, a marine fossil, a beached whale—somewhere, lingering, was just a hint of what she might have been. Like the image on the signet ring, still alluring and exciting. Half of her was gone, her skeleton shape made primordial with river slime—but in her prime, Hatton knew she would have been maybe eighty feet long and thirty feet wide, hurtling across breezy oceans, newly painted, brass fittings polished like diamonds, and down below, the hold stuffed to the gill with rum, sugar, wheat, turpentine, coal, spices, or . . .

Men and women?

Was this one of Mr. Hecker's ships? But that was impossible, wasn't it? Because the mill owner's fleet had sailed on a mercy mission from Donegal to America—hadn't it?

Inspector Grey must have read his mind. He held his hand over his eyes to shield the sun. "I recognize the name on the side of the ship. Do you see it? *The Best of British*. There's a romanticized painting in the office at the mill. Not the huge Millais painted in Ardara, but a smallish thing, used to disguise his safe. One of my officers noticed it later, and not very original, I must say, to hide your money that way. But if this was one of Hecker's vessels, then how the devil did the ship end up here? In Essex? Wouldn't it be in America or Canada?"

"Not necessarily. The vessels came back to England, didn't they? And as far as any name's concerned, I'm afraid it's you who's imagining things, this time, Inspector. There's no name. It's a prison hulk, or what's left of it, anyway. Or an old hospital ship, like the *Dreadnought*. There are plenty of wrecks, further along toward the coast and upriver in Greenwich."

Grey shook his head, squinting. "I could have sworn . . ."

"It doesn't matter either way. Come on . . . hurry . . ." said Roumande, using an old rope ladder to clamber up the side.

And he was right because the ship was empty now, a hollow cask. The echo of her cargo, long silenced. Hatton pulled himself up onto the deck, panting for breath in the terrible heat, and ahead of him, a hatch fastened with a rusty padlock. There were flies in the air—a black buzzing veil. Roumande began spluttering, spitting them out, waving them aside. Grey was bent over the side, being sick, then turned around, his kerchief pressed to his mouth as Hatton stood firm. But as he bent down, he swallowed hard, because in terms of stinks, this was a record. Fighting back his own stomach, he tried the hatch. "It's locked."

"Get back, Adolphus," said Roumande, who was a size thirteen and a half. Hatton did as he was told and his friend brought his boot down. *Bang.* By which time Grey had recovered himself. "Something's cooked in the weather. Wouldn't you say so, Professor?" Pushing past, disappearing into the hold with, "I need light, here. Quickly . . ."

Against a flickering candle, Monsieur Pomeroy was sitting upright on a stool. Jutting out between the torn material, a razor sharp rib, a wiry elbow, and in his yawn, a tongue covered in, "What's this? His last supper?"

Maggots crawled out of the dead man's eyeballs, squirmed under his fingernails.

But Hatton simply beckoned for the lantern. "It's grass, Inspector. Mixed with Indian corn, and here, do you see, this stain's from a blackberry."

"What sort of diet is this?"

"A famine diet. Grass, corn, and a berry, if you're lucky. But if you look at the tongue and the cuts around his mouth . . ." Hatton pulled the mouth further open, using the tip of a scalpel. "There's a couple of teeth shattered. Someone's been force-feeding him. Little by little, like torture but not enough to sustain him. He's starved to death down here . . ."

The chef had been bound to his chair with a crisscross of emerald ribbons, and beyond the putrefying corpse, Hatton could see lined up on a worktop, a number of bowls and a jug filled to the brim with pencils, brushes, and quills. As the hold flickered into light, it looked like a church—a place of worship for a Dark Ages anchorite. And fastened to a beam with a nail, a picture of a girl, on the cusp of life, with blood-red hair plaited with the brightest of green ribbons. Behind her, not the hop fields of Essex, but mountains, gushing falls, and agate forests. And nearer in the foreground, a place of graves, Celtic crosses, a little church, verdant meadows dotted with the wildest of orange flowers.

"What have we here?" said Inspector Grey, bending down and helping himself to a littering of pastel-colored recipe cards. "*Ardara, Donegal, October 1847.* This particular recipe is for cooking Indian corn, and signed," the policeman cleared his throat and spoke as if he was addressing an audience, "*On Behalf of the British Government Emergency Feeding Plan by Monsieur Gustave Pomeroy.* So, how long's he been dead, do you think?"

"It's difficult to tell in this place. His body's begun to decay, sped up by this weather, which is why the stomach has popped. This gas is dangerous, noxious, so be careful, gentlemen. But I'll need to do an autopsy back at the morgue to tell you anything more definitive."

Roumande leaned over the body, his hand over his mouth, but his voice strong and clear, "What about the mites, Adolphus?"

The mites, of course, thought Hatton. The maggots in the cadaver were fat, ready to burst themselves, added to which there were already flies in the air, meaning they'd started hatching only days ago. Maggots presented themselves in three squirming stages before they metamorphosed into these revolting fliers.

"Roumande's right," he said, flitting a fly away. "This is larvae from blowflies that live on the dead and take nine days to hatch. The flies wouldn't have found the corpse immediately, locked down here, suggesting his time of death was probably about two weeks ago. So yes, the stink, the state of the body and the mites suggests to me he's been dead two weeks, which would have timed Pomeroy's death perfectly for the anniversary of . . ."

"Drogheda." Grey's voice was flat in the fetid air. "Suggesting our killers know a great deal about nutrition . . ."

No, thought Hatton, not nutrition—something else. Something much closer to home. Something anatomical—this killer knows the workings of the human body.

"So why didn't they hoist this poor man up on a mast," said the inspector, his kerchief still pressed to his nose. "Or move the chef to Piccadilly? Put him somewhere, anywhere, if it was *a point* the gang were making? They left him here, in this lonely place—"

"Maybe the gang were intent upon the bomb, as the boy said, and the murder of Monsieur Pomeroy was something else entirely . . ."

"Not connected? What do you mean by that?"

"Has it occurred to you," said Hatton, "that the bombers aren't necessarily the Ribbonmen?"

"Who, then?" demanded Grey. "If not them, bloody well who, then?"

Roumande was over on the other side of the hold by now, rattling and opening drawers.

"What does every ship have?" he asked, his voice sounding disembodied in the gloom.

"Masts," said Grey, through the flickering darkness.

"A captain?" answered Hatton still intent upon the body, digging for worms, scraping the skin with his scalpel, checking under Pomeroy's fingernails.

"A log? There must be one somewhere because every ship has a log, dammit," Roumande said, moving his hand around to find a couple more paintbrushes among ancient rat droppings and, "Could this be a log, Inspector?"

The book was black, covered in dust, torn leather, musty pages. With bated breath, Roumade opened it, to see a world forgotten. With each flick of the page—the currents of the winds, the movements of the stars, stores taken aboard and jettisoned, their type and quantity. "We're in luck. It's definitely a ship's log," said Roumande. "But not from this clipper, but an old vessel called *The Liberty*, which sailed to a place called Isle de Coudres off the coast of Canada, ten years ago, from Ardara, Donegal."

Hatton was thinking of that comment in the garden—*a cousin in Canada, she'd said*—as Roumande read, "First Entry, December 12, 1848. *The Liberty*. Destination, Isle de Coudres, Canada. Ship's Owner, . . . Jesus . . ." he stumbled, then quickly repeated, "Ship's Owner: T. W. Hecker. Cargo: Turpentine. Passengers: Four hundred and twenty. State and Condition of the Crew and Company: Fit to Travel. It's signed by the Portside Physician."

Grey's voice—"Cat got your tongue? Who was the damn doctor?"

Roumande tore a page from the logbook and shoved it at Hatton—"His name is clear and there's no mistake, Adolphus, because his signature's a hand we see quarterly. His obsession is infectious diseases—smallpox, typhus, cholera . . ."

Hatton knew at once, as he read, "'*Fit to Travel—signed by the portside physician—Dr. Algernon Buchanan.*'"

"Buchanan is next . . ." Hatton said the words plainly but inside he reeled. The sick bowl? The retching? There must have been grains of arsenic or some other kind of poison in the vomit, but he'd missed it, so intent was he on helping the man. "I thought it was food poisoning."

Grey grabbed the logbook. "What the devil are you two talking about?"

"We need to go. We need to go, right now."

"Wait." Roumande wrestled the logbook back. "Good job you're wearing your lavender gloves, Inspector. Daylight's better for my purposes, and if *The Liberty* is at the heart of things, then maybe . . . just maybe . . . one hard piece of forensic evidence . . . what do you think, Adolphus? Is there time to spare?"

"Do it," said Hatton, because one piece of forensic evidence would be enough to tell him for sure what was becoming horribly clear. The terrible stomach cramps, the vomiting, the clammy skin, the man's sore throat. It wasn't the salmon that caused poor Dr. Buchanan's illness last night. And that speech of his—

"It covers all my most groundbreaking moments, from the very early days, as a younger man sleeves rolled up and investigating typhus along the coast, to my latest and most important crusade, which as you know is the smallpox inoculation program for workhouse children."

The coast? The coasts of England were fair-weather places, where patients were sent to recover their health, but the beaches of Ireland must have been another place entirely. Littered with the dying.

"I believe Dr. Buchanan worked in Ireland, along the coast in Donegal. Perhaps he knew Gabriel McCarthy and the others and was part of this works committee. And the key to that picture at the mill wasn't the land, Inspector. It was *the sea* . . . always, the sea. The ship on the signet ring, this logbook, a wreck on an island, four hundred twenty passengers signed fit to travel? Hecker's vessels were used for emigration, but did they go willingly? And what happened on the ship? *The Liberty?* Did it even reach Canada? And somebody gave him a duck, Inspector. A Canadian duck . . . a wigeon, of all things . . . an anonymous gift, from a grateful patient, he said . . ."

The inspector was incredulous. "That wretched duck? Last seen quaking in the hospital fountain? What on earth has that poor creature got to do with any of this?"

Well, wasn't it obvious, thought Hatton, but he only said, "Quack. Somebody's calling London's leading physician a quack. A liar, a swindler, a fraud, a fake. He must have been there on the beaches in Donegal when the ships sailed. He signed a paper saying over four hundred men, women, and children were fit to travel, but what if they were nothing of the kind? They must have been sick, malnourished, covered in lice, dying already, then crammed in the hold, like animals."

The inspector lit a cigarillo. "Like a fucking slave ship, Hatton."

"We need to find out what happened to *The Liberty*. Thirty pieces of silver? The gombeen betrayed those people, but how? I need to find Buchanan, if he's still alive, and ask him."

Roumande was still on deck above them, as Grey spoke, "Some of the ships that sailed to America were nicknamed 'coffin ships.' I never thought much of it at the time. Just the Irish up to their blarney again, I thought, with ridiculous stories about how they were dying on them."

"Coffin ships? These people didn't go willingly, *did they*, Inspector? Are the Fenians right? Were these people forced from the land and sent to their deaths, knowingly? Was the government involved in trying to wipe out a race, just like the article says it was? Is that why these men were punished? A country-wide attempt to rid Ireland of its own people, starting with the weakest people, the hungriest, the most remote, the least able to protect themselves—starting with Ardara?"

"One piece of hard forensic evidence is what I need, Hatton—not supposition—just one piece, that's all I'm—"

A beaming face appeared upside down at the entrance of the hold.

"Don't tell me your chief diener isn't a genius. Senility, indeed? I'll give you senility, Professor. I have a print, as clear as clear can be . . ."

Roumande jumped down into the hold, the logbook, his personal triumph, which he pushed into the astonished men's faces. "Herschel was right, Adolphus. Less powder, less ink, a finer brush, flypaper, lay it absolutely flat, press down with an eraser and thus . . ."

Hatton moved the lamp over to examine the virgin piece of paper, with the replicated print to see—two double loops, a tented arch, and a whorl, almost falling off the tip of the finger denoting . . . what was it? An artistic temperament, loyalty, passion. Hatton and Roumande looked at each other.

"So," said the inspector. "You have a print. Excellent. Now you just need to match it to one of my prisoners and I think we have more than enough evidence to ensure that even you, Adolphus, will sleep well tonight. You'll not mind the banging of the gibbet for that wretched boy, will you? You'll close your eyes and slumber like a baby, in the full knowledge that I was right."

"You're wrong," said Hatton, flicking through the ancient pages, looking for a name to match the print—once and for all—and as he did a green ticket flittered to the floor. The inspector picked it up. "Half a shilling, all the way to Canada. A regular bargain, I'd say. Perhaps Mr. Mahoney sold the tickets? Many did, along the beaches from where the coffin ships left. What do you mean, I'm wrong?"

"The murderer isn't one of your prisoner's, Inspector, because this print, I'm afraid, we know."

"It's that widow, isn't it? She's as guilty as sin," said the inspector. "Shame to hang a lovely thing like her, but I'm afraid she's up to her neck in it." As the inspector spoke, he moved a flickering candle toward the watercolor. "So what about this girl in the picture here? A passenger? Known to Sorcha McCarthy, perhaps? A sister? A cousin? I can just about read . . . here, look . . . I think it says, Kitty."

Katherine. His sister's name was Katherine—Kitty. The sister who was dead when the farm failed. It wasn't Provence. It was Ireland.

Hatton ran his finger down the passenger list and quickly found "Kitty O'Shaughnessy, a twelve-year-old orphan traveling with her younger brother. Age eight, name of Paddy. *Paddy meaning Patrick . . .*" Of course, but then why Sorcha? What were they to each other? Was he the cousin in Canada with his stories of fishing, bear hunting, log cabins? Did he get on that ship, as an orphan? Grow up in Canada, and alter his name? Adopt a French accent? It was possible.

Hatton took the picture down from the beam and traced the young girl's name, thinking, *Kitty, Kitty O'Shaughnessy.* "We have the fingerprint—clear and distinctive—and we know where to match it. And I can give you more than one piece of evidence, Inspector. I'll test the brushes at St. Bart's, but I bet five guineas I'll find traces of poison in the pots. Strychnine is made from nux-vomica—a plant—which will have been mixed here into a paste, and I suspect we'll find arsenic as well, which as you know brings on terrible stomach cramps and mirrors cholera. And syringes are two a penny in a hospital."

"The killer works in a hospital?"

"I'll explain everything on the way, Inspector, but we need to leave here as quickly as possible. Dr. Buchanan survived last night but he won't survive another."

The carriage hurtled back to London.

Inspector Grey popped a candied opium into his mouth. "You pick up this apprentice of yours and I'll head for the docks, because I'm willing to bet right this minute O'Brian's trying to get out of England. Maybe sail to America. But not on my watch, Hatton, and not while Disraeli's on my back. Even if Patrice is the ribbon killer, O'Brian's the bomber."

"Whatever you say, Inspector." Hatton and Roumande looked at each other as Grey jumped from the carriage at the corner of Salmon Lane. "I want you to check in hourly with The Yard, understand? Mark any telegram urgent. Somebody will find me. Good luck—"

And the inspector was gone, disappearing into a throng of ship cranes, loading barrels, muscle-bound stevedores.

But Hatton had only one thought in his head. Buchanan. It was seven o'clock in the evening now, giving the poor man, what? A few hours at the most, if he was in the last stages of arsenic poisoning or maybe this time, thought Hatton, the killer would do something quicker. Like a slam to the back of the head with a hammer? Or a grab from behind, as Dr. Buchanan left the hospital, an old man, unsteady on his feet. The killer was strong, mendacious, and clever. A jaunty, "How the devil are you, monsieur?" *A twist of the arm, a slice to the jugular. Over.*

"I'll go straight to the morgue, Adolphus. I might yet catch him there."

"Good thinking, Albert. I'll try Buchanan's office."

Roumande charged to the North Wing, and Hatton made his way quickly along the South Wing corridors to find the door to Buchanan's office was shut. Hatton put his ear to the door, readying himself. Utter silence. He turned the handle with a dull click and pushed the door slowly to see the wood-paneled room. His eyes scouring a well-swept fireplace, a side table littered with a small collection of stethoscopes, and in the center of the room, a Persian carpet, a large teak desk covered in . . . feathers . . . blood-soaked feathers. The duck's blank eyes, yellow slits; its head decapitated and left on the desk amidst a pool of dark blood, and written in the blood, amongst the abandoned coffee cups and biscuit crumbs—*Quackkk*.

Hatton sat down at the desk and saw splayed out in front of him Dr. Buchnan's treasured article for the October edition of *The Lancet*. He slumped in the chair and read quickly all of Buchanan's personal history. His inoculation program for work house children, his endless papers on typhus victims, and his so-called groundbreaking work on cholera. The research done at a place Hatton knew. *Funded by the Works Committee, Ardara, Donegal, July 1847.*

Analyzing as it did, estimated infectious disease levels among those deemed suitable for urgent emigration, as laid out in HM government's Gregory Clause. When these people boarded *The Liberty*, they were dying already, he thought. Hatton peered at one of the Wedgwood coffee cups to see thick grains—so easily disguised as sugar—but it wasn't sugar, was it?

"Open up!"

"No need to bang so hard, Professor. I'm coming." Roumande peeled the door open, bleary-eyed and rubbing the back of his head.

"My God. Was he here? Was he just here? Jesus, Albert. Have we missed him? Which way did he go?"

Roumande made a groaning sound. "We won't catch him, Adolphus, unless we know where he's going. He's not traveling by foot and I've been out like a light for a good ten minutes, but I suppose I should be grateful he didn't kill me. Yes, he was here . . . waiting behind the door, then gone in a flash. And all this is my fault."

"Your fault? What are you talking about? Never mind all that, Albert. Arsenic is easily scraped from flypaper. You said it yourself, didn't you? That we're practically eating the stuff? That's how he's poisoning Dr. Buchanan. Right under our noses, scraping off the flypaper and putting arsenic in the coffee, whilst he sketched the poor man in his office among the biscuits, the tea, the silver pot, making jokes—all the time smiling and watching him die." Hatton looked at his friend who was ashen, about to collapse at any minute. "Sit down here, Albert, before you fall down," Hatton said, as he unraveled the watercolor from the shipwreck. "We should have known, because look—it's drawn in exactly the same style as the girl we have hanging on the wall. *Sleeping Beauty?*"

Hatton smoothed the picture flat, his thoughts whizzing around his head, but as he said it, he knew he was right. Patrice was the killer. There wasn't any doubt. And the fingerprint was enough to send him to the gallows.

"The print, Roumande. Where is it?"

Roumande rubbed the back of his head. "That's why he hit me. He's taken the logbook, too. One last sitting, Dr. Buchanan begged only this morning, out of the city somewhere, saying the evening light is best for portraits and I encouraged it. Oh, and he might be a killer but he's not without a sense of humor. He's took the fingerprint right out of my hand but left the beads with a note, addressed to me." Roumande took a sip of porter, and rubbed his head, read, "*To Monsieur Albert Roumande, For Your Own Learning and Erudition, Sir*—and see here, he's marked page one hundred and twenty-three of the *New World Flora* book." Roumande sighed, put his head in his hands. "Do you think I'm getting old, Adolphus?"

"Of course not. Why, just look at the way you shimmied up the rigging . . ."

"Naive, then? Foolish?"

"No, no, Albert."

"It's kind of you to say so, but . . ." Roumande rose from his chair and staggered over to the trestle table. "Put the beads under the Zeiss, Adolphus, but I already know my knowledge was there all the time, right at the back of my head, I just didn't file it properly. We have an old dresser which was my wife's. Came with us from Paris, years ago, and mahogany has a distinct burnish to it. The wood of the rosary beads isn't the same at all. It's a type of slow-growing cedar."

"You're bleeding, Albert."

"Bleeding? Am I?" Roumande didn't seem to care. "Knowledge of botany was a clue, but not the flowers or the hops. It was the beads, always the beads." And at once, Hatton realized that Sorcha's insistence on getting them back had been verging on the desperate—the surest sign of guilt.

Hatton checked the reference book. "You're right. The molecular pattern matches almost exactly, a coastal Canadian Red Wood. *Sequoia sempervirens.* These beads are from Canada, and though Patrice was born in Ireland, in 1848, he sailed to the New World on *The Liberty,* and found himself on Isle de Coudre where he grew up, grew bold, learned a new language—a perfect disguise—and armed with the logbook, made his way back to England."

Roumande laughed at his own idiocy, then said, *"Ouch,"* still rubbing his head, continuing, "The islands of eastern Canada are full of disease, brought to the portsides by immigrants, and it occurred to me, even before I took that print on the shipwreck, that Patrice was very reluctant to do the fingerprinting and . . ."

But all Hatton could think was, *she knew.* She knew all the time, she helped him, and that's why Patrice was always hovering around her hospital bed, asking Hatton questions as to her welfare. They were cousins.

"And the Irish went to Canada during the famine, didn't they? Irish orphans, spread across Canada like a stain, and along the way they were helped by French families, other Catholics, who live near the Lawrence. It seems so obvious, in retrospect."

Roumande nodded. "He said he was from Provence, but that accent of his? It was so polished off. It was almost Parisian in its intonation, but then, again, not so. The girls and I teased him about it. But now I know he smoothed it down for a purpose—"

Just like me, thought Hatton, who once had a thick country accent, but had rubbed it away, keen to get up the next step of the ladder and blend into the melee that was London Society.

Roumande looked so disappointed. "Was I blind?"

"Yes, Albert. We were both blind. You wanted to think the best of him, a young man full of zest and a real interest in forensics, who you welcomed into your family. And I was blinded by her. His first French words were probably learned on one of the islands. His name was Patrick O'Shaughnessy and at age eight he sailed on *The Liberty* to Isle de Coudres, the French-speaking part of Canada. Something happened on that ship which haunted him, haunted his victims, too. That's why they let him in, offered him a drink. He either won their trust somehow, or they simply recognized him and were guilt-ridden."

"Patrice was the visitor? And she paved the way?"

Hatton nodded. "He had no family, he was an orphan, and then he lost his only sister. He had a terrible score to settle."

Roumande went over to the picture, the one of the cholera girl. "Which is why he was so troubled by the girl we cut, Adolphus. She reminded him of someone close to him. Someone he lost? I thought it odd at the time, how Patrice was a body collector but couldn't bear for the girl to be cut, yet he could happily stomach the others."

Hatton leaned against his desk. "He knew about religion,

plants, and by working closely with us, the nature of forensics. We gave him enough knowledge to cover his tracks and keep one step ahead of us. He came to us because he wanted to kill Dr. Buchanan. I didn't tell you at the time, but Sorcha fainted when Patrice came to the house, as soon as she saw him. I thought it was grief, but I now know it was simply fear that he should be so bold, or he might in fact be caught. She helped him, didn't she?"

Roumande looked at his hands.

Hatton said, "Before we find Buchanan, I need to go to her, Albert."

But when Hatton got to the ward she was already gone, leaving only an empty bed and a note under her pillow addressed in the plainest of hands to *Professor Adolphus Hatton, Esquire*. Hatton sat on the end of the bed, putting the paper to his parched lips and then read:

My Dear Adolphus

I don't ask for you to forgive me. But I know I owe you an explanation, because you saved my life, and believe me when I say that in another time and place we might have been happy together—but there's no point thinking like that now, is there? I am just a foolish girl, and despite all that we have done, that remains the heart of me.

My story is a sad one and perhaps will win some sympathy. It is impossible to put into words what I felt, because they took away my father, my mother, my brothers and sisters. Nothing was left by 1848—just the voices of the dead and me, an empty shell. Ardara was ransacked, tumbled, burnt to the ground, and when you uttered those words, Mortui vivos docent—*never a truer word was said. Because four hundred and twenty dead voices were calling me. And they were calling Patrice, too. They called him all the way from Canada—across the hurling sea—where he sought me out here in London and told me what to do. When I first laid eyes on him, he reminded me of those terrible times, and who I really was.*

On the morning of the tumbling, men came with rifles in their hands, twitching for blood and more than blood. Though she could barely stand from hunger, my mother was raped by that animal, the gombeen man who had come to herd us to the ships.

Patrick's sister Kitty was drowned. She was signed fit to travel by your eminent quack, Dr. Buchanan, but of course, she had typhus, and on route to Canada was locked in the hold, and when that ship hit the rocks off Isle de Coudres? Well, he tells me the screaming was terrible. It haunts him still. I mop his brow, I hold his hand but nothing will comfort him save one thing.

Revenge is a wild kind of justice, they say.

His real name is Patrick by the way and we are first cousins. Once you found the beads—a foolish mistake to discard them like that in the rookeries—we knew it was only a matter of time till you discovered the truth about us. But blood is thicker than water, you see.

It pains me that you will call me a murderer, but I am proud of what I did. An eye for an eye, a tooth for a tooth, a life for a life? Isn't that what the dead teach the living? And it was no crime surely, compared to what those monsters did to us?

You see, I let my cousin in that fateful night to deal with Gabriel, my do-gooder husband, fool that he was. I also visited Mr. Hecker and gave him a draught. I lured the chef to the island. He was Catholic, and lonely you see, and it was easy for me. He thought I'd come back from the dead, he thought I was a ghost, a chimera, a vision—he was overwhelmed by me. He paid the price.

Fearing your forensics, we tried our best to leave no trace—except the glitter, of course, which Paddy spread everywhere to lead you to others who wanted to be martyrs anyway. But in the end, you're not a fool and we weren't quite good enough for a man like you. Once you had the beads in your hand, and the botany book, it really was just a matter of time. And time is like sand—it runs out as we must run. But please, don't try to follow us. We're still ahead of you and there's another who's demanding our attention. It must be done. Revenge is a wild kind of justice.

But as I write this note, despite what you think of me now, I will always be your dearest, and most respectfully, friend forever.

Sorcha O'Shaughnessy

Hatton folded the note, knowing she was gone—but then a hand on his shoulder, the light touch of a true friend.

"We need to hurry. Dr. Buchanan could still be alive, Adolphus. We must go—"

Work. Work is what I must do. No more of her. Hatton concentrated. "You say, Patrice isn't traveling by foot?"

"Just before he coshed me, I heard a horse whinny, outside in the yard."

"How would he get Dr. Buchanan to go with him? Didn't you say that you encouraged them to do one last picture somewhere out of the city."

"My fault . . . all of this is my fault."

"Never mind all that. Think, Albert. Think really hard. Did Dr. Buchanan say where?"

Albert thought for a second, his head splitting with pain. "I can't be certain, but there was a discussion about the Celtic monument for cholera victims being a wonderful backdrop. It's a site for remembrance, just beyond Highgate village, near some old plague meadows, I believe."

"A monument, you say? I know the place. Up high on a hill, north of Highgate. The cross can be seen for miles. It sits perched on top of a plague pit tumulus, doesn't it?"

"I believe it does."

"Call a carriage, Albert," said Hatton. "And bring your gun from the mortuary. Bring mine, as well. That's where they've gone—I just know it."

24

HIGHGATE

They would leave for Canada tomorrow, but in the meantime, they'd dug at least six feet down into the old plague pit, but still the old man seemed to be squirming, the earth shifting above him. Sorcha said, a little crossly, "I think he's still alive. We need to finish him off. Hurry."

"Don't worry, cousin," said Patrice. "A few more shovels of earth . . ."

But the doctor seemed unwilling to die. At one point, up came a desperate hand flailing around, which Patrice had to whack again and again with a spade, practically chopping it off, before a foot appeared at the other end of the grave. It was almost comic in its timing and she couldn't help but laugh.

But the earth was definitely still shifting a little, Sorcha thought. But perhaps it was just the bugs, the black flies, and the worms? Her own father had died this way. During the forced emigration, he'd hid her from the British down deep in a bog hole, the two of them, lasting three days and two nights before baying bloodhounds sniffed them out, screaming blue bloody murder.

"Get out, O'Shaughnessy. We know you're there. Hecker's ship, or the gallows? What'll it be . . ."

He whispered in the dark, "I'll get up there first, child, and distract them. Are you ready?"

"But what'll I do, Da?"

"Get your head down, head for the hills, keep running, and whatever you do, whatever happens, girl, don't look back, I'll be right behind you . . ."

It took just one glance over a shoulder to see soldiers smash her darling da with a rifle butt back into the wormy ground. But she kept running, through gushing streams, tearing briars, scrambling for her life, over rocks and jagged stones till she saw a wide green valley, like a dream, and a Georgian house, splendid on a peaceful mountainside with the vista of the sea—wide waves breaking the Atlantic. *Saoirse*, she thought, freedom. Desperate with hunger, she lay down on the steps of the magnificent house—*no more running*—and Gabriel must have found her there, a lost lamb, and took her in, fed, her, clothed her, and eventually bedded her. But she was a shell, an empty shell, and he meant nothing. Just another ticket to who knows where.

Ten years later, her cousin had his hat pulled down, a looming shadow on the wall in the garden at White Lodge.

"Why, if it isn't my darling cousin. Sorcha O'Shaughnessy? Remember me? Sure, it's only Paddy . . ."

He'd come all the way from Canada on a ship, he said, and crept up on her when she was painting an oil—to ease her troubled spirit—in one of the outhouses, but as she turned around, she knew at once what this visitor wanted—*her*—because blood is thicker than water.

Paddy put her right about everything, including her husband, who she'd foolishly thought as her savior.

"Your savior? Are you mad? A fucking traitor to his own people, more like. And you let him touch you? Bed you? You should hang your head in shame, cousin, because when he comes to your bed, he stinks of the dead."

"What should I do? How can I redeem myself? Tell me?" she said, sick to her stomach.

"Move out of his room, never let him touch you again, and then, sure, listen to your long-lost cousin. It's God's will."

She sat down on the milking chair in the outhouse and listened as Paddy continued on the subject of her husband. "Gabriel was in charge of the whole thing, Sorcha. I was a stable boy at the big house, I heard them talking. Hecker, Pomeroy, that quack of a doctor—all sitting round a table, and your man at the helm. A tumbling of the whole area and to get what? Money from Mr. Hecker for the land cleared, so he could buy enough food to feed the few carefully chosen tenants McCarthy said he could support. Which was ten . . . just ten fucking people out of four hundred and thirty . . . and your name was on his list, cousin."

He told her all that he'd heard, crouched down, at an opened window:

"The estate is in debt and the simple fact is, gentlemen, I cannot feed everyone. According to Monsieur Pomeroy's nutritional forecasts, based on his expertise with workhouse diets for the British government, with the crops all failed and a harsh winter on its way, I can only afford to keep ten carefully selected tenants at the most. The rest will have to go. Which is where you come in, Mr. Hecker. In return for your land, we want safe passage for these cottiers. Your vessels—they are seaworthy, I hope?"

"Of course, they are. What do you take me, for?"

"*A man who likes to turn a quick profit, Mr. Hecker.*"

Laughter.

"*Do you have a man who can organize things? The people are weak, but they might resist. I don't want a riot. I don't want blood on my hands.*"

Mr. Hecker again.

"*There's a man called Mahoney, a gombeen man, who lives by himself up the side of a mountain somewhere. Much hated by the locals, but efficient. He does a little work for me and can offer the incentives for those who must leave—land when they get there, cabins, that sort of thing . . .*"

A thump on the table.

"*That man's a hooligan. A lying scoundrel. People say he murdered his own brother. He's only just been released from prison for some other offense involving a young woman. Jesus, Mr. Hecker, is there nobody else but him . . .*"

"*Sometimes when you want to catch vermin, Mr. McCarthy, you need a rat catcher.*"

A chair pushed over:

"*I shan't listen to this anymore. This is a bad idea . . . forget I ever invited you in . . . the Ardara tenants will stay here and starve, if necessary, but I shan't entertain that gombeen man . . .*"

Whispering.

And then.

"*I'm glad you see sense, because beggars cannot be choosers, McCarthy. Choose ten and let the rest go. It's your duty, sir. You've heard the British government's view on this. It's better the people go to Canada, where they have a chance to live—and if it's my ships you use, then I choose the men to organize the emigration on my own terms. Dr. Buchanan here is an eminent physician and very reliable. You have to trust me . . . when it comes to exporting men, I know what I'm damn well doing . . .*"

The scratching of a pen. The clink of glasses.

"*Very well. It's a deal, but you will tell no lies. The state of the cabins, the conditions when they get there, because these*"

people are weak and it's a hellish voyage and reports say daily,
the islands of Canada are full of cholera. And that only last
week a vessel hit the treacherous rocks off the coast of New-
foundland and five hundred perished, never even reached the
coastline . . ."

"*You have my word, McCarthy . . ."*

She put her hands to her ears, but Patrice continued:

"Go ahead and stop your ears, cousin, but that's what I
heard. Gabriel played God, walking the line along the beaches,
his fingers twitching his pistol in case a riot broke out. But we
could barely stand, never mind fight, as he decided with Dr. Buchanan who should stay and who should go. I was in the line. He
sent my sister to her death in that coffin they called a ship, for it
was a leaking vessel and not fit for sea. No wonder it went down.
Most of us died when it hit the rocks off Isle de Coudres. A few
of us survived to tell the tale and, of course, this logbook, which
rolled up on the shore in an oak chest, unsullied and testament
to everything. Open it up and read the prayers of the dead. The
survival of this logbook is a miracle . . . God's gift, Sorcha, and
it's speaking to us—it's our destiny."

There was a soft breeze in the air and a ruffle over the parched
grasses of the plague pit meadows. A lark rose on a melodious
note. She tilted her head and listened—but the whispering had
stopped.

At last.

Wonderful, endless silence which she broke with, "The doctor must surely be dead by now, hurry. Quickly, cousin . . . we
need to go . . ."

But Patrice was unwilling, saying they'd made enough mistakes already, and that men could survive for a good ten minutes
if an air pocket got in the way, and they had to be sure. No more

mistakes. But she was trembling. "We'll give it five more seconds, Paddy. But then we run and we keep on running . . ."

"Where is this place?"

"Up ahead. A mile beyond the village. Are the guns loaded, Albert?"

Roumande nodded, his finger ready, heavy on the trigger.

The friends moved quickly, but with stealth, through the rustling grasses. Up ahead, scudding storm clouds—pewter morphing into thunder. A white crack across the sky. The parched meadows suddenly black, the heavy swell of raindrops—*splat, splat, splat*—slow but steady, and up ahead—high on a grassy tumulus, under the shadow of a Celtic cross—two figures they recognized, lit up like firecrackers.

"It's them . . ."

Another crack, fork lightning connecting to the earth, breaking through the sky, into a prism of mauve, sulphur, azure—and the figures were gone, vapors in the air.

"They're running away, Albert . . ."

"So where the devil's Buchanan?"

"Patrice was leveling the ground, Albert. He had a spade. Buchanan's just been buried. Quick. C'mon . . ."

The two men threaded their way, quickly, heads down, their backs lashed with the pelting rain, stumbling over molehills and a meadow full of tumuli—dead bodies overgrown with three hundred years of grass. Roumande hurled himself behind the biggest. "Get your head down, Adophus, and I can get him from here . . . that's Patrice, heading left . . . I've got him in the viewing finder . . . like a damn Jack rabbit . . . she's going right . . . she's limping . . . quick . . ."

"You go after him, Albert. I'm heading to the mound because Dr. Buchanan could still be alive. It's worth a try . . ."

"And the girl?" asked Roumande.

"Leave Sorcha to me," insisted Hatton. "She's injured, still weak, and she'll leave prints that will be easy to track. Those stitches on her face aren't healed, and if she exerts herself, they'll split, then splatter the grass in blood. But Dr. Buchanan first. You have to let me try . . . I've let him down once already . . ."

"If you're sure, Adolphus?"

"I'm sure," answered Hatton, determined.

Roumande stood up, heading left with his gun, the trigger ready. Hatton bolted ten yards straight ahead, then scrambled up to the top of a tumulus, with a quick, flitting glance left to see Sorcha McCarthy, way off—a pathetic, rain-soaked figure, slowly threading her way downhill toward a stream.

The earth was fresh. The discarded spade was ready. Hatton grabbed it, tears in his eyes, remembering his father's last moment on earth. He came too late on that ominous carriage from London, but not this time.

Dig, dig, Addie.

His sister's voice.

Dig, put your back into it, Addie.

Mary's voice.

Black earth. Five and half feet down to see—worms, old bones from years ago, the Black Death, plague people . . .

Keep going, lad. You're a farmer's son. Come on now. Not too proud to dig, are you?

His father's voice, and swishing the earth away, choking back his tears, to see—a face, the flicker of an eye. Dr. Buchanan.

Breathe. Breathe . . .

He's not dead. He's not quite dead . . .

Using dexterous fingers, quickly digging the earth from the old man's mouth, giving him air, a kiss of life—the old man sobbing like a baby now, pressed to Hatton's beating heart.

"My God . . . my God . . . they buried me alive . . . Hatton? Is that you, Adolphus . . ."

"It's me, Dr. Buchanan . . . I'm here . . . I'll always be here for you, sir . . ."

"I made a terrible mistake . . . people died on that ship . . . *The Liberty* . . . they punished me . . . oh, God . . . bless, you my son . . ."

"Stay here . . . I have to go . . . I have to go now, sir . . . just gather your strength . . . I'll be back . . . I promise you . . ."

Roumande was a bulky man, forty-six in May, but he was fast and better than fast, he was a damn good shot. He'd shimmied, his mouth eating earth, shifting his big body, like a frog, splayed out, invisible, snaking across stones, molehills, tumuli, his viewing finder to his eye, hidden by the high scorched grass, his loaded pistol ready, until he reached another, younger man, who was without water, exhausted, with his back turned, panting in the heat—

"Put the gun down, Patrice. Put it down. Right now . . ."

Was it simply bravado that made Patrice turn around and say, "Well, well, well. No flies on you, monsieur. You caught us up, then? But you're too late. Dr. Buchanan is dead already and you'll be next."

"It's over, Patrice. Lay your gun down and come with grace . . ."

"Grace?"

Patrice shook his head at Roumande like he was a fool. "Do you know, monsieur, it's a shame that it should end like this, because I really liked you, which is why I didn't kill you back there in the morgue. You were almost like a father, really. And as for those girls, those beautiful girls of yours . . ."

"Leave me girls out of this and put your damn gun down. We've sent a message to The Yard, and these meadows will be swarming with Specials any minute . . . there's no way out . . . whichever way you go, they'll find you. How on earth did you ever think you could get away with it?"

Patrice laughed, standing under a huge oak tree, his finger twitching on a trigger. "Get away with it? You helped me. Showed me every trick in the book, Albert." He tapped the side of his head. "Learning and erudition, monsieur. I couldn't resist that. One in the eye, for the ignorant apprentice, *n'est ce pas?*"

"But why? If you survived *The Liberty* and saw all those terrible deaths, why more deaths? What did it achieve, Patrice?"

Patrice put his eye to the viewing finder, readied himself, as the sky got darker, the rain fell down, the lightning setting the earth on fire. *Crack.* Fork lightning, as he smiled. "Achieve? I'd say that was obvious, wouldn't you, monsieur, or should I say, and this be Paddy speakin' to yer now . . ." His voice switched suddenly into a rasping Donegal accent. "Sure, I knew no better, me be'n a poor Irish lad, one up from an animal, no better than a savage, yer honor . . . killing and death is all I know . . ." *Crack.* A wave of thunder across the shimmering grasses.

"Killing me won't bring your sister back."

"Then let me go, then . . ."

"You know I can't do that, Patrice . . ."

"Very well. It's a pity because I raised myself, fed myself, clothed myself, shooting game in Canada, lived like a wild man in the woods, and I'm an excellent shot, and even through this finder, I can see your gray hair, Albert. Your failing eyes, your trembling hands, but are you ready . . ."

"Ready."

Roumande counted for both of them—as a matter of honor—

Une.

Deux.

Crack.

Patrice went up like a firecracker. A burning effigy. A hot explosion of sparks, his body on fire, the tree on fire, the grass on fire, the earth on fire. Roumande wrenched his coat off, ran, threw it on him, rolled him in the dirt. But struck by lightning, Patrice was dying, just one word on singed lips, "*Sssss* . . . or was it "*Ffff.* . . ." Roumande bent down, said something like a prayer and listened. "What are you saying, lad?"

"Ssss . . ."

Hatton raced down the hill, to see her twisting and turning around ancient gravestones, her thin body pummeled by the rain but not enough rain to stop the blood trail that was leading to a stream, a canopy of trees. Hatton was long-limbed, fast, determined, and she was stumbling, limping, slipping across some moss-covered stepping-stones. But what was he doing? Catching or saving her? He didn't know, he wasn't sure, but as she scrambled up the other side of the bank, he was after her. Her heels sending little pebbles flying into the water, scaring the fish away, and above them, ribbons of evening light, and in the leaves, a peep, peep, peep of a bird and the snap of a branch.

"Sorcha?" he cried. A flash of black hair, she suddenly found her strength, knowing she might die, and ran like the wind up the grassy bank, but he was a damn good hunter when he put his mind to it. "Got you!" he said, as the girl—and she was a girl despite her strange appearance, with her ripped face, her curling locks caked in blood—fell to her knees then and turned around to face him saying, "*Saoirse* . . ." Her breathing came in sharp little rasps as he held her to the ground. He grabbed her wrists tighter. "How could you?" "*Saoirse,* please, Adolphus . . . if you love me . . ." "Love you?" "*Saorise,* please. I beg you . . ." He held her there for a few more seconds, pinned beneath him, his legs straddling her body. She pulled him forward, kissed him. "Please, please . . . have pity . . . Addy . . ." There was a storm above them, electric in the air, a crack of thunder, clouds rolling in. His breath running faster than hers.

25

"I'll never see her again, will I?"

Roumande shook his head as Hatton crossed the bloody
floor of the mortuary toward a large cadaver on the slab. It had
come their way yesterday, for general dissection work. "So who's
that?" he asked, not really caring at all.

Roumande was preparing the corpse, washing it down with
chloride of lime as he said, "The journalist, John O'Rourke. He
was hung from a gibbet in the Old Bailey, along with that poor
little boy, despite our protestations to The Yard. It's a disgrace.
He was one year older than my son."

Yes, I know, thought Hatton. *And I'm bitterly ashamed.*
He'd heard the prison bell ring, announcing the hanging, but
couldn't go, he couldn't face it, but soon learned from the hospital gossips that it was a terrible sight because the rope was too
long and the boy was too light. That the hood filled with blood
and the boy twitched on the gibbet for a good fifteen minutes
before the end came.

Hatton had moved like a ghost, laying his scalpel down and
making his way slowly to the chapel, to do what? *Revenge is a*

wild kind of justice, he'd thought as he genuflected in front of the altar, in a show of what? Contempt? Mockery?

But today Hatton thought, *I did nothing, nothing for that child. Another death on my hands*—as his mind drifted back to Sorcha. "She really has gone, hasn't she?"

Roumande knew it was best, under the circumstances, to say nothing more about the girl. False comfort helped no one. And it was times like this when it was best to give the professor space, a little time for the contemplation of love and what it meant when it ended.

Hatton sat on his chair by the grate where a huge, comforting fire was lit, because even though it was still summer, he felt cold all the time. Roumande said, "It will take time, Adolphus. But you have to accept that she's gone from your life."

Yes, but Inspector Grey hadn't.

"What do you mean, she's gone?" Inspector Grey had said when he arrived at the plague meadow, two hours too late. *"She can't have just gone? She must be somewhere? If you're lying to me, Adolphus, there'll be hell to pay. You let her go, didn't you?"*

But Inspector Grey had other matters to deal with, far more pressing. A singed killer at his feet and two more ready to hang. The successful conclusion to the Ribbon Murders Case, ensuring that Grey was no longer just "inspector" anymore.

"Chief Inspector," he preened, a few days later. "Free meals all over town. Champagne all round. Chief Inspector Jeremiah Grey? How the devil does that sound, Hatton? Mr. Tescalini is a very proud man."

"It's very fitting, Chief Inspector. Like one of your suits."

"Yes, isn't it," said Grey as he leaned forward, sneering. "We all suffer from affairs of the heart, Adolphus, and I know what you did. But I shan't breathe a word. It will remain our little secret, eh, Professor Hatton?"

Yes, the threat weighed heavily and Hatton knew that as long as he kept Sorcha's letter, there was always a chance for the threat to weigh heavier still. So reluctantly, he stood up and threw the letter in the fire, watching it burn, a funeral pyre. And when it was nothing but ash, he said, "I'm not feeling so well, Albert. I'm going home."

"You did your best, Adolphus. It's all we can do in the end. Dr. Buchanan is up and about, by the way. He has been sent to Clacton for sea air, and just before he left, he made special mention of you and our department, Professor."

Did he care? But fighting his despondency, Hatton still said, "In what capacity?"

"A fivefold increase in our budget, Adolphus, which means we can hire a toxicologist, a part-time phrenologist, and really get going on this fingerprinting thing."

"Of course," Hatton said, pushing his derby down on his head, and lighting a penny smoke, a habit he'd now adopted. He puffed the bitter weed out, grimaced. "You're right. I'll see you tomorrow, Albert."

Because this day was over, but another would surely begin—without her.

Hatton left the morgue, and walked with his head down, crushing the weeds which struggled up through the pavers. Bright orange hawkweed and the blue specks of speedwell trying to catch the last drop of a soon-to-be-ending summer.

14 Gower Street.

He opened the door to the lodging house and, once inside his room, lay on his bed, looking at the cracks in the ceiling, utterly spent but hearing a voice in his head—"*Death stalks us. Death stalks all of us, Professor.*"

Historical Afterword

A WORD ABOUT INSPECTOR GREY
AND SCOTLAND YARD

In the nineteenth century, Scotland Yard was based at Number 4 Whitehall Place, the number of detectives increasing to around twelve men by the mid 1850s. The population of Great Britain was expanding rapidly, and by 1858, London was the largest city on the earth, fueled by Industrialization and the great wealth generated by The British Empire. With these dramatic economic changes came a burgeoning middle class, intent on protecting its property, and the flip side of that—desperate poverty, particularly in the rookeries (the slums). With increased city dwelling came an inevitable increase in crime—armed robbery, garrotting, vice, pickpocketing, and, of course, murder.

Inspector Grey is a figment of the imagination and it wasn't normal for a detective—even a senior one, like Jeremiah Grey—to have an assistant. His yearly salary would have been in the region of three to five hundred pounds a year, tops. Not nearly enough to keep him in Savile Row suits, opium bonbons, a morphine habit, presumably lodgings somewhere (tastefully decorated, of course), never mind a servant. However, for the purpose of the story, I felt Inspector Grey really ought to have one.

DRUG CITY

Drug-taking was widespread in nineteenth-century London. The Victorians enjoyed not just large amounts of alcohol (the water wasn't safe to drink, anyway) and spoonfuls of laudanum (opium mixed in a syrup), but also cannabis, coca from South America, mescaline, and with the invention of the hypodermic needle in the 1840s, morphine and heroin. Hot off the narcotic-filled creative brilliance of the Romantic poets, Victorian writers such as Dequincy, Dickens, and later Conan Doyle were all influenced in their work, to a greater or lesser extent, by drug-taking. For many Londoners, drugs undoubtedly lessened the pain of existing and the harsh realities of urban life in the 1800s. Added to which, all sorts of drugs were widely available dressed up as lotions, potions, eye drops, pills, and pick-me-up "tonics" to treat a whole range of illnesses and maladies—headaches, coughs, feminine "hysteria" (PMS), you name it. And on the whole, simply bought over the druggist counter, perfectly legally. This inevitably led to an increasing number of addicts. Opium-spiked bonbons—a favorite of Inspector Grey's—were a regular treat for many.

SICK CITY

The opening theme of this novel is cholera. London suffered from a number of outbreaks from this horrible disease during the 1840s and '50s. Most Victorians believed the disease was carried in the air—the so-called miasma—but it was the work of Dr. John Snow (dead from overwork by June 1858) and his colleagues, Mr. William Farr (the government's chief statistician), who together isolated the true roots of cholera though their groundbreaking medical research, during an outbreak in 1854 at

The Broad Street Pump in Soho. They discovered through painstaking detective work that the disease traveled via the mouth from feces in contaminated water. However, the miasma theory continued to hold sway long after their work was completed.

A WORD ABOUT THE PAINTING IN MR. HECKER'S MILL BY MILLAIS

Sir John Everett Millais was an English painter and one of the founders of the Pre-Raphaelite movement. Amongst other things, he painted landscapes and was much beloved by Victorian gentlemen.

As with all historical novels, I did a great deal of research to get the detail right. I hope I've succeeded but, of course, I'm not infallible and will stand to be corrected—although not in a Newgate dock. Here are some of the places and books that helped me: The Wellcome Trust Museum; *The Medical Detective*, by Sandra Hempel; *London in the Nineteenth Century*, by Jerry White; *London, A Biography*, by Peter Ackroyd; and *The Great Hunger*, by Cecil Woodham Smith. For more on the Victorians and my work, please visit my Web site at www.demeredith.com